10650024

The Randolph Legacy

Forge Books by Eileen Charbonneau

Waltzing in Ragtime

The Randolph Legacy

A Tom Doherty Associates Book/New York

THE RANDOLPH LEGACY

This book is printed on acid-free paper.

A Forge Book
Published by Tom Doherty Associates, Inc.
175 Fifth Avenue
New York, NY 10010

Forge® is a registered trademark of Tom Doherty Associates, Inc.

Library of Congress Cataloging-in-Publication Data

Charbonneau, Eileen.
The Randolph Legacy / Eileen Charbonneau. —1st ed.
p. cm.
"A Tom Doherty Associates book."
ISBN 0-312-86332-2
I. Title.
PS3553.H318R36 1997
813' .54—dc21 97-3788
CIP

First Edition: August 1997

Printed in the United States of America

0 9 8 7 6 5 4 3 2 1

For Abigail and Marya, Virginians along with everything else,
thanks for your sweet and gracious company over
our second Southern sojourn.

Acknowledgments

The Randolph Legacy had a catalytic beginning when my daughter and I were entranced by the collection of miniature sailing ships at the Mariners' Museum in Newport News, Virginia. I hope this book honors the memory of August Crabtree (1905–1994), whose artistry in his own wonderful collection of models was my inspiration for Ethan's efforts.

I am grateful to Betsy Tunis, whose wonderful writing helped me figure out how to begin; readers like poet Patricia Annie Rogers, whose voice I will always hear when I read this book; editors; readers; and dear friends who said, "Get your writing done, Eileen, I'll take the kids for a few hours." Bless you all: Natalia Aponte, Diane Michele Crawford, Charlie Rineheimer, Juilene Osborne McKnight, Dolores Oiler, Margie Rhoadhouse, Susie Shackleford, Laurie Alice Eakes, Donna Cawthron, Jim Green, Majorie Gemmill, Lisa Winters, Donna Blum, Nancy Meissner, Laurie Maxwell Tenney, Florence Kay, Jean Gold, Barbara Ward Lazarsky, Lisa and Alex deBritain, Shelia Chapelle, Robin O'Brien, Janet Bixby, Mitze Flyte, Anne Kelleher Bush, Ann Adelman, Kathleen Ernst, Patricia P. Knoll, Susan King, Kathy Caskie, Christine Whittemore, Deborah Barnhart, Cindy Haak, Meredith Bean McMath, Nicholas W. Quick, Jan Robison, Scott and Alison Meyer, Bruce Wilder, and Carolyn Krebs.

The Randolph Legacy

Prologue

October 1805
Off Cape Trafalgar, Spain

The bosun's whistle shrieked.

"All hands stand by to witness punishment!"

Grim-faced marine guards brought the prisoner to the uppermost deck, the execution yard. Though limping from the gash in his knee, he was ruddy-cheeked, and looked well fed. They said sailors on the American merchant ships ate salt pork and beef washed down with tankards of beer. Perhaps he had even enjoyed plum duff before he'd been impressed into His Majesty's Royal Navy. If the number of lashes was reduced because of his youth, he might survive, Maupin thought.

Why did he care? He had his own problems. Chief among them was to stay alive on this stinking English man-of-war until his release could be negotiated. They had lost the battle, but Maupin had seen the great Nelson fall, downed by a sniper. He had that story for his next port's whore, if he could only stay alive.

The shrill whistle sounded again. All but the prisoner snapped to attention. His eyes darted everywhere. A salt sea wind blew across the deck, sending his dark hair out of its neat queue and into his powder-burned face.

The soles of his bare feet were bleeding, as if they'd never been toughened by deckwork or climbing rigging. And his legs were pale below his breeches. Maupin turned the puzzle of those pale legs over in his mind. When the boy's short blue jacket was pulled off, another puzzle joined it.

The shirt beneath it was beautiful. Even the sound of it ripping down from his shoulders was beautiful. Its generous yardage billowed in the breeze, adding a touch of grace to the grim occasion. They all noticed it—the captain of the *Standard*, its officers, squad of marines, common seamen, and Maupin's fellow prisoners-of-war alike. They were over four hundred in number, he estimated. They all watched the dance of the beautiful shirt with the awed reverence of the faithful at church. Even from his distance Maupin could see that the material was rare cotton muslin, lovingly washed soft by a mother, a sister.

The boy deserved better—a quick fall into the unforgiving Atlantic, a clean bayonet-point through his heart, even the full blast of the cannon whose fire had singed his face. Not this. He was so young and had only made the mistake of choosing his country, whose navy was David to the Goliath that was George the Third's might on the sea.

The infant United States was not even the enemy that day, Maupin's France was. Maupin had watched, struck dumb in the middle of combat by the curious spectacle of the two arguing. "I will fight for no flag not my own!" The American had shouted his defiance. The captain, furious, had shifted his aim from Maupin to the boy himself. The young seaman would have had his quick end if the cannon hadn't exploded. Maupin owed his life to their argument.

Now the French were defeated and Captain Willis had his opportunity back.

"Master-at-arms!" the captain shouted, though the officer was standing just beside him. "You will read number fourteen of the Articles of War."

The reedy voice carried over the deck. " 'No private in the navy shall disobey the lawful orders of his superior officer, on pain of death.' "

The captain nodded toward the prisoner. "Admit your cowardice. Bend to your sovereign, and I will show you mercy."

"Unlawful orders," the boy said hoarsely, grasping at the words of the proclamation in his own defense. "Not my war, not my country. I am American."

"His Majesty's lash will be applied until you are convinced otherwise."

The prisoner cast his dazed eyes over the deck. "Lash?" he whispered, as if the miserable assemblage would tell him, *No, it's all a jest, young friend.* Instead, the captain stepped forward.

"The lash. Until you beg for your English birthright."

Willis was worse than most, Maupin could see that now. There was something beyond hardness in his ferret eyes as they passed over the prisoner's form. Even if he lived, this boy would never be safe.

Did he see the same? "Free trade and sailors' rights!" He proclaimed his country's latest slogan in the voice of a child, not even a squawking adolescent. Was he yet twelve? Maupin wondered, swallowing down bile. *What does it matter?* he scolded himself. *There is nothing I can do.*

But other slogans that stole foolish children's lives linked themselves together in a strange whip-ended dance through Maupin's brain. Join or Die. Give Me Liberty or Give Me Death in this glorious Age of Reason, liberty, equality, fraternity.

The drum started.

The quartermaster stretched the prisoner's arms over his head and secured them to the square frame of woodwork. At the captain's nod, the boatswain's mate swept the cat-o'-nine-tails around his thick neck, then brought it with the whole force of his body upon its mark. The lashes tore skin. Welting it first, then streaking it red.

The boy made no sound, only lifted himself on the toes of his wounded leg in a strange, graceful dance as the lashes struck. After the first seven, his head leaned on the webbed grating. His hair no longer blew in the breeze laced with the scents of tar, sawdust, vinegar, fresh blood. Its glistening brown locks were plastered to his face.

After a dozen strokes, the whipping seaman paused, drew his thickly muscled forearm across his lip, and looked to the captain. "What are you stopping for, boatswain's mate? Lay on," he was told.

Later, a small cry came though the sickening stillness between strokes. Was the prisoner calling him? How could that be? He had given none his name. Again. No, not his name, Maupin realized, but *"Mama"* in that drawling American accent.

Despite what Maupin had seen in his years in service to the Revolution, then Napoleon, he desperately wanted to turn his eyes away. But the lieutenant's crop had already brought two of his fellow prisoners back to full attention.

After stroke thirty-nine, the boy's body twitched violently, before it collapsed. One hand slipped through the leather thong, made for a thicker wrist. All of his weight landed on his right leg, which twisted, then snapped, dangling at an impossible angle from the wounded knee. The prisoner weaved there, a broken marionette. The drumbeat stopped, as did the sweat-soaked man who held the cat. Silence. Except for the echo, inside Maupin's head. His name, called by a child.

"Water. Bring him back," Captain Willis said.

No one moved. Officers and seamen alike seemed afraid to approach.

Maupin felt a shove at his shoulder. The dough-faced ship's surgeon, his uniform stained brown and smelling metallic, set a water bucket in his hands. They approached together.

The prisoner was smaller, somehow. Smaller than he looked at a distance. Maupin swept the matted hair back and found a face that was serenity itself. His eyebrows were burned off, but audaciously thick lashes still framed closed lids. The face reminded Maupin of that of a stone angel he'd lopped off the south portal of the cathedral at Chartres in an excess of revolutionary zeal. His fingers found this angel's throat. He turned to the captain of the HMF *Standard.*

"Dead," he said.

"That's not possible. Surgeon, water. Revive him. His heart—"

"It's stopped, sir," the medical officer confirmed, his watery eyes hesitant.

"Failed!" the captain shouted.

"I beg your pardon, sir?"

"It failed. The prisoner's heart failed. That's how your report will read. He would not bend. He broke. A failure. A failure of the heart. Do you understand?"

"Aye, Captain."

The Englishmen's fear shone from their faces like the glittering medals on Admiral Nelson's coat. Maupin felt as the French sniper must have felt—the one who caught sight of those medals and brought Nelson down. It was his turn to be the sniper, to capture a moment of glory, Maupin decided. He would salvage something from the defeat off Trafalgar. And somehow, the foolish American boy became a countryman.

The executioner untied the remaining leather thong at the boy's wrist with the gentle manner usually reserved for the living. "Let me have him," Maupin demanded, although as a prisoner himself, he had no right to demand anything.

The executioner stepped aside and let the body fall over Maupin's shoulders.

He took note of the boy's proportions as he descended the steep stairs, the surgeon behind him. Four and a half feet, weighing about seven stone, perhaps one hundredweight, he judged. He would need the sense of the American when he wrapped a substitute body-form in the boy's blankets, sewed his hammock closed over it. They would commit that, not him, to the sea. It was a trick every sailor knew.

Maupin stopped outside the sick bay on the berth deck, where the wounded marines of both sides groaned.

The surgeon's mouth twisted before he spoke. "I must be mad as an inmate of Bedlam," he said. "Take him down to the hold."

Four bells into Midwatch. It was the time of Captain Willis's most sound sleep. Maupin wrapped the boy's shivering form in the blue blanket and headed for the quarterdeck. He was lighter than the substitute mass of rags and ballast they'd cast into the waves a month before.

Maupin found his way blocked by the boatswain's mate who had rendered the lashes. He pushed Maupin against the stairwell, lifted the blanket.

"God's blood," he breathed. Maupin felt his mouth go dry, his mind freeze.

"I did not sign up to kill children, Frenchman," he growled, and stepped aside.

When he climbed onto the quarterdeck, Maupin found a secluded area in the shadow of a launch. He sat and laid his burden at his side. Though he'd tried to ease their journey out of the hold by spooning rum-and-lime-juice grog into the boy's mouth, the face was now contorted with suffering.

"Look at the stars, my young friend. Tell me if they are not worth a little trouble?"

The eyes searched the sky, settling on a point.

"Ah, *très bien*!" Maupin exclaimed. "Every man should know how to find the North Star."

The eyes scanned again—deliberately, Maupin thought, systematically. Was he charting their position? Did he know astronomical navigation? "Who are you?" Maupin asked softly.

The boy's dark, pained eyes clouded with confusion. He bit down hard on his lip. A guttural sound escaped as a seizure started. It wasn't as severe as the fits of the first days. The Frenchman could even hold him without fear that he would bite an earlobe off or a finger to the bone.

"C'est bien, bien, mon petit cousin," he crooned, rocking, waiting for the seizure to loosen its grip. *"Bien, bien,* so that we are never any trouble to those who tolerate us. And we must never wake the giant from his slumber, yes?"

Was he a fool for saving the American, as the surgeon said? Would the child be a simpleminded cripple, if he survived his injuries? Maupin fought the notion. The eyes were not those of a simpleton. They read the stars.

The fit ended, leaving the boy exhausted. "Never mind, then, with names, and the past," Maupin told him. "Perhaps you and I, we need to be rechristened as we expatriate ourselves to nationalize with the universe. We are in an alliance, no? Like the old one between our countries. I am Lafayette to your Washington, *petit général*, so *en garde* for free trade and sailors' rights! I will serve you as faithfully, nobly forgetting your country's abandonment during our own revolution!"

The corners of the boy's mouth went almost imperceptibly up.

"Ah, this you like, young Washington? Be warned—I will be a hard taskmaster on your journey to manhood. But when your resourceful President Jefferson comes to your rescue, you will speak French like a native of La Rochelle, the finest seaport in all of France!"

Smiling. Yes—Maupin was sure of it.

"You will know how to choose a wine, cook oysters, fight a man, and give and take a compliment. A few card tricks, much poetry, and the names of a dozen flowers. With this knowledge you will charm the ladies. Though you must remember that the only one whose love is free is that of your *maman*. . . ."

A tic started beside the boy's right eye. He'd been calling his mother, then, as he bore the lash? "*Eh bien,* now," Maupin scolded, "the past has no more dominion over us, remember? We are newborn."

The spasm stopped. Slowly, the boy reached trembling fingers to his own face. He looked surprised to find it.

More, his eyes beckoned.

Maupin continued the game, giving them a future together, though his charge was more a shade of the underworld than a being of flesh and blood and possibility. The new Lafayette babbled on about finding a good tailor and being a conscientious guest, stopping razor cuts properly and taking a woman's meaning to heart when she says no.

Suddenly, a silver spray of starlight streaked across the cold sky of the North Atlantic. "*Regardez!* Opportunity, Washington. Wish," he urged. "Wish for what you desire more than anything."

The boy's eyes followed the sharp radiance. "Dance," he whispered. "To dance."

He could speak. There, he was not an imbecile. The boy could speak. Maupin snorted out his laughter. "What? You are an odd fellow. No fortune? Fame? The hand of some beautiful Helen of Troy?"

The boy's eyes fired. "To dance," he maintained.

"Very well, *petit général.* You have had your fill of all the others, yes? You want for only simple pleasures. Good. Those are all we'll manage for a while."

Maupin glanced at the fractured leg, wrapped in an eighteen-tail bandage, splinted by a surgeon better at hacking off limbs. "To dance," he echoed. "For that, perhaps we need a comet."

He'd fathered a child by Madeline, once. Long ago. The milk-saturated smile of that newborn was somehow like the boy's as he drifted off to sleep that night. Maupin drew the threadbare blanket over lanced shoulders, wondering what had possessed him to speak as he had. It was ridiculous, indulging the child. Maupin was a reasonable man of thirty-eight years. He should have known better than to spark those young, trusting eyes with hope. But then, what was the harm? Madeline and their child had not survived that bitter winter. The boy would surely not last this one.

1

Henry Washington

1

April 1815

One night of peaceful sleep. Judith Mercer petitioned for it, silently waiting for the Divine Presence. It did not visit. A soft, formless drowsiness did. Then, as sleep descended, the nightmare came.

Black Africans, so crowded they could neither stand nor sit, shamed by their own filth until buckets hailed down fetid water from above. Some were shackled with iron collars, with arm and leg fetters secured by pins. Their feet were large, all out of proportion to thin, brittle-boned limbs, barely clothed. Their eyes, deep-set and glassy, held the essence of suffering.

Judith, a child again, stood in their midst. As she felt the panic rising in her throat, she remembered they were from God, no matter how dark and fearful their appearance. She raised her arms over their defeated heads.

"Brothers, sisters," she called them quietly in that voice her mother had said was her gift. "What can I do for you?"

"Remember," they said.

Judith woke, listened for her father's contented breathing, there in their small storage room on the orlop deck. As soon as she could no longer hear her heartbeat, she rose, placed her warm, dove gray cloak over her shoulders. She climbed flights of steep stairs until she could see the night sky.

Two bells announced the second half-hour of Midwatch. On the port side of the forecastle, Second Lieutenant Mitchell was the only officer on the watch. His fingers touching the brim of his hat confirmed to Judith the captain's promise that she would be free and safe anywhere on the HMF *Standard,* at any time. Mitchell's smile was as lopsided as his one-epaulet shoulders. All but a core remnant of her fear dissipated into the salt sea air. Judith crossed the deck to the starboard side.

None of the common sailors got more than four hours of sleep at a time on the *Standard*, their night-watch pattern so different from that of the pampered officers. Judith felt the practice was cruel, and based solely on that hallowed bane of government institution, "precedent." She resolved to write a letter to the British Admiralty on the subject before the Atlantic crossing was over.

Yet she could not feel sorry for the seamen as she walked among them tonight, under a hail of spring stars. Judith felt immensely glad to be going home at last, after the war had stranded her on the wrong side of the Atlantic. *Wrong side.* Was that the proper way for a Friend to see it? she wondered. Tonight she didn't care. She was an American Friend, going home at last.

She and her father had lived in London the first year, then extended their mission, visiting many Friends' Meetings throughout the British Isles, but she had always felt the honored stranger. Now, the pull of the sails toward her homeland was making her feel content and rested at one hour past midnight, and moments past a nightmare. No, not a nightmare. A revelation, whose meaning would come with the help of the Divine Presence.

Judith heard a sound she thought was the wind in the sails. Then the softness became laced with a rich baritone voice singing:

Sur le pont d'Avignon
L'on y danse, l'on y danse,
Sur le pont d'Avignon
L'on y danse, tout en ronde

She turned the corner. There, in the shadow of the mizzenmast, she saw the singer. He was bent over yards of sail. His deft fingers pulled the needle with its coarse thread through the canvas to the rhythm of his sprightly song.

Judith was taught that singing was frivolous, ornamental. But this song had a practical purpose. Would that help absolve her of the distinct pleasure she received in hearing it?

The sailmender's needle slid through startled fingers.

His ragged clothing draped rather than fit his painfully thin frame. He pulled off a worn cap. A thick crop of hair blew into his bearded face. That face, with its gaunt shadows, suddenly put Judith in mind of the starving, sunken-eyed people of her dream. "Put thy cap on," she implored, crushing the ties of her cape as the sharp wind blew back her hood.

The sailor complied. Had she frightened him? "Forgive me," she said softly. "Judith is my name. Judith Mercer. My father and I are taking our passage to America aboard thy ship. We are of the Society of Friends. Thou needs not bow, remove thy hat, or use any titles or formality with us."

He tilted his head, curiosity seeming to overcome his fear. His eyes closed slowly, their long lashes meeting as he pondered. They were young eyes, Judith realized, when he opened them again. " 'Thee, thou, thy.' For 'you, your.' Yes?"

"In the singular. We use a simplified American form of the old speech, the speech of our Friend forebears." Judith stepped closer. She looked down at even stitches and the leather thimbles over the sailor's long fingers. "Thy work is fine."

"Thank you."

"What was thy song about?" she asked.

"Dancing." He smiled, showing even teeth. The smile, the better angle, transformed him from a hollow-eyed skeleton to a young man who needed only more food, a good wash, and a new suit of clothes.

Judith sat beside him on the bench. "What is thy name?"

"Washington."

"Thou sings French like a native, Washington."

He gifted her with one of his transformational smiles. "Fayette taught me," he said.

"Ah, the cordial gentleman who is the surgeon's mate. He gave me the ginger root that has sustained my father over his seasickness."

"He is well now, your father?"

"Almost."

Washington nodded, picked up the dangling needle, and began drawing it through the canvas again. "And what sustains you?" he asked quietly.

"I have not been ill."

"But troubled out of your sleep?"

"Only by a dream."

He frowned. "Why did you not take an officer's cabin when you came aboard? Surely one was offered."

"My father and I are doing what little we can to deliver the Americans at Dartmoor Prison without delay."

"By sleeping in steerage?"

"It's a gesture of protest. Elizabeth Fry, an English Friend who is seeking prison reform, suggested it."

"For how long have the Americans been at Dartmoor?"

"Some since early in the war. Three years."

"You have seen them?"

"Yes. My father and I ministered to them."

"What does that mean?"

"We brought them food, clothes. We wrote their letters home. We will deliver them to their families in America. We talked to members of government about their treatment, about hastening their release."

"Why?"

"Because we're Friends. Quakers."

"And the prisoners are of your religion?"

"No, none are. We are forbidden to be in military service. But they are suffering as a result of injustice."

He looked up from his work with different smile. Not his radiant one. This was a small smile, the shared-secret smile of a child.

"That's good work. I will talk to them," he promised.

"To whom?" Judith asked, perplexed.

"The black people. The ones in your dream."

Judith sat back, startled speechless.

He went on sewing. "This frigate was a slaver, back before it was outfitted to fight Napoleon. I sleep in the hold, below you. They were packed in the ship back then, the slaves. When I was a child, the echoes of them, they frightened me, with their large feet, their eyes. But they would stroke my head when Fayette was on watch, and I was alone and afraid. Fayette, he is a man of reason, and calls them my *revenants*, 'the ones who come back.' In English they are . . . ?"

"Ghosts."

"Yes. Just so. Ghosts." He shrugged. "I do not know why they came to you. But I will talk with them on it, yes?"

There was a comfort to watching his graceful plunges into the canvas, out again. Through her shock, Judith sensed that he knew this, and went on sewing steadily, for them both.

"Washington. How long has thou been aboard the *Standard*?"

A stitch faltered. "A long time."

"How long?"

He scratched the side of his head impatiently, then went back to the steady rhythm of his stitches. "I don't know."

"Where did thou live before, in America?" Judith tried.

"I don't remember."

"In America, Washington. The South."

"South?"

"Yes. I am from Pennsylvania. Thy speech is slower, rounder than mine, though phrased by the influence of Monsieur Fayette, I suspect."

She waited. He looked at her, intensely interested, as if they were talking about someone else. She persisted. "I have not seen thee on the forecastle before."

"I don't come up on the open decks except for now, Midwatch."

"But thou is not a holder, living below. Thou is a sheet anchor man, with thy sewing?"

"No. Fayette's the sheet anchor man, and the surgeon's chief assistant, and the yeoman's trusted mate. He used to be a topman, he was captain of the mizzenmast—up aloft there, next to the stars. His fingers can't climb now. Stiff, you understand? I help him with the sails, with the numbers in the yeoman's book."

"But how is thou listed?"

"Listed?" He looked as if the very notion was absurd. "As ship's *revenant,* perhaps. That is what you thought me to be, yes?"

"Friend Washington, thou teases me quite as mercilessly as Monsieur Fayette."

He shrugged his thin, graceful shoulders again. "I am his apprentice, after all," he said.

Judith fought back a smile at his evasion, and kept her voice serious. "When did thou join the crew?"

"Join?" His voice went hard. "I did not join."

"Impressed," she realized suddenly.

"That is what Fayette says. I was sick. Before that I don't remember, except for pictures."

"Pictures?"

He touched the side of his head at the temple. There was no secret smile. He did not look up at her at all, only at his work, which quickened a fraction. "There is the dancing one," he offered quietly, his voice small and pained. "Two women who smell like you, like roses. Above me. I am standing on their feet. We are laughing, laughing and dancing. I wonder, which one is my . . ." The thread caught. "Is my—"

"Mother?" Judith prompted.

The needle jabbed an unthimbled finger. Three spots of bright red blood stained the canvas. Judith reached for his hand, pressed the puncture wound between her finger and thumb. She looked into eyes that were almost fathomless and bright with stubbornly unshed tears, bright with a pain which far outweighed that caused by the small wound.

"I am not stupid," he whispered fiercely. "Not lame-brained, simpleton, imbecile. I only don't remember!"

"Yes. My dear Washington. I understand."

"Pardon!" he whispered. "Fayette taught me better than this, how to speak with a lady. But you are as beautiful as the moon."

He was looking at her hair, Judith realized. The wind that had shoved her hood back had revealed what she had always held within her cap. She had not attended to her hair before coming aloft. Now it blew freely about her face, reminding Judith of that night, twenty years ago, when her childhood ended so abruptly. She'd torn at it until her scalp was bleeding, that night. By the end of the year her flaxen strands had gone as silver as a crone's. How could he find her beautiful?

Judith followed Washington's shifted glance to the licorice-scented man standing behind them. Without his charming smile, the surgeon's mate seemed older.

"Your father is well enough to be left unattended, Judith Mercer?"

"He sleeps soundly, yes." Her clear voice answered the Frenchman's implied accusation.

His hand took hold of the younger man's shoulder. "It grows colder. Time to go."

"I have not finished."

"Finish tomorrow."

The sailor freed himself of Judith's hand. She felt the pull of his drying blood between her fingers. She sensed the Frenchman's anger.

"Washington has been pleasant company for me, Fayette," she said.

"That is good to hear," he said stiffly before turning back to the young sailmender.

"Fayette, I have yet to search off the stern," Washington said.

"Neither did you finish mending the sail."

"But I worked with diligence. Did I not, Judith Mercer?" Washington pulled her into their controversy with a good-natured smile.

"I agree to the truth of what thee says," Judith affirmed.

"Mr. Carney is keeping watch there, off the stern. Would you join us, Judith? We watch the sea together, Fayette and I." He turned to the larger man. "Could we invite her, Fayette?"

The Frenchman sighed like an indulging parent. "It seems you already have, *petit général.*"

Judith had suspected the possibility of warmth behind the man's cynical smile. Her American countryman made it flower.

Judith watched Fayette's large-boned form bend, then gently lift Washington, as if he were a child who had fallen asleep by the hearth. She caught sight of the cruel track of a scar that coursed up the sailmender's right leg and disappeared under the white duck of his trousers. His right foot was twisted inward, useless. Judith lifted the cloak's hood over her hair, her shocked eyes. He couldn't walk. Washington was crippled. How could that be?

"Coming?" Fayette called in an indifferent tone, but daring her with his eyes.

Judith rose and followed the men.

The poop deck was virtually deserted. Judith watched Fayette nod curtly to a single red-coated marine guard. Between the lanterns stood the compact Mr. Carney. He gave Fayette a casual, palms-in salute, then smiled at Judith.

"Ah, and don't the three of ye look like a regular, strolling-of-a-Sabbath-afternoon family up here?" he exclaimed, pulling off his neckerchief and dusting a place for them on the signal-flag locker. Word had already traveled up two decks that she'd met young Washington, their ship's ghost, Judith realized.

"Have they come tonight, Mr. Carney?" Washington asked as Fayette placed him beside Judith.

"Feast your eyes over the side, lad. We've got our sign of a smooth voyage to America now, all right." The grizzled man turned to Judith. "That should quiet the few who are still grousing about a female aboard, Miss Mer—"

"Judith, Friend Carney," she reminded him.

"Judith." He nodded solemnly.

All their attention was soon absorbed by the sleek, moon illuminated bodies leaping and splashing behind the *Standard*.

"Spinners!" Washington cried out.

"Aye, lad, your favorite."

"What are they?" Judith asked, catching the ties of her cloak as she looked over the side. "Sharks?"

"Nay," Washington exhaled a more playful version of Fayette's disgusted snort. "Dolphins! Not fish, but breathers, like us, Judith. They click and whistle and sing like the whales."

"They are whales," Fayette said in his haughtiest tone. "Group?" he demanded.

"Cetaceans," Washington said happily, not taking his eyes from the flashing streaks.

"Family?"

"Delphinidae."

"Species?" Fayette persisted. Behind him, the old sheet-anchor man gave Judith a helpless shrug.

"Well?" Fayette demanded.

"Delphinus delphis," Washington answered effortlessly, still watching

the moon-drenched surface of the Atlantic. " 'Spinners.' too, because they sometimes spin on their side when they leap. Oh, look at that one, Judith—she's doing it to greet you!"

Judith sighted the dolphin he'd meant the instant the smaller calf at the animal's side imitated the same acrobatic movement. Delighted, Judith let out a skittering burst of laughter.

"A greeting dance, is it?" Fayette demanded. "You read the dolphins' minds now, do you?"

"And what if I do?" his pupil challenged. "Someday I will swim with them perhaps, yes?"

"*Mais oui,* soon after I throw you overboard, you pompous—"

Suddenly, Fayette's body stiffened with the sound of the shrill whistle. Judith turned to see the marine guard click his heels and salute.

"Merde," she heard the Frenchman growl low in his throat before she felt the sudden warm press at her back. Her cloak flared behind her. But there was no wind. She tried to turn, but Fayette took her arm fiercely. His voice was low, calm, desperate. "Please, Judith." She looked up into his startling green eyes. "Please," he said again, as she felt another hand's fingers press the small of her back. She was hiding Washington there, against her nightgown, she realized.

Carney joined Fayette and together they blocked her from the blur of red and white that was the approaching captain. Both men lifted their hands in formal salute.

"Frenchman!" Captain Willis shouted. "Where is he?"

"Who, Captain?"

"That face! I've sent three servants to scour the ledge around my windows! There! He's there, behind—" He pushed the men's shoulders apart to discover her. "Miss Mercer," he stammered. Judith stared at the captain of the HMF *Standard* in shock. He was hatless, and his nightshirt was yanked into misbuttoned trousers. He resembled a wild man, despite the jacket of his suit of office drawn hastily across his broad shoulders. Worse was the intemperate look he now struggled to control within his small eyes.

"Friend Willis." Judith forced herself to smile.

Carney stepped forward. "Mr. Lafayette and me, we were just bringing Miss Mercer up for a look at the dolphins, Captain," he said affably. "Sign of luck for the rest of our crossing! Could it be them you seen from your cabin's windows, sir?"

"Dolphins?" Captain Willis said, enraged. "I know the difference between dolphins and—"

"And what, sir?" Fayette asked, a predatory gleam in his eyes.

The captain met Fayette's look with unmasked hatred.

Judith felt Washington's fingers press her back in silent appeal. She found her voice.

"Friend Willis," she called, "I did not know the difference between these wondrous creatures and sharks, imagine! My companions have been explaining them to me. Friend Carney says—"

The captain moved closer. "Miss Mercer. Divine, chattering Miss Mercer." Judith smelled spirits and degeneration. "Perhaps you'd enjoy a closer look at our splashing camp followers? I understand you and your father are well versed in botany. Does your scientific inquiry extend to animals as well? Shall I call for my pistol and personally shoot a specimen for your further inspection?"

Washington's hold was compounded by his burning face at her back. Judith felt more than heard his low growl.

"Miss Mercer had just expressed her wish for me to bring some ginger root to her father, Captain," Fayette said evenly.

"Oh? Attending dear Papa with our French turncoat, are we?" The captain stumbled back. "A pity. Another time, perhaps?"

"No," Judith said. "No other time. I honor the wondrous sight of the dolphins living."

He waved his hands spasmodically in the air. "As you wish," he said in a high, almost giddy voice. "Everything aboard must be as you wish—the Admiralty has commanded it!"

He danced back on his toes, bumping into the approaching soldier. He turned on the man viciously. "Who in hell are you?" he demanded.

"Sergeant Meany of the Marine Guard, sir."

"Damn you stinking foot soldiers! Where's Mitchell? Where in hell's my first lieutenant?"

"Here, Captain."

Lieutenant Mitchell appeared, as if from the air itself. He had a heavy, ermine-collared dressing gown over his arm. "Captain, it's a cold watch, sir, and I thought you'd be needing—"

"Just so, just so." The captain gathered what was left of his dignity and stumbled away on his second-in-command's arm.

"It's a good thing the war's over," Judith heard the marine guard mutter in disgust, "I'd be hard put to follow that one's command."

He walked back to his post as Carney and Fayette freed Washington from the cover of her cloak. Without his warmth against her back, Judith shivered. She saw Fayette's gnarled fingers sweep through the man's hair before he pressed Washington's head to his chest in a quick, wrestling embrace.

"*Mon dieu,* those dolphins will be the death of you!" he said gruffly, pushing him away again.

"Nay, Fayette. They are life-giving, like this lady," Washington said.

Fayette yanked the young man into his arms. "Below. Now. Carney, bring her," he ordered abruptly, then finally looked at Judith. She watched him force his agitated breathing to calmness. "Would you wait for my return before you retire to your quarters?" he asked quietly.

"I will."

"Thank you."

Once Carney left her back on the forecastle, Judith sat. None of the *Standard*'s crew approached, though she could hear their whispers swarm around her. She watched a cloud obscure the moon.

"You have made an indelible impression on my young friend, Quakeress."

Judith lifted her head. The Frenchman's cynical smile had returned. "No less than he has on me."

"Yes. He told me of your shared African slaves. He will intercede, and so help you find your peace."

"Intercede?"

"The Light, Judith Mercer. Is that not what you seek in each of your fellows?"

"It is."

"Are you troubled by the darkness of their skins? Is there no holy light in Africans?"

"What does thou know of our Society's philosophy?"

"Enough to admire your threat to corrupt social order, and your Pennsylvania Experiment, based on Reason."

"Reason?"

"Yes. Voltaire says—"

"Thou has read thy Voltaire, thy Rousseau, perhaps, Fayette. They bent Quaker philosophy to shape their own ends. Read our George Fox or William Penn. The Pennsylvania Experiment was based on personal enlightenment, not Reason."

"Is this true? Will you leave me only with what I despise, gentle lady? Your Society's retreat from government, and your intolerance?"

"Intolerance?" The sweet tenor of her voice would not give her passion away, Judith decided. She buried her fisted hands in the folds of her skirts. "We are a society based on tolerance."

"That is the shame of it. To be so tolerant of all others while subjecting your own community to so many precepts of speech, dress, behavior. This is disappointing in a people who started with such revolutionary zeal."

"Perhaps we should lop heads off, or overrun Europe with armies, instead of plodding so uneventfully toward the Light?"

His eyes boldly swept her trembling shoulders and hidden fists. Then he threw back his head and laughed. "This will be the best Atlantic crossing of my life, I think, Judith Mercer. We shall have a grand adventure, the three of us!"

Judith felt the anger melting from her heart like spring snow. "Fayette," she summoned. "That young sailor—he is the reason a French prisoner-of-war changed his allegiance and now serves aboard the *Standard*."

He turned away. His voice, when it finally came, was a hollow whisper. "What else could I do? He was a child, ten years ago. No one came for him. He had only me. So when the time for my release approached, I signed on."

"It was difficult," she whispered, touching his arm.

"Not so difficult."

"Can he not walk at all?"

He faced her, his cynical smile returning. "The surgeon wanted his leg. Perhaps it would have been best. It still pains him. But phantom limbs do, too, I'm told. If only I had known more about healing than killing then. The bandages, you see, they were too loosely placed and—" He swept his hand across his mouth abruptly. "No, he cannot walk at all."

"Why wasn't he discharged, sent home? He's an American. He—"

"He was discharged—D.D."

"What does that mean?"

"Discharged, dead."

There was no mirth now in the Frenchman's sharp green eyes. But when the shiver rode up Judith's arms, a measure of kindness, part of the kindness that hovered between him and Washington, broke through.

"Who is he, Fayette?" she whispered.

"That, my dear lady, is the puzzle locked inside him. Our puzzle, perhaps, now."

"He tried to make me swear, Papa," Judith exclaimed as she brought Eli Mercer his ginger tea that morning. "Swear not to tell any officer, or the master of the watch, or the purser, or anchor's mate—a vast list of persons who know nothing of the young man's existence. To them, as well as to Captain Willis, Washington is a rumor, a haunt. For ten years he's been hidden on this vast vessel, imagine!"

"Extraordinary."

"Only select members of the officers and crew trusted by Fayette know Washington to be real. When he said that thou and I must be sworn into their society, I told him that we Friends do not take oaths. My agreement would have to suffice."

"Did he accept this?"

"Not without a stream of French words, which I feel he was using to spare my ears of their English translation."

Eli Mercer rested his hand on his daughter's shoulder. He appeared to be searching his breast pocket. No, Judith realized as she heard the sputtering sound of her father's laughter, he was not searching for anything at all.

"Papa, what is thy source of such amusement?" she demanded.

He sighed elaborately, for a Quaker. "Whenever I think about settling these old bones on a small farm, events intervene to tell me it's not our will but the Creator's that shapes our ends, rough-hew them as we may."

"That's prettily said, Papa!"

"Shakespeare said a version of it before me, sweetling."

"Thou is not reading that English . . . playwright!" she said with mock menace in her voice.

Eli laughed. "Not since my Fighting Quaker days. Not since I was welcomed back, repentant, at Meeting. But some turns of phrase have lasted, here." He tapped the side of his head as his eyes went wistful. Judith cherished this look that recalled her father before she was born, before the horror that had changed both their lives forever.

His wistful expression transformed itself back to familiar Quaker purpose. He smiled. "I feel a mission, Judith. I will, as ever, be standing by in wonder, thy humble assistant."

"But, Papa, between this dream and these strange men, what am I being called upon to do?"

"I don't feel that is the source of thy agitation, daughter. Consider this—Traveling Friend Judith Mercer is piqued."

"Piqued?"

"The tables have been turned. Thou, who has astounded people everywhere with thy ability to see into the darkest corners of their hearts, are now being called upon to take guidance from a young man who is comforted by the same vision that frightens thee. Whoever says the Creator has no humor, eh, Judith?"

2

"Wake up, *petit général.* Your *toilette* awaits you."

Washington shifted in his hammock. He counted the five bells of the night watch. "Too early. Leave me alone, Fayette," he grumbled.

"*Allons! Allons!* You must finish mending that sail for your ancient papa."

Washington opened his eyes. The familiar, child's fear—do not leave me!—stung him. "You are not old, Fayette," he told his friend.

"Best to hope not, while I have the razor at your throat."

Washington focused on the steaming rags, the worn strop, and gleaming metal. "*Non. Allons donc!* No shave," he declared firmly.

"What? You proclaim undying love for a woman you will not so much as shave for?"

Washington placed his lame leg over the edge of his hammock.

"I talked with the black people, Fayette," he said. "They promised not to disturb Judith Mercer's sleep anymore."

"Leaving room for thoughts of you."

Washington frowned. "She will sleep now, in the night, I think. She is not an owl, like me."

"Come, before all the heat is gone from these towels." Fayette eased him out of the hammock, carried him into the candle's light.

Washington sensed his friend's strained back. Was he too great a burden? How could that be? He was more than twenty years old, Fayette said. Surely he had stopped growing by now. He must eat less.

Fayette lowered him to the damp floorboards, propping him against an overturned shot box. Washington felt his face being swaddled in steaming rags.

"Why don't ladies like beards, Fayette?" he asked, enjoying the muffled, dreamlike tone the rags gave his voice.

The Frenchman removed their warmth and brushed the lathered soap along his jaw. The friction against his stubbly beard made foam. "Why not ask our beautiful Quakeress tonight?"

"Do you truly think she will come again?"

"Do you want to look like an unkempt scarecrow if she does?"

Washington grunted as the razor slid under his ear.

"She is beautiful, is she not, Fayette?" he asked.

"Mais oui."

"Why does she not know this?"

"She knows it. Religious women are obliged to pretend they do not."

"Was Clarisse religious?"

"Clarisse?" Fayette laughed. "Hardly. Why?"

"She used to call out names of her angels and saints when we loved each other. Why do you stop? Am I finished, then, Fayette?"

His friend's voice was tired. "You are so far from finished that I sometimes despair," he said. Washington felt the blade sweep up his throat. "Now listen to me," Fayette demanded. "You must not talk of Clarisse before Judith Mercer."

"Why not? Clarisse said women do not see the world as men do. They do not always assume a crippled mind or heart when a body is so. A woman values a man who is good and gentle and has hands that can do those things she showed me, to cause us both delight."

"Washington, Clarisse's favors were bought for the purpose of initiating you into your manhood. You were only with her three hours, for the love of God!"

"And I could not even speak at first, I was so afraid of her. But by the end—"

"This is not the same. You must keep your hands off Judith Mercer."

"It was she tending me when you came upon us, I tell you! Because of the blood, the small wound. And she was brave, like Clarisse, when she hid me under her cloak, no? I did not touch her, not in that way, Fayette, though my fingers ached there, so close against her shirt."

"*Gown*. Women wear gowns."

"Gown. Skin, just beneath. Soft, fragrant, how could I not notice? But I did not touch her, I swear it to you."

"Do not swear."

"Why not?"

"Judith Mercer's religion forbids swearing."

Washington laughed. "But between ourselves, may we not—?"

"Enough. Enough with your infernal questions!"

"Fayette, you are as nervous as a cat. Perhaps I should stay below tonight. I can finish mending the sail by candlelight."

"After my barber's skill has produced such good results without so much as a cut? *Zut alors!* I should have left you looking like the ungrateful American barbarian you are. Put a drop of this at your neck and wrists."

"What is—" Washington drew back with a start when Fayette pulled the cork from the small bottle. "Clove oil? I must smell like I have a toothache to win this woman?"

"No, like you don't live in the bowels of a leaking frigate. And pull this through that mane before I shave your head as well."

Washington looked down at the wide-toothed whalebone comb that Fayette had slapped into his hand. "It's for nothing. She will sleep dreamless. She will forget us."

"Have you become some visionary seer now? You must add that title to 'friend of slave *revenants* and dolphins and lover of all the women of the wide world around'! Soon you will not desire mere mortals such as I about your grand personage."

The silence crackled between the two men. Finally, the quiet voice, the one akin to Washington's as a child, spoke. *Do you love her, too?* it asked. *Is that why you are acting so strangely?*

Washington watched the older man walk out of the single candle's circle of light. He sat on the mahogany chair with the gold filigree that was their only piece of furniture besides the rough shelves. The shelves held Washington's ships and their books. They'd both preferred books to any other luxuries, even tobacco, until five years ago, on Fayette's shore leave in Lima.

Washington remembered laughing when he saw the French revolutionary drag his throne into their cramped quarters. Since that time the chair had become the place where Fayette sat when he needed privacy. Washington had learned not to violate his elder's time in the chair.

Now Fayette looked stunned and defeated there. His fine head of sun-bleached hair was buried between gnarled and scar-riddled fingers that could no longer climb the mast, but ministered tenderly to the new mast-men's injuries. Washington could not see his friend's green eyes. As a boy he used to fancy Fayette's eyes belonged to the great, wild cat he became in the dark. When the cat was there, Washington could sleep well, protected.

The man that the frightened boy had become pulled himself quietly toward the leg of Fayette's gold-leaf chair. He combed his hair out of his eyes, then wiped the trickle of sweat that slid down his clean-shaven face.

"C'est vrai, mais oui."

No response. He tried English. "You are right, of course. I am a worthy subject of your despair. My time with one woman has made me a crowing cock, a donkey braying. *Clémence?*"

The older man sat back, staring out into the small space that had confined them both for a decade.

"I will not talk so much, but listen to your good counsel, and follow your precepts. Do not be angry with me."

The spines of their books, the bleached-bone gleam of Washington's miniature ships, pulsed through the darkness. The seventh bell of the night watch sounded dimly from above. Finally, Fayette let his hand rest lightly on the thicket of dark hair hovering contritely at his knee.

"I am not angry with you, *petit général*," he said.

"*Bon. Très bien. Tu es un—*"

"English—speak English only! Have you forgotten your own language? Your contractions?"

"Contract—?"

"Don't! Won't! Di'n't!"

"Di'n't?"

"You think in French, I see it!"

"What harm is there in that?"

"Your own people will take you for a foreigner."

"You are my people, Fayette," Washington said softly, "only you."

"What? You birthed yourself from my head, then?"

Washington grinned. "Like Athena?"

"Athena, there! You knew of the goddess Athena before me."

"No. Yes. I don't know!"

"But you do, addlebrain."

The name stung at Washington like a whipping northwest wind. He folded his arms. "Keep your insults to yourself," he grunted.

Fayette smiled, looking smugly satisfied. "There. That part of you should remain French."

"What part?"

"Your pride, *mon général.*"

The leather thimbles absorbed another assault. Why was he jabbing himself so much? The lantern's light was good. There was no need for anticipation, for nervousness. She was not going to come.

Washington worked more quickly, hoping to finish within an hour. He'd lose himself in his shipbuilding then. A ketch. That would be next. He had sketched designs for it, a miniature of the one he'd seen merrily rocking fore and aft in the harbor at Galway Bay. Where were those drawings? What would he use to represent the stout chain of the ketch's mainstay?

The soft, pearly gray of Judith Mercer's cloak touched his arm. "I have brought mending. May I work with thee?"

He lifted his head, but couldn't find his voice in either language. He only managed to touch the place beside him on the bench. She sat there, and opened her deep-scarlet cloth bag.

Its color reminded him of Clarisse's final petticoat, the one that swept by his face as she danced for him. She had promised to come again, but she had not come. Instead, she had married a merchant who could give her a fine life. He must not think of Clarisse, Fayette said, because she was happy, and did not think of him. Still, she had promised. Were her other words lies, too?

Promises and swearing offended this woman sitting close enough for him to smell the salt sea air mingling with her scent. Her scent was more tart tonight, from something she liked to eat. Lemons, he thought. It was offset by what she pressed into her moist places—dried roses. The thought of those moist places was making him hard. *Merde!* His body held such dominion over him. Washington returned to his work with a will.

After an eternity of minutes, he glanced not at Judith Mercer but at the white shirt—or was it a gown?—in her lap. "Good seam," he said, feeling every inch the idiot.

"That is high praise."

Her cape's hood fell back. Her wondrous hair was hidden inside a plain white cap tonight. It reminded Washington of the kind the women wore selling their tulips along the dock of Amsterdam. He wished he could find this woman one of those flowers, a red one that would send the reflection of its color to her lips. Moving lips.

". . . Am I, Washington?"

"Are you?" he echoed, confused.

"Distracting thee? From thy work?"

"No, no. I am—I'm finished. Fayette will help me fold the sail later, at the end of the watch."

"Where is Fayette?"

"Below. He often sleeps now. He works very hard all day, and says I snore. I don't believe it. He likes to be rid of me for a little while, I think. Did your dream return?"

"No. Did thou speak to thy—friends?"

He grinned. "They told me you had opened your heart to them and listened. They would have allowed you to sleep from now on anyway."

"My thanks, just the same."

"You're welcome. May I see your needle?"

She handed it to him. He held it close to his eyes.

"So fine and sharp," he marveled.

"These needles have quite spoiled me, I'm afraid. I grew so accustomed to their delicacy, their ease and precision, I indulged myself in a lifetime supply before leaving London. Not very patriotic, my father scolds. He has succumbed to no English finery, but I—" She frowned. Her lower lip was more full than the upper one. Washington imagined the feel of those lips on his own.

"Forgive me, I do not usually prattle on so about frivolous things," she was saying now.

"Art is not frivolous."

"My mending is art?"

"Yes."

She laughed a full, musical laugh then. Soprano. No, deeper. Alto soprano. Washington lost himself in its sound. He wanted it all for himself, not for those on the outskirts of their lantern's circle of light—the masters of the Midwatch, the seamen throwing dice in the shadows, the ones aloft among the rigging. "May I finish the seam, Judith?" he asked. "My hands are clean, see?" He removed the leather thimbles from his left fingers to demonstrate.

Curiosity joined the mirth in her ever-changing gray eyes. "So they are. Not a trace of tar tonight, Friend Washington. And thou are scented somehow—savory?"

He ground his teeth. "That was Fayette's idea. I feel like a cured slab of meat. He has been very peculiar lately."

She laughed, handing him the garment. He examined the seam. "It has ripped here before," he observed.

"At the shoulder? Yes. Always reaching, that's Papa."

Belonging to her father. A shirt, then. "I will show you a lockstitch."

He was amazed at the way the gleaming needle eased among the strands of the shirt's weave. He followed Judith Mercer's straight stitches to the rip's end. Then he doubled back on them, and around the selvage. "Loop, see? Then lock."

She leaned in closer. "Do it again."

He did, more slowly.

"Let me try!"

He held the cloth between his fingers as she plunged the needle through. She was so close, a wisp of her hair glanced his chin. The silver strands were soft but strong, he could feel that even through the heat of his blush. Those strands, they would work well in the task he had in mind for them, he was sure of it.

She sighed. The rose part of her scent intensified. "I've gone too wide, haven't I?"

"Try placing them closer. And do not—don't—" he amended, "pull so tightly."

She went back to her task, absorbed. Could she hear his heart? Would the sound frighten her away? He tried to think of the design for the ketch, of keeping watch for unfamiliar officers, of anything he'd once thought important.

"There!" she called, triumphant. "What genius thou has!"

He exaggerated a scowl. "I am not an artist?"

"An artist in the Quaker tradition. An artist of thy life."

"Judith"—he summoned laughing eyes—"tell me what that means."

"We Friends desire to be remembered by our deeds, so our lives become our art. We take great joy in a well-planted field, a straight, strong seam. We see God in these things."

"But why do you not see God in plays, painting, poetry, songs?"

A whisper of a sigh escaped her. "Fayette has been speaking of our morning talks on deck?"

He bowed his head. "Yes."

"Washington, my father and I have tried to convince him that we Friends do not denounce. We have a loving approach to life. It's just that, for us, we see what thou calls art as an imitation of life, and so distracting from life itself. No, we have no poets, as thy dear friend reminds me daily. But we have fine botanists, scientists, and husbandmen."

"You would not like my ships."

"Ships?"

"I make them out of bones, scraps, things others throw away. They are not useful, my ships. They do not even sail."

"But perhaps they would be useful for teaching. Teaching children about ships, navigation?"

"Do you have children, Judith?"

She lowered her eyes. "No. There is only my father and me. But I visit many children."

"As you visited the prisoners at Dartmoor?"

"Yes."

"And these children you visit, they would like my ships? Learn from them? So you will give me your hair?"

Judith touched her cloak's hood. "My hair?"

He shook his head. "I am not doing this in the correct way."

She touched his arm. "Do not be distressed. Speak plainly."

Washington let the calming warmth of her touch spread through him. "I cannot raise the sails on my ships. I had found nothing fine enough, or strong enough, or light enough. The combination of all three, you understand? Until I saw your hair. It would flow through one of your needles, it would become the lines my ships need to raise the sails. To be complete."

Her hand left his arm. "I would be privileged to contribute the leavings of my brush for thy purpose," she said.

"And this would not violate your precepts?"

Judith laughed again. Hers was a religion of joy, Washington decided. Why did Fayette scorn it so? She pulled a bound book from her scarlet bag. Washington felt a familiar tingling at the tips of his fingers that the sight of a book always produced.

"Look," Judith Mercer said. "Nature's own art, the shadow."

Centered on the first creamy white page was a black paper silhouette. A portly gentleman in a wide hat stood, his attention absorbed by a broad leaf in his hands.

"Who is that?"

"Eli Mercer. My father. He collected plants during our time in London. The windowsills were full, vines around every doorway."

"Who made this, Judith?"

"I did. In partnership with nature's shadow, of course. I'll bring Papa tomorrow night, so thou can judge the image with reality."

"Good," he said, meaning it, but hoping she would not bring Eli Mercer every night.

"But he needs his sleep, so I'm afraid you'll have to suffer my company alone for most of the crossing."

His smile widened. A spot of color appeared at her cheek as she returned her attention to her black paper sheets. "It is a simple craft, but I take joy in finding details to heighten, illuminate my subjects." She turned the page.

"There's Stanley, the captain of the forecastle!" Washington exclaimed.

"Yes! How do you know him?"

"By his swinging waistcoat, his wild hair, his hold on the rope." Washington turned the next page eagerly. "And here's the purser with a tight grip on his keys and lips both. And First Lieutenant Mitchell, tilted from wearing only one epaulet—so long has been his wait for promotion! Judith, how do you do this?"

She leaned over the book, pointing her slender fingers at slit collars backed with white paper and delicately cut buttonholes. Her deep, richly toned voice explained the craft that had captured the crew of the *Standard* as they engaged in their daily living.

"Shall I bring my scissors and my black paper tomorrow?" she asked.

"And I'll bring one of my ships. We can raise the sails together, yes?"

3

Captain Willis spun the fine crystal glass by its stem. The mulatto servant in satin livery poured brandy to fill it again.

The captain's sneering smile cut through the ugly saber-scars. Despite his manners and the polished reflection of his quarters, this was a man who'd abused his privilege of power, Judith sensed. And he bore the intemperate palsy of the hunted. How much longer would this interminable meal last? She watched the steam rising from her tea.

Judith usually slept during this time, the dog watch between four and eight in the evening, so that she could join Washington later under the stairs. Tonight, she'd planned to craft his silhouette as he carved the graceful Irish ketch.

"I fear I do not command your full attention, Miss Mercer."

Judith lifted the cup, swallowed. The tea burned her throat.

"Tending my health has turned my daughter into a night owl, Captain Willis," Eli Mercer explained, smiling pleasantly.

Judith pressed her father's hand. Eli would protect the knowledge of Washington's existence as fiercely as she did.

The captain changed tack. "My officers praise your daughter's reading of the story of Noah and the Flood to the seamen."

"We've felt warmly accepted by all the ship's company."

The sneer, again. "I, too, sought upon occasion to enlighten, and even to make merry with my men. While at our common diversions I must have seemed the loving, even indulgent, father of this ark. Then I would need to 'ship my quarterdeck face' as we say, to become lord again. No more. It was not fair to the men. I saw hope in their eyes. Hope of rising above their station. Worse, I saw thoughts that they may, in some capacity, be my equal."

"Art thou attempting to goad us into debate, Friend?" Eli Mercer asked, the tone of his voice remaining banter-light. He even used the older English Quakerisms in his speech. Judith wondered if she would ever achieve her father's diplomatic skills.

"Debate?"

"Our Society is based on equality."

"Actual equality, not an ideal?"

"Just so."

The silent servant filled Judith's cup. "My father and I have no quarterdeck faces to ship," she affirmed sharply.

Captain Willis leaned across the table, his dress uniform advancing on her in the polished brass, too. "Ah, now, at long last a taste of fire, Miss Mercer! Your indignation is somewhat legendary. It persuaded even the British Admiralty to overrule my objections and permit you to board the *Standard* for the crossing."

"We didn't meet with thy approval?" Judith asked.

"And I have made you so welcome you never suspected my initial opposition! You will report as much, I trust, in one of your future missives to the Admiralty. I know there will be several. With many admonitions."

"Suggestions."

"Of course, suggestions. Gentle persuasion. Quakers. Why was the *Standard* chosen as your escort over the waves to your native land? Did you wonder?"

"I did not."

"Allow me to enlighten you. This ship has roamed the French and Barbary coasts unmolested in times of heaviest fighting. Our twenty-four-pound guns have remained silent through the late unfortunate hostilities between your United States and Great Britain. Silent since our glorious victory over the French at Trafalgar, to be precise. Ten years. The wisdom that presides over our Admiralty must have imagined this frigate the safest of passenger barges for your return." He swallowed his glass empty again and turned to Judith's father. "We are something of a Quaker man-of-war, wouldn't you say, Eli Mercer?"

Her father smiled. "Were thy ship's magazine empty, perhaps."

The captain glared at them both. "Is that another step in your loathsome process?"

"Friend?"

The sneer returned. "Will you heave my ammunition overboard? I'd best keep my sentries on guard against this devious Friend and his daughter, practicing her own black art in her charming silhouettes. What if you should convert my men, Mercers? A crew of Quakers does not suit a man-of-war."

Cruel laughter erupted before he demanded more brandy with that curious, silent twirl of the glassware's stem. "Tell me, Judith Mercer, do you think the American ships are run substantially different from His Majesty's?"

Judith thought of Washington's eyes, which still were full of his love of the sea despite his long captivity. His time in his American vessel must have given him that. "I am not well versed on that subject," she said quietly.

"The ideal of equality is maintained in your sacred documents, but its actual practice is not. Slavery, for instance?"

"We feel everyone is on his own path in the journey toward the Light." Her father came to her aid.

"Or the darkness. Don't you people acknowledge the existence of Hell, of punishment?"

"Acknowledge it, of course," Judith replied. "We do not choose to dwell on the darkness."

"Is it as easy as that, woman?"

Open your heart to him. She prodded her fear to unlock her paralyzed throat. "That choice stems from our will. And free will is God's blessing, is it not, Friend Willis?"

He leaned across the table again. "What if the darkness has a life, a will of its own? What if it visits nightly?"

Judith felt a spark of the Light pierce through the darkness, through her fear. "Speak to it," she urged in a faint whisper.

"What?"

"Speak to it, find what it requires of thee."

He turned abruptly. His boots sounded hard, even on the Persian carpet, as he prowled around his heavy chestnut furniture. His sword rattled in its shaft. "I know what it requires of me, woman! I should have been made a commodore after Trafalgar. By now I should be on my way into the Admiralty! Instead, I am cursed, pitied, laughed at by enemies, attached to this useless frigate like a Roman galley slave. That's what my demon requires of me!"

Her father laid his hand protectively over Judith's arm. "Thou could resign thy commission," he said.

The captain stood his ground. "Go down, sir? Admit defeat by the hands of an insolent boy who did not know his place?"

"What boy?" Judith whispered, her heart racing.

"You know very well what boy, Quakeress! The one who would not fight! You know the story, you've heard it from that arrogant Frenchman. Have a care who you choose as your friends along this voyage, Mercers. Lafayette, indeed. His name is no more Lafayette than mine is

Nelson! He signed on to escape the guillotine's blade, most likely. He could have jumped ashore on any continent. He must have made powerful enemies around the globe!"

"Or perhaps powerful friends here," Judith said.

"Oh, they speak well enough of him below, with his salves and remedies—that's kept the lash more than once from that crafty Frenchman's back. But I have my eye on him. I've had my eye on him since he carried the body off."

"Body?"

"The cat-o'-nine-tails did not kill that boy, his own unyielding heart did! Don't let any tell you differently. I was going to make that powder monkey my cot boy after the battle. He would have lived here, serving me with those fine-boned hands."

"From where did this boy come?" Judith asked.

"The *Ida Lee*. He was weeping like a child over a dead midshipman. It was supposed to be a warning shot. It was off, that's all. Such things can't be helped. The boarding of the *Ida Lee* was my sworn duty! We were heading toward Trafalgar shorthanded; I had to supplement the crew."

He shrugged—a heavy act in his medal-laden uniform—before turning his back on her scrutiny. He leaned on the shining brass railing, and looked over the calm sea beyond the cabin windows.

More. Tell me all of it, she demanded silently.

"I picked him up myself, by the scruff of his neck—he was that small," he began. " 'I will provide you with someone to serve who is worthy of your tears,' I told him. He didn't answer. He didn't speak a word to me until his defiance during the battle.

"Soon after the boarding, the *Ida Lee* sank in a gale off the Bermudas, all hands lost. I had saved him, Miss Mercer, saved him from that fate, by taking him on the *Standard*! Why do those angry, accusing eyes visit me nightly? This ship is a man-of-war. Why does he glide around its glorious purpose—war?

"I gave him control of the lashes. He only had to pledge allegiance—to me, to his new country. Boys that young are green branches; they can mend, they can be taught to grow in a different direction. But not him. His leg cracked, his heart followed. Weakness. A failure of the heart. He was a suicide, then, wasn't he?" He turned from the window abruptly. "What does your Society of Friends think of suicides, Miss Mercer?"

Judith touched her forehead. "I am terribly fatigued and must beg to be released."

His smile creased through the saber scars. "Released? Released? You are hardly my captive, dear lady. Of course you are free to go. Go, come, all decks, all times, as the Admiralty ordered. Even I am not that free. But of course you are used to freedom. You are an American."

When she felt her foot slip on the step, a firm grip took her elbow. It eased her down.

"*Mon dieu,* Judith, you are as pale as a lily."

Fayette's concerned eyes so relieved her she rested her head against his broad chest. His arms enfolded her. There. Safe. "They said thou was on duty in sick bay," she said.

"I'm just going off. Where's your father? Are you ill?"

"I must see him, Fayette."

He looked behind him. Satisfied by the empty silence, he pulled her into the shadows. "Now? Why? He's sleeping."

"Please."

He shook his head, but took her arm. They descended the stairwell until there were no more steps. They stood in the lowest caverns of the *Standard.* Judith smelled apples, the cold iron of the anchor and chain, earthy potatoes, and briny seawater as they walked past the lockers. At the far end of the dank hallway, she saw a small, rounded door. Fayette retrieved a key from his vest pocket.

"He's locked in?" she asked.

The Frenchman frowned. "The curious are locked out. He has a key. Tied around his neck."

He opened the door, stooping to enter. Judith's head touched the planked ceiling. The room was nothing like she'd imagined, nothing like a dungeon, except for the darkness.

As her eyes adjusted, they scanned a capacious gilt armchair, some tacked-up netting studded with conch shells. And shelves. They were set low, as if for a child, or a man who could not walk. Books—an astonishing number, perhaps a hundred. Beside them were Washington's wondrous miniature ships, their white sails raised on lines woven from her nightly hair-leavings. She had never seen the ships like this, together in their graceful beauty. They had helped keep him sane through his captivity, Judith realized. That alone would have been enough to give them full Quaker purpose.

A breeze from the hallway cleared the air. Fayette raised his lantern. Suspended from the low ceiling hung a hammock. From it, even breathing sounded. Judith stepped closer.

Washington shifted and sighed deeply. No blanket covered him, only a rough gray frock, mended many times with his even stitches. Judith felt a distinct rush of pleasure being able to see him like this, unobserved except for Fayette's wary eye.

Any lingering distrust of Fayette had been vanquished during Judith's time in the captain's cabin. The Frenchman was her ally. He was the reason the cocooned dreamer was alive, and so much more at peace than he who lived in splendor above.

Judith laced her fingers in the strings of the hammock. She pushed, watching fondly. Fayette's hand glided gently down her spine before his fingers fanned out at the small of her back. An intimate gesture. Judith didn't stiffen. Beneath their joint gaze, Washington smiled in his sleep. His cheekbones were sharp, his frame not meant to carry so little weight. It would all be remedied—the thought birthed itself in Judith Mercer's heart—once she brought him home.

He opened his eyes. "Judith?"

"Yes," she whispered, sweeping the hair back from his forehead. "It's only me, collecting my wager from Fayette. No snoring comes from thy hammock."

"Wager? He will not even allow me to swear, and you two are wagering?"

"Shhh," she whispered, rocking. "Back to sleep now."

"You'll come? On deck? Tonight?"

"I'll come."

"When do you sleep, Judith?"

Fayette shook his head. *"Les questions, seulement les questions. Avoir sommeil, petit général,"* he admonished.

Once Washington's eyes closed again, Judith felt dazed, underwater, which in fact, there in the hold, she was. Fayette led her from their quarters, locked the door. They climbed to the deck above. They walked past the sick bay and the counting room of the purser's steward to the apothecary. The somber man behind the half-door had his head in a medical treatise.

"Thrumming," Fayette summoned. "I need a remedy."

Thrumming's hollow cheeks compressed further as he surveyed Judith. "Hmmm. I would bleed her first."

"I'll consider your suggestion. Would you like to take a promenade of the deck?"

Thrumming nodded, put his book under his arm, and left.

Fayette brought Judith inside the small room, and lifted her onto its lonely surgeon's stool.

"Fayette," she protested, "I'm not ill."

"Shhh," he admonished, as lightly as he had Washington. Then he set to work.

Tiers of shelves crowded with green bottles and gallipots lined all four sides of the cubicle. Beneath the shelves, drawers were inscribed in Latin. From one, Fayette removed a gnarled root. He added powder, and began to mash them together in a mortar.

Judith watched, oddly comforted. He had been doing this a long time—standing, harnessed by the small space, patiently making up remedies.

"My father and I dined with the captain," she said.

"I see."

"His darkness, Fayette. Thou cannot protect Washington from it much longer."

"I know." He ground something black beneath the pestle.

"Thou art not Lafayette. His name is not Washington. Who is he?" Judith demanded. "Why is he on this ship?"

Fayette looked up, amused. "What's this, anger?"

"Bluntness. We Quakers are known for being blunt, remember?"

"Your knotted fists betray you, Judith."

"Anger, then! At—"

"Anger? From a gentle persuader seeking the seed of Truth within this poor fellow here beside you?"

Judith concentrated on the stiff fingers in her lap. He was right; that was the worst of her humiliation. This rationalist Frenchman was right. "I ask thy forgiveness," she said softly.

He uncorked a bottle and added its liquid to his concoction. It smelled like blackberries. He stirred, then poured it all into a chipped crockery cup. He put it in Judith's hand. "Drink."

The draught was curiously sweet, spiced by ginger and licorice. She finished it in the second swallow. "What was that, Fayette?"

"A love potion."

"Thou cannot resist teasing me, even now?"

"No, *rose blanc.*"

"Rose—?"

"White rose. Have none of your lovers ever called you by the names of flowers?"

Her hands were now folded in her lap. "Stop."

He sighed. "Very well. But you will not be so without mercy as to disallow me my dreams?"

Safe. He was teasing her again. She met his eyes.

"And who was I, in thy dream?" she challenged.

"My dream?"

"The one as we stood beside the hammock?"

He exhaled an exasperated snort. "You are like him, do you know that? Chipping away at my rational being with your infernal visions!" He took in a pained breath. "Madeline and I, we used to lean over the cradle together like that. Exactly like that. Not quite believing."

"Believing what?"

"Our good fortune."

"She was a Friend, thy Madeline," Judith realized.

"Disowned when she married me—Reason, the Devil himself."

"Thy wife, child, are they . . . ?"

"A lifetime ago I lost them, back when you were playing with your dolls."

Judith felt a warm glow pass between her and this charming, provoking man. He didn't even think her older than her years, as most men did, because of her hair's early graying. He had erred on the other side.

"I am two and thirty." She protested his idea of the vast difference between their ages.

"My daughter would be eight and twenty come spring. You were playing with your dolls then? Surely you had a poppet at four, dear Judith? Do concede me that. Allow me to win one argument with you."

She nodded, remembering the doll her mother made her. A faceless doll, and dressed plain, of course—but how she'd treasured her baby, and the real one that her mother birthed soon after, and the three who came after him. She treasured them still, though they were becoming as faceless as the doll.

Judith watched the broad-shouldered man return his remedies to their proper drawers.

"Has he become ours somehow, then, Fayette?" Judith whispered. "Is that why we fight so?"

"Perhaps."

"Thy potion was not necessary," she told him. "I did love thee already. Since I saw the brother thee is to my countryman," she said, reverting to the more informal American turn of her people's speech.

"And your countryman? Do you love him, Judith? Not with this obligatory, universal Quaker love you bestow on me, but with the passion that springs from your heart? I fear my Washington will not survive out in the wide world without that love."

"He is not in the wide world. He is in this place of terrible risk. What of his survival here? If the captain should know . . ."

"He is a demon of the captain's own guilty mind, whom he wrestles nightly. To the others—both the ones who think Washington a crippled imbecile, and the ones trusted with the truth?—to them he is a charm against their own deaths. Sea battles rage around the globe, but this ship has not fired a shot since Trafalgar."

"The captain rails about this."

"I did not make any of it so. I am a rational man. I only take advantage of the consequences, for the sake of my friend."

"It's coming to an end. We both know that, don't we?"

"You've become a second demon to Willis, I know that!" he proclaimed, pacing the few steps the small space allowed him. "Perhaps he believes you to be that other Judith, the apocryphal giant-killer, who slew the mighty Holofernes for the Israelites. Your Inner Light is your sword, yes? What did it slice out of the captain tonight? Come, Judith, I am sure you went through your own terror and found all manner of—"

"Washington was impressed from the *Ida Lee.*"

"His ship. You learned his American ship? I'm damned."

Judith frowned. "That I doubt. But I'm sure thou will find aspects of Heaven to complain about."

Fayette threw back his head and gave out a blast of laughter. She should have ignored his impiety, Judith decided, but she did enjoy the sound.

"Washington was weeping over the loss of a midshipman when they took him from his American vessel," Judith continued.

Fayette sobered. "The other boy, the boy with his face."

"Boy?"

"When he was fevered from the lashes, he called out for another boy. Sometimes he'd call him the boy with his face, sometimes the boy with no face. So, he was a midshipman aboard the *Ida Lee*, this other. What else, what else?"

Judith's fingers flew to her temples. "Let me think, baneful man! Oh, yes. What are powder monkeys?"

"The messengers to the cannons during an engagement. They bring fresh gunpowder from the magazine. Powder monkeys are a very short-lived breed."

"Captain Willis called Washington one of them."

"Ah. That would explain the burns on his face. Cannon blast. From before the battle off Trafalgar, then? But, Judith, does the United States teach her powder monkeys Latin and Greek and celestial navigation?"

"Was not thyself his tutor in those subjects?"

"No. I come from bourgeois shopkeepers. My father was only concerned that I learned English, the language of commerce, and my numbers, an ability at which Washington exceeds me. My further education was through Paris literary and social salons, the maxims of Camfort and the ravings of Danton, before I awoke one morning a citizen marine. This powder monkey who reads to me from *Plutarch's Lives*, he of the beautiful shirt—who was he, Judith? Was the *Ida Lee* of the American navy or was she merchant marine?"

"I don't know. But the captain said she sank off the Bermudas. Washington is now her only survivor."

At this news the Frenchman's eyes went melancholy. "Perhaps he has people, then, after all."

"People? I don't understand."

"That is why no one's ever come for him, inquired about him all these years. The messengers, those who could have told your government how he was taken, where he is, they are all dead themselves." His green eyes sparked. "All but you, Judith."

"Me?"

"He's from the South of the United States, you said?"

"I think so, though his speech is so influenced by thine own—"

"You must travel your southland; you must find his people."

"It's a very large area, Fayette."

"How large?"

"Larger than all of France; and beyond the seaboard, much of it is still wilderness."

"Ah, but this is nothing, not for you! Your father will be your aide-de-camp. First you and I, in the time we have left, we will badger our Washington's muddled head about his remembrances. His dreams, you must ask him about those pictures in his head, traces of his childhood are in them. Night and day we will badger him!" He laughed. "Shall we pledge it together, Mother?"

Judith was startled by the appellation. It connected itself with Washington's picture of two dancing mothers. She was his third, the Quaker one, the one who didn't dance. The name linked her to Fayette, in the same capacity as his Madeline. Dearly.

She took the Frenchman's outstretched hand to seal their pact. No, not a pact—she must not swear. She took it in friendship. Warm. He caressed her fingers between his big hands with a delicacy she didn't think he possessed.

"Find his people, Judith," he said. "Bring him home."

Her lips parted. Not in objection to the task, but at the sudden, searing thought of being left alone, without him, to do it.

He came closer. Her feet dangled like a schoolgirl's from the stool. She was no schoolgirl. She was a grown woman who had convinced herself she could live a full life without this. He touched her cheek, watching her eyes, always watching, as he lowered his mouth to hers.

Their chaste kiss lingered, somehow mingling her licorice love potion with his lime-and-rum grog. His fingers glided down her neck, deftly maintaining intimacy as his lips left hers.

"Perhaps your parents should not have chosen such a fierce model in your namesake, *chère* Judith," he whispered at her ear. "Perhaps you were gifted with too much of that lady's fire to remain light only? Should gentle Ruth or David's wise Abigail have guided their selection?"

Judith found her voice. "My deficiencies are my own, Fayette. Leave my parents blameless."

His mouth discharged another snort of laughter before he took up her hand and deftly, defiantly, kissed protesting fingers. "There," he conceded. "Some humor, even if you people have no art. I suppose I could be giving Washington to a blasted Calvinist."

"Giving?"

"You heard me. He is yours."

This was the old Fayette—cynical, angry—and Judith was waking reluctantly to spar with him again. "Why?"

"Because you are right. It grows less safe for him daily. I should have somehow gotten him ashore years ago, but I've seen how the lame are treated out there, and every time I thought of not being able to protect him, of that fine spirit broken, I chose the evils we already knew. Foolish."

"Fayette . . ."

"You must hurry. My joints ache so I can barely lift the small weight he is. Washington cannot survive without me, and I am long past my prime out here on the sea."

Judith felt a bone-numbing cold invade her being. "Dear God. Don't say that," she whispered.

His index finger gently traced the line that appeared in her forehead. "No grief. Yours are not a grieving people, remember? The ten years aboard this cursed English frigate have been the brightest of my life after Madeline. My *petit général* has exceeded me. Could a father want for more? When he was a child, I told him that his fine, principled President Jefferson would rescue him. We were too patient, yes? No one came. Now is your turn, Judith Mercer. Find his people, tell them he lives, and make them procure his release. Help him find himself with them, after." His eyes went sad. "Protect him from his enemies, brave little Quakeress, because I have never been able to teach him guile. In return he will love you forever, in whatever mode you desire."

4

"The steaming of the pudding plumps the raisins," Washington explained. "It mixes with the oats, makes the pudding taste—"

"Delicious," Judith finished for him. Washington watched their honored guest swallow the cracker mashed in boiled water. "Thy plum duff is delicious, Washington."

Judith was good at the game he and his friend had played with their food for years.

How beautifully she graced the chestnut-and-gold filigree of Fayette's chair. How could he find the courage to steal her soul? He could barely steal glances. Why must he do this? he'd asked his friend. *"In war as in love, we must achieve contact to triumph."* Fayette had proclaimed Napoleon's maxim. And he'd only snorted when Washington pointed out that Napoleon was now in lonely exile.

When Judith had met with him on deck, her changeling gray eyes transmuted with the density of the night air, with the color of her garment. But they took on no color here in the blacks and whites and grays of their home below the waterline.

Judith was not used to their quarters. She should not stay any longer. Couldn't Fayette see that? They must fetch her father to bring her to her berth, and, tomorrow, to her own country. No, not that; not gone. Washington fought the notion of her being gone from them. He must not think of that. Not yet.

Standing beside Washington's hammock, Fayette grinned. "You are succumbing to it, Judith," he warned.

She raised her head. Washington pretended he'd see that defiant gesture for a lifetime, that he'd continue to mediate the altercations between these two people he loved best in the world.

"Succumbing? To what?" she demanded.

"To the power of Washington's imagination," Fayette parried, his light eyes flashing. "It has turned our meager fare into a feast of oysters and quail eggs and plum duff, our humble ration of grog into the finest wine of Champagne. And has made you, dear Judith, the most desired woman since Helen of Troy."

Her mouth curved into a smile. It was not the taut, wary one she usually wore when sparring with Fayette. It was wide, open, astounding Washington more than Fayette's improper words.

Judith raised the bleached-bone cup Washington had made for her, looking past the delicately carved tulips in its rim. Her eyes turned green, suddenly. From where did the color come? The green serge of her gown? Washington blinked. She and Fayette laughed like doting parents over a dreamy child. He was not a child. It stung at him, their laughter.

"I can hardly protest, not tonight," she said in that bell-clear voice. "Not when thy fine-wrought imagination has given thee a life in thy captivity, dear Washington." Judith raised the cup higher, to his friend. "And it has helped transform this bitter revolutionary into the most devoted of fathers."

Judith watched the men's cups touch the rim of hers. What was she saying? The overseers of her Monthly Meeting would not approve of these words, praising imagination. The cup in her hand lost Washington's fanciful design and became bone again—ugly, broken, like the bones of his leg. What was happening to it?—to her? The hazy film of a vision enshrouded them all.

Judith glanced desperately past the men's faces to seek her stability in the sight of the miniature ships. Their masts were shredding. Her hair strands whipped and lashed at the fine cloth sails. The ships plowed into each other, then shattered as they hit the floor. A voice, abandoned and lost, repeated the French words over and over.

"Catch her, Fayette." Washington's urgent whisper cut through the haze of Judith Mercer's vision. Too late. She fell on the bones.

Judith felt a cold wetness at her temples, and the familiar scent of cloves. She opened her eyes. Washington returned her smile. She was not lying on bones, but on his hammock stretched out there on the floor. The vision was over, her eyes clear, everything in place again. Washington's deft hands were both at work, one fanning her face with a torn page of one of their precious books, the other gliding something over her lips. "Sip, Judith," he urged.

She did. "What is it?"

"Ice. Fayette went into the officers' provisions for it. He's locking up now, and fetching your father."

The sliver of ice melted. Washington's fingertips tasted of the steel of his needles. "There," he said. "Your color returns."

Judith took his arm and sat up slowly. She felt better there, on the floor with him, away from the pomp of Fayette's chair. How tenderly, how calmly he cared for her, after she must have frightened him to the marrow. What a wonderful doctor he would make, her Washington. She raised her hand to her brow. "I was saying something, wasn't I? Something foolish. . . ."

"Not foolish. You were making us the artists of our lives. Fayette was the foolish one, comparing you to the Grecian queen, embarrassing a religious woman by calling attention to her beauty. It was rude, and he has taught me better. I apologize for him."

The face that had been forlorn and drifting all night now found its focus in indignation. Judith let out a small rush of laughter that somehow ended in a sob.

"Now, don't do that," he admonished. "Fayette will think I was not a gentleman, and made you cry."

"I'm not crying."

"No? What is this?" He turned her face to the candlelight.

"The ice. The last drops of the ice."

Washington came closer. His tongue swiped her cheek and followed up the side of her face. "Salt," he declared. "Tears. For whom do you weep, Judith? What did you see in your vision?"

How could she hide it from him? "Thy ships, falling from the shelf, breaking," she whispered. "Bones, all the bones broken. And French words. *Plus tard*. What does that mean, Washington?"

He spoke gently. " 'Later,' it means only *later*. Some rough seas ahead, is it? We must tie the ships down to the shelf, yes? Do not cry. They are not worth your tears."

"Yes, of course." Her voice shook out the words. "Foolish. Didn't I tell thee I was being—"

"I love you, Judith," Washington whispered. "Across the water, beyond time and the stars and remembrance, I love you."

She swept his gleaming hair off his brow. It was a mother's or sister's gesture, and he knew it. Judith felt the searing heat of his anger as he caught her hand, pressed it to his face, kissed into its palm. Deeply, tasting her sweat, her skin. He traced her life line with the tip of his hard, unyielding tongue, leaving her breasts tingling, her body faint with longing. He knew what he was doing. He knew exactly.

"Washington," she gasped out. "Stop."

He did, lowering his head until she could only see the spiraling crown of his hair.

"I do not please you," he whispered.

"You do please me. And you know you do," she said, abandoning her Quaker "thou." "Washington, you are not an innocent."

He raised his head. His man-child eyes, already too wide, too beautiful, went wider still. "Is that required in your religion?"

"When? How?" she heard herself demanding.

"Only once! And she was full of courage, like you. . . . No, not like you, nothing like you. Fayette says I must not talk of her, because you will think of it as a sin because it was not sanctified, and the money he paid for her favors, and—"

"You miss her. You loved her?"

"No. Yes. She said she would come back, she promised! Did she lie? Am I so hideous, so damaged?" He ground his teeth in frustration. "Wrong. I'm doing it all wrong."

"Doing what, impossible man?"

"You are angry?"

"Yes!"

"As angry as you get with Fayette?"

"Fully as angry!"

His mood underwent a sea change. "This is good!" He laughed. Then he kissed her.

Judith felt the urgent breath bursting from his nostrils across her wet cheek. When she shivered, his lips pressed harder against her yielding mouth. She felt his even, gleaming teeth under her tongue's bold sweep. Her fingers raked the abundance of his hair shamelessly as he probed her mouth. The kiss sweetened with the raisins of his imaginary plum duff. Joy followed on the heels of surprise, both unfettered by thought. He pressed so close she felt the taut sinew of his muscles, the bones underneath, the strong heartbeat, farther still. Fayette's kiss in the apothecary had paved her way toward this one, she thought, when it ended.

"What have you done?" she whispered.

He smiled, taking her hands in his, swinging them in a small, graceful arc. "Stolen your soul," he admitted, like a boy caught pulling the tail of a cat. "A small part only, but you will have to come back to us for its return."

"I will come back," she said. "But not for my soul. I'll come to bring thee home."

"I cannot leave without Fayette, Judith."

"I know," she whispered.

Fayette slouched in the doorway, his shoulder pressed to the rafter. *"Mon dieu!"*—he announced his presence. "For this I have bribed the yeoman for ice with my medal of the Egyptian campaign? For a woman with rose cheeks, full of life and health?"

He stormed in, stepping over their clasped hands. Eli Mercer, his shirt tucked hastily into his breeches, followed.

"I'm well now, Papa." Judith assured his anxious eyes as she took his hand, linking her father to her flushed young lover.

Fayette snatched the worn book from the floor. "My Molière!" he shouted at his charge. "You could have just as easily torn pages from your bloody Shakespeare!"

The *Standard*'s bow shrouded in mist as the launch pulled farther toward shore. Judith raised her arm to the men's farewell.

The English frigate had performed its small duty of delivering the Quakers and the letters of the men at Dartmoor. It would sail on. Captain Willis stood in full-dress uniform on the quarterdeck, ramrod-straight as if he were made of tin.

He'd remained beside Judith during her farewells, and so she could only hold Fayette's hand a little longer than the rest as she gave him her gift. He'd stared down at the black cut paper.

His silhouette placed him high on the mizzenmast, where he'd served in his prime. It had been Washington's suggestion to place him there. Judith had not been sure Fayette would view it with approval. She should have relied on the younger man's instincts. As Fayette regarded her gift, his sharp eyes had lost their icy cynicism. For one lovely moment, they'd almost darkened. It was as if he'd turned part of himself into Washington, so that she could see them both for this last time.

From her native shore, with the packet of the Dartmoor prisoners' letters under her arm, Judith looked out to sea. The land sounds were strange, as was the solid dock beneath her feet.

"The coach waits," her father urged. "They cannot see thee any longer," he said more quietly, touching her arm.

"Go on," she said. "I'm coming."

As his footfalls faded, she whispered the last verse of a lullaby. Practical songs, lullabies, used for the purpose of drawing children to rest. Had her mother sung them? She must have—from whom else had Judith caught the words?

Take time to rest, my ray of hope,
In the garden of Dramore.
Take heed, young eaglet,

Till thy wings
Are feathered fit to soar.
A little rest and then the world
Is full of work to do.

Sleep, Washington, through the dog and night watches. Sleep and stay engaged with thy sails and ships until I return, she sang.

Judith walked to the waiting coach.

"I believe we should bring the Dartmoor prisoners' letters to James Madison, Papa, so he can touch the lingering effects of his war. Our new mission of securing Washington's release may as well commence there too."

5

Dolley Madison, born into a Quaker family, had been expelled from the Society when she'd married James Madison. If she bore any Friend ill will as a result, it was not apparent. There was much Quaker criticism of this flamboyant wife of a wartime president. But Judith recognized her as a kindred spirit in a satin Empire-waist gown, gold-embroidered headband, and ostrich plumes.

"How many died?" Judith asked the president's wife.

"Six. There were sixty wounded."

"Perhaps we should have stayed."

The lively blue eyes darkened with compassion. "You could not have prevented it, my dear."

Soon after Judith had been entrusted with the Dartmoor letters, there had been a riot at the prison. The carnage had taken place in the sweet, budding month of April, the very night she met Washington sewing his sails.

"Sometimes it seems this war will never be over," Mrs. Madison said. "The president has arranged for special couriers to deliver the letters you've brought, Judith, along with his assurance that surviving kinsmen will be home soon."

Then her face lit with the legendary, winning smile that made her either her husband's greatest asset or the new capital city's most notorious seductress. But Mrs. Madison's personal courage could no longer be held in doubt since she'd saved the country's sacred documents as the British burned Washington around her. Now she presided over her quarters at the rainbow-hued rooms of Octagon House.

Fayette would love it here, Judith thought, with its bold reflective colors and fantail windows that made the house the embodiment of his philosophy of Enlightenment. She wished he were sitting beside her, Dolley Madison's charming, male match. "You are now free to search for the family of your impressed sailor," the president's wife proclaimed. "I envy you!"

"Me?"

"Here, in my graciously loaned exile from the president's house, I feed, charm, and entertain diplomats who have great power over the lives of those prisoners you serve. If the men I amuse could exchange places with the Mercer family for one day, I think they would come to realize that they have been fed and charmed enough."

The hostess's long-gloved hand opened the folder in her lap. "And now, let me give you a small reward for the work of your generous heart." She handed over the paper inside. Judith read its contents. "My. How beautifully your eyes change color, my dear," the president's wife observed.

"Mrs. Madison. This is—"

"A list of the officers and crew of the lamented American merchant ship, the *Ida Lee*. Thirty of them were boys under the age of fifteen. All came out of the South. Their names are marked. It is still a large number, but I feel sure your sailmender is among them."

Judith scanned the list. Jarvis, Cowper, Burnett, Jameson, Morris. All of the boys the names belonged to were dead now—as dead as the six prisoners at Dartmoor, but one. Would she be too late for him, too? She finally lifted her head, remembered her manners. "I thank thee," she whispered.

"Let the results of my intrigue ease your sorrow. And when you find your captive's family, come flying back to me and I will begin charming vain men of the British government to procure his release."

At their small suite of rooms across the river in Alexandria, Judith's father listened intently. "Papa, imagine how even Dolley Madison acquired such information with this city in ruins around her."

He stroked his chin. "That makes three gifts."

"Three?"

"Did thee not unpack thy trunk since we arrived, Judith?"

"Not all of it. We were so busy, then I was called before the president's wife so quickly that the last few things—"

"Including thy green serge gown."

"Have the moths gotten at the weave? Or mildew?"

"It is unharmed. But among its folded layers I found two gifts to place beside Dolley Madison's." He reached into a drawer and brought forth a delicate silhouette. Judith recognized herself immediately, her scissors in her hands. She was in the process of cutting the figure of Fayette flying about the lines of the mizzenmast. How had Washington fashioned this clever image without her knowledge?

"Thee taught him well," her father said softly. "And here, look what else found its way into thy trunk."

Eli reached into the drawer again. He placed a miniature two-masted brig into her hands. She had never seen this model. It was twice the size of the largest of Washington's others. She could barely contain it between her hands, though it was lighter than it looked. Judith's eyes scanned the masts, quarter galleries, and into the windowed stern lit by glowing lanterns. There she found a room furnished with miniature tapestries, chests, a table with tiny candles on top, three stout chairs around.

"Judith—" Her father called her out of her fascination. "Thee has not yet observed the figurehead of thy worthy vessel."

A white-haired mermaid modestly attired in green serge scales and seaweed led the vessel, holding the twined flags of France and the United States and a tricolor ribbon pronouncing her name: *Survivor.*

Fayette *had* wished for something to take Washington's mind off their time with Judith Mercer. But a gale out of the Gulf of Mexico was not ideal. He strapped the injured in their sick-bay berths as the *Standard* pitched again. There was no use in trying to stop the several leaks from the gundeck. The pots would overturn in the next swell. Sick, injured, and caretakers alike, would have to dry out later.

The latest ship's-surgeon, not yet bestowed with his sea legs, was himself ill, but working his way around to all their patients. Perhaps now he could slip below, Fayette thought, to check for flooding in their hold cabin, to make sure Washington was secure.

He'd only reached the stairwell before a drenched midshipman grabbed his shoulder. He was on his first tour, this one. Stephenson. Small, about the size Washington had been after Trafalgar. Stephenson had attached himself to a bigger, boastful boy. The two had become inseparable. Until now.

Young Stephenson's eyes were swollen. "Mr. Fayette, you used to be captain of the mizzenmast," he yelled. Though two decks removed from the waves' roar, yelling was necessary. "I would count it as a great favor if you would cast your word on bringing Jamie down!"

"Down from where?"

"He's on the yard above the mizzen sail, sir. While we were bringing in the sheet, his ripped. He lost his balance. Now he's caught, as in some devil's grip. He's not let us near. Kicked me back. Sent Mr. Truxum down bleeding."

Fayette glanced down the stairwell. He saw the gleam of water in the hold. How much? Only a few inches, surely. Washington was secured high in his hammock, he told himself, sleeping through the storm as he'd slept through many others. Still, a pang of concern stung. Fayette turned from the hold, followed Stephenson topside.

One look at the midshipman wedged between the yard and mast confirmed Fayette's first instincts. "The grip he's in is one of his own fear," he told Stephenson.

A fork of lightning hit the main skysail. Its accompanying thunderclap dislodged the midshipman. "Aw, then, Jamie," Fayette heard the boy sigh before his friend took a desperate hold of the tattered, flying sail. The wind and rain battered him against the mast. But his grip held.

"Merde." Fayette yanked off his coat and boots. With them, years seemed to peel away. He laughed at the incredulous faces of the topmen, at Stephenson's openmouthed stare.

"I only meant for you to call him down, Mr. Fayette!"

"There's no hearing in this wind."

Fayette passed the battered men who had tried to haul the midshipman down before him, and began to climb the ropes. This was foolish. He was an old man, they were laughing at him. And he was risking Washington's life as well as his own, he realized, the sharp pang returning. But Stephenson was now helpless, dangling. And the ropes felt good again under his feet.

Fayette glanced down, not at the deck—he knew better—but at his legs. Pale. Pale from tromping below in boots, as pale as Washington's when he had borne his lashes at the gratings. Boots, of course—that's why his legs were so pale, long ago. Washington had been used to wearing boots.

Fayette reached the fighting top. He rested, looking up through the rain. Still twenty feet to the boy.

He began composing a letter to Judith Mercer in his mind as he resumed his climb, telling her of his epiphany, directing her where to look on the *Ida Lee*'s list of officers and seamen for their Washington.

He thought of kissing her. He hadn't meant to. Saint Michael, the sweet, wounded beauty of her! What would it be like to be a man to love a woman like Judith Mercer for a lifetime, as Washington would?

He reached out to the dangling boy. The midshipman turned slowly, like a hanged man. His eyes were closed.

"Jamie?"

They flickered open.

"It's me, Fayette."

"The Frenchman?"

"That's right. It is time to go down."

"Good."

Fayette heard a rip. He glanced up at the canvas sail. Shredding. Not along a seam line, not along any of the stitches his Washington had made. But along a sun-bleached, weak part of the canvas. A stiff wind pulled the boy out of his reach. Fayette waited. Patiently. When had he learned to be so patient? If he had been this patient at twenty, the Chartres angel would still have his head.

Washington woke with a start, choking. Drowning—he was drowning! He yanked his head up, coughed. He'd fallen out of his hammock, that's all. A storm, above, causing the flooding. Sitting up, he tasted salt water and blood. He touched under his nose, winced. There. A small cut. Nothing. It was nothing.

Washington wondered what hour it was. No bells sounded to tell him, not in a storm. Where was Fayette? He glanced at the wall, the shelves. Their books, his ships, were safe.

Washington felt for the key strung around his neck. If he placed it in the door's lock, would the rest of the sea come tumbling in? Perhaps a multitude of water rats drawn by the smell of fresh blood? Would they be too many to kill with his knife?

Stop it. Fayette said his vivid imagination had the power of both life and death. They would laugh about this wild leap of his mind when Fayette returned. The pumps would suck out the water and they would drink a little grog to warm themselves again.

He was so cold.

He should get out of the water. He should clean himself, find dry clothes, climb into Fayette's chair, whose seat was still above the flood. But he crawled to a far wall, sat back against it, staring at the door, shivering. He let the blood flow into his mouth and wondered why he felt so helpless and afraid.

The boy Jamie was bigger than Washington had been ten years ago, and heavier. Fayette questioned if he were cutting both their lives away as he sliced at the canvas. But when the midshipman fell against him, Fayette felt the boy take a firm hold at his shoulder. He was not deadweight, at least.

"There, good," Fayette assured him. "Now, together we descend to the fighting top. We'll ride out this fine storm there, yes?"

Jamie looked down. His hand slipped from Fayette's shoulder.

Fayette barely had time to grab Jamie's wrist as he fainted. He was an anchor now, one that made Fayette feel as though the tendons in his shoulder were bursting. Still, he held on, for they were swinging over the hard, unforgiving main deck of the *Standard*. "There now," Fayette crooned down at the boy.

The wind answered, blowing them over the small square of the fighting top. His tortured hand released. He heard the sound of the boy's body landing on the top deck. Fayette smiled. *A good landing. Not even any broken bones,* he thought. *It will not be so difficult to bring this young one back to life. Not so difficult as ten years ago.*

The boy lying on the top deck dissolved from his sight. Then the ship itself was gone. In their place were green hills. They were like the rolls of the ocean, seen from the top of the mizzenmast. Fayette's vision was as clear as his eyes had given him in his prime. He heard Judith's voice, exclaiming both joy and pain as she gazed over the same green mountains. Washington stood behind her, unseen. How different he looked, standing. How handsome his *petit général* was, Fayette thought, his eyes misting. Or perhaps it was misting there, in the rolling waves of the valleys below.

He reached out to them. Judith stumbled.

"Take your lady's burden," Fayette instructed Washington impatiently.

Judith laughed, raising her shining eyes to Fayette's. She shook her head. "Go on, Fayette," she told him, before she threw her head back and a wild, ecstatic sound burst from her. He'd never heard anything like it.

Yes, he had. Madeline had cried out like that, once.

The wind changed direction. Judith's cry became the faint sounds of warning from below. But the arm that had held the boy so tenaciously would not obey his mind's command. *Hold on. Grip. Grip the ropes.* They could not.

There was no pain as he fell. The pain came, of course, in the landing. It sent him through the gratings and onto the gundeck. He heard the brutal cracking of his bones.

He looked up into the face of Lieutenant Mitchell, the first officer he'd trusted with the knowledge of Washington's existence. He heard the voices, even through the pain.

"Take him to the hold."

"The hold, sir?"

"As carefully as you can. And hurry, while the captain is busy at the wheel."

Washington heard footsteps. Many of them, not just Fayette's. No, none of them were Fayette's. When the door opened, the opposite of his imaginings happened: The water on his side drained out. He watched its flow. That was why he saw only the sailors' bare feet, the officers' booted ones, until they laid Fayette down.

Washington leaned over him. His fingers ached to give Fayette comfort, but knew they would only add to his friend's torment.

"Where's his coat?" Washington demanded. "He's cold."

The midshipman with swollen eyes handed it to him.

Washington placed it carefully over the broad chest.

Fayette opened his eyes in the swinging lantern's light. His mouth twitched into a smile. "Fell out of your hammock, did you?"

Washington shrugged, smearing the fresh blood from his nose and lip across the back of his hand.

"Have Thrumming make you up a salve."

Washington nodded, the tears flowing down his face.

"Now," his friend admonished, "you knew this day would come."

"Plus tard," Washington heard the abandoned child whisper.

"Listen to me. You are not without friends. They will do their best to keep you safe until Judith comes. I saw her, *petit général.* And I saw you, beside her. Standing. Imagine!"

"Fayette—"

"My name is Maupin. Henri Maupin, Washington. And I have finally had one of your confounded visions. Of green mountains and mist. A beautiful land. You will love it. It will remind you of the sea."

He coughed, splattering Washington's shirtfront with blood. His eyes focused on their shells, books, and the miniature ships. "We did not do so badly with what we had, did we?"

"No. Not so badly," Washington confirmed.

"So. I have given you my vision. Now bring me home."

Washington pulled in a halting breath. "No area in the world around is blessed with light that can compare with that of the city of La Rochelle," he began, in French, the description he had been told for years of Fayette's birthplace. "The harbor with its two towers—Saint Nicholas and the Tour de la Chaîne glistens now, do you see it? The arcaded streets bring back those times, medieval, sober, yet delicately noble. Do you hear centuries of lively argument among the Plantagenets and Bourbons and Catholics and Huguenots? Do you hear the cries of the people crushed under Richelieu's siege? Best, best of all . . ." His voice squawked like an adolescent, but recovered quickly. ". . . the Hôtel de la Bourse is a masterpiece, its facade decorated with the sterns of ships and maritime trophies and . . . Fayette?" he called softly. "Fayette, you are very rude, I haven't even gotten to—"

He could not stop his tears. He felt one of the sailors kneel beside him. Washington leaned into the man's side, for the moment it would take to regain his composure. Then he would reach out and close the lids over Fayette's stilled green eyes. But the moment never came.

What came felt oddly familiar. A hand grabbed his shirt, fisted it, throttling him.

"Foolish, foolish, powder monkey!"

The grip tightened. Washington struggled to breathe as he felt himself lifted to his feet.

"He's but a helpless cripple, sir," he heard Lieutenant Mitchell say. "An orphan Fayette picked up. In Lima, I believe."

The massive hands released Washington to the damp floorboards.

"Is that so, Lieutenant?" The captain advanced on his second-in-command. "Is that what you believe?"

The captain's way was blocked by Fayette's body, still staring silently at the rafters. The captain kicked it with disgust. "Throw this rubbish overboard," he instructed.

Washington grabbed for his friend's coat. *"Non! Plus tard! Plus tard!"* he called.

The captain turned. "A Peruvian who speaks French?"

He tore down the back of Washington's shirt savagely. "A Peruvian who wears the whitened scars of the Royal Navy's cat-o'-nine-tails?"

Washington felt the captain's boot nail his shoulder to the floorboards with the force of his massive weight.

"Bring him on the main deck," Willis instructed the seamen. "In a cage, and in irons. He'll never get near my windows again."

Washington struggled to stay upright between the two marines as they dragged him up the stairwell. His mind could only hold on to one thought, but it did so tenaciously. He'd failed Fayette. He hadn't closed his eyes.

Behind him, he heard wild laughter, then his ships crashing together under the unholy sweep of the captain's long arm. They fell to the floorboards, bones again.

6

It was not so different from his other Midwatch times on the deck. He could see the stars beyond the cold iron of the cage. And the new surgeon tended to his lip almost as gently as Fayette would have done.

"Rest," the surgeon advised, speaking very slowly. "When the sun comes out, it will hurt your eyes and burn your skin, because you're not used to it. Drink all the water they allow you, keep yourself covered, and seek what shade you can find. Do you understand me?"

" 'Course he understands you, he ain't a fool!" Carney, the sheet anchor man, barked; then he seemed to think better of it. "Beg pardon, sir," he apologized. "Mighty trying day."

"It has been that."

"The lad here's had the worst of it."

The surgeon looked into Washington's eyes for the first time. "My—my condolences," he muttered.

Washington nodded. "Thank you, sir," he said quietly.

The surgeon shook his head, then glanced over at Carney. "Most of it is done?" he asked the grizzled seaman.

"It is, sir."

"And you'll lock him in, after?"

"We will."

"I didn't see you here. I don't know about any of this."

Washington watched the surgeon disappear into the darkness. He'd neglected to lock the rusted door of the cage. Carney entered, squatted his already square frame. He'd always reminded Washington of a squeeze box.

"How about helping us with the services, lad?"

"Services?"

"For Fayette."

Washington looked away, stung again by open, staring eyes.

"We'll finish the shroud ourselves, if it pains you."

"I don't understand. Did you not—"

"No, he ain't in the waves yet. That was just rags and ballast, an old trick. Fayette used it to keep you amongst us. That were a fine thing he done, and we were all with him in it. Well, he deserved no less. We got him, waiting for you to make him proper."

Carney signaled, and two other sailors hoisted their burden from the launch boat. They carried it into the cage.

Washington looked down at the clean canvas, the neat stitches that reached to Fayette's neck. The face was no longer seared with pain. His friend's mane of leonine hair was mostly silver. Only traces of gold remained. When had that happened? There was even a vestige of Fayette's cynical smile frozen there for eternity. Someone had closed the eyes. Washington laid his hand on his friend's shoulder.

"Cold," he whispered.

"Had him on ice, down in officers' provisions. The least they could do for him, after he saved one of their hides, eh?" Carney tousled Washington's hair, the way the sheet anchor men used to when he was a boy. He smiled, ignoring the sting at his lip. He was forgetting his manners. "Good work." He complimented the stitches.

"Thank you, sir." The two sheet-men pulled the caps from their heads almost in unison. How strange, Washington thought, anyone calling him "sir."

Carney handed him two pennies. Washington placed them over Fayette's eyelids. Then he kissed each weather-beaten cheek.

He took up the dangling needle and worked at the last of the stitches. Fayette's face began to disappear under the canvas. Washington tried to think of something to say or sing. He tried to remember one of Judith's Bible verses. But only snatches of François Villon's "Ballad of Dead Ladies" came to mind. He whispered them softly as the chain between his hands kept time.

Qui commanda que Buridan
Fust gecté en ung sac en Saine?
Mais où sont les neiges d'antan?

The verses' dancing cadence, the haunting Old French refrain of *"Where are the snows of yesteryear?"* helped the rhythm, helped him pull careful, locked-in stitches.

Prince, n'enquerez de sepmaine
Où elles sont, ne de cest an,
Que ce reffrain ne vous remaine:
Mais où sont les neiges d'antan!

He doubled the stitches back until they found Fayette's nose through the canvas. That nose had snorted in frustration as he taught Washington to speak French, had breathed in scents of times and places of his landed past. The stories had made his student, who had no past before this ship, breathe La Rochelle too. Washington plunged the needle through the cartilage.

When Washington had first seen Fayette performing the mutilation on a dead sailor, he'd been shocked. . . .

"Why do you do that, Fayette?"

"It's said that this will keep the dead man from floating back up to the surface to haunt his comrades."

"Is this true?"

He'd shrugged. "It is a good story, *n'est-ce pas*? That is more important than literal truth."

"But isn't it unreasonable, superstitious?"

His friend had frowned. "Perhaps. But be more tolerant of comforts for the living, *petit général*," he'd advised.

Washington locked in the last stitch, thereby ensuring Fayette's peace on the ocean floor, his new home.

"May flights of angels sing you to your rest, Henri Maupin," Washington whispered, in English. Where did those words come from? Shakespeare, the only Englishman who could approach Molière, Fayette said. A death, in one of the tragedies. Which? They were all so full of deaths.

Around him, men replaced their caps. A young midshipman wept. He helped the others carry Fayette away. Washington listened closely as they slipped the shrouded corpse, almost without a splash, into the waves.

* * *

The stars came out later, along with a blowing cold wind that made Washington shiver against iron bars that afforded no warmth. He tried to cover his back, but the tear the captain had made in his shirt resisted his efforts. Washington felt someone staring at his ugly knots of scars. He turned. Fayette's worn coat touched his shoulder.

"Monsieur Fayette got Jamie down," the midshipman said. He thrust the coat between the bars, and was gone.

Washington pulled it over his shoulders, buried his face in the weave and its scents of rum and salt and licorice. Finally, as dawn was breaking in the eastern sky, he fell asleep.

Judith heard the horse's piercing scream. She pulled her cloak from its peg on the tavern wall and took up a lantern before running out into the night.

When she reached the wooden bridge, one of the landau's four horses was whinnying wildly, its foot driven through the rotting wood. But two men with powerful shoulders, one the driver and the other a clear-eyed black servant, succeeded in calming the animal.

When he saw Judith, the servant gave a quick nod and glanced toward the rolled-up hood of the vehicle. She placed her hand on the carriage door, latched in a graceful French design.

"Inside!" she called.

"My grandson has injured his lip," a deep voice, calm despite its worried tone, called out. "Are the horses secure?"

"Yes. I will be happy to guide thy party around them."

"What does the odometer read?"

"Odometer?"

"On the wheel, just before you."

Judith found a wooden box. What looked like a clockface with only one hand was attached to the wheel. She placed the lantern closer, intrigued. "Six and eight-tenths," she said. She heard the sound of a scribbled calculation.

"Ah. Only one-tenth of a mile to Pierson's Tavern, then. Ellen, Cornelia—might you assist your cousin?"

"Yes, Grandpapa," Judith heard bright voices affirm.

"Good." The door opened. Judith could see dark shapes inside. "I will avail myself of the arm of this lady," the speaker said, "and we shall get out of Burwell's way."

He glanced at the man still working to calm the lead team. A signal passed between master and servant without words, and as fast as quicksilver. Judith admired it, as she admired the well-dressed gentleman who took her arm. He was very tall, over six feet. Though she judged him to be past seventy, his grip was strong, and his lively, deep-set eyes held vast measures of intelligence, tempered by kindness. He turned to the two young women who emerged from the coach with a boy of about twelve between them. One held a handkerchief to the boy's face, though he struggled against it. "It's almost stopped bleeding, Grandpapa," he called out in frustration. "Tell them to let me be!"

The gentleman approached, calmly drew the handkerchief down, and inspected. "Quite accurate, Francis. I will allow you to keep pressure on the wound yourself, if you will show respect for all our valiant ladies by walking between Cornelia and Ellen. Agreed?"

Francis raised his dark eyes to Judith's and smiled shyly. "Yes, Grandfather," he said. The young women looked at each other over their cousin's head, and nodded, satisfied. Judith felt the tenderness among the four catch her in its overflow. She cast out a quick prayer to find such a family for Washington, soon. A family like this one would be worth the frustrations and sadness that had beset her search.

After consulting briefly with his coachman and servant, the old gentleman reached for Judith's arm again. They led their small expedition back to the tavern. Under the man's low-crowned hat, Judith saw glints of red in his white hair, worn undressed, like her father's.

"Now, tell me what brought you out and to our assistance ahead of the tavern keeper. You're not—" A thought struck him, Judith could see it fire his eyes. "Pierson hasn't finally taken a wife?"

She laughed. "No. Judith Mercer is my name. My father and I are thy fellow guests. I heard the horse. Is it badly injured?"

"Burwell will do his best. That concern, your dress and speech lead me to a more well-founded speculation, Miss Mercer: That you and your father are Quakers."

"We are Traveling Friends, yes."

"Ah, my life long I have admired the Friends' fair, equitable, and reasonable settlement of Pennsylvania."

A fond remembrance of Fayette gently pierced Judith's heart with sorrow. "Thee has read thy Voltaire, thy Rousseau on that subject?"

"Of course! But also William Penn and George Fox."

"That's good, as thee does not wish to spend the evening arguing with me when thy fine family—"

"Squire!" The tavern keeper ran, breathless, toward their small party. "Squire, had I known! Had I but known it was you! Let me take your arm, sir—are you injured?"

Her companion held firmly to Judith. "I am under the care of this lady, and with her assistance will find our way to your establishment, Mr. Pierson. Your time would be better served by fetching your carpentry tools to mend the bridge over Beaver Creek."

"Of course, Squire. By morning's light my sons and I—"

"Tonight, Mr. Pierson, before it catches any more hapless travelers."

"Aye, Squire, just as you say!"

Judith watched the tavern keeper disappear. She wondered how the heretofore lumbering fellow could attain such speed. "Thou art a man of considerable influence." She spoke her astonishment, even slipping into more formal use of her language.

Her companion smiled. "At one time, perhaps, Miss Mercer. Now I gladly exert what influence is left me to cheer your kind heart." His granddaughters were smiling, too, behind their gloved hands.

Young Francis's cut lip was indeed not deep or severe. Once inside the tavern, Cornelia cleaned the wound, then Judith pressed it with a measure of her father's supply of shepherd's purse. The boy's grandfather watched, the line of worry creasing his fine, high forehead eased by Eli Mercer's assurances about the healing properties of the herb. But soon their voices faded as Judith felt the odd sensation that she was comforting not Francis, but Washington. Why? Because his eyes were dark and guileless? Or was it that her longing always grew more intense after the fall of night, Washington's time? And when her doubts about her mission settled in.

Benjamin Morris's father had told her that his son had lost three fingers to frostbite at sea before he'd signed on the *Ida Lee*. The next name on Mrs. Madison's list—the Jarvis boy—had had a large birthmark on his right cheek, and so was not Washington. Judith felt herself opening old wounds of grief instead of bestowing the light of hope to one family who had grieved without cause. And she had many more families to visit, from a settlement at the base of the Alleghenies to a lighthouse on the Maryland shore. She heard Washington's voice. "Hurry, Judith." Her hands trembled against the poultice.

"Must I wear the leaf, Miss Mercer?" the boy asked, becoming young Francis again, annoyed at being the only injured member of his family.

"Indeed not. What wondrous healing power is thine, Francis! The wound is hardly swelling."

"Do you hear, Grandpapa?" he called.

"I do. Let us hope Samson is faring as well."

"I will consult with Burwell on him, sir," the boy offered eagerly.

He was stayed by his grandfather's hand, gnarled, Judith could see, with arthritis. "Rest by the fire, child. Burwell will report on Samson's condition soon."

The boy walked to the hard-backed bench by the hearth and sulked, avoiding his cousins' attempts to draw him into their conversation.

Judith left the common room's company long enough to fetch Washington's large model of the brigantine ship. When she returned, the sisters chatted together across a table set with a hearty stew for four. The man everyone called "the Squire" was absorbed by her father's botanical collection. His grandson still stared into the fire, his swollen lip adding to his brooding look. Judith approached the young man cautiously.

"Francis, may I show thee something?" she asked quietly.

He made room for her on the bench, turning toward her treasure. His eyes lit with interest. He soon gave up his sullen silence to join a conversation on the circumstances of Washington's creation.

"May I look more closely at your gift?" the voice of the Squire soon intoned behind them.

Judith turned to him, tall and majestic and burnished gold by the hearth-fire light. She placed the ship in his hands. He studied Washington's creation through the magnifying glass he'd been using to study her father's plants.

"Extraordinary craftsmanship. But, my dear Miss Mercer," he said, the astonishment giving his well-modulated voice even more timbre, "we must ponder together why the captain's quarters of this vessel is the study of Windover, Winthrop Randolph's plantation on the James River."

Judith felt a catch in her throat. "It is? Thee knows this man?"

"My granddaughters Ellen and Cornelia are Randolphs, as was my own mother. Winthrop Randolph is a distant kinsman. Of the branch of the family which holds me beneath contempt, but not as vocal about it as others of the line. He's even older than I. Windover is not far, perhaps a day's ride from here."

"Does Winthrop Randolph have a family?"

"His wife Anne. She's a Blair. Yes, I believe so, a Blair. They had three sons and a charming daughter. Two of the sons remain; one was lost."

"How?"

"In a shipwreck—"

"—off Bermuda, a merchant ship, the *Ida Lee*, in the year eighteen hundred and five," Judith finished, breathless, for him. "Thy kinsman

Mr. Randolph's son was impressed into the Royal Navy, before the wreck."

A fire of indignation spread from the man's eyes to his entire long frame. "Impressed, Judith Mercer?" he almost roared.

"Yes. I seek to free him of his long captivity aboard the HMF *Standard*. I have Dolley—I have Mrs. James Madison's assistance in the matter."

A smile warmed the old man's fiery indignation. "You have Thomas Jefferson's as well," he promised.

Washington awoke to the coat being pulled away. His hand grabbed the sleeve at the last possible moment, and held. Through the weave, the clang of his wrist irons, he felt the captain's white-hot anger.

"Who gave you this?"

Washington maintained his silence. He would not give up the midshipman's name, even if he knew it. Though the sunlight hurt his eyes, Washington stared, trying to remember the hardened face before his. This was Captain Willis, the man who stole him away, who had him whipped to within the measure of his young life, long ago, Fayette said. The slumbering giant. He should remember, but he didn't.

The captain released Fayette's coat. Did that mean there was a spark of Judith's Light in him? Washington wondered. The giant's eyes were so sleep-starved that Washington felt sorry for him. Captain Willis motioned to the guard. "Who had the Midwatch?" he demanded.

"Collins, sir."

"Have him flogged. Twelve lashes. On the gundeck."

"But, Captain—"

"Now, Sergeant."

"Will the nature of his transgression be made known to him, sir?"

"He knows his transgression. If he allows the prisoner free access of this ship again, I will have him keel-hauled, you may tell him that."

"Free access? Sir, the man is crippled, chained, and caged!"

"And your prisoner will maintain his fast until trial," the captain said as if the sergeant had not spoken.

The surgeon came forward. "Captain Willis, he needs water," he proclaimed.

The captain looked at the cloudless sky. "Perhaps it will rain," he said.

7

Judith's hand grasped her father's as they sat in the full-size version of the captain's quarters on Washington's *Survivor.*

It was not where guests were received at Windover, but where business was done, this room in the back of the house, away from the splendid great hall and receiving rooms that faced the river. This was where the overseer was instructed, the contracts signed. The heavy tapestries smelled faintly of tobacco. It was a male domain, and the silent woman sitting at the accounts desk couldn't have looked more out of place in the hold of the *Standard.*

Anne Blair Randolph was used to cocooning herself, Judith thought, of living in a place somewhere back behind her lustrous eyes. Light eyes. It was the shape of her face, her generous lower lip she shared with her last-born. Or was Judith grasping at resemblances?

She banished the hint of doubt and concentrated on the woman. The whiteness of her skin was made even more dramatic by the deep crimson of her gown. But the sad, beautiful mistress of Windover Plantation possessed a delicacy for which she herself was partially responsible, Judith sensed.

Her eldest sons flanked her. One was portly, and looked older than his mother, with jaundiced sags of dissipation, frown lines, and a set, pugnacious jaw that marred his handsomeness. Tall, almost towering, he dressed in well-made, bright brocades. The other son's face was sharper, more intelligent, but it was cowed by his elder brother, to whom his eyes were continually referring. An Anglican clergyman with a century-old family church, but with neither tithes nor a congregation to fill it. That was how Thomas Jefferson had described the second Randolph son. The only trace of Clayton Randolph's calling was his sober black suit of clothes. Tall, large-boned men, these Randolphs, with light eyes and hair. Not like her Washington at all.

Judith despaired of either man believing her. And they would not allow her to see their father, palsied with age and illness upstairs. Her hope lay with the woman.

"Miss Mercer, Mr. Mercer," Clayton Randolph said in a practiced, almost toneless voice. "Perhaps you can understand our distress. The federal government is scouring the seas for this vessel, bent on the release of a man we have yet to be convinced is our kinsman. That is hardly fair to us, is it?"

Eli Mercer nodded graciously. "How we wish the constraints of time had made our visit less startling."

The woman glanced at the letter in her elder son's hands. She touched his arm. "Mr. Jefferson has recommended—"

"Mother, Mr. Jefferson would like to salvage heroic stories from this miserable war for his friend Madison." Clayton Randolph looked pointedly at Judith. "We buried our brother ten years ago," he said.

"Sally did not," Anne Randolph spoke just above a whisper. "Sally would not even wear mourning."

Winthrop Randolph the younger stretched his hand across his chin. Not long, or fine. "Ethan was a gregarious child, Miss Mercer. He very well might have described his home to this man. While at sea, among boys, the classes sometimes mix. My brother still sported as one with our servants at the time he went to sea. I'll concede that your sailmender may have served with him. But Ethan Randolph was no powder monkey. He was an officer, a midshipman aboard my father's flagship. And he went down with it."

Anne Randolph's gaze finally met Judith's eyes. "He was only ten when he went away to his Norfolk training, then to sea at twelve. He did so love the sea. He did so want to please my husband."

"Don't think on it, Mother, you'll only distress yourself." Anne Randolph's eldest son admonished her as if she were the child. She nodded, but turned the brigantine, and stared at Judith's rendition of Washington's silhouette as if she could breathe life into it.

"May we speak with thy daughter, Mrs. Randolph?" Judith tried.

A trace of a smile appeared on the woman's face. "Our Sally is only yesterday delivered of a child. A fine new daughter."

"There is no need to disturb Mrs. Gibson at this delicate time," Clayton proclaimed. He had been put in charge of his sister, Judith surmised, just as his brother reined their mother.

A young house servant in starched linen knocked and entered the room, breathless. "Your pardon, mistress . . ." she began.

Clayton Randolph frowned deeply. "What is it, Phoebe?"

"I come from Miss Sally. She wants the Quaker lady and her daddy come up see her."

"How has she learned of their presence here?"

"I don't rightly know, sir."

"Winthrop!" Judith heard the deep-throated shriek sailing down the elegant curved staircase. "You bring those people to me before I pull the rafters down!"

Phoebe smiled at Judith's amazement. "Miss Sally, she be plenty mighty 'round her birthing times," she explained.

The quartermasters sat Washington on the Peruvian chair. One left to summon the captain. The others stood guard, their long shadows protecting him from the sun's direct heat. It was so warm there in the waist of the ship's deck. Still, Washington needed Fayette's coat for the remnants of the Frenchman's courage it still possessed.

The men of the *Standard* assembled in benchrow sections, according to rank. So many faces. Some looked disgusted, some sympathetic, some wore unreadable masks.

It had rained. Yesterday, or perhaps the day before. Washington had raised his face to it, tried to catch it in his hands. After the rain came more of the relentless heat of the South Atlantic. Through it, sailors had risked flogging to slip him water.

Collins, his guard of the Midwatch, sat in the officers' section. Washington tried to show him how to anchor his arms at his thighs and lean forward, taking the pressure off his welted back. Collins followed his example, releasing a slight smile.

All but Washington stood as the captain, in full-dress uniform, left his cabin. He approached the rail above them, motioned his officers and crew to their ease.

The trial began.

Captain Willis called his witnesses. Washington recognized none. They gave disjointed testimonies with haunted, ferretlike eyes. They spoke about Fayette and Washington as foreigners, whispering to each other in sedition, in French, even when Fayette was dying. The words, the vaulting space of the high blue sky, the heat of the sun left Washington's head spinning. He anchored it between his hands.

"Chaplain," Captain Willis called, "swear in the prisoner."

Washington lifted his head. Judith did not believe in swearing. It was an insult, she'd said, to the truth that dwelt inside, to be sworn. A Child of the Light spoke the truth always, never swore. But he wasn't a Child of Light. He was a Deist like Fayette, ruled by smatterings of Reason, the gift of a creator who had long since lost interest in individual creations. And he was ruled by his dreams—the ones in his sleep, and the waking ones that Judith called visions. But he would never be like Judith, who talked with God. So perhaps it did not matter if he swore.

The chaplain's detached eyes warmed a little. "Don't be afraid," he said quietly, offering the black book. "Place your hand here."

Washington followed his instruction.

"Do you swear to tell the truth, the whole truth, and nothing but the truth, so help you God?" he intoned.

Where was the chaplain's god? Washington wondered. In that book? The chaplain's eyes narrowed with impatience.

"Well?" he demanded.

"Yes," Washington said. "I do!"

"Good, then. From both of us, the truth."

Muffled laughter. Had he caused this? The captain waved the small man away, and approached the rail above the quarterdeck.

"Prisoner. What is your name?" he demanded.

"Washington."

"And your Christian name?"

Washington's eyes stayed focused on the intensity of the captain's gaze as his mind searched. Nothing. He would have to name himself, he reasoned. "Henri—Henry," he amended.

"You are French?"

"No. I am American."

"From where?"

He must not lie. What had Judith told him? Judith never lied. "The South," he said.

"The South? In which of the United States were you born?"

He hesitated. The captain laughed. It was a cruel sound. Washington did, from somewhere deep in his dreams, remember the sound of that laughter. "You are a rather empty-headed spy!"

Washington took in a steely breath. He was not stupid. There was no need for any of them to think him stupid, empty-headed, not anymore. He took a deep breath. "The United States of America are Delaware, Pennsylvania, New Jersey, Georgia, Connecticut, Massachusetts, Maryland, South Carolina, New Hampshire, Virginia, New York, North Carolina, Rhode Island, the District of Columbia, Vermont, Kentucky, Tennessee, and Ohio." He listed the names by order of their admission into the Union.

"Louisiana," the captain corrected quietly, as if to a dinner guest. "Louisiana is now a state."

"Is it?" Washington asked, as if he was that guest.

"Since eighteen hundred and twelve."

The new Henry Washington remembered the purchase of land. President Jefferson bought a vast territory, no one knew how vast, from the

French emperor Napoleon, for whom Fayette used to fight. Had all that land become a state? So much had happened. His flag had another star. And the war, the second war between his country and Britain, was over. *Hurry, Judith,* he thought—filled with the intensity of his need to go home, to embrace those places that were only stars and stripes and names to him.

Washington absorbed the strength that Fayette had left in his chair, in his coat. He lifted his head higher. "I know my country," he told Captain Willis.

"Then you know your American ship."

"No. I don't remember it."

"It was manned by a crew of British deserters, not Americans."

"I was sick—"

"You were dead! They told me you were dead!"

"I don't remember before I was sick." Henry Washington's quiet tone cut through the captain's mounting hysteria.

"Then how are you so sure of your nationality, powder monkey?"

"Fayette told me—"

"The Frenchman? He was captured after I pulled you off that merchant ship. In the battle off Trafalgar we captured him, so how did he know anything of you?"

"He knew. I know."

"He was your master, this man who called himself Lafayette?"

"No. My friend."

"I see. Did he teach you to speak French?"

"Yes."

"Did he fill your young mind with notions of a Franco-American alliance? Did he teach you to spy?"

"We did not spy."

" 'We'? Can you speak for your friend, Henry Washington? Were you with him always? He left this ship. What did he do on shore leave? Where did he go? Who were his contacts, his sources of information? How did he do it? God damn you both to the fires of Hell! How did he keep this ship out of the conflicts of a decade?"

Washington thought of Fayette listening to the outlandish claims and smiling. He found himself doing the same.

"Something amuses you?"

Washington's smile grew wider. He was infected now, somehow, by the chair, the coat. It was as if he were Fayette, already dead, and unafraid. "It is ridiculous, this notion of spying. Fayette gave up his country. He gave up his life on any land so that I would not die."

Captain Willis left his place behind the brass rail and approached his prisoner. Even then Washington did not feel any fear. "Do you know how long you have prowled His Majesty's ship?" he demanded.

"I have not prowled. I am not able to prowl."

He came closer. Washington smelled drink on him. Strong drink. "How has your face appeared outside my window?"

"Your window?"

"That look of ignorance is very well practiced, Mr. Washington. But we both know you are no cripple. Raise him from the chair," he commanded two men. They obeyed.

"Now, stand away."

The surgeon rose. "But, Captain—"

"Away from him, I said!"

When they released him, Washington stood on his healthy leg as long as he'd ever remembered. It was long enough even to feel the hot air sift though the weave of his worn duck trousers, and to turn his wish to dance into a need. Now, without Fayette's arms supporting him, it was a need that pressed at his core, even as his good leg buckled.

The surgeon pulled Fayette's coat from his back drenched in sweat. No coat, no chair. Washington shivered without his amulets.

"I'm so thirsty," he whispered.

The surgeon nodded. "Captain," he called out, "this man is incapable of being a threat to you, or to anyone. Look."

He cut the trouser leg. Washington felt the silence weigh on him. He closed his eyes as he felt the stares. Just above his leg irons, the stitches began carving a drunken path up his shortened, misshapen leg, stopping at the scarred knee. The sight even stunned the captain to silence. For a moment.

"It was the Frenchman!" he bellowed. "You can crawl, powder monkey. He put you out there nightly, he brought you to my window!"

"He never did."

"You are under oath, Henry Washington."

"He never did," he repeated, louder.

"How did you get there after that damned Frenchman became food for the sharks? Who assisted you? Was it Collins? He will stand on the gallows beside you!"

"It was no one, so help—how is it said?—so help me, God." He glanced up at the chaplain. "Is that what these words are? A prayer?"

"Be still," the small man urged nervously, but Washington couldn't stop. *Illuminate.* They were all listening. *Remember.* "I saw a fine room once," his dry voice croaked out now. "Tapestries on the walls. Is that what I was seeing? But you were not there, Captain. It was only a dream, wasn't it? Fayette? Judith? *Quel dommage,* the dreams are the best I can do at remembering."

First Lieutenant Mitchell stepped forward. "Captain, I beg you to recess the court. The prisoner is not well."

Captain Willis's wild eyes underwent a sea change. He smiled benignly. "Nonsense. The accused recites American states like a schoolboy. He's in perfect health, and capable of treason. For which I find him guilty, and sentence him to hang, at first light, as soon as we are in sight of the beloved country he knows so well."

"Sir, may I remind you that the evidence is circumstantial at best and points not to this man at all, but to the one already dead?"

"You may indeed, Lieutenant." Captain Willis turned and called out over the assemblage, "The trial has concluded."

"Cease. No more," Washington whispered.

"Don't be such a coward, man! Heat exhaustion requires strong countermeasures! You should be grateful that the captain has relieved the surgeon and put me in sole charge of your health. There. It's done now. Raise your arm."

Thrumming stuffed lint into the wound, then handed the bowl of blood to Collins. "Here," he said. "Overboard."

Washington took the officer's sleeve. "Tell the sharks it's but to appetize," he whispered. "Main course at first light." Collins didn't laugh. Had he forgotten how to tell a joke? Washington wondered, disappointed. Or was Collins angry with him about the welts on his back? The midshipman stationed outside his cage snorted a short burst. Washington felt better.

When Thrumming returned to his apothecary below, Washington flung the lint from his arm's wound and tried to sit up. The midshipman entered the cage, assisted him. "Don't eat the food," he advised.

"Why?"

"It's laced with purgatives. So you'll be empty. So you won't shit on the captain when you get strung up."

"Zut alors," Washington spat. "No peace from that man."

The boy leaned forward. "I—I won't let them hang you, sir."

Washington looked more closely at the boy. He was the one who'd wept at Fayette's services. "What is your name?"

"Stephenson."

"Stephenson, listen to me. Fayette would not like noble, futile gestures. He'd bother me about it for all of eternity. You would not wish such a fate on me, would you?"

"No, sir."

"There, then. Now, if you could find me some decent drinking water, so that I can go about the work of replacing the blood that idiot keeps robbing from my veins, I would be very grateful."

"Aye, sir." He turned, but glanced back. "Mr. Washington?"

"I am only Washington."

"You sound like Monsieur Fayette."

He smiled. "Well. I am his heir."

The young midshipman brought water as the first star appeared in the cooling evening sky. Washington sipped at it, imagining it to be the sparkling wine of Champagne that Fayette raved over. They had played at drinking it many times. Washington almost explained their game to the boy, but did not trust his voice to remain steady through the telling. "Join me, Stephenson," was as far as he ventured.

The boy did. Soon the young officer's troubled glance was skirting the iron bars of Washington's cage as he spoke. "It seems to me that the world is upside down here."

"It is. But it will right itself again."

"In time? For you?"

"Perhaps. Perhaps our captain will regret letting me within sight of my country, yes? Where are we putting in?"

"At Norfolk. To repair the masts that were downed in the gale. Do you think the Quaker lady—"

"Judith." Her bountiful heart might grieve. But she must not think them spies. And he must release her from his dream of a future together. His future was ending at first light. Hers must go on.

"Stephenson, might you procure me pen and paper? Could you get a letter of mine to that lady? Out from Norfolk, posted to her Quaker Meeting in Philadelphia? Can I trust you with that?"

"Monsieur Fayette got Jamie down, sir," he said. "Be assured."

Soon Washington was alone again, at his favorite time of the night. But his hand seemed paralyzed above the paper.

Dearest Judith, he finally wrote.

Fayette's end came suddenly. It was caused in doing what he loved the most—restoring foolish youth to safety, though he would tell us he wanted one last flight across the mizzenmast near the stars, I think.

It appears I am to be granted a less noble demise. We were neither pious nor pure men, Judith, but we are blameless of the crimes for which we are condemned.

It is my hope that you will think upon us seldom, but in

those times, not without some measure of fondness, as we were, by God's oversight and your generous heart, graced by your love.

With my last breath I will release that stolen soul to her home. She carries my affection to her mistress as bonding agent.

—H. Washington

As he held the letter drying between his fingers, Washington heard a ship approach, then hail the *Standard*. He listened carefully, and judged it to be a small vessel, a harbor ketch or schooner. The hailing master spoke American English.

Washington watched the conference between the master and the captain, then saw the rage enter Captain Willis's face as he approached the cage. "Damned woman. That damned woman," he muttered.

Washington folded the letter quickly, but a flash of the paper caught the captain's eye. He yanked it from his grasp. The ink bottle crushed beneath his foot.

Washington drifted off. So tired. This was his time, the night. Perhaps his last night; how could he sleep? But no one was poking, prodding, bleeding him. They'd even removed his chains. He slept deep, dreamless, like a child with decades instead of hours of life left to him. Until he sensed Captain Willis again beside him, there in the cage. And something else. Death.

"You seduced her," his voice hissed.

He opened his eyes. "Who?"

"That woman. That damned Quakeress."

"No. I love her. How could I not love her? But I did not—"

"Seduced! Defiled her, you and the Frenchman, both! I have it in your letter—'mistress' . . . 'stolen soul' . . . I will say I saw you—the three of you, in unspeakable, unnatural acts. I will say that corrupt fascination is what accounts for her devotion to your cause. She will be disgraced, disowned by her father, ostracized from her community."

"It's not true."

Willis's smile made Washington's teeth ache. "I am a captain in His Majesty's Royal Navy, Henry Washington. A hero at Trafalgar. Who are you? A convicted spy. A crippled coward, the marks of your disgrace on your back. Who will be believed?"

"You must not hurt Judith."

"It's you will hurt her, if you're alive tomorrow, when she comes with her officials, her papers. Another choice, my pretty cot-boy. Here's a final choice, a last chance at honor." He slipped the knife into Washington's hand. "The Romans did this. The ones who weren't cowards."

Then he was gone. Washington looked down. A fine thing, the knife was. Its handle was delicately carved ivory, swirling with interlocking circles. Its blade was short and sharp. Bounty, Washington sensed, from some past campaign. The knife was bounty. That's what he himself had been, long ago. The captain's bounty impressed off another ship. What ship? The one with the boy. The boy with his face, then no face. The knife's point slashed across the memory, slashed across the blue delta of veins in his wrist. Not Judith. Not Judith, too. He watched the blood well up, spill out.

Not deep enough. Again. He was no coward. He must try again.

But when he grasped the knife's handle, it shouted at him, its voice annoyed, full of strange clicks. The language was not English or French, though its disapproving tone reminded him of Fayette's.

Washington dropped the knife, pressed three fingers against the wound in his wrist. He felt the pulse of life beneath it.

The lullaby of the black people whose echoes lived with him in the hold began. He felt tears sting the corners of his eyes, and welcomed them. So kind. Why were they so kind to him?

He caught the unmistakable scents of dampness and wormy fruit. The hold, his dark, familiar place. Shouts of men and machinery sounded above. No hammock, but something incredibly soft; a cloud, perhaps, held him. A light blanket covered him further. One more smell approached, crowding out all the others. It made him think he was dead. Plum duff.

He opened his eyes and saw Judith Mercer.

"I did not lie," he told her. "I named myself Henry for Fayette, but I did not lie."

"Thou art hereafter Ethan." Her fingers combed his hair back from his brow. "Ethan Randolph, who has a mother and father, two brothers and a sister, and a fine house on a beautiful river."

"Where?"

"In the Commonwealth of Virginia."

"These people."

"The Randolphs."

"They want me, Judith?"

"Of course they do!" she said quickly—too quickly, he thought. "And thy sister, thy beautiful, courageous Sally, has a husband and children now."

"Children?"

"Three."

He looked at the empty shelves of his quarters. "My ships are gone. I'll make others for the children. Would that be good, Judith?"

"Yes, beloved. That would be splendid."

He reached up to touch her face, saw the strip of gauze around his wrist, and remembered. "They must not hurt you."

"No one will hurt me."

"The captain said he would use my letter to ruin you with slander, unless I—"

"Oh, Ethan." Her voice cracked over his new name, and she bowed her head as tears slipped down her cheeks.

"Our black people prevented it, Judith. Scolded me without mercy! Don't cry."

She lifted her head, but the tears continued. "Captain Willis had no power over thee once he entered United States' waters, and he knew it. Lieutenant Mitchell could stand his madness no more. He and the surgeon signed papers attesting impaired judgment. The lieutenant arrested Captain Willis, held him secure in his cabin."

"But the letter—"

"It was found by Lieutenant Mitchell, and delivered. I thank thee for a fine letter, a beautiful letter. Captain Willis cannot hurt us with it. He cannot hurt anyone anymore. He hanged himself this morning before I came aboard."

Washington let her words sink into his being, become reality. "Fayette called you a giant-killer," he said in an awed whisper.

She frowned. "I am no kind of killer."

"He meant no offense. Don't be angry with us, Judith. Fayette, I do not say it correctly, tell her about what you—" he called, as if his friend were sitting on his empty chair. "I forgot," he whispered. "*Mon dieu*, Judith, I forgot."

She stroked his brow and spoke softly. "I wish I could see our Fayette's face now, I wish I could laugh at his astonishment as he is led toward the Light he spent so much of his energies denying."

"Who will lead him, do you think, Judith?"

"His Madeline, perhaps?"

The new Ethan Randolph felt the weight of his loss change in density. Its color went from bloodred to rose.

"Eat," Judith commanded. "Tomorrow, the clothes thy brother ordered will be ready, and thee will be on thy way home." She put a spoon into the steaming bowl in her lap.

"These Randolphs. Do they know I don't remember them, Judith?"

"Yes."

"Are they angry with me?"

"No. Only, they will need time, as thou does."

"Ethan. Why was I given that name? Who gave it to me? From whom did I learn the constellations?"

Judith laughed. "I don't know, beloved! Thou must ask the Randolphs these things."

"You will come too?"

"Yes. Now eat."

"What is that?"

"Plum duff, of course."

The portion she spooned into him was full of raisins, oats, and a sweet, vanilla-based syrup. He let it skate about his mouth, savoring all its flavors separately, then in combination, before he allowed himself to swallow it.

"Judith?" he whispered, as she held another spoonful at his lips.

"Hmmm?"

"Are you sure I'm not dead?"

2

Ethan Randolph

8

The white linen shirt reached his knees. Above its hem was an em-broidered set of three letters. The large russet *R* was flanked by an *E* and a *B* in crimson. The *B* must initial his middle name. Ethan wondered what it was, and who had fashioned the beautiful monogram. He was a grown man who didn't know his middle name. Who would want such a man in his family? He tucked the shirt into the trousers, fastened the braces, pulled on the gray-and-white-striped waistcoat. The waistcoat had ivory buttons, like the handle of Captain Willis's knife.

Exhausted, Ethan sat back in Fayette's chair, and pondered the dizzying array of neckerchiefs and cravats, the merino wool coat beside them. He would rather wear Fayette's coat.

A swift knock sounded at the door. He thought it belonged to the newly balanced Captain Mitchell, but he raised his eyes to a stranger.

The heavyset man was dressed in an array of mustards, olives, and browns that complemented his light hair. He was very tall. He had to stoop inside the small compartment. After tucking his high hat stiffly under his arm, he stared at Ethan for a long time. His expression, sour to start with, grew more displeased. The room was crowded with this man, as it never had been with Ethan's friends.

"You don't even know how to dress yourself properly!" he accused.

"Sir?"

" 'Sir?' " he mimicked. "Oh, yes. You don't remember me."

"I—"

"Isn't that the conceit your little Quakeress has connived to get her orphan reunited with a suitable family?"

Ethan's throat tightened. "Judith did not—"

"Oh, but Judith did, young man! Judith involved Madison and Jefferson and all of Washington in her first round. Even I will have to sing 'hail the fallen hero' to their tune. For a time only, I warn you. I will make you sorry you ever schemed entrance into my family."

* * *

Judith Mercer boarded the *Standard* on Stephenson's arm. She was about to ask the source of his worried look when Captain Mitchell rushed to her side.

"Thank all that's holy you've come!"

"What is it? Ethan's not ill?"

"I don't know! He's locked himself in his quarters since Stephenson went to help him dress this morning. Every one of us has pleaded. I've had to turn away the ambassador to Great Britain and his dismal, formal apology."

"What does he say?"

"The ambassador? He was most displeased—"

"Ethan, Captain Mitchell. What does Ethan say?"

"Oh, that he'll open the door to no one but you."

She smiled. "Well, I'd best get below decks, then?"

"Oh. Oh, yes, quite right."

Stephenson led her all the way to the rounded door before he tipped his hat, apologized awkwardly for doing so, and left her there. She knocked softly. "Ethan," she called. "It's Judith."

She heard his key enter the lock, turn. She waited on the other side until he'd made his way back to Fayette's Peruvian throne. "Come," he whispered.

She was struck by the way his clothes made him disappear even against the brightly gilded chair. Why had they ordered so much black? The color turned Ethan's already pale skin translucent and accentuated the dark circles under his eyes. Winthrop was behind it, she was sure.

The pantaloons were loose on him, as if the tailor did not believe the measurements he was given. The many yards of muslin neckerchiefs remained untouched, and his shirt was open. The fine cutaway coat fit him badly, too large everywhere except the arms, which were short enough to show the bandage around his wrist. Winthrop, definitely.

Worst of all was Ethan's expression. His grief over Lafayette's loss was there, reined in behind his beautiful eyes. But there was something else, too, something deeply troubled. Why? He would know the complexities of his new life soon enough.

He sat there in Quaker-like stillness. She loved his stillness, and wondered if any of the other Randolphs had it. Or was it his alone, born in captivity? Judith walked to him. He raised his head, and took hold of her hands. His were cold and bloodless, like his face. Dark hair fell in waves to his shoulders. The younger American men wore their hair this way now, free, without a queue. She wanted to tell him this, to chatter on and on. He squeezed her hands.

"Judith, I think Captain Mitchell, the crew—they would allow me to stay on board," he said quietly.

Anything. She was ready for anything. But not this. "What?" Her voice cracked so badly Ethan winced.

"I have a skill. I'm good at mending the sails, you said so yourself, remember? They'd treat me decently now, wouldn't they? And I love the sea, Judith, I've always loved the—"

She flew away from him, pacing the small space. "One of them got in here!" she realized, turning. "One of them bribed his way into thy cabin. It was Winthrop, it had to be!"

He winced again. "That man is my father?"

She looked at his eyes, at the slant of his brows, always winsome, now distressed. His mother's had the same bent. "He is the younger Winthrop Randolph, thy brother. Thy eldest brother."

He shook his head. "No. These are not my people, Judith. I think you made a mistake."

She fought to keep her voice calm. "Ethan, listen to me. Winthrop has many fears. That thee wants to steal—"

"I don't want anything from him, from any of them."

"They would have to possess the hardest of hearts not to see that soon. But thou must give them a chance. Thy brothers are almost a generation thy elder, Ethan, and so different from thee."

"And Sally Gibson?"

"With Sally, the years between you don't mean so much. Thy sister is forever young."

"Like you."

Judith should have said something, denying it, but she was so happy for the slight smile that played about his bruised lip. "If only thy sister had come instead of Winthrop. And she would have if she hadn't so soon delivered a child."

"The children."

Judith could see him remembering his nieces with a stab at his resolve to remain on board the *Standard*. Of that she would take full advantage. "Yes, the children. How dost thou think of abandoning them before you've even met?"

He frowned, guessing her ploy, she thought. "Judith, I have not come to be a burden to these people. I have a trade here on the *Standard*, I have a certain acceptance. Can I find a trade there, on land, in my own country? I do not ask for promises, but I need to know the truth of it. I need to know if there's any possibility of my becoming worthwhile. Out there."

When she reached for the gaunt curve of his cheek, he kissed into the palm of her hand, then rested his face there. "Yes," she whispered, unable to explain a worth that would never have anything to do with his clothes, his wealth, his family and religion, all the things that would forever keep them apart. "Yes, of course," she said, louder.

"I have become a great burden to you, Judith Mercer," he observed, like a wind condition, without regret or apology. Then he smiled. "I suppose I must hold on to your soul a little longer."

Judith finished winding his white muffling, then tied the black silk cravat around it. "Thee is very handsome."

"No I'm not," he disagreed. "But at least my attire doesn't frighten you now."

"Frighten me?"

"When you first came in it did."

Was she so transparent? "It was the color, the black. We Quakers don't wear black. We have no mourning."

"I offend you? Should I wear Fayette's coat?"

"No. Thee must show respect for thy own people now, Ethan, not mine."

A tapping sounded at the door. Judith opened it to Captain Mitchell and Winthrop Randolph. Behind them walked a tall, muscular black man of about fifty. He had to stoop even farther than Fayette had, so she judged his height in excess of six feet. His eyes made quick contact with hers, then lowered to study Ethan's twisted leg. With interest, perhaps even sympathy. Without disgust.

But as the captain and Winthrop talked, a glistening line of sweat stood out on the servant's broad forehead. Something was wrong.

Winthrop Randolph finished his instructions. "Now, Aaron will assist your ascent to—"

"I can't, master," the black man blurted out.

"What are you saying?"

"This place. A bad place, sir. It grabs at my strength."

"What is this nonsense?"

The servant went to his knees beside Fayette's chair, clutching his middle. Ethan reached out, taking his shoulder. "Yes," he said, "I understand."

Winthrop Randolph's eyes narrowed. "Understand what? Get up,

Aaron," he demanded. "Carry this man topside or you'll face a whipping the likes of which—"

"No," Ethan commanded in a white-hot voice Judith had not heard before. "No more whippings."

Captain Mitchell sighed. "Amen to that," he said, under his breath, as if his old superior officer were still beside him.

The black man moaned. Ethan spoke calmly above its unearthly sound. "If you'll escort my brother topside, Captain," he said, "we will meet you there shortly."

Captain Mitchell nodded, then hustled Winthrop from the hold.

With only the three of them in the room, Aaron raised his head. "There be other folk here. Suffering, dying," he gasped out.

"We know," Ethan said. "We've seen them too, haven't we, Judith?"

"Yes," she whispered.

Ethan squeezed the man's broad shoulder. "Go up to the gundeck, sir," he urged gently. "It's cooler. It might be less troubling."

"But, how—?"

"Judith will help me; go on."

Aaron stumbled out of the cabin on Judith's arm. She returned, and soon they heard him move up the stairs with an ever-quickening step. Judith turned to Ethan.

"Blood memory," he whispered. "Is that man a slave, Judith?"

"Yes."

"Belonging to the place on the river? Windover?"

She nodded.

"Are there more?"

"Yes."

He winced. "Many?"

She nodded again. "Nearly two hundred."

Judith heard the barest sigh escape him. He handed her Fayette's coat, the only inheritance he was bringing from his years on board the *Standard*. She draped it over her arm before assisting him to his feet. He was an easy burden, weighing less than herself, she judged. It was hard to judge his height, but he was not a tall man like his brothers. Even his undamaged leg was not strong, and buckled before they reached the stairs. There Judith heard him mutter a soft French blasphemy before he slid down, breathless, on the last step.

"Ethan," she pleaded. "Allow me to fetch—"

"I will not be the cause of any whippings," his new, steely voice insisted. "Just stay ahead of me, Judith. I'll manage. I'm strong." He smiled ruefully, surveying his crumpled form as if it didn't belong to him. "Well, I'm stronger than I look. It's not so far, not if your face is just beyond me."

She released his cravat, unwound the cloth, then opened his carefully folded high collar. She ripped a yard's length, tied one end to his right wrist, the other end to her own. He smiled.

"Ethan Randolph. Dost thou find me amusing?" she demanded, as imperiously as a Quaker could manage.

"You make good use of my brother's strangling neckwear."

Ethan's arms were the strongest part of him, Judith realized, as he lifted himself over each wooden step. His fine coat smeared with tar and dirt. Twice he caught his sleeve on nails, ripping the wool.

Finally, as they neared the cannon level, large hands reached past her. They lifted Ethan to the deck's gunpowder-scented quiet.

Aaron clucked his tongue severely. "You looking like you been giving the bullfrogs a merry chase down in the salt marsh!" he chided.

"Salt marsh, sir?"

"Ain't the likes of me a sir, Master Ethan. You's the sir," Aaron explained as he brushed the worst smudges from the black coat. "You don't recollect that? Or me?"

"I do not. I'm sorry."

Aaron took the ripped neckerchief Judith offered and wiped the sweat from his charge's face. "No need for any sorrying," he crooned in a deep voice, rich with melody, before lifting Ethan Randolph high in his arms. "Lord, Lord. You don't got the heft of the straw man in the garden, young master! My Martha, how she gonna love the job of fillin' you out!"

Ethan smiled. "You are feeling better?" he asked quietly.

"I am, sir, thank you."

Her Washington was being protected again, Judith realized. By a man as strong as Fayette was in his prime.

An array of officers in full-dress blues, their medals gleaming, took Ethan Randolph's hand, shook it. Some offered stiff apologies. His brother stood, erect and pompous, like them. Others offered welcome, tinged with pity. He knew that look. Fayette bore that look, back in his first memory. They didn't expect him to live, then? Ethan glanced back over Aaron's shoulder at the crew of the *Standard*. They saluted him smartly, though he was never one of them. Mr. Thrumming scowled, but Stephenson waved, as did Fayette's old compatriots, the sheet anchor men.

"Beloved ghost," Judith whispered wistfully at his ear.

"Is that what I was?"

She nodded, her eyes bright. Ethan was glad for this woman, Judith Mercer, and for the strong, kind arms of the bondsman. Without them, he might have gone back to the only home he remembered, despite the scandal it would cause these strangers on the deck—the ones whose sunstruck medals hurt his eyes.

The shoreline was crowded with people waving small American flags. Too small to count for the new state, the new star. Mustered militiamen fired their rifles above the sails of the *Standard*. The marines of the *Standard* fired back.

"Quite the spectacle," Winthrop Randolph said at Judith's ear.

She ignored him pointedly, Ethan thought. Eli Mercer rushed forward. "It's wondrous good to see thee again, Washington," he said.

Ethan grinned, remembering how much he liked Judith's hearty, forthright father. Eli Mercer's hand held that of a little girl. He set her before him. This must be his sister's eldest child, who Judith said was waiting onshore. Ethan had only caught rare glimpses of children, at a distance from docksides around the world. He was fascinated by this one, but wondered how to behave. Aaron lowered Ethan to her height. The girl's golden curls shone beneath her high bonnet. Her simple muslin frock was caught at the waist by a yellow ribbon. It flared about her when she made a full curtsy. How beautiful she was, this miniature.

"Your ship with Grandfather's study inside is most cleverly made, Uncle," she said.

"That is very kind of you to say, Elizabeth."

Her eyes brightened further. "My family calls me Betsy."

"May I?"

"I would be pleased if you did, sir." She made another curtsy. "Mother says I should give you these."

He took the three small silk flowers. This child would lead him to his ageless sister, whom Judith said had never buried him.

"Mama sprinkled them with—"

"Rosewater."

"Yes." The girl tilted her head as he inhaled the scent, then dropped the silk roses into Judith's waiting fingers.

"Do you dance, Betsy?" he whispered. "Do you stand on your mother's slippers and dance?"

"Oh yes, ever since I was very little! I teach Alice that way, too. Mama promises we will do the same with the new baby. Her name is

Charlotte, and she hardly cries at all! Will your leg become better, Uncle? Will you dance with us too?"

"I now have a powerful reason to desire it so."

Judith wove the flowers' stems through the first buttonhole of his waistcoat. Betsy leaned in against his ear as she did. "Mama loves your lady, Uncle Ethan," she confided. "And she doesn't care for the other wives at all!"

A man pressed gentle taps at her shoulder. Ethan looked up. The sun shone off spectacles.

"This is my papa, Barton Gibson. He is a land surveyor and has worked his trade in every one of the United States and Commonwealths! Someday I will travel with him."

The man squatted down beside his daughter. He was tanned and handsome and brimming with health. "A pleasure, sir. A distinct and miraculous pleasure." Ethan saw his laughing eyes now. They were the right kind of eyes for a man so rich in dancing women, he decided.

Barton Gibson drew another man into their circle. "And may I present Dr. Jordan Foster, a skilled physician and surgeon and esteemed friend."

Ethan felt cold suddenly. He thought of the bleedings, the purgatives, the badly set bones growing gnarled, misshapen, lame. He buried his head in the bondsman's broad chest, scented with corn and licorice, and the salty remnants of the slave's own shipboard terror. "No doctors," he whispered. "Tell them. Please. No more doctors."

"Young master," he heard Aaron's voice, "Dr. Jordan, he got the healing in his hands. He and your mama done got your brothers and Miss Sally and all of mine through the measles in a terrible time, back before you was born. Come," he coaxed, "give him your hand, child."

"Thy sister sends him," Judith intoned like a prayer at his ear.

He did not raise his head, and so he heard the gentle, sad voice first. "Ethan," it called. "I would not hurt you for the world, son."

He lifted his head. He saw eyes, dark like his own, set deep in a kind face. The man was dressed in plain, well-made clothes. His rich brown hair was graying at the sides—a soft, shining silver. He had a neatly trimmed beard, reminding Ethan of a Dutch merchant painted in one of Fayette's books. Jordan Foster took Ethan's arm in a gentle hold. The touch penetrated his sleeve with a soothing warmth.

"We will be guests at Dr. Foster's house for a few days," Judith told him, "so thee might rest before we bring thee home."

"Je regrette—" He blinked. "Pardon," he amended. "That is most generous of you."

"Not at all." Dr. Foster's warmth penetrated deeper.

Soft cries exploded from the edge of the crowd. "She's here!" and "She came!" The woman in the emerald satin spenser trimmed with Russian sable approached. Her silk gown sported a jabot at the bosom, her headdress was gold. All stood aside but Betsy Gibson, who curtsied low, then escorted the splendid woman to her uncle.

She smiled at Judith, and offered her gloved hand to Ethan. He took it and without thinking, he kissed her middle knuckle. Her exotic-smelling fingers curled around his.

"Why, Mr. Randolph, for what purpose is French etiquette taught aboard a British man-of-war?"

"For the express purpose of pleasing you, *madame*."

He liked the way the beautiful woman's chin dimpled before she finally released his hand with a slight squeeze. "I think I should require all senators and members of the Congress to ship out on a tour of duty at once.

"But as for you, sir," she tapped his shoulder lightly, "this lady and her father have gone to considerable effort on your behalf. It would not be wise to cross them or me now. And I require a complete recovery before you call on me."

"You have been very kind, Mrs. President." Winthrop Randolph spoke up behind them.

"Ah no," Dolley Madison said, casting a dismissing glance in his direction before returning her eyes to Ethan. "It's your brother who has proved to be the hope left to us from the Pandora's box of this warring era, Mr. Randolph. I charge you to help him to thrive again on his native soil. With his health restored and his gracious manners intact, I don't believe anything will be beyond his reach."

9

The first night in Dr. Foster's house, Ethan Randolph dreamed vividly, of two children whose portraits, painted on rough board, hung with a fair-haired woman's over the room's writing desk.

The children approached the handsome sleigh bed, then pulled him to his feet. They showed him a game played with a stick and a hoop. The woman smiled at their antics, playing a soft tune on the three-stringed instrument in her lap. The air was scented with pine. Ethan gave up trying to make the children understand that he was lame because he realized, just before the dream ended, that he was not. He awoke feeling so refreshed and whole, the pain in his leg surprised him.

Eli Mercer, dressed in his traveling clothes, sat by the bed.

"I did wake thee, Friend Ethan?"

"No. You are as still as Judith."

Eli smiled. "Or she is as still as her father?"

"Of course, that way around." Ethan rubbed the side of his face that had been buried in the soft pillow. "I am no lark."

"True. A night owl, thee. Who kindly tended to my Judith in her distress while this lark slept. I have not forgotten. I've come to ask that of thee while I am gone for our Meeting in Philadelphia."

"Ask? I don't understand."

"Oh, I know my Judith is a grown woman who has, on her missions, stood unafraid before admirals and prime ministers and generals and jailers. And with the Randolphs, she will help thee find thy place. But when thee becomes a father thyself the understanding will come fully, yet thy generous heart sees it even now, I feel it."

" 'Sees'?" Ethan prompted.

"That Judith will be my little girl as long as I draw the breath of life."

"Ah, yes."

"You are kindred spirits in your marred childhoods, Ethan."

"Judith's childhood was marred? How?"

"In time, I will tell thee all. For now I ask—not Ethan Randolph, who neither of us knows—but Henry Washington, whom we cherish, to look after Judith in my absence."

This man was more than respectful of him, Ethan realized. Eli Mercer was seeing through his broken body, seeing a whole man. Trusting that man with his daughter's care. He would never forget it. "You have my assurance," he said, careful not to swear.

"I shall travel north with a contented heart." He placed his hands on his knees, pushing himself up onto his sturdy legs with an ease Ethan envied. "Well, Judith will walk me to my horse. Your worthy doctor waits patiently to—"

"Eli? I will see you again."

"If God grants me that pleasure. I will summon Friend Jordan Foster. He will speed thee on thy way to health, son, I feel it."

Ethan tried to lose himself in Eli Mercer's words after he closed the door. The physician approached with a curt greeting. He lifted the covers, then Ethan's nightshirt from his leg. He frowned.

"Miss Mercer said you would not lean on her as much as you should have, aboard ship," he said. "Do you think that's the cause?"

"Cause, sir?"

"Of the inflammation. The pain you will not complain about?"

The doctor probed his leg lightly with his hands. Ethan suddenly realized he didn't know this place, or this man. Where were his instruments? All surgeons had instruments. Cold, iron instruments. Where was Judith? *"Où est ma femme, s'il vous plaît?"* he blurted.

The doctor looked up, startled. "I'm sorry. I don't understand the French language."

"Was I speaking in French?"

"Yes."

"Where . . ." he began, then forgot to translate the rest as he felt the woman's hand on his shoulder—felt only. There was no one in the room with them. "Please, Dr. Foster. Who are the people, the painted people here on your wall?" Ethan asked, to distract himself from this new fear of the unseen woman and her pine-scented air.

"My wife and children."

"This is your bed, then? Your own room?"

"It's yours whenever you come." Jordan Foster's fingers lifted Ethan's eyelids.

"Where are your wife and the children?"

"I buried them in the Ohio Territory."

Ethan thought of the scented air. "Among the pine."

"How did you . . . ? The painting. You saw the pine trees in the painting." He answered his own question. "Yes, I buried them there."

The doctor thumped Ethan's back, the gnarled vines of scars without comment.

"Did your wife play a stringed box, Dr. Foster?" Ethan asked quietly. "Placed in her lap? Did the music sound like laughter?"

The probing hands finally stilled. "A dulcimer. How in Heaven's name did you know that?"

"She played it for me. Well, for us, your children and me, in a dream. Last night. She must have been a generous lady to do that, to play her music for a stranger."

The doctor rested his head in his hand.

Manners, Ethan reminded himself. "I am sorry for your loss. I should have said that first. I am not so good at the proper order of things."

Jordan Foster raised his head. That twitch beside his mouth—was it a smile? "Perhaps she knew that you would not always be a stranger," he whispered. "You are still afraid of me, aren't you? Afraid I will hurt you?"

"Perhaps my fear is that you will not hurt me. The hurt necessary, yes?"

"What do you mean?"

"Necessary hurt? Is that not how to say it? The hurt to help me walk? You have hope for this?" he asked quietly.

The doctor rubbed at the frown line between his eyes. "The leg bones were set improperly, so long ago." His tone turned clipped, rational, impatient, like Fayette's sometimes became. "The bones grew together. The fracture at the ankle was ignored, so the right foot turned inward. Muscle tone—well, there's some muscle tone, more than I would have thought. You have not stood in so many years."

"I have crawled, all over our cabin. Fayette said I crawled faster than sand crabs on the beach at—"

"Listen to me! Anything short of doing terrible violence that would most likely not work—"

"But I am young, and will be stronger soon," Ethan pressed. "Perhaps, then, the chance of success will be better?"

"No chance, no hope!" The doctor turned away suddenly. "I'm very sorry."

A charged silence dwelt between them.

"Dr. Foster." Ethan finally broke it. "Please do not allow your concern to exceed mine. Even if there is no hope, even if the Randolphs do not accept me as I am, Eli and Judith will help me."

"Help you?"

"To discover a place, here on land. To achieve usefulness. I am not too old to find a trade, and through it fashion a life, do you think, sir?"

The doctor smiled. "I did not find my life's station until I was older than you are now."

"How old am I?"

"You will turn three and twenty at harvest time this year. On the thirtieth day of September."

"Will I? How is it you can tell me this? Did we know each other in the time I cannot remember?"

"No. You'll not find me in your dreams, your memory traces. I was away at my training in Scotland when your mother was good enough to write to me with the news of your birth. I was far from home. And lonely. It was a bright moment, her news. One remembers such moments."

Ethan couldn't imagine the sad-eyed man looking any more lonely. *Manners.* He smiled. "Well. I am happy to have occasioned this moment, however inadvertently. The earlier Randolphs you knew only?"

"Yes."

Why? Ethan wanted to know. But could not manage to question this man whose eyes were becoming sadder still. Manners, again. "So, then. You are not a stranger to me now. That is my very great fortune."

The doctor smiled. A rare thing; he did not do it often, Ethan surmised. "I would consider it a privilege if you allow me to help you find your purpose as well," he offered.

Ethan shook his head, perplexed. "This woman Mrs. Gibson has a fine friend in you, sir," he said.

" 'This woman'? Ethan, Sally is your sister. And what is this fretting about the Randolphs? They are your family."

"Perhaps."

"Not perhaps. You are Ethan Randolph."

"Dr. Foster, I am not blind. The brothers elder—no, that is not correct—the elder brothers, they are against me, even Judith concedes that. I do not make a good case for myself, do I? No memory, barely sounding American. And I look nothing like them, do I?"

Dr. Foster took Ethan's arm in that same curious warm hold as when they met. "You favor your mother," he said.

"I do?"

"Yes."

"Will that help her, do you think?"

"Help?"

"Anne Randolph buried herself when she buried me, Judith says. I'm afraid of this lady, Dr. Foster," he admitted, reluctantly. "More even than Winthrop, who is dangerous in his anger. What if Anne Randolph prefers to keep us both buried? Without being deemed worthy of my mother's love, how can I hope to win Judith?"

The doctor smiled slowly. "You love Miss Mercer?"

"Is it not obvious?"

"I . . . Well, I noted a certain devotion . . ."

Ethan laughed. "I love her so much that I, who have annoyed you all with my constant questions, am struck dumb by the power of it!" His grin faded. "Did you love the dulcimer woman that way, sir?"

"No. But her heart expanded to accommodate my limitations."

"I have heard the music of that heart. I'm grateful."

"I—I'd best fetch your lady, before you confound what little sense I have left."

It was something Fayette might have said, in response to one of his visions. But this shy, sad-eyed man was not Fayette. Why had he trusted those eyes? Because he had not hurt him with dreaded instruments or purges? Because his wife and children had gifted him with a beautiful dream? Was that enough for so much trust?

As Dr. Foster approached the bedroom door, it burst open. Betsy Gibson entered, her skirts flying, followed by Aaron holding a covered tray.

"I have poached the eggs for you myself this morning, Uncle Ethan," the little girl proclaimed, "as Mama instructed. I'm to watch you eat every scrap, you must not hide any remains under your linen!"

The child's spirit lifted his own. "If I am to have your company, *petit chou,* I will gladly eat the linen as well."

Betsy stopped, leaned her elbows on the high, goosedown mattress of the bed, and regarded him curiously. "What do you call me, Uncle?"

"*Petit* is, in English, 'small,'" Ethan thought aloud. Perhaps he would think in English again, if he thought aloud. "Small *chou. Chou*—'vegetable.' "

"I am a small vegetable? What vegetable? Corn, squash, beans?"

"No, no. An elegant vegetable, a beautiful vegetable, the finest vegetable in all of France. Cabbage!"

Betsy Gibson giggled, then clapped her hands under her chin. "Me, cabbage? What a notion!" she said.

He touched the child's hair. Soft. Not as strong as Judith's. Was all children's hair like Betsy Gibson's? Were all children as dazzling? Beyond the child, Ethan watched Judith in conference with the doctor in the doorway. Her cheeks were still tear-stained from her farewell to her father, but she, too, looked as bright as the morning beyond the windows.

Satisfied with his appetite, Betsy dusted the errant crumbs from his sheets, took Aaron's hand, and skipped down the hallway.

Ethan fretted, now that he was alone with Judith. "What will Dr. Foster tell these Randolph people? That this broken-down sailor claiming to be their son and brother asks questions like a relentless magpie? That he has visions of the dead?"

"Friend Jordan Foster is no one's spy, Ethan. Trust him," she insisted, placing her fingers over his heart.

Ethan tried to frown like Fayette. He loved her closeness, her touch. "This doctor, he lied about my leg," he said.

"Lied? What do you mean?"

"He says he can't help me to walk. He's the only one who can, I think. But he is afraid."

"Why?"

"He thinks he'll hurt me. He is the only doctor who has not hurt me, Judith. I am most bewildered by this man."

Judith spoke in the quiet tone to which he had learned to pay careful heed. "Even Mrs. Madison knows him by reputation, and approved of thy sister's choice. He was schooled in Scotland as a physician and a surgeon and teacher of medicine. After he lost his family, he served the wounded in the late war. His skills saved many lives and limbs, Mrs. Madison says."

"Why has he taken us in like this?"

"He tutored your brothers and sister many years ago."

"Yes, Aaron said that, didn't he? Why did Dr. Foster not stay in service to the Randolphs?"

"He was not a doctor then, but a young man, like thee, seeking to further his own education. Thy father was grateful for his help during an epidemic. He provided the means for Friend Jordan's advanced studies."

Ethan smiled. "A good investment. But my father's wealth is based on slave labor, is it not, Judith?"

She looked down at her lap. "Yes."

He slipped his hand into hers. "This offends us both."

"It is my hope that thee will always feel this way, Ethan, without ceasing to love thy family."

He frowned. "I don't know my family. Perhaps my family has no wish to know me. But I know you, and Eli, and—" He spoke a thought as it dawned on him. Was he losing her already? "Is that why your father has gone north this morning, Judith? The Philadelphia Quakers—are they now distressed that you found me, because my family holds slaves in bondage?"

Her steel eyes met his. "Our Society is based on recognition of the Light in everyone, on—"

"Tolerance, of course." He shook his head. "There is so much I don't understand."

"Thee is not yet a full day on dry land, beloved." She stroked his brow in that familiar way he loved. "My father has gone to report on our three-year mission abroad. He will find us a home, and seek to establish our livelihoods in Philadelphia."

"Livelihoods? Don't you preach?"

"Yes, we are both ministers of our Monthly Meeting," she explained. "But the Meeting doesn't support any ministers, except on our travels.

Now that our English mission has finally ended, we make our own way in the world."

"You do? How?"

"We were farmers, when I was a child. Since our move to the city, Father has a small trade as an herbalist. I craft my silhouettes, and I'm ashamed to admit it to one so much better skilled, but I take in mending."

"People pay for such things?"

"Wealthy people, in cities, yes."

He nodded, enjoying her closeness, enjoying the full, rich silence around them. But thoughts invaded his contentment. Were her people tolerant enough to approve of his stolen kiss, her *"beloveds"*? If he could win her love, would they tolerate her marriage to a slave owner's son, even if he renounced his family and took up her mending trade beside her?

Though the woman stood on the wide, open porch of the Windover plantation house, she was bathed in shadows. Ethan's tongue thickened in his mouth.

Aaron carried him off the schooner and over Windover's dock. "Master Ethan, that be your mama."

Her abundant hair, iron-gray shot through rich amber, was dressed simply, elegantly, in lace. Her lavender chemise sifted over a slender, stately form. Anne Randolph moved down the wide steps with the grace of a dancer, more grace than he could ever hope to achieve. She would turn him out. For that alone, she would turn him out.

Her eyes changed. Not the way Judith's did, with her surroundings. This woman's eyes veiled, as if she had dozens of invisible lids she could place over their green brilliance. The intricate complexity of her beauty wove around him like an enchantment. Warm mixed with cold on her like snow on a sheltering tree.

When she met them, she looked not into his eyes, but at the space between them. An artifice, an imitation of directness. "Mr. Washington," she said softly—and it was sealed, what they should call him in her presence. "Welcome."

"Thank you," he said carefully. Were the words in English? Yes.

Behind her strutted a man in clerical black. He resembled Winthrop in height, but was without his imposing size.

"My second son, Clayton."

Clayton Randolph bowed stiffly.

"Grandmama!" Betsy called. She jumped down from her father's arms to bound toward the woman's welcome. "Mrs. Madison visited Uncle Ethan three times, once with a bright-plumage bird on her shoulder! We ate ice creams every day she came!"

"How delightful, darling. But we must bring our guest inside now, he looks tired."

"He's not our guest, Grandmama! He's your little boy who was lost, come home. Don't you know him?"

Anne Randolph's eyes met his at last. "I'm sorry, Mr. Washington, for the child."

"She has been a treasure, *madame*."

"I will apologize for—" She bit her lower lip and he caught a glimpse of the girl she'd once been. "—for myself, then. This has all happened too suddenly for me."

"You are most brave and generous to entertain the possibility that I may be your son. And I would consider myself the most fortunate of men if it proves so."

He bowed his head, unable to maintain this taut, rational equilibrium under the veiled scrutiny of those eyes. He felt the light, trembling touch of her fingers on his shoulder. Long fingers, like his own. Cold. Was she afraid too? Of what? That he was not her son? Or that he was?

Her elder sons quickly flanked her, taking each arm. Winthrop glared. Clayton raised his eyebrow with what seemed detached curiosity.

"Well, if you're not going to kiss him," Betsy proclaimed, folding her arms, "I shall have to bring him to Mama."

The entry of the airy, splendid house was a dazzling shine of marble, cream-painted wood, and urn finials. In their midst was a brass chandelier and a staircase that spiraled up from two directions. Ethan felt more dizzy than the first time he'd experienced the sun on the wide deck of the *Standard*.

"Stop. Please," he whispered to the bondsman.

Aaron halted midstep. Judith felt Ethan's face with the back of her hand. A simple gesture, he knew, to assure herself of his health. The affection behind it eased his lightheadedness. "I don't know this place, these people. Judith, might we go? I don't know them."

He brought her ministering hand to his lips, then gave it the kiss he longed to give his mother. The one Anne Randolph did not invite.

"Betsy," Judith called the little girl, who was already halfway to the first landing, "would thee show us to thy grandpapa's study?"

His niece took her hand. Ethan noticed for the first time how Judith's clothes contrasted with those of the Randolphs. The cloth was more textured, of plain color and simple lines, without ornamentation. How directly it complemented her beauty, without distracting his already tired eyes with swirls and variations of color and design. He was still following the flow of the folds from her waistband when Aaron placed him on a chair in the small room. The bondsman opened heavy green drapery from the windows.

The sunlight entered the room selectively, lighting two tapestries depicting a medieval harvest celebration, the carved mahogany chests, and the long trestle table with silver candlesticks on each end.

"Familiar?" Judith asked him softly.

He felt he had shrunk to the size of the tip of his smallest finger. Impossible. He was sitting in the captain's quarters of the two-masted brig he'd made aboard the *Standard*, the one Fayette had placed in Judith's bag. "Only in dreams," he whispered.

She stooped beside his chair. "A source of comfort, then?"

"The color, it's wrong."

Aaron joined Judith. "What about the color, sir?" he asked.

"Not green. The walls should be rose, that rose," he pointed to a reveler's tunic in the old tapestry.

The black man grinned. "The younger Master Winthrop had us paint this room, just last month." He lowered his voice. "He don't think his daddy's going to be well enough ever to see what he done. Walls will shake when the old master comes down, I say!"

"Are you ready to see my mama now, Uncle?" Betsy said, tugging at his sleeve.

Ethan smiled. "Yes. I must compliment Mrs. Gibson on her excellent taste in daughters."

Sally Gibson's room faced the south side of the house. It was bright in the afternoon sun. The high Palladian windows overlooked an expansive boxwood maze that hedged pathways through gardens alive with early summer flowers. Fayette had taught him the names of some flowers. It was too late for the jonquils, crocus, and hyacinth, but the purple and yellow irises were in full bloom.

The woman standing by the windows was swaddled in pale green folds of a cashmere shawl. She turned as they entered. The sun dappled shadows across her form. She looked like the rest of them—imposing, light-eyed, hair kissed by the sun. But the features that had hardened in her brothers were distinctive on her, and tempered by kindness. Aaron placed Ethan on the brocade sofa.

The woman walked slowly to him, the train of her chemise the only whisper in the room. Ethan lost the sense of Judith beside him, then Aaron. Even his niece had gone silently. Sally Gibson sat. Her recovering, distended body was full of mystery. Her eyes were as green as Anne Randolph's. But without veils, without confusion.

She gently lifted the hair from the side of his face burned by the cannon's blast off Trafalgar. Warm lips pressed a kiss there, though it had long since healed, though his brows had grown in again over whitened scars.

"Mother called it a great injustice—you getting eyelashes women would swoon over, while she and I were gifted so sparsely."

"Did she?" he whispered.

A flood welled up, faster and worse than any that had ever invaded the hold of the *Standard*. The woman blurred.

She held out her arms as his body betrayed him, shaking, sputtering. It began to wrack itself free of sobs. She allowed it, welcomed it, holding him close. Ethan smelled the milk soaking her bodice. He knew that smell. "You're safe now, sweet boy," the woman promised. "You're home."

The gull screamed. How had the bird gotten so far belowdecks? "Fayette," he called, "the gull, she's caught, let her out!"

He opened his eyes. Judith had his shoulders. "No, no. Not caught. Hungry," she assured him. "And not a gull, a baby."

"A . . . ?"

"A baby," she said again.

He took her wrist, steadying himself to its pulse. "Baby?"

"Yes, silly."

She left him, walked to the windows where Sally Gibson was in a draped chair, her new daughter at her breast. A tray sat close by, the mingling aromas of beef stock, vegetables, yeast bread, and honey-smoked ham tantalizing.

Judith put a white blanket over her shoulder, then took the tiny bundle from her mother's arms. Sally sat back, smiled at him. Affection shone from her eyes. Was this glorious woman who'd held him, then sang him to sleep, his sister? What had gained him her love? he wondered, astonished.

Betsy rose from where she'd been stacking alphabet blocks with a child who was a smaller version of herself. No, this one had her father's pointed chin, Ethan realized as they took each other's hands and approached with Judith and the baby.

Betsy stopped them all, then stepped ahead. "Uncle Ethan, may I present my sisters Alice and Charlotte? Alice, you'd better curtsy so he knows you are neither a bird nor a cabbage," she instructed.

Alice obeyed formally.

Ethan sat up higher. "A pleasure, ladies," he said.

He took the younger child's offered hand and watched her light eyes fire with indignation. "Like Mrs. President Mad'son, if you please," Alice insisted.

"Like—?"

"Kiss my hand!"

He looked over the curly head at the child's mother. *"If you please,"* Sally mouthed silently, mimicking. He kissed the dimpled knuckles, stifling a smile.

Judith sat beside him. "Charlotte," she whispered. He peered into the blankets in her arms, left breathless by the tiny face, the perfect fingers, the sweet scent that emanated from Charlotte Gibson. "Oh, Judith," he finally whispered. "Let's steal them all."

Alice turned on her older sister, her eyes wide with horror. "See? He is a pirate, and not our uncle at all!"

"Of course he's our uncle, he only used to be a pirate."

"He doesn't look anything like an uncle. He's dark and clever and foreign, like a pirate."

Their mother swooped down. "What a notion, you silly creatures!"

"But, Mama, Uncle Winthrop says he's come to steal—"

"Return to your game," she told them in a low, calm voice that had molten lava behind it.

"But you said we might feed him when he woke," Betsy cajoled softly. "We've been playing so quietly, and he does look awfully hungry."

Their mother's frown lightened. "Very well. Betsy, you may pour the soup. Alice, prepare a cold plate."

Ethan watched the miniatures go about their tasks. He smiled at their mother.

"It seems I have become one of your chicks, Sally."

Her eyes danced at his voice trying on her given name. "You were my first chick. Mama gave me a practice baby when I was thirteen." He looked away, then felt Sally's touch on his arm. "Ethan. You will remember," she promised.

Who will I be then? he wanted to ask her. She seemed so sure of everything, this tall, kind woman. Could she tell him that? Could she tell him if Judith would love that man, her brother?

After filling his plate, Betsy led her younger sister back to their play. "You make fine children, *madame*," Ethan told their mother.

Her smile made both cheeks dimple. "Well, Barton did play his part." She laughed, then stopped abruptly, touching her face. "I mean—Ethan, you do know how babies . . . ?"

"Oh, he knows," Judith told her with a sly smile. "He had a very fine French teacher in Monsieur Fayette."

Ethan felt the color rise to the roots of his hair as the women laughed. From her snug place in Judith's arms, the seabird baby belched like a sailor.

10

Aaron set Ethan down gently on the chair beside the old man's bed. The face buried in white damask showed all of his eighty-five years. Winthrop Randolph was a wizened stranger to Ethan, Judith knew that immediately.

"Get me my spectacles!" the old man shouted to no one in particular. "Let me have a look at him."

Judith watched his wife, sons, and servants scurry about—all but Ethan himself, who reached up to the spectacles perched on his father's bald forehead. He gently drew them down to his eyes. The man gave him a long, sour, disapproving stare.

"So, you've come back," he said.

"Yes, sir."

"You look terrible. Didn't they feed you?"

"I—"

"Didn't speak up! Didn't I always tell you to speak up, or the wolves of the world would devour you? Never mind, you're back. Tell your mother to stop looking at me with those wounded eyes, won't you?"

Ethan turned. Anne Randolph, who was standing beside the door, bit her lip and slipped outside the room.

"Leave her." His father called him back. "Come closer, you young scoundrel. Couldn't get enough of the sea, could you?"

"I believe I've had enough of it for now, sir."

A rasping sound erupted from the old man's throat. Then his eyes found Judith. "Who's this woman you're holding on to like she can keep you from the gates of Hell?" he demanded.

Sally Gibson touched Judith's back like a comforting sister. Aaron adjusted the old man's bedcovers. "She be Miss Judith, sir, the fine lady who got the child home to us."

"Is she yours, then, Ethan?"

"No, sir."

"Well, who does she belong to?"

"To no one but herself."

"Nonsense. You've been to France, I hear it in your voice and idiotic notions both! I told that captain to keep a tight rein on you and your fanciful head. She's your mistress, this Frenchwoman?"

"She's—"

"Why didn't you feed my son, woman?" He railed at Judith suddenly. "Can't you cook?"

"Not at all well, I fear."

"Well," he sniffed, "Your English is fair."

"I thank thee," Judith said with a smile.

"It's of little consequence, your cooking skill. We don't eat snails and frogs here anyway. We have our Martha, who is the best *chef de cuisine* on either side of the river, make no mistake. I'll give her to you as a wedding present."

Judith's smile disappeared.

The old man's eyes narrowed further. "Crafty French," he grumbled. "All right. You may have the whole family, if you live close, and deliver Martha back for special occasions. Like christenings. How would that be?"

His eyes swept across Judith's form before they returned to his son's flushed face. "You're in America now, young rogue, not some French port of call. Marry her. I approve. Good teeth, wide hips, and direct, with a saucy look about the eyes besides. Your brothers and their silly, twittering wives have been no use at all. I can't wait forever to see this estate securely based in the next generation!"

"You don't understand . . ." Ethan began.

"What do you want now? Aren't your woman's well-placed silences enough?" Annoyance made his father's voice rise in pitch. "Well? Shall I kill the fatted calf, Prodigal Son? A week of dancing to make your brothers even more envious of the ways I've indulged you, wild child of my old age? Go, plan it. Dance your little bride's legs off, then plant me a grandson!" His light eyes waited for a response. The room was silent. "Come home in ill humor, have you? Ethan"—he warned now—"do not you get into one of your mother's moods!"

The room stayed in its hushed silence until Aaron spoke. "Master Ethan's not up to any dancing. He come home crippled, sir."

"Crippled? Nonsense. No son of mine is crippled!"

Ethan leaned into the cool palm of Judith's hand.

"See here, woman." His father appealed to her, his voice tempered quiet. "I'm all blow. A spray, no substance. Tell him that, will you? What else is left to me at my age, eh? I only mean— Listen, child," he summoned Ethan gruffly, "you remember how to ride?"

"Ride?"

"Horses, ride horses! What in blazes is the matter with you?"

"I don't know."

"Don't know? Don't know?" The old man looked around in confusion at his sons and daughter. "What doesn't he know?" he demanded.

"I don't know anything, any of you!" Ethan shouted. His darting eyes found no anchor. "I know only Judith." His eyes finally steadied on the old man's. "She is a Quaker, a holy woman, and you have insulted her in assuming her my paramour. Then you barter me, with human beings as bounty, which she thinks of as an abomination."

Silence. Finally his father spoke. "A French Quaker?"

"She is from Pennsylvania, not France!"

"There's no need to shout, boy. I can hear you."

Sally giggled softly. Judith's mouth turned up. Their laughter drenched the room like a summer rain.

The master of Windover raised his hand. "If this family of pileated woodpeckers will indulge me!" he stormed them silent.

He cast his piercing eyes on Judith. "Though forgiveness is a commendable trait of your people, Miss— What's her name, Sally?"

"Mercer," his daughter answered. "Judith Mercer."

"Miss Mercer. I would not be surprised if you think my youngest child is no candidate for your affections, given this exhibition. Let me assure you upon the subject of his heredity. In accordance with my recollection, he always favored his mother in looks and gentle temperament both.

"As you have seen demonstrated, he has also a streak of choleric anger when the subject is your honor. For this I hope you will forgive him, and that some of that forgiveness he might deem to share with his much more grievously sinning father."

Judith bowed her head to mask her smile. "I accept thy apology, Winthrop Randolph," she said.

He grinned broadly. "No spendthrift chatter out of this one. Good choice, son!"

"Father . . ." Ethan warned.

"Look at how straight he sits!" the old man proclaimed with sudden ferocity. " 'Crippled,' nonsense! We'll get him back up on a horse, won't we, Aaron? That will be the start of his cure."

Aaron sighed. "After my Martha gets the boy a little cushioning for his bones, you think, master?"

"Yes. Exactly! Blasted British starved him! First things first, of course. Proper food, up on a horse, then down on your feet. You'd like that, wouldn't you, son?"

"Yes, sir, but—"

"No qualifiers! Weakens speech! Didn't that damned Boston tutor cram that into you?"

Aaron leaned over his master again. "Mr. Foster crammed the first three, sir," he reminded the old man good-naturedly. "Before you sent him off to Scotland, to learn his doctorin'?"

"Foster, yes. The one who didn't leave, when the sickness came."

"That's right, sir. Now, Master Ethan was borned after the sickness, had his sister Miss Sally schoolin' him, then went to Norfolk, to learn your business from the counting men, then—"

"I know who it is, you great fool!" Winthrop Randolph thundered.

When he turned to his youngest son, his expression softened. He almost smiled. "Don't fret about your imperfect memory of your imperfect family. Even I don't remember everything." He cast his eyes over Judith's form again. "And I haven't been to France."

Against her own judgment, Judith Mercer smiled at the old man. Perhaps he had been a terror to a family who still feared him, but now she felt Ethan had an ally in this most unlikely of fathers.

Ethan loved the quiet of the library, the smell of the book bindings. He pulled the book his sister had set out for him from the shelf. Its pages had been turned many times. By them, together, she'd said, back when she was his teacher. Of course, he remembered the contents. He and Fayette had read all of Shakespeare. He closed the book. He'd reward himself with sonnets after he finished the first few letters. He began the task his niece had set out for him.

Soon he heard echoed snoring. "Aaron?" Ethan called.

The servant jumped up from the empty hearth. "You needs something, Master Ethan?"

"I thought you left with Judith. Why don't you go home?"

"Home, sir?"

"To Martha, your family? You have children?"

"We do, sir. Five. Three girls. Two boys."

"I should like to meet them."

"You done grew up with them, young master."

"Then you must help me. Tell me their names, so I don't appear as rude as I am. Tomorrow, not tonight. It's very late. Go home now."

"But I be your personal servant, sir. So long as you awake, I be awake." The big man stifled a yawn. "Standing by."

"There's no need to subject you to my habits. You must go home. To your wife, your own bed."

"I'll sleep outside the door, if'n you's sure you don't need me—"

"Listen, I don't understand any of this, except it's wrong."

"Wrong, sir? Has Aaron done wrong by you?"

Ethan ran his hand through his hair. "I am not helpless."

"Never said that, did I, sir?"

"The man who took care of me aboard the ship, he was my friend. I've never had a servant."

" 'Cepting back in the days here, what you disremember," the bondsman said.

"That's right."

"And you didn't understand so good then, either, Master Ethan, if you pardon my sayin' so."

"I didn't? I was troublesome to you, Aaron?"

"Oh, a tender sort of trouble, sir. You was too fond of us. Martha would have to shoo you toward your own folk. Weren't your fault, sir, you was just a child, born in the middle of our young. You left us before it all could be hammered in, you see?"

"Hammered in?"

"The difference 'twixt us, sir. White and black, masters and slaves. It was going to take some mighty hammerin' with you, my Martha always said. You was one stubborn child. She weren't happy about you being turned to your brothers' ways with us, either. She see'd you off at that *Ida Lee* ship proud, happy, not like your mama, all fretful. You would come back, my Martha said, on account of you was born in the sack, a water baby—she had to pierce it open herself, so's you can take your first breaths of life."

"She was midwife?"

"Yes, sir, for you all. Now, your mama, Miss Anne, she rolled up her pretty sleeves for each of ours as well, and the two grandbabies come of late, I'm proud to say."

Ethan couldn't imagine his elegant mother rolling up her sleeves in a slave cabin. Holding people in bondage was more complicated than Eli and Judith knew, he thought. "What did that mean, being born that way?" he asked.

"In the sack? That you would never die drowneded, is what! Watching that fine ship *Ida Lee,* my woman, she speaks. She say maybe one of her African grandfathers take care of you there on the water, and you never learn to beat us down. Right then you went and hugged her, in front of them white folk! My Martha, she took it hard, your passing, almost as hard as— Well, hard."

"Almost as hard as what?"

"As you was a one of our own, I reckon, sir," Aaron said, not looking up. "You still ain't learned, Master Ethan. We be feared for you."

Ethan touched the man's mighty shoulder, to assure himself he'd heard the whispered words.

"This difference, you mean? How to treat you all like property? I'm not interested in such lessons," he said, looking through the wavy panes of glass at the crescent moon.

The man, for all his physical power, smiled shyly. Then he leaned in closer. "You got to hide this before your brothers, sir. They'll be trying some late hammering. And you, sir," he glanced along Ethan's leg, "you borne enough already."

"I don't know how to hide it."

"You too polite with me, with all of us niggers. Got to forget them French manners 'mongst us. Learn to look as if we ain't there."

"What?"

"Watch Master Winthrop the younger, sir. He's the best at it."

Ethan frowned. "I see too much of him already."

Aaron shook his head. "My Martha says there weren't never any dissemble in you."

"Will you go home to her, man!"

"I cannot, sir."

"Cannot?"

"Not without a pass. I dare not travels away from my duties without a pass with say-so."

"Who must write you one?"

"Why, you could, master."

"Why didn't you tell me that when I first tried to be rid of you?"

"You didn't ask, sir."

Ethan pulled the lap desk toward him, dipped the pen and hastily scribbled a note, and handed it to his servant. "Get out! Get out!"

"That be good, master. Much better!"

"Better? *Mon dieu,* I'm growling like my father!"

"Your daddy don't cuss near so pretty, sir." Aaron turned as he reached the paneled doors of the library. "Be back at first light for to see to your needs. Martha and me—we thank you, sir."

Ethan watched the bondsman jaunt past the window, envying his muscled calves, the power of his stride. Had he followed those strides as a child?

He rested his head against the cool glass before he went back to his correspondence. After a while he realized his handwriting was easing out of the cramped, tiny letters necessary when he was Fayette's student. Here there was an endless supply of cream-colored paper, an endless supply of everything, even human beings who thought it natural to sleep in cold fireplaces.

Ethan sprinkled sand on the script of the seventh letter, then rewarded himself for his diligence. His fingers slid through the pages of the small volume of sonnets.

He heard the whisper of silk.

"Mr. Washington?"

He raised his eyes to Anne Randolph's form in the doorway. Her voice was more delicate coming through the darkness. Her tunic shimmered over the linen chemise. "Is no one with you here, sir?"

"No one."

She entered the room farther, but kept searching the shadows. "And where's Aaron?"

His jaw set. "He's one of the no ones, *madame.* I gave him a pass to go home to his own bed. This meets with your approval?"

"Of course. It's just that—what if you need him?"

"I won't need him before daylight, Mrs. Randolph."

"You must go to bed."

"I can sleep here. I can sleep anywhere—a sailor's habit."

"Are you not fatigued?"

"No. I kept night hours on the *Standard.* Another habit. Working on the Midwatch."

She walked closer. "You write to your friends?"

"Your friends, who were good enough to call on me in Norfolk." He offered her the unsealed missives. "I have signed none. I am not ashamed of the name you call me. But it occurs to me that they would not know Henry Washington. Still, I will sign them as you wish."

"As I wish?"

"Of course."

She scanned the letters' headings. Stopped. "You have written to Jordan Foster. Did he visit you?"

"We stayed at his home for three days. Didn't Sal— Didn't Mrs. Gibson tell you?"

"No."

Secrets, Ethan thought. So many secrets, but he did not guess at this one, between daughter and mother. Anne Randolph sat beside him. "Mr. Washington, have I distressed you?"

"I have betrayed her. I have betrayed the only one of you who believes I belong here," he whispered.

She touched his hand. "You have not, be assured. I'm glad Sally had you brought to Jordan. He's a very fine doctor, and a very fine man. Did he examine your leg?"

"Yes."

"He offers you hope, I trust?"

"He offers me everything but hope."

"Sir?"

"He'll need to break the bones, reset them, if I'm to have any chance of walking, of . . ." He lost himself in her eyes, wondering again if she was one of the dancers.

"Of what, sir?"

He looked away. "Making my way in the world, without any pity."

He felt her move closer.

"Shall I invite Dr. Foster to Windover? Would you like that?"

More veils gone. The ice was melting, the spring coming by way of the doctor from Norfolk. "Yes, Mrs. Randolph," he said softly. "I would like that very much."

She stood, swept past him, looking out at the ancient oak beyond the library's windows. Her hands were trembling. "He'll be interested in your general health, of course, so you must make us all appear good nurses and eat well. We'll leave you plenty of time together when he comes. Time to talk." She turned abruptly. "Does Jordan think you're my son, sir?"

"I believe so."

"Then he will deem me very guarded, as Sally does. He will chide me for listening to Winthrop and Clayton." A veil returned. "My sons have advised that I not meet alone with you," she said.

"Do you trust their judgment?"

"Yes."

"I will go back to Mr. Shakespeare's sonnets, then, and you will be out of danger."

He found his place in the book, but the words would not enter his understanding. The woman had not moved. Yet he felt her anger.

"Your presence here is most disruptive."

He raised his head. "I will depart upon your wish."

"Windover is not run in accordance with my wishes."

"I will depart upon your wish," he repeated, his eyes watching hers, his heart aching for another veil to lift.

It did. "What do you want?" she asked, her voice breaking.

"Not this," he whispered, driving the anger away. "Dear lady, not to be the cause of any pain."

She came closer, touching her pale fingers to his callused sailor's hands.

"There, there," she whispered. "I am not as fragile as I look. Write, Mr. Washington. We will decide how to sign the letters later."

When he nodded, the long fingers touched his face.

"A beard?" she said, her voice a wisp on the night air as she felt the day's stubble on his cheek. "My boy, my bright boy, your age. With a man's beard. Such a long time it's been."

11

"I thought the sea was supposed to give you an appetite!" the old man boomed across the table.

"Sir?"

"Look at your brothers! Look at the portrait of me in my prime—a hearty twenty-stone weight of muscle and vitality. Even your sister restores herself after childbirth. Meat does that, child, meat! Don't turn your nose up at it the way you do my tobacco!"

Ethan engrossed himself in cutting the deep-red liver. Sally frowned. Sharp-eyed Clara signaled a servant to bring him more. She dominated Hester, Clayton's wife, just as his brother Winthrop dominated Clayton.

Hester's face made him think of a porcelain doll's. When she nodded, the red curls at her cheeks bobbed to life. "My, Mr. Washington's transgressions have had a restorative, blood-warming effect on you, Father dear!" she observed.

"Washington? Who's Washington, you silly woman? I'm talking to Ethan!" He looked around the table. "Sally calls him Ethan." His eyes narrowed. "And you use the name, don't you, Quakeress?"

"I do," Judith agreed.

"Lying is against the Quaker religion. That's why your woman can't fawn on me like your brothers' bookend deceivers, Ethan. Also why she's free to deliver her lectures about impoverishing ourselves by freeing our blacks. It's what their religion bade them do. That's why the Quakers no longer run Pennsylvania, isn't that right, Clayton?"

"I think that theory is original with you, Father," the black-clad man said primly. His clergyman son seemed to have perfected the method of making his father lose interest in him, Ethan thought, as the old man's eyes again found him.

"Now, Prodigal, what's this I hear from young Ruffin about you siding with him in disapproving of my tobacco?"

Ethan cast a glance at the oldest Randolph son and knew the source of the information. Winthrop's eyes challenged him to deny it. "Mr. Ruffin's ideas on crop rotation made sense to me, and I said as much, sir," he began. "I am not trying to interfere with any of your practices—"

"Time-honored practices."

"Honored by time, but not success. Your records show yields descending in both quantity and quality."

The patriarch rubbed a gnarled finger against his chin. "A few early frosts, or inadequate rainfalls, perhaps."

"It's more consistent than that, sir. There's a pattern of—"

"Who gave you permission to study this household's records?" the younger Winthrop Randolph challenged, half rising to his feet.

"I did," his father answered for Ethan, "in that room you are going to have your people paint the original color, usurper." He dismissed his eldest son with a wave of his hand. Clara pursed her lips in tight resignation. It had been her idea, then, the changes in the study.

Aaron had been right; the rafters shook with the old man's anger when he'd found out. Now his eyes danced with a mischievous glee as he focused on Ethan. "You know he's eaten with envy, don't you?"

"Who is, sir?"

"Young Ruffin. Those blackguards in Washington reached a peace just as he was ready to jump into the war. Itching to fight, he always was, remember?"

"No."

"Of course you do! Even when you were boys, he was envious of you in uniform! How he sulked when you were made midshipman on the

Ida Lee! At the Harrison barbecue. Remember? It's like yesterday to me, and I'm eighty-five! You must remember!"

"I'm sorry."

"Father," Sally demanded, "isn't it enough we have him back?"

"No, it is not enough! I am not going to leave him to be smothered by the rest of you! No legs to stand on, talking like a Frenchman, and with an addled mind besides! Where is that damned doctor? He must help. Didn't I buy him the best education before he traipsed off to the territories to waste it on heathen Indians?"

"Dr. Foster, among Indians?" Ethan asked.

Winthrop Randolph frowned at Sally. "There, again! Listen to what catches his fancy! We've got to get this child on his feet so he stops these peculiar bends of the mind.

"Ethan!" he summoned. "Eat, while I explain Ruffin's envy. To wit: He lives on after we thought you were lost, missing every opportunity to make war. Then you come home to us, doted on by presidents past and present, hero of no less than the Battle of Trafalgar, slayer of your own mad English captain—"

"I didn't kill anyone," Ethan whispered, reaching for Judith's hand under the table's linen. He felt what the old man accused. Addle-brained. Confused. But he hadn't killed anyone, had he?

"That hardly matters!" Winthrop Randolph insisted. "It is what's believed, what's driving Ruffin to distraction."

"Mr. Ruffin has been kind, and patient, and—"

"He wants to see you fail, Ethan. That's why he's giving out such cockeyed advice."

"He only gave it after I asked him about Elwood."

"Elwood?"

"Aaron's youngest son, sir. He gets the tobacco sickness. I was concerned, and—"

"What? Are you interfering with Windover's people?" Winthrop the younger boomed, rising all the way to his feet this time. The silver plate of cheeses and fruit dropped from the serving girl's hands. Aaron's daughter, Elwood's sister—Phoebe. All of Aaron and Martha's children were house servants or craftsmen, except for Elwood. The tray's contents crashed to the floor.

"There!" Winthrop crowed, as if the action had underlined his point. "That's the only sickness any of your people suffer from, Father! Clumsiness, laziness! And the cure for that is the strap. Send this one to our place, Mother. Clara will return her to you with more grace about her person."

Ethan watched the young slavewoman's eyes fill with fear. How had his simple mention of the health of her brother led to this?

Anne Randolph stood, turned Phoebe toward the doorway, and dismissed her. She faced her eldest son. "I am still able to manage my own household, Winthrop." The veiled eyes of the mistress of Windover challenged both him and her daughters-in-law.

Clara nodded coldly. Hester waved her handkerchief in frilly surrender.

Mrs. Randolph entered in the way that was becoming her habit, after a quiet knock at the bedroom door. He was finishing a letter to Jordan Foster with yet another request to visit Windover. He could sign himself "Washington" to those letters. And the ones to Eli Mercer. Judith's father and Jordan Foster understood his predicament.

"The roast calf's-liver was not to your liking tonight, was it?"

He smiled uneasily, a twinge of pain at his middle. "It was more that I was not to its liking."

"Still, you finished the portion, at my husband's prompting. You must not do that. He will only find something else to be displeased about. It is not his age or illness that causes this disagreeableness. It is a lifetime trait. You have seen it in ample evidence, so has Miss Mercer. You attempted to please him at supper, and caused yourself distress. Here." She placed a small cake at his side. "The ginger will soothe your indisposition. Eat it slowly."

"Yes, *madame*."

She glazed her forehead with her middle finger. Gracefully. Everything this woman did was graceful. "I'm being insufferable."

He grinned wider. "Not at all. Will you sit?"

"If I can be good company."

"You always are."

"There. Now I know you don't have a lifetime of memories of me."

His laughter startled her. He stifled it, breaking off a piece of the confection. He placed the cake on his tongue, let it flavor his mouth before chewing slowly, an old habit, checking for weevils, mold. There. He felt better already, distracted by the sweetness of molasses, the tang of the spice.

"You are quite correct about Elwood," she said quietly. "He is plagued with the tobacco sickness."

"All his life?" he asked quietly.

"No, only since working in the fields. He was his brother Micah's apprentice at the forge. Until he tried to run away."

"I see."

"Perhaps our joint concern might prove beneficial, if we both tread lightly."

He smiled. "I am used to treading lightly around giants."

"Good. If you will work to free a few acres for— What would you have us plant?"

"Corn, beans, squash. Food."

"Then I will see if I can persuade our giant that Elwood's time of punishment might better be spent in those fields."

Ethan listened closely. For what? Related tones? Remembrances of other times they schemed like this around the old man's temper? "You are fond of Aaron and Martha's family," he observed.

"They are as much Windover's heirs as you or I."

He didn't know what was more shocking—her statement, or including him within it, as if she believed he was her son. She had shocked herself. The veils were down; she was standing, leaving him. He took her hand.

"Help me to understand this, Mrs. Randolph. Tell me about the time of the measles." he asked her quietly. "How you saved all the children."

"Who told you that?"

"Aaron and Martha. Any of the black people would put his hand in the fire for you since then, they say."

"Don't say 'black people,' " she reprimanded gently.

"No? 'Slaves,' then?"

"Gracious, no. 'Servants.' There are slaves, of course. Ones with wicked, greedy masters. But not here, not at Windover. Not even in the fields. Here the Negroes are our people, part of our family. Our servants."

She's been looking through that veil a long time, he decided. Perhaps she'd come to believe it as her naked sight. There was no use mentioning Elwood's flight. He stayed the course of their conversation instead. "When Aaron and Martha tell about the measles, I get to bask in your reflected glow."

"Mr. Washington, you do have odd notions!"

"You looked a little like Sally just then."

She touched her cheek. "Did I?"

"I mean, the other way around, of course." He shrugged. "Or perhaps it is only that you both have chosen 'odd' as my most descriptive trait."

"Nonsense. Sally adores you."

"She adores her little brother. The one born after all the sickness."

There. That smile appeared, that rare smile he would stand on his head to see. "Tell it," he urged. "Tell about the epidemic."

She leaned her back against the chair's green cushion. "My husband was abroad in England that winter. Winthrop was eighteen; Clayton, fifteen. It struck them first. Sally was only twelve. She had a mild case, a blessing for me, because once she recovered, her brothers had the worst of their fevers."

Her eyes fired with remembrance. "All of the overseers, hired tutors, dancing masters, even the tinkermen were running off, avoiding our part of the Tidewater in fear. But not Jordan Foster. He prevented my sons from destroying themselves in their pain, I think. It was rampant throughout the servants' quarters, too. So I helped Aaron and Martha in the cabins as they helped Jordan and myself in the big house. We were the only plantation to come through the epidemic without deaths."

"You were running the place?"

"Yes. With my husband gone, my sons so ill, and our neighbors in the same throes, how could I have done less with all of them assisting me with every drop of their own sweat? Windover survived."

"It thrived, as it never did before or since."

"You must not add to already exaggerated accounts."

"You found something good, didn't you, *madame*? You found your own strength, within that terrible time?"

"I . . . haven't thought of it that way."

"And Dr. Foster found his calling."

Her eyes went wistful. "Martha and Aaron were right. He had the healing in his hands."

"Do you still think of Dr. Foster fondly? As in days gone by?"

She looked startled by the question, then peered at him more closely. "What are you up to?" she charged. Already this woman knew him too well, he feared.

"Why will he not come? I thought once you invited him, he would."

"Dr. Foster has obligations. Be patient."

"It's not his obligations keeping him away. What is it?" He sounded like a willful, petulant child. Is that who he'd been?

"He's never come back to Windover," she said quietly.

"Never? Why?"

Her mouth formed that impenetrable line. "You think it such a curse, such a hardship, to be without memory? Think on his memories! Think of being able to help save us all, and then watch his own die."

"The lady with the dulcimer, the children," he remembered.

"He spoke to you of them? Of his family?"

Her eyes were so sparked with gold he was afraid to tell her his visit was not with Dr. Foster, but with his dead. He nodded.

"Did he love them? Did he know enough to love them?" she demanded, almost fiercely.

"He has regrets."

She looked away. "Regrets, of course. We all have regrets. We who are blessed with memory."

She regarded him coldly then, wondering, he knew, if she was telling these things to a stranger. Neither Ethan's name, nor his old one fit her lips anymore. He wondered if she would cease calling him anything, and so bury him, too. Out. He must get out, before that.

"Jordan Foster will listen to you." He tried another tack, his French-trained reason. The Boston-bred doctor from Norfolk was her chance to be rid of him. Jordan Foster would kill or cure him. Either way, he would leave her to her everlasting grief. Let her understand that. "If you intercede, I'm sure he'll consider doing what is necessary to help me walk again."

"I could not possibly—"

"You trusted him with teaching your children," he pressed. "And together you preserved the whole plantation at the time of the measles epidemic. Sally says he saved soldiers' limbs in the last war. Will you write to him on my behalf, about performing the surgery necessary?"

"You ask a difficult thing."

"But I am willing to take the risks—"

"You do not think of him!"

"Him?"

"Him, yes, him, you selfish boy! He believes you are my son! How will he live with himself should you die under his knife?"

Her cheeks had gone from flushed to white. He smiled uneasily. "Well. Then he will at least be rid of this bothersome magpie who—"

Her slap yanked his head back hard enough to hear his neck crack, to make the side of his face numb. It began to sting.

Anne Randolph stared at her hand as if it didn't belong to her. "My dear God," she said in a splintered whisper.

He lowered his head, so she wouldn't have the pain of looking at him. "I only wanted to make you laugh," he whispered. "I only ever want to make you laugh."

"Don't you understand? You are almost him to me now."

"Who?" He wanted the word. He wanted his name from her lips just once, for his pain.

"Ethan. My Ethan. You must not talk of taking risks, dying. Not now, not when you've just barely come back."

"Almost, almost back. Sally says her belief is strong enough for us both. It is not, is it? It is not for you, or for me. I am your heir in that. My dreams, my remembrances are tricks, explained away by your sons. They think me a simpleton, they think Judith the dark mistress of a scheme. I lack the experience of most men my age, my body is crippled. But I need to know myself, Anne Randolph, as badly as you need to know me. Dr. Foster, he has the key, does he not?"

"Don't, please."

Tears came with her pleading. But he would not take the blame for them, not this time. His face still stung. He would not bury himself to ease her pain. "I'm not your little boy. I'm a man, *m-madame*," he stammered.

"You can't do it!" Anne Randolph said, astonished. "You can't do it, either. You can't call me Mother!"

"I'm sorry."

"No. Don't be sorry for it. We are kindred spirits in that, too. Both lost. There's comfort. Yes?" she imitated his French cadence.

He sighed. "You find odd sources of comfort."

She laughed, kissing his cheek where she'd slapped him moments before. What would Judith make of this exchange? He suddenly felt very tired. Anne Randolph rose, gracefully glided among the windows, closing the shutters. Gliding, like a dancer. Around and around. No, that dancing was a dream, only a dream. Then she was there again, this beautiful woman, putting his legs up, covering him with a quilt.

"Rest now, stubborn sailor," Anne Randolph whispered. "You've won. I will converse with your father on this."

12

Judith watched as Ethan pulled off his riding glove and massaged behind Cavalier's ears. "Perhaps you are not so old, nor I so lame, yes?" he said, laughing. "Perhaps we will confound them."

You have confounded them, Judith thought, with a mixture of sadness and delight as she watched him replace the glove. Ethan sat high in the saddle, for all the world like a powerful young centaur. He would stay in the saddle forever, if Windover didn't also have his mother, his sister and her beautiful children, and its library.

The horse and its rider disappeared beyond the giant oak, on their favorite trail, along the high ridge that overlooked the James River. The falls were there, and the salt marsh. The James led to the Atlantic, Ethan's link to who he used to be: Washington, Fayette's child.

What did he think of that other world, the one they visited daily? It was beyond the orchard of fruit trees, the poplars, cypress, crepe myrtle—the hardworking world of Windover's slaves.

Judith returned her attention to her letter.

> Father, though I praise his progress, let me not give the impression that our Washington has conformed to his family's ways. Ethan has forgotten none of his skill or resourcefulness. He casts about the heaps of discarded refuse in the slave quarters for materials for his ships. His brothers and their wives chide him for not engaging in more useful activity, but I think in their hearts they are glad that he refuses what his aged father pushes him toward, the stewardship of Windover itself. Now our Washington's handsome vessels are gifts to grateful household children of all colors.
>
> He is withdrawn with his own family, however—a beggar at the feast, despite the remarkable remembrances. His brothers' animosity is an undercurrent, growing more powerful as the women's love for him grows.

"Miss Mercer, I should like a word with you."

Judith raised her head to see the afternoon sun blocking Clayton Randolph's form. "Of course," she said quietly. It had been a long time since she'd reminded the clergyman to use no title with her name. If her father had been here, with his gently persuasive ways, he'd have been more successful.

"We have prepared an offer."

"Offer?"

"You have been our guests the better part of the season. As harvest approaches, we will no longer have the time to be patient. Despite all you see, my father is not cash-rich, not since the loss of the *Ida Lee*, Jefferson's embargo, Madison's war. But my brother and I agree to a small fee so that your sailor can learn some trade. He is not a dull boy, I'm sure he can apprentice himself to some worthy Quaker person. He seems inclined toward your notions. I'm sure with some patient instruction—"

"What dost thou say, Clayton Randolph?" Judith whispered.

He came closer. "He may have the horses—Patchwork and Cavalier both. And a stipend for a five-year apprenticeship. But you must go."

"Go?"

"Be reasonable, woman! He doesn't remember us. We don't accept him as our own."

"His mother—"

"*My* mother has been turned away from reality for a great many years now. This vain hope, and my sister's stubborn belief, neither will stand. They are women. And our aged father? He will be humiliated if he resists our decision. We'll have him examined for competency. He will be ruled against. None of the results of your scheming will stand. Not in court. Would you destroy this family, Miss Mercer?"

Judith felt as if her head was between a vise. The truth was the small, lonely voice whispered among the babble inside. Clayton Randolph's voice turned almost kind, its tone right for a man of God. The words were not. "This is the best you can do. Make him one of your own. You get to keep him, then, don't you? You must see—"

"The truth."

"Then look down your nose. Do not commit the sin of pride again."

"Pride?"

"Come, Miss Mercer. We are not that unalike. You had Jefferson, Madison, and your spotless reputation behind you. You couldn't let go of your notion then, of course. My brother and I, we understood. But time has passed. This is your chance to make all right. Your sailmender would go. He would do anything you advised, you know that."

"If that is so, I must not abuse my influence."

"Who is being abused now? My mother and sister! My father looking for his lost ship and fortune as well as his son in this man's eyes! And he himself, caught without memory or bearing, infirm in body and mind!"

"How dare thou speak him so? He is not infirm!"

"You women may have Jordan Foster coming today. But we have well-paid physicians who will swear otherwise, about the young man as well as the old one."

Judith bit back her words, buried her fists in her skirts. Clayton Randolph crossed the boundary he'd always maintained between them to whisper at her ear:

"You have not failed, Miss Mercer. It's your subject who has failed you. Cut your losses. Take your prize convert and go home. Our offer stands until harvesting begins. After that we will give you the fight of your life. And you will lose."

When Judith had finally gained control of herself, he'd gone. She stared down at the letter in her lap. She could not see the words. She could only see Ethan, in plain attire, smiling at her. Ethan, a convinced Quaker. As her father's new son, he'd replace her brothers and sisters, those little bodies growing cold as the stone around the hearth. She'd carried the coldness of her murdered family inside her so long. With Ethan as her helpmeet, in her bed over winter nights, she'd never be cold again. The vision was a sweet possibility. Was it a holy one?

Martha nudged Judith's side with a basket smelling of freshly baked bread.

"Where they off to now?" she demanded.

Judith wiped her eyes hastily with the backs of her hands. "Ethan's riding Cavalier today. They'll return soon. Sit with me, Martha. I'm just finishing." Judith made room for her on the quilt.

"You and Master Ethan and your letters. Post rider's never had so much work at the place! Who's this one for?"

"My father."

"He's done found a place for you up north, Miss Judith? That be his news?"

Judith glanced down. "Yes. Yes, he has."

"Don't tell Master Ethan. Not today. He be so happy today, with his doctor finally comin'."

Her father had not questioned how long she'd chosen to remain at Windover. But their Monthly Meeting soon would. Judith felt Martha's hand at her shoulder and instinctively pressed her cheek against it.

This woman and her Aaron were the pillars of the other half of Windover. Aaron's wife breathed warmth—from her kind face to a lean but soft body that sloped into a lap that Judith had seen fit three children at once. Her coppery tone and high cheekbones spoke of a Cherokee slave ancestor mixed with Africans. Martha was Anne Randolph's age. The two had been girls together a half century before. Their lives continued to intertwine when Martha was sent to Windower as part of her young mistress's dowry. Now—wars, children, epidemics later—the slave-woman looked as resilient as Anne Randolph looked delicate. Still, both had survived, together, their stations in life. Judith wondered at it.

Horse, rider, and a watchful Aaron came into view again. Together, the two women watched. Martha frowned, shaking her high head.

"Too soon for Cavalier. Should of stayed on Patchwork longer. Master Ethan not near fattened up enough for Cavalier's spills."

"Your latest bounty should help, Martha."

The woman looked down at the basket. "I trust you with a secret, Miss Judith. Ain't my fancy white bread's got him filling out. It's corn." She lifted a linen cloth to reveal a plain, round loaf of grainy yellow beside a hunk of cheese and bottle of red wine.

"Corn? But you don't serve corn at the big house."

"When Master Ethan brings you down to quarters for your Bible stories? He has that man of mine sneak him in my kitchen for spoon bread and boiled-up corn besides! He's got a mighty taste for it. Shall I leave you some?"

"Yes, please."

Judith was grateful for Martha's trust. If Ethan's brothers found out this taste for food deemed fit only for slaves and farm animals, they would surely use it against him. Ethan Randolph's sole enemies remained his brothers and their wives, the straight-backed Hester and fussy Clara. Even their influence was dwindling daily. Clayton knew it, hence his offer.

Ethan rode to the women. He leaned over the saddle, and removed his hat. "Martha," he said, then placing his hat back on his head, "Judith."

"Master Ethan," Martha shouted. "You disrespectful of your lady?"

"No, I—"

"You get that hat off your head 'fore I knock it off."

"But, Martha—" he beseeched.

"You don't needs to take no sass from him, Miss Judith." She sniffed. "He only the third son."

Judith laughed, knowing Martha would not dare tease Ethan's brothers with such banter. That set him apart from his family, too.

"Judith," Ethan demanded, "tell her!"

"Ethan is greeting a Quaker in a perfectly proper fashion, Martha," she finally admitted.

"Even a lady?"

"We make no distinction."

The black woman considered her words. "So that be the price of having your women speak out at meetings? You don't get no bows, no tipped hats, no hands to help you from carriages?"

Judith smiled slowly. "Perhaps that is the price," she realized.

"Did your daddy once farm with the labor of slaves, Miss Judith?"

"Yes," she said quietly.

"Did he free his people? Is that why you be poor?"

"We're not poor, Martha."

"You got no home. You dress poor."

"We choose to dress plain. We'll have a home soon."

"Do Quakers follow Jesus? I loves your Moses stories, Miss Judith, but do Quakers go by the same as the Baptist preacher's Bible?"

"The same."

Ethan cocked his head. "For what do you barter with Judith now?" he demanded of Aaron's wife.

The woman's face sliced into a grin of delight. "Me, master? What would I wants? Already got us our Bible stories, reading that singing-strong voice of Miss Judith here. Serves to balance out you and your card tricks corruptin' the young ones of a Saturday evenin'."

"How long did you keep the lamp burning learning cat's-tail yourself, you great Tartuffe?"

"You sassin' me now?" she stormed, shaking her finger at him. "Better not take to sassin' me, young master! Not as rail-thin a man you still is! And not the cook your woman ain't till I shows her the ways of my kitchen."

Judith laughed. "Martha, if thee succeeds where legions of angelic women have failed, thee will die seeing God."

"I see the Almighty's works already, miss," the servant whispered, her bantering suddenly sobered as they watched Ethan dismount into Aaron's arms. "I see them in the changes you two done brought this mournful place."

There were changes—dizzying changes, Judith thought. The elder Winthrop Randolph was recovering from the illness all thought would be his last. Ethan's sad, beautiful mother was even moving out of the habits of her grief. The servants doted on this third son of their master to the last man, woman, and child. Was it real affection? Did they see in him a kindred spirit in his own captivity? Or another master to be flattered into favor?

Only Jordan Foster had disappointed Ethan, in declining his mother's invitation to visit, though he was the most diligent of Ethan's correspondents. Today, even that disappointment would end. It was all meant to be, wasn't it? Not the future Clayton Randolph described.

It was not a burst of pride that had turned her into an avenging angel aboard the *Standard*, when he'd whispered that these were not his people. When he'd spoken of staying at sea. It was not pride. It was the Truth, wasn't it? Judith wished her father were here to help her sort through her doubts.

Martha deposited her bounty of the warm, covered loaf of corn bread, cheese, wine, and glasses on the cloth beneath the willow tree. Aaron walked both Cavalier and his wife to the big house to deliver her remaining loaves.

Judith placed her writing supplies into their box. It was her favorite time, under the dappled shade beside Ethan. She would think no more of changes today. Nor of leavetaking.

Ethan removed his coat and she caught the scent of summer honeysuckle his nieces had pressed in the pocket of his rose-and-gold-brocaded waistcoat before the ride.

"I didn't know your family owned slaves, Judith," he said, leaning back on his elbows.

She stopped breaking off the cheese. "It was a long time ago. Before I was born. I am not impoverished."

He put up his hands. "I was not thinking of that. Judith, listen. I remember no childhood with these people. Will I never learn yours? I wish to know your family, your Society. I wish to know the little girl from where your beauty, your generosity, your unshakable faith comes."

She looked away. He touched her hand. "Is this rude?"

"No more than thee lying in this shade with me, escaping thy brothers' visit."

He scowled. "They don't come to see me. They come to put more doubts in Anne Randolph's mind. And their wives take inventory so they can accuse me of stealing the silver, perhaps, yes?" He grinned. "That's a very becoming hat."

Judith lowered her head. "It's Sally's. I'll tell her thee admires it. Eat."

"I admire you."

She put the cheese closer, trying to hide the pleasure she took from his open, guileless affection. But she must distract it, because they were alone. "Truly? Such an unfinished woman?" she tried. "I feel honored that Martha has decided to make a cook of me."

He smiled, sipping his wine. She was not distracting him at all.

"She even trusted me with a certain taste you have for—"

"Corn bread!" he exclaimed, breaking off an end even as she uncovered it. "I thought I smelled it!"

His gleaming teeth tore through the crust with abandon, so opposite the slow, careful way he sometimes still chewed his food. His appetite was different out here under the tree, and with simple, hearty fare from Martha's kitchen house.

His eyes sobered. "You deserve their trust, Judith. But I . . ."

"Thee?" She prompted his usually eloquent tongue.

"Why are they so good to me? If I am a Randolph, I am their oppressor."

"Hardly that!"

"They allow me to play with the children, listen to their speech, their music. When I watch them dance, see their feet stamp out patterned rhythms, I think . . ."

"What, love?"

"That the black people call us with these rhythms, the way the ones in the hold of the *Standard* did."

"You and your mother have Elwood tending beans instead of working in the curing barns. He is not dizzy there, and sleeps all night again, Martha says."

"That's not enough."

He was torn, Judith sensed. His heart was beginning a painful, righteous struggle, just as she was leaving his sphere of influence.

"And you changed the subject!" he accused her suddenly.

"Subject?"

"You. The subject was Judith Mercer. And I don't want Bible stories."

"I know. Heathen," she teased.

"Mais non." He set his jaw stubbornly. "I am a Deist, like Fayette, my father, my brother. My real family."

"Thee is not fair to—"

"Confound you, woman, how do you do it?" he stormed. "Hush up and listen to me now. I need Judith stories to hold on to when you've gone home. They're calling for you, aren't they, in Philadelphia, that haven for lawbreaking, slave-stealing Quakers and runaways? And you miss your father."

Tears stung at the corners of her eyes. "Thee needs to eat more," she insisted. "Martha says—"

He knocked her offering from her hand. "Martha! Moses! Plagues, escape of the Israelites!"

"What?"

"There—in your Bible stories. Those are the ones you read them. Escape. Always escape from slavery. Have you planted the seeds of sedition in our people's hearts?"

" 'Our people'?" she echoed.

"Yes, our people." He advanced on her across the quilt, gracefully, his lame leg merely a part of his stealth. "Our people are treated better than you Northerners treat your hired hands, your city poor, even in mighty Philadelphia!" His accent changed completely, the French clip disappearing from his Virginia drawl. "Our servants are protected members of our household. We live as Abraham and Isaac and our biblical fathers lived, Miss Mercer, you must see the righteousness of that."

He almost convinced her, until she realized he was parroting his father's pronouncements too exactly. Judith giggled in relief. "Ethan, stop! You are being most disrespect—"

But his mouth was over hers, stealing a playful kiss, tasting of the wine, of the summer day. She must not allow this. She'd barely caught her breath before he kissed her again, longer, stopping only when the blast from her nostrils hit his cheek. He grinned wide. "Had you going, didn't I, Judith Mercer? Had that indignation you cast at my brothers, my poor invalid father—I had it fired!"

She whacked his shoulder soundly. "Deceiver!" she accused, trying to cover her hot blush. The sun had given his skin a healthy glow, and had streaked a few flaxen highlights through his chestnut hair. Randolph highlights.

The smile disappeared. "What else is left the powerless but deceit?" he asked quietly.

She touched his face. "Oh, Ethan," she whispered. "What have I done? Where am I leaving thee?"

"Don't leave me, Judith. Don't leave me here."

He pulled the loose tie under the straw hat and knocked it from Judith's head in one fluid motion. Her lips parted. He cupped his hand around the back of her neck where her hair was carefully braided inside the white cap. "Judith," he whispered ardently, "save me from dinner conversations filled with biblical patriarchy and the fluctuating price of tobacco."

Kisses. Swift, stolen kisses to her chin, cheek, earlobe. "In return . . ." He took her weight fully into his arms, arms strengthened by his control of the horses. He purred against the weave of gray homespun and shift, through to her skin.

He must talk, she must make him talk—not this sweet, warm sound that was filling her being with yearning. One hand went to her hip, pulled her closer against his freshly muscled thigh, another gift of his father's horses. "In return, let me please you," he whispered against her neck. "Let me spend my life pleasing you."

He lowered his head. With only the slightest touch he rubbed his cheek against the nipple of one breast. She felt both grow hard, responding. *No.* His shoulders. There, beneath her hands. *Push, Judith. Push him away. Say no, even if it causes pain. He doesn't understand. He is a man—young, French, beautiful, so beautiful and strong and scented with desire.* It was her responsibility. *Shoulders, Judith, not hair*—not lacing her fingers through his hair, pulling him closer, feeling his tongue's caress through the weave of her bodice.

"Ethan, this is—"

"What, love? What is it?"

She gasped, her blood singing. "Wondrous."

No, not what she'd meant to say, not at all. And what was this sudden, languid drowsiness in her limbs, this triumph in his eyes? He laughed, kissing her sweetly behind her ear, then along her neck as his fingers wove along her gown's seam, then lifted the hem to caress her legs beneath. It began again, the delight, the desire for him to be impossibly close. Inside her. What was he doing? Something carnal, something a French whore had taught him. Judith Mercer didn't want such things. She wondered who she was.

She was in his shimmering web, her bodice as wet as a nursing mother's, her gown up past her knees, her pumping heart caught between joy and fear. Did he know that? Yes, he knew. He stroked her cheek with his long, leather-and-honeysuckle-scented finger. With infinite care he replaced the hem of her skirt to her ankles, though his breathing was ragged, like her own.

Judith had felt his young, powerful urge to continue, to spread her legs and put himself inside her. Even the terror of that, of her ruination, had melted like snow under a summer sun. Why? Because his guileless eyes told her she was safe. Only joy was left. Judith felt her love for this man, who could perform that miracle, deepening.

Could she do these things to him in return? She reached for the elegant jawline that matched his mother's, took it between her hands. She kissed him—long, hard, fervent. She was soaring, but did not recognize the vision. Was this his dream she'd been cast into? Was he joining Fayette atop the mizzenmast?

The kiss ended. They stared at each other for what seemed like a lifetime. Finally, Ethan's startled look left, and he smiled that shared-secret smile of their first meeting. "I feel a part of my soul missing, Judith Mercer. And I'll haunt you for its return in Heaven, Hell, or Philadelphia."

She began to cry.

His eyes turned almost black. "What are you doing? *Sacre-bleu,* stop that!" he demanded.

She tried, but the torrent only got worse when she heard Betsy and Alice, the ships he'd made them held over their heads, singing down the pathway.

". . . L'on y danse, l'on y danse . . ."

Ethan sat up, pulled the handkerchief from his waistcoat and threw it at her. "Each time we kiss, you cry! First your father sees this, now my nieces! They will be sure to report *tout de suite* to my sister that I leave you howling. You're giving me a terrible reputation!"

"I'm sorry," she implored, blowing her nose. "If it had only not been *'Sur le pont d'Avignon'*!"

He grunted. "It's the only song I know without scandalous lyrics. What else was I to teach them?"

"Oh, Ethan," she said, sniffing.

"Don't 'Oh, Ethan' me, you silly woman. If it were not for the sweetness of your kisses and the fine weave of your hair for my masts, I'd send you home to your father!"

"Would thee?" she demanded, wading up his fine coat. "Is that what I am? A mouth to kiss? Hair for thy masts?"

"Breasts," he assured her. "Your breasts are very fine, too. Even clothed."

She stood, threw his coat to the ground, and trampled it. He laughed. "Better, better," he murmured. "Alice, Betsy!" he called out to the little girls. "Guard me from this wild woman!"

But Alice leaped to Judith's side. Her sister fisted her hands at her hips as she gazed down at him. Her eyes narrowed with suspicion. "Uncle Ethan, you've been very naughty!" Betsy pronounced.

He cast Judith a sidelong look, and caught her hot blush in its sights, she knew.

"Naughty, *petit chou*?"

"Because you are outside riding so long!"

"Mama says you must come home!" Alice commanded. "You must change clothes, to look more proper, for Uncle Winthrop's gone to fetch Dr. Foster from the docks."

"Jordan! He's here?"

Judith watched Ethan's face brighten in anticipation of seeing his friend again. Sally, Dr. Foster, his mother—she was leaving him with a triumvirate of allies to ease his entry into the life of a family he might never remember.

Alice took her hand. "You're so cold, Judith," she whispered, concerned.

"I'm always cold, little one."

"Not always," Ethan reminded her, with his mischievous boy's grin.

"Take Judith home," Betsy commanded Alice. "I'll call Aaron to fetch Uncle Ethan."

Judith walked a few steps before she turned, looked back at him. How was the afternoon's sunlight slanted to make his face glow like that? she wondered. The glow made him seem so vulnerable, much more than his lame leg had ever accomplished. His eyebrow arched to the hair rakishly pulled back from his forehead. Had she done that?

"Go on, go on," he dismissed her.

* * *

Ethan watched the straight, even skirts of Judith's pearl homespun glide against her form. Had he done too much there, on the quilt? As strong as she was, there was that part of her so fragile. Had his hunger frightened her even as she rose to her pleasure?

Worry superseded even the pride he felt at having helped Judith accomplish— What did Clarisse call them? A woman's rushes. Every properly instructed man should be able to help a woman find many of these rushes before he seeks his own fulfillment between her thighs. He thought of her languid smile. Yes. Little deaths. Rushes.

They were part of courting, seduction. The man must be a very good lover, because women didn't need men, Clarisse said. His hands and tongue and kisses were letting Judith know he as a husband would be worth all the pain that would also be part of their lives. But was it the same for American women? What about Quaker ones? He must ask Sally these things. Sally would know, and guide him.

Was Clarisse speaking the truth about his leg not being of consequence to the women who loved him? The Randolph brothers sneered behind their hands at his riding being good exercise for half a man. Is that why he'd continued with Judith on the quilt? To show her he was not half a man? His face flushed with shame at the possibility. He must ask her forgiveness, if this was so.

It would change. It would all change after today. Jordan Foster had come. He had the skill to do what was necessary to help Ethan walk again. He needed only to get past the barrier that was holding the physician back. Ethan must convince him to do the things needed, no matter the cost.

He would dance with this woman Judith Mercer, Ethan silently promised the air between them. He would dance, and wed, and together they would climb ladders of delight. Perhaps children would come of their climbing. Children as beautiful as Sally's. His niece tugged on his arm.

"Think of what Dr. Foster would suppose once he saw you not only riding, but with me in your charge. He would have to help you!"

"Indeed," he agreed. "And a healed leg would serve to make little Alice no longer think me a pirate, yes? You will intercede for me with Jordan Foster, then, *petit chou*?"

"Oui, mon uncle!"

"Oncle," he corrected.

"Oncle."

"Très bien."

"Mama and Grandmama and Miss Judith will intercede as well."

Ethan grinned. "No wonder the physician resisted coming to Windover so long. He does not stand a chance against my women."

He plunged his arms through his trampled coatsleeves, as Betsy found his hat. Aaron approached, with Cavalier.

"Can't run, even trot him, sir, 'specially not with Miss Betsy on with you," the bondsman warned, frowning.

Ethan placed his good leg in the stirrup, then swung the lame one over. He stood poised above the saddle, waiting for Aaron to lift his niece aboard, then anchor him on the other side. He'd feel as secure as any two-legged horseman astride the mount then. He loved that feeling, the sheer physical pleasure of it.

But he sensed something wrong at once in Cavalier's shaking head, the nervous back-and-forth dance his feet did.

"No. Wait," he said, as the big man lifted his niece. But the words didn't come fast enough. Betsy's small weight landed on the saddle.

The horse reared. Betsy grabbed Ethan's middle. He searched the ground for Aaron, but found only a blur of him as Cavalier bolted.

The horse leaped along the ledge where the trail led down to the salt marsh. Betsy screamed. Ethan tucked her head deeper. His good leg was buckling under the strain of their combined weights. He would go down. If Aaron didn't catch her, he would take this child down with him. He pulled slightly on the reins and felt the horse's pain. But there, Aaron's powerful sprinting legs were close.

"Take my arm, Betsy," Ethan coaxed the terrified girl. "Only my arm, *petit chou*."

He felt her grip ease from his middle and grasp his forearm. "Good, good," he said. "There's Aaron—see him?"

"Yes, but—"

"You must let go when I say, Elizabeth."

He could not hold the reins and her at once, so he knew it would have to happen quickly. He lifted her over the saddle, and aimed for Aaron's steady arms. "Now," he called.

When Ethan's strength finally failed and he landed alone in the saddle, Cavalier screamed as if burned to his veins. The horse leaped toward the ledge. Then he stopped, lowered his head. The reins tore through Ethan's hands. He got a quick, confused vision of the deck of the *Standard*. He was falling. Falling as Fayette had fallen.

A gift came after the terror: a fleeting feeling of flight. It was exciting, seductive. Ethan wanted it to last forever. He heard something rip, felt the assault of the ground spoiling it all. Still, as the darkness came, he struggled to form the thought. *The pain's not in the fall, but in the landing*. And the fall was Judith's word: *Wondrous*.

13

"Uncle Ethan?"

He had to open his eyes, it was a little girl—the cabbage or the gull or the one who thought him a pirate. She called again. He saw only the dense blackness of his own eyelashes. He struggled to untangle them. There. The cabbage, her pretty dress torn. He smiled. "Aaron caught you, *petit chou*?" he asked.

She nodded.

"Where is he?"

"Here, master." Aaron's voice, from his other side.

"You're bleeding," Betsy cried softly.

Yes, he felt the flow from his scalp, looked at his hand, drenched red where it hovered, close by. Frightening the child. "It is not so bad. Head wounds bleed more. Did your mother never tell you this?"

"My papa did once, when Alice cut her lip."

"You see? I shall have a fancy scar and you will tell the story of our wild ride ever after, yes?"

He turned his head, looking for Aaron, and felt a searing wave of pain. His garbled struggle not to cry out made the small face disappear. When it washed back, Aaron was with her, holding a wet neckerchief to Ethan's head and crooning in African cadences.

"Come back, young master. There. Stay with us now. We likes your talk, keep talking."

"Under the saddle," Ethan said, remembering the riderless horse.

"Cavalier's saddle, sir?"

"Yes. Sharp, hurting. Help him, Aaron."

"I will, sir," he promised.

A filmy vision overlapped the reality that was his niece and Aaron tending him. "Judith?" he whispered.

"You wants your lady, sir?"

"Yes. She is in Sally's flower garden, with the doctor." He released the small fingers, hoping he hadn't squeezed them too hard. "Go with Aaron, Betsy," he told her.

"But—"

"I'll be all right. Go on."

He felt their fading steps, heard the bondsman's deep, melodious bass voice answering Betsy's protests. "No, he ain't alone, child! He got all them ragged black angels of his lookin' after him whilst we fetch the doctor and Miss Judith."

Aaron saw them too, then? Of course. He'd felt them before, when they were on board the *Standard*, hadn't he? The filmy apparitions turned into seabirds, squawking, curious. He was Washington again, and ravished by longing for the open sea. He didn't want to die here. He wanted the ocean to take him as it did Fayette. How far away was the ocean?

He felt his head. Under the cold handkerchief the wound's flow was down to a trickle. Slowly, he rose to his elbows, looked down. Pain. The worst pain. There. He yanked Aaron's coat back.

"Mon . . . dieu."

He didn't think his lame leg's ugliness still had the power to shock him. But the sight of the ripped, blood-soaked trousers, the muscle and frayed cartilage protruding, made the red wine, the bread and cheese he'd eaten with Judith on the quilt come up his throat. It spilled over his chin and across his opened shirt.

Initials were there, on the shirt's hem. He would not die nameless this time. Ethan Randolph of Windover, on the James River in the Commonwealth of Virginia, the United States of America. Who was that? A boy, who wrote letters to his mother, his sister, that's all. He'd died long ago. It didn't matter anymore. He was Washington. Who would sew him into his hammock, who would pierce the cartilage of his nose? That didn't matter, either. His hands found the root of a scrub pine. He began to pull himself toward the sea.

—Where are you going, my friend?

Ethan couldn't think of an answer that would not offend Fayette's rational mind, so he just watched his face, gloriously happy to be seeing him again. "I'm lost here, Fayette," he finally whispered.

The heel of his friend's hand, pressing into the head wound, smelled of the depths of the sea.

—You have hit that stubborn skull hard enough this time. Had I known this, I would have thrown you from the mizzenmast long ago and saved my poor back, yes?

Ethan reached out.

—*Stay still now, so they can find you,* Fayette instructed.

Ethan heard voices in the distance. He struggled to keep his eyes open. "Don't go," he implored.

—*I am here,* Fayette promised, before his face turned into Jordan Foster's.

Ethan grabbed his waistcoat, fisted it. He growled back the pain. "You have no choice now," he said.

"You have not provided the best of conditions."

"The sea heals."

"Broken skulls? Compound fractures?"

"Everything. You helped the soldiers. In the war? The one I missed? You have seen the likes of me before."

Jordan Foster shook his head. "I've never seen the likes of you."

The doctor's face swam out of focus. "Don't take my leg," Ethan charged, while he still had a voice, a grip.

Roses. Intense, from her moist places, where she was sweating. Judith. "Ethan. Behave yourself," she commanded. "Dr. Foster won't do anything without telling you first. Agreed?"

"Agreed." He heard the doctor echo his voice.

Ethan watched Jordan Foster open his portable chest and hand Judith an ugly-looking root. "Between his teeth, Miss Mercer," he instructed, "so he does not bite off that brazen tongue while we reduce the fracture." The root did not taste ugly; it tasted of licorice. The physician took Ethan's face. "It will be very painful, for a moment. But after, you will feel much better, I promise."

Ethan nodded, anchoring his eyes on Judith's face. Aaron gently shifted him to his side. Micah and Elwood flexed Ethan's thigh and knee. The doctor was stationed at his ankle. Ethan knew which pair of hands were Jordan Foster's. Long, experienced. As the men reined him, those hands did their work. Pulled. Unbearable pain. His teeth ground into the root.

Relief. Better. He did feel better, Ethan wanted to tell the doctor's anxious eyes. But the thicket of lashes descended again.

"Ethan?"

He heard, but couldn't summon the strength to answer, to open his eyes. He felt Judith gently loosen his jaw's hold, remove the root.

"I'm going to do it now, while he's fainted."

But he wasn't fainted, he wanted to tell them, as he felt Judith's warmth slip away. Aaron took her place. Then the doctor's long hands again, at his ankle, turning, turning. Snap. His bones, breaking. He bolted, fighting Aaron's hold, and heard Dr. Foster's sharp surprise.

"Good God, I thought—"

"Don't stop."

"Ethan—"

"Finish!"

Was this what he'd begged for? Ethan clenched his teeth together, but the cry escaped. A million more cracks echoed inside his head before the darkness finally came.

Then he was sailing the James, his head in Judith's lap. Windover's slaves stood onshore, their lanterns held high, singing softly, as their ancestors sang for him in the bowels of the *Standard*.

Why were they so good to him? He tried to ask Judith again, but heard only a guttural moan from the cloth remnant in his mouth. Aaron poured something into it. Whiskey. American whiskey, made from corn. Bourbon. It tasted like liquid fire at first, then it eased the edges of the glaring pain. It let him see that Judith's eyes were the pale green of the surrounding marsh, like the mermaid's he'd carved on the bow of the *Survivor*.

His finger found her rolled-up sleeve, tugged for her attention. She took the cloth from his mouth. He caught her scent.

"Lemons," he murmured. "Just how close has this gotten to you, mistress?"

Silence. Her brow arched. "Closer than thee has. Yet," she parried back at him.

Laughter. Even from the doctor this time.

His mother and sister waited at the dock. Clayton, too, with the unfamiliar scent of gunpowder about him. How was it dark so quickly? Anne Randolph had forgotten her shawl. "Mother," Ethan tried to reprimand, "it's too cold for—"

"My son is cold!" she shouted, and within a breath a patched slave's coat was draping his chest. Too much movement. And bourbon. He closed his eyes.

He caught the scent of books, heard the fire's crackle. The physician's calm voice called again. "Ethan. See where you are?"

"How did the bed get in the library?"

"Your mother's idea."

She came into view over the doctor's shoulder, her eyes red, swollen, but her beautiful voice clear. "You sleep here more often than in your room, don't you? Now you can have your books close. And Aaron will not have to climb the stairs all day with volumes."

"You are thoughtful toward us both, *madame*."

Anne Randolph sat on the bed, touched his soiled shirtfront with a mother's tenderness.

"Ruined," he apologized.

"We'll wash it. Won't we, Sally?"

Together the two women, the mother and sister of that boy, removed his foul coat, unbuttoned and slipped off the silk waistcoat. He didn't know them, he knew only Judith. Where had Judith gone? They began to remove his shirt. No, only Judith. There was something under it. Something they should not see, the mother, the sister. But the bourbon made his mind slow. "Don't," he warned, too late.

They stared at the diamond-patterned scars of his punishment. "Good God," Anne Randolph whispered.

"What did I do wrong?" the boy inside him asked her.

"No-nothing," she assured him. She was the wrong person to ask. Her affection for her son was free. She would love him no matter what he'd done.

Judith shook her head at Phoebe's request to relieve her. She would not let any crowd her away from him. She had her lifetime to sleep. Now, on this third day after the fall, Ethan's grip on her hand was strong, secure, as Dr. Foster applied the dressing to his leg wound.

"Tighter," Ethan urged.

Jordan Foster looked exhausted, out of patience with him. "Are you still telling me my business?" he demanded.

"When first it broke, Fayette said that the ship's-surgeon's bandage was too loose. There was fresh bleeding, displaced bones. Displaced bones grew together, and I went lame. Tell him, Judith."

"Judith doesn't have to tell me anything. I have eyes!"

"I only meant—"

"Listen to me. If the dressings are too tight, blood is decreased, and will increase inflammation, possibly excite a fever, leading to—"

"Tighter," Ethan cajoled again, smiling. "The head wound will kill me first, I promise. Nobody will say it was your fault, if it's the head wound, yes? 'He was a little crazy already,' they'll say. 'Did not even know his own name.' Your reputation will remain spotless. My gift to you, Doctor, for all your trouble. An intact reputation."

"You are too kind," Jordan Foster whispered, without looking up.

Ethan smiled. "Not at all, sir."

The doctor completed the dressing in silence, then plunged past Aaron and Betsy on his way through the room cast in twilight. Ethan turned to Judith.

"Am I so hard on him?"

"He's worried about you. And so tired."

"Of course. I'm an idiot. Find him, Judith. Tell him I'm sorry. Make him sleep."

Judith hesitated. He looked so pale. Or perhaps it was only her fear, and the descending night?

"Go on, go on!" he urged impatiently. "Aaron and Betsy remain here, my keepers. They will see I don't go dancing!"

She squeezed his hand. It was moist, cold. Judith put down her sewing. "I'm going." She frowned. "Pest."

Ethan hoped Judith would find the doctor. She would say his apology better. Jordan Foster would listen to her and rest. Perhaps that would restore his humor, if the blasted man had any humor. Ethan watched the shadows play on the works of Pope, Milton. A small girl appeared, gently lifting the hair from his forehead.

"It will be a lovely scar, Uncle Ethan," she told him. "Just as you said. Dr. Foster makes stitches as even as your own on the masts of our boats."

"Ships," he corrected her.

She giggled behind her hand. "Ships," she said.

How he loved this child. What was her name? Whose child was she? He couldn't think. He couldn't think at all well suddenly. "I am so . . ." He couldn't remember the word.

"Thirsty?"

"Yes."

"I'll call Aaron. He's just by the window."

The black man held his neck gently. Once he'd poured the contents of the cup down his throat, his large, work-callused hands wiped Ethan's mouth with linen, set his head back in the pillows. What did this man do with those hands? Boots. He made shoes and boots, the boots he'd gone to sea wearing. Or was that a dream, or a story the boy with his face once told him? That boy. What was his name? No, it wasn't there, in his head. But there was another name. Of another boy, who looked like this man.

"Aaron?"

"Yes, sir?"

"Where's Aubrey?"

The servant's eyes softened. "Why, we done lost him, Master Ethan. He drowned under the falls, four years back," he explained.

"Drowned? How could he drown? Aubrey taught me to swim."

"That he did, sir. Our Aubrey, he hit his head. Diving from the rocks, we expect, like the two of you used to do together. Hit hisself here."

He felt the bondsman's touch, just above his own wound. It caught him in a wave of grief. "I'm sorry," he whispered, turning his head to the wall. He felt the tear streak across his face and down his neck.

"Miss Betsy,"—he heard Aaron summon the little girl who'd gone back to her ships—"you call your mama and grandma in here, if you please, child. Tell them Master Ethan is shedding off his disremem-berin'."

Her eyes widened with interest. "Shedding? Like a snake?"

"Yes, miss." The servant followed the track of Ethan's tear with the back of his huge hand. "Good Lord. Call the doctor, and Miss Judith, too. This boy's gone powerful warm."

Hands, arms, black and white, holding him still. Don't cry out. Children in the house. Don't frighten the children. Where was Judith? She wouldn't let them take his leg without asking. There, her scent: worried, more roses than lemons.

"What's wrong with me now?" he demanded of the doctor.

"Fever. You're having some fever convulsions."

"It's not my leg?"

"No, not your blasted leg!" Jordan Foster shouted.

The head wound *was* killing him, then? Ethan's laugh caught in his throat. Was that why they all gathered around the bed, staring at him? Women whose eyes he couldn't bear to meet. Even his elderly father was there, bundled in his dressing gown, and uncharacteristically silent. And those other men, the ones who'd never wanted him here. The sharp-faced one even looked sad.

Was he dying? Is that what they were all waiting for? No one would tell him the truth, no one except— "Judith?" he called.

"I'm here, love."

"What is this place?"

"Your home. Windover."

"No. You made a mistake. Windover. The place on the river. This was the dream. I'm sure of it now. I don't belong here. I have to go back to the ship."

"What?"

"The sails. The sails are ripping, Judith. Cannon fire. They need me."

"What sails?"

"My ship's."

"What ship?"

"The *Standard.*"

"No, not Washington's ship. Not the *Standard.* It's the *Ida Lee*, Ethan Randolph's ship. Let the sails rip, Ethan. Go back. Go back to the *Ida Lee.*"

"Why do you and Fayette bother me about this woman? I don't know her, I told you!"

"Not a woman. A ship of the American merchant marine."

He closed his eyes. Yes. She was right. It was all there now, back behind his eyes. They shot open. "Judith, it's too fast, it's coming too fast. I don't have room for it all. I'll lose you. I'll lose you and Fayette."

Sally took Judith's arm. "For the love of God," she pleaded. "Another's starting. Don't."

"This is the only way," Judith whispered, holding his shoulder as the twitching he couldn't control took over his face.

Anne Randolph moved to the doctor's side. "She's right," she whispered. "God help us all, she's right."

Judith looked to Jordan Foster. *He will stop me,* she thought. But her Inner Light directed her now.

"Aaron, you must keep him still," the doctor commanded.

"I will, sir," Aaron promised from Ethan's legs, still untouched by the spasms that were riding through his upper body with frightening regularity. The fit left him, as the others had, dazed and exhausted. But he hadn't uttered a cry of pain.

Judith held up their clasped hands. "Beloved, I will not let thee forget the *Standard,* or me, or Fayette. Hold on to me. Good. Tighter. Now add to us. There is room."

"No."

"Yes. Add. What happened? What happened aboard the *Ida Lee*?"

His voice was the haunted whisper of a child. "I killed him."

"Who?" she asked through her shock. "Ethan, who did thee kill?"

"The other boy, the one with my face. No, not my face, no face."

"You hear him, woman?" Winthrop lashed out suddenly at Sally. "You hear who your children dote on? Not our brother. Our brother's murderer!"

Judith kept her voice steady, though tears streaked down her face. "Who was the boy? What happened to him?"

"Fayette said I could forget. He said I was newborn. I am Washington!"

"But someone else, too. Someone aboard the *Ida Lee.* A boy of twelve years. Which boy?"

"I don't know."

"What were your duties?"

"Leave me alone!"

"I cannot. Forgive me, but I cannot."

Another convulsion started. He thrashed about the bed, leaving sweat and bloodstains on the fine linen pillow. But he did not release his hold on her hand, even when the spasm spent itself and he lay still, whispering through clenched teeth.

"He loved the brass buttons on my coat. He wanted to wear my boots, the ones Aaron made. I wanted to climb masts, like him. To bring the powder to the cannons during drills. We could do it, he said. We could switch, just for the day, an ordinary day, when the officers wouldn't look twice at either of us. We were the same height, coloring. But my boots were too big for his feet. And it wasn't an ordinary day. No warning. From the frigate. Fired on us. Again." He closed his eyes tightly against the sound. "Again."

"The *Standard* was firing?"

"Yes. I should have been standing there, where he was, at my post. The blast blew my boots off his feet. His face—faceless, without features, blown away, red and writhing, Judith! It should have been mine."

Judith leaned in closer. "Thee did not kill him," her voice soothed. "The guns did. There was nothing thee could do."

"Nothing?"

"You were children. You were both children, caught in the crossfire of nations."

His eyes opened. "We were?"

"Yes, love."

"You never lie, Judith. Are you sure?"

"I'm sure. Ethan, remember Willis?"

"The captain with the empty eyes."

"And the battle off Trafalgar?"

"Yes. Everything was on fire. As it is now. So hot, it is so hot, Judith."

"I know, my darling." She bathed his face.

"I would not kill that man," he murmured, "the man who took me up to see the stars."

"Fayette."

"Yes, Fayette, when he wore the blue uniform. I was American. My country was not at war with his. The captain was so angry that I would not kill him. After the battle, they bound my hands, strapped me to the gratings. I didn't understand why. No one on the *Ida Lee* was ever even struck, you see? Then came the lashes. Why did they do that? I was only a boy, a boy who did not remember anything except dancing atop Sally and Mama's slippers."

His sister stifled a sob with the back of her hand.

"I regret nothing," he said fiercely. "What if I had killed Fayette, who made me the hero of my own life, when I was just a spoiled midshipman, an ignorant, slogan-spouting boy?"

"Fayette had another name," Judith whispered.

"Yes. He told me. Maupin. Henri Maupin."

"So dost thee, Washington. Tell Henri Maupin thy name."

"Ethan," he said slowly. "The only one of us given Mother's family name. Her brother's name. The one who fought in the Revolution, under Lafayette. Ethan Blair. I am Ethan Blair Randolph."

"Yes. Come home now," Judith whispered, though she knew it would be the beginning of their good-bye. Her mission was ending. "Come home to thy family, Ethan. They've been waiting such a long time for thee."

14

Judith Mercer's eyes were closed, her hand held Ethan's shoulder, trembling, in need—the way it never would have been had she thought him awake. Her lips formed silent words—of what, supplication? Her fierce beauty intensified when she spoke with her God. Ethan remained still, waiting until she was in his world again.

She looked down at him, startled. "Ethan! I didn't realize—"

"I love to watch you pray."

She looked away, her touch lightening.

"I was rude to you, wasn't I, when you came down to the river for me? Something about your petticoat? I apologize."

She smiled. "There is no need. I was rude right back."

"So, that's not why you pray so much now? For tolerance toward your ill-bred patient?"

She laughed. "What a notion!" Did she know she was imitating his sister's favorite expression of amused astonishment? She touched his face. "Ethan, I pray, asking for strength to face my future."

"Future?"

"I have received a letter. From a member of my Meeting. My father is ill."

His hands took hers, pulled her slowly against his chest, against the scent of his fresh linen shirt. Judith fit there, ignoring the cold iron brace that anchored him to the bed. She acted as if the contraption was inconsequential, as his lameness had been aboard the *Standard,* as his position in a slaveholding family was here. Would he ever deserve this woman's love? He tucked her head under his chin.

"Tell me of this," he whispered.

"A cold; Papa wrote himself. Nothing of consequence, he said. But it went into his lungs. His letters don't complain at all. But a member of another Meeting, Prescott Lyman, now writes that he has taken charge of my father's health and brought him out of the city, to his farm. He is most uncomfortable, this man claims. He urges me to come."

Ethan breathed in her dried roses. "At first light. Take the fastest coach, the swiftest horses. Take Dr. Foster. He'll—"

Judith broke from the haven of his arms. "Thou must stop this ordering about of Dr. Foster. He is not thy servant!"

Ethan raised his hands. "I will ask him," he amended quickly.

"And thy mother—"

"Will agree that this is a providential opportunity to demonstrate this family's debt to yours. Go pack."

"I'm sorry," she whispered.

"Hush, hush. I have too many doting females. I will be glad to be rid of their taskmaster!"

When she bit her lip, he pulled her into his arms again. They held on to each other in silence. Then he whispered into the errant strands of silver at her temples, "There can be no joyous reunion without parting, yes?"

She nodded.

"The women can secure my chains while Martha force-feeds me. When I am better, I will visit with you and Eli."

"Beloved, if that were possible—"

"Possible? It will be necessary, essential!" He took her hands between his, kissed them. "Before you both go off on another mission and forget all about me."

"Thou, Ethan Randolph, art the expert at forgetting!" she accused.

He looked stricken. "You are cutting out my heart now, haughty Quaker."

Her eyes went wide. "I banter only. I didn't mean—"

"Cutting out an invalid's heart. Surely that is an offense, even in your godless religion, Miss Mercer."

His cadence, his drawl, his dancing eyes gave him away. "Invalid," she scoffed. "Thee is well enough to tease me without mercy, Ethan Ran—!"

He stole his last kiss then, extinguishing any anger left in her with the sweet explorations of his tongue. *Remember, Judith,* he needed the kiss to tell her. *Remember this, and the promise of it.* Her face was growing warm, there, between his hands. *Pull away first,* Clarisse had told him of courting kisses. *Leave her breathless, wanting.* He barely managed to remain his first lover's student. "Peace, then," he whispered gruffly. "Until spring."

"Spring."

She pulled herself out of his arms and ran to the door.

"Do you feel my hot grief at your back, Judith Mercer?" he called after her.

He watched her stand stock-still. Then she turned. She was trying to keep her eyes off his ruined leg, and her mind from his mother's will never again to allow him out of her sight. And she was a little afraid of him now, because the half of his life he remembered made him a new man, one she did not know and perhaps would not like if she did.

Ethan shook his head slowly. How did he know these things? How did he sense the patterns of her thoughts?

"Judith?" he whispered. "Your mind—"

"My mind, Ethan?"

How could he tell her? That he'd been listening to her thoughts? Perhaps he should not. "The diverse turnings of your mind," he whispered. "Write them to me. Write everything."

After she'd softly closed the door, he fisted his covers and pounded at the soft featherbed. He should have requested, not demanded. Demands belonged to the spoiled boy springing up inside him, one he was not sure he liked so much, either.

The elder Randolph brothers and their wives stood before Judith in the faded opulence of the entry hall. Winthrop's smile was grim as he dismissed his wife and sister-in-law. Then he turned the same countenance on Judith. "Well. You've got your Truth, but lost your convert. A bittersweet victory at best, Miss Mercer."

"I am not interested in victories."

"No? Fortunate. For you will never have him now. He's ours."

She was so startled by the ferocity in his voice that she took the arm his brother offered. But Clayton, the mediator, the one who'd never raised his voice, shocked her further. His lips almost touched her ear as they passed the last pineapple carved over an archway. "This family eats its young, its infirm, Miss Mercer. As I'm sure you've observed while serving your Truth."

He spun her outside to the house servants then, who kissed her hands, urging her return. Aaron and Martha, they would protect him. They were slaves themselves, but they would do their best. Would it be enough?

Once the brick dovecote faded from view, Judith finally leaned back in the horsehair-padded seat. She tasted Ethan's kiss. She listened again to his parting words, and those of his parents and his sister for comfort. Sally had hugged her, whispering, "God sent you, Judith."

What Ethan's sister didn't acknowledge was what Judith saw clearly: God was now propelling her away. The gates of Windover had closed with such finality.

What a pair she and the brooding physician were going to be all the way to Pennsylvania. Judith felt sorry for the coachman.

"Has your father had pneumonia before, Miss Mercer?" Jordan Foster asked, startling her.

"No."

"Frequent colds? Influenza?"

"Not frequent, no."

"His age?"

"Threescore years come Ninth Month—September," she amended.

"Has he ever endured surgery? Or broken any bones?"

"No."

"You would describe his health as good?"

"Excellent. Oh, but he can't abide radishes," she thought fondly. "And is more prone to the travel sickness than I." The doctor was watching her intently. "But, excellent," she finished.

"He loves you," Jordan Foster said.

"Friend Jordan?"

"Ethan loves you."

She was caught by the small space, by his candor.

"I don't think—"

"You don't have to think. It's not a thinking matter. What will it mean? You are an acknowledged leader in your religion—"

"We have no leaders."

"Do not play humility games with me, young woman. You are admired at home and abroad for your work, your clear sight into the human heart. Now look to your own."

Not more attack, not from him whom she thought safe, whom she needed. "I cannot. Not now, with my father ill."

He sighed, patted her hand awkwardly. "I will do all I can for your father, do you understand?"

"Wilt thou?" she challenged. "Even though traveling to Pennsylvania is the last thing thou wishes to be doing?"

The doctor looked caught now, like an animal in a trap. "I'm angry, yes. But how could I refuse, when Ethan's got those formidable Randolph women behind him? What the fall and I did to his knee, his ankle—it will require a long period of immobility. Without my attendance . . ." Judith could taste his bitterness. "He's a young, restless man," Jordan Foster finished. "He could spoil even his slim chance of recovery."

"Thee does not trust him?"

"It's not a matter of—"

"But it is, Friend. He gave thee his word. And Fayette schooled him on the sacredness of his word."

"This man Fayette. I wish I'd known him."

"Thee does," she assured him.

"What are you saying?"

Judith wondered as much herself. "After Fayette was killed," she began hesitantly, "it was as if Ethan absorbed parts of him. At first I thought they were parts that he needed, to survive. Now I feel other gifts of Fayette returning."

"Gifts? Like Deism?"

Judith almost smiled. "Belief, philosophy, was one of our sparring points onboard the *Standard*, of course. Oh," she realized. "My own views of the two men merging are hardly in line with any standard Christian doctrine, I suspect. Do I shock thee, then, Friend?"

Jordan Foster shook his head before resting it on the seatback. Judith saw the trial the past week had been on him. Dark circles spoke of worried nights beside Ethan's bed.

"So many years in captivity. How did they survive, Miss Mercer? Why is there no hardness about the boy?"

"There is his stillness. A stillness that I have only seen in the most devout at Meeting." She laughed. "When I am being quite recalcitrant in not concentrating on my own Inner Light enough!"

The doctor smiled. He was a handsome man, Judith realized. His beard, his habitual, taciturn sadness could not mask eyes alive with intelligence and curiosity. Judith began to think the way home might not be so fraught with their separate miseries, after all.

Jordan Foster's chin made the same lift as Ethan's did before he spoke. "I have known no Quakers. Are you typical in your humor?"

"Humor?"

"Yes. Full, rich humor, without a hint of primness. It surprises me. It delights Ethan. Can you feel his delight in you?"

"I'm not insensible, Friend Jordan." He was going to apologize again. Judith sought to head it off with a laugh. "Though it is my serious nature he himself delights in teasing," she finished.

He frowned. At himself this time, Judith sensed. "I should not have badgered you. I have never been the most charming man among women. Please forgive my intrusion into your heart."

Judith smiled. "Fayette was the most charming man I've ever known. Yet he was more blunt than thee is when the subject was Ethan's happiness. I take no offense."

The doctor gave her a weary smile. "You are a very generous woman. To endure everything you have. And now the grief of parting."

"Friends don't grieve, or mourn, or wear bl—" *Black.* She could not form the simple word. *Instruct, Judith. Instruct this man, he is open for instruction. . . .* The gentle physician pulled her into his arms. "This is not grief for that scoundrel of a Frenchman!" she insisted, even as she buried her head against his chest.

"No," he agreed.

"Nor at parting. His mother told me Ethan is a most d-diligent correspondent!" Her tears released the scent from the physician's shirt. Salt, sweat, lavender. He smelled like Ethan. No, the two men had the same laundress at Windover, that was all. Still, Judith took comfort in the shared scent, even in the midst of her humiliation. "This is—" She tried again.

His long fingers grazed her cheek. "Not grief, of course, Judith Mercer," he conspired with her lie.

Sally climbed onto Ethan's bed, placing Charlotte between them. It was a beautiful day for his sister's journey, he saw it from the temperature gauge outside his window, and the barometer he'd consulted earlier that morning. Richmond. Sally lived in Richmond now, with her handsome, bespectacled husband, her family. She was going home. Not leaving him. Going home. Ethan touched Charlotte's palm. She fisted his finger in her tiny hand.

"Like a rose petal. Do all babies' skins feel this way, Sally?"

"The well ones, yes."

Charlotte was in her third month of life. Both mother and child were rosy with the glow of health. Sally's full breasts were laced inside her chemise, so that she could free them easily to feed her baby on the schooner. His sister was leaving him so far behind.

"Well, you've made this room your own. The library suits you, Ethan. You will not grow cramped when it's your classroom, I trust."

"Classroom?"

"Betsy and Alice must keep up their studies."

"You're leaving your girls here at Windover?"

"Until Christmas. While Barton and I settle the baby in. If you agree to teach them."

He looked down at the iron bracing that made his right leg immobile. No walks, no sun, no riding. It was not a life to share with healthy children. "Sally, I cannot—"

"Nonsense. You had me. Now they have you. And all the books I used with you. Aaron's brought them down from the nursery." She frowned. "You do remember our lessons, don't you?"

"I never forgot them."

She leaned back on his pillows as if the library ceiling was the sky of their childhood. "Even the constellations."

"The constellations were simple. I saw them nightly aboard ship," he maintained, to vex her, to keep her and her gurgling baby there for as long as he could. He was still a spoiled child when it came to his sister's affections, he realized.

She rolled to her side and leaned up on her elbow. "So teaching my daughters should be perfectly simple," she admonished.

His face sobered. "My own education did not far exceed theirs."

"You believe yourself deficient? After climbing on my lap with your *Mother Goose* before you could walk? After all of my work with that insatiable little head over the years that followed?"

"You were the best teacher any child could hope for."

"I had the best teacher myself. Father only allowed me to sit in on Jordan's lessons because I would probably marry some blockheaded planter, and would need to tutor his sons myself."

"I'm glad you have not fulfilled his expectations on either count. And I'm fortunate you were such a good student."

"My teacher will guide you, perhaps."

"I'm too old now, Sally. Even for a man more patient that your Dr. Foster."

"He's not my Dr. Foster."

"No? Who finally charmed him into going to Pennsylvania?"

"You slander me! It's Mama had to ask him."

"And he wouldn't have budged without her leave."

"Ah. You saw that, did you?"

"I'd have to be blind as well as crippled not to see that."

She squeezed his hand. "Don't. Self-pity does not become you."

She had him. "I ask your pardon," he whispered.

She smoothed down the spiraling crown of his hair. "Ethan, schooling didn't make Jordan Foster a good physician. His own suffering allowed him to care so well for others. Yours may do the same for you."

"I? A physician?"

"Why not? Under Jordan's—"

"He would never consider it. He can barely stand my company."

His sister gave out an exasperated sound as she stood, then walked to the windows. "Must I always be the go-between?" she demanded of the clear early autumn Tidewater sky.

"What do you mean, Sally?" Ethan asked her, baffled.

She looked to the river. Did her daughter sense this tension between them? Ethan wondered as he stroked her fussing baby's cheek. Charlotte pulled his smallest finger into her mouth and suckled.

"They are packing up the boat. I need your answer," Sally said from the windows. "Will you dishonor me as your teacher and insult your time with Monsieur Maupin as well? You owe us both, brother!"

He stared at her defiant stance, her fired eyes. He shook his head and laughed, enjoying his defeat.

She returned and sat beside him on the bed, taking his face in her hands. "Oh, Ethan, it is so good to hear that sound again. I was beginning to think your laughter died with Washington."

The smile left his face. "Washington's not dead, Sally."

She patted his cheek lightly. "Then ask your charming Mr. Washington to add French to the subjects I taught you, and that will go far toward repayment of keeping your memory alive all these years."

"Oh, now I must pay for lighthouse-keeper duty?"

She sat higher, fisted a hand at her hip. "You will sour my milk, Ethan Blair."

"I will?" he whispered, stunned.

She swooped, kissing Charlotte's forehead. "No. I'm teasing you, brother dear."

The sweet smell from her bodice rose between them. "You see?" he challenged. "You see how ignorant I am?"

The baby whimpered, no longer content with his finger. Sally had her on her breast before the sound could turn into a cry. Ethan watched, fascinated.

"Oh, bother me not with your ignorance," she said. But her annoyance was decreasing in ferocity with every suck her daughter pulled on her breast. His sister was growing as languid and contented as a cat in the sun. Was her baby's suckling doing that?

"You have such bounty about you, Sally," he observed.

She smiled at him fondly. "I glory in my nursing. But it is temporary, this bounty. Betsy, then Alice, taught me that. Temporary, just as this brace's hold on you is. Patience, brother. Your flowering is yet ahead of you."

"Do you think so? Dr. Foster only frowns."

"Do you doubt me yet? Perhaps you're right. I should renew my search. Perhaps Betsy and Alice deserve a more clever tutor."

His sister traced the side of his face fondly.

"Only you tolerate me in this house, Sally." He let his fear slip out. "Only you ever did."

Her fine brows slanted in sympathy. "Perhaps I can stay a few more days. Until your first letter from Judith comes? All these desertions—"

"No."

He was behaving badly toward his sister after all her gifts. He covered his shame in a laugh. "My long-suffering brother-in-law has done without you long enough. As it is I will send home his daughters sounding like tiny French revolutionaries. Thank you, Sally," he whispered, pressing her hand to his cheek. "Now show the little gull her home, and stop worrying about me."

15

Ethan heard the soft sounds of a dulcimer. How had the doctor's wife found him here in the library of Windover? Her children took hold of his hands, pulled. "I can't," he told them. "I must stay still. I promised your—" He was plunging into the salt marsh again. "Father!" he called, clutching at the air.

Ethan saw the strong fingers entwined with his own. "You wants me to fetch your daddy, master?"

"Aaron. I didn't fall?"

"No, sir. Still harnessed in fine. You's dreaming is all."

"Dreaming, yes." He released the massive hand.

The servant wore his heavy apron, and smelled of leather. Ethan breathed it in, remembering that smell at this time of year. "How is your work progressing?" he asked.

Aaron smiled as he plumped the pillows and shifted Ethan to his side. "Your healing naps be workin' out real fine for me gettin' everybody in shoes for the winter."

"I can sew, Aaron. I used to mend the sails on my ship."

"Yes, sir."

Ethan looked at his hands. The calluses were fading, the summer color leaving them. They were becoming useless gentleman's hands. "If any shoes need mending, if a strap breaks or some stitching bursts . . . Children grow out of shoes, don't they? You might use my help, then, when I don't sleep so damned much?"

"If'n you offered help, sir."

"I do. If you please, Aaron."

The servant shook his head. "There's no '*If you please*–ing' me, sir. Don't you be talking that way in front of your folk or they be sending you on back to the Frenchies, your remembers returned or not."

"What am I to do?" Ethan heard himself shout. "Order you to make this terror of my own uselessness go away?"

"Easy, child. I was only just funnin'—"

"I am not a child! I am a man of twenty-two years. A man with a skill. I have a skill, God damn it!" What was he doing? Ethan wondered. Aaron, who could break him in two between those powerful hands, was cowering. Ethan lowered his voice. "I have an ungovernable temper as well. Forgive me."

"Yes sir," the servant said, as if he'd been given an order. Had he given one? Ethan took in a breath, and tried again. "There are all these new people inside me, Aaron. Son, brother, uncle, teacher."

"But not cripple. That one you'll be growing out of, sir. That's what I been thinking on, whilst I work at my bench."

Aaron pointed with his chin to the table piled with books and the Gibson sisters' bright watercolor drawings. Beside them stood a pair of gleaming brown leather boots. Pride in his work shone from their craftsman's dark eyes. "Bet you never seen the like!"

"They're mine?"

Aaron laughed. "Won't fit nobody else in this world around, sir! I took especial care, on account of you ain't had a decent pair since the last I made you, back in the year of our Lord eighteen hundred and five. I done followed what Dr. Foster said before he left to tend Miss Judith's daddy, too."

"What did Dr. Foster say?"

"Oh, not nothing 'bout boots, you can be sure! No, he mostly talk about that cage holding your leg steady, and how to keep you clean and still. 'I expect Master Ethan knows plenty about still from bein' on that slaver so many years,' I told him, sure enough!

"Well, he talk about your hurt leg, sir. In that mournful way of his. Muscles ain't been used, cramped space, bad food—all that I knows already from my grandmammy's stories 'bout the slavers. Then our Mr. Jordan, he says something new. That bad leg, it's rebroke, mending again, maybe straight and strong enough to hold you. But it be shorter than the other now, he says. Sets me to thinking. About after your bones mend. How I might help your legs hold you good and steady."

Ethan looked at the right boot's construction. Both heel and sole were about an inch thick, with an extra layer.

"I'll work down the leather of that one," Aaron continued, "to get you balanced, so's you can walk, see?"

"Yes."

"It's for your bad leg only, sir. Don't go mixing them boots up or you'll get yourself one mean limp!"

"I'm a long way, even from limping," Ethan said quietly.

He felt Aaron's powerful hand at his shoulder. "I knows that, sir. But you ain't havin' them fever fits no more, are you?"

"No."

"Dizziness left your head, didn't it?"

"Yes. Just now—I was dreaming, not dizzy."

"And dreams be good things. Favors from God."

"Are they?"

"I believe so, sir. You always been a good dreamer." His hand hovered around Ethan's head scar, but he seemed to think better of touching it. He straightened the bedcovers instead. "And you done shed off your disrememberin'! You knows us all again. Next, I expect the cage comes off Dr. Foster's work. So these here boots—they'll sit here, 'minding you what all the mending time is for. I figure you needs something real, waiting."

Ethan admired the clever craftsmanship. He saw himself pulling the boots on, and standing. His imagination was not sufficient for walking. But he did see himself stepping into a stirrup, and mounting a horse. He could do that, without a blasted leg. "How does Cavalier fare, Aaron?" he asked. "Who rides him now?"

The servant was silent so long that Ethan wasn't sure he'd heard. "Didn't no one tell you about Cavalier?" Aaron finally whispered.

"Tell me what?" He refused to believe what was in the man's eyes. "Aaron, you promised you'd take care of him."

"I was helping the doctor with you."

"What happened to Cavalier?" he whispered.

"Your brother shot him, sir."

"No. No one shot him."

"Master—"

"No one shot him, do you hear me!"

"Sayin' that will not make it so, young master! You says you ain't a child no more. Sure, you used to think I could move the stars through the sky for you, back when. Well, I can't change what done happened. If I'm lookin' at a man, he knows that."

Ethan's eyes steadied themselves on the fine tatted lace of his pillowcase as he clenched his jaw.

"Was it Winthrop?" he finally whispered.

"No, sir, the other. Master Clayton, sir."

"Clayton. He smelled of gunpowder," Ethan remembered.

"Said the horse was lame—"

"He wasn't lame. Under his saddle—something was hurting him. A thistle, a thorn."

"Maybe Master Clayton needed to blame the animal."

"Pas mal! Merde!" Ethan ground his teeth.

"You laying down a curse on your brother, sir?" Aaron whispered against Ethan's rapid-fire French.

"No. I'm cussing."

"Them ain't pretty, like the ones you lay on your daddy, sir."

"God's blood. Cavalier. That's why. My brothers, their wives," Ethan realized, feeling equal parts of rage and fear, "they're trying to kill me."

"I didn't say that!"

"But you think it."

"I don't think that, sir, no, sir!"

Ethan's mind raced on. "You won't leave my side when they're here," he accused. "And I caught you sniffing, tasting my food the one time Hester brought the tray. Liar!"

Ethan sensed a fire burning through the servant's fear of him. A fire of indignation. "Miss Hester, she ground out too much pepper. Didn't want my Martha blamed when your daddy see you don't touch your meat!"

This was a more worthy man than his two brothers put together, Ethan thought. "Who was your mother?" he demanded suddenly.

Aaron looked caught off-balance. The resonant timbre of the slave's voice lost none of its power as its volume reduced to a whisper. "Hagar was, sir."

Ethan closed his eyes in his effort to concentrate. "She wore black, always black, except for a cardinal's feather, here." He pressed two fingertips to the hair beside his own temple.

"My ma done passed over 'fore you weaned yourself from Miss Anne, Master Ethan. How is it you remember that?"

"And your father? Who was he?"

"Never said. Hagar raised me by her own self, sir."

"And you are formed straight and tall and powerful—like my father in the dining-room portrait, my father in his prime. And despite your strength, your build, he kept you out of the fields, he allowed you a trade. Aubrey was following you in it. Now Micah is a fine smith. Your daughters are house servants. My father trusts you as no other. We're brothers, aren't we, Aaron?"

"Can't rightly say, sir."

"You were born before any of us. You're the eldest."

"I'm Hagar's child, Master Ethan. Only hers."

"No wonder you understand Winthrop and Clayton when I falter." Ethan looked down at the hands that had ministered to his needs so gently. They were his father's hands, on a finer man than his father would ever be. Ethan felt like a child beside him. A blustering, helpless child in a crippled man's body. Not fit for anything, least of all Judith's love. He never felt like this onboard the *Ida Lee,* or even the *Standard.*

"Master Ethan. You have a right to your anger, it be righteous anger, if'n—" Aaron stopped abruptly, wiped his powerful hand across his mouth. "Lord Almighty, I ain't ought be talking like this, I knows my place. You don't, but I does!"

"Help me, Aaron."

"I can't. Black can't testify against white, it ain't lawful."

"I don't mean in court. I've had enough with courts, trials, laws. I need to stay alive. I need to get to Judith."

"Listen, master—"

"Don't call me that!" Ethan shouted, then ground his teeth together, cursing his temper, and that he was again using it against this man. "Not when we're like this—alone," he amended quietly.

"Young Ethan," the slave said with difficulty, but pride in his eyes.

"Your brothers—it was maybe a stumble, a spill, they wanted, is what I'm thinking. Not the hurt you got. Master Clayton, he's sorry. You see yourself how sorry—"

"For Betsy, perhaps. He almost had an innocent child's blood on his hands. Not for me. He killed a fine horse. How does that make him sorry for anything?"

"It don't. But it makes him a'feared maybe, sir."

"Of what?"

"Of being found out. Master Clayton, he knows now he done wrong, not by some stranger trying to take your place here, no, sir. He caused harm to his own brother returned."

"Brother! They never cared a whit for me, no matter what I did to please them. I've got to get out. I don't belong. I never did."

"Now, master, don't be forgetting your poor mama, your sister, her little ones in your teachin' care. They's all your blood kin."

"And you, Aaron. Aaron. Double A–R–O–N," he said and saw his small hand guiding the servant's mammoth one, teaching him to write in the dirt floor of the old first house of Windover Plantation. "You and your family are my kin." Ethan's expression grew wistful, remembering the quick minds of all his secret students. "Aubrey," he realized suddenly, "Aubrey was my nephew, then, wasn't he? My elder nephew. I wish I'd known."

"Would not have changed anything between you, I don't believe. You an' our Aubrey, you's were peas in a pod." The black man looked away and spoke to the empty fireplace grate. "Ethan. Martha and me, we's proud of the way you turning out by way of that French gentleman. Proud, like you was our own."

"I am your own. And I'll see you free. I swear on our common blood I'll see you and yours free."

Aaron reached out his powerful arm and bridged it to Ethan's shoulder. "Them words, they got to stay in secret places. Like the place you taught us our letters, and numbers. In days which we have all forgot, ain't we?"

"You didn't—"

Aaron cast his big hand skyward, the way he used to, rarely, when Ethan was a child, to get his undivided attention. "We have all forgot," he repeated. "On account of the late slave risings, and the law against us reading or writing, or any teachin' us such like, we forgot. For all our sakes. You knows what I be sayin', sir?"

"Oh. Yes." Ethan shrugged sheepishly.

"That be a good thing." Aaron squeezed Ethan's shoulder. "Now, when the doctor come back, and we work with your leg through the winter? The first of some changes comin' after that, I do believe. A joinin', maybe? With a powerful force to the North?"

Ethan felt himself color like a boy. "If I can win her."

"You see I made these boots handsome, don't you, sir? And no mournful color, neither. Them Quakers, they don't wear no mournful colors, Miss Judith says. Them boots will help you find your way to Pennsylvania, I expect, sir, in the fullness of time."

Dr. Foster joined Judith near the well. The scent of a Northern harvest was still in the air.

"It has been a great benefit having thee here, Friend," she said, as they walked toward the field where dull orange pumpkins peeked from their browning vines.

He grunted. "Your father has a command of botanical remedies that exceeds my own. And he was over the worst before we arrived."

"Perhaps he needed your reassurance, then."

"Leave your father blameless in this."

"Blameless?"

"He did not write that letter of urgent summons."

"Prescott Lyman assures me that my father had not the strength—"

"To conspire with your courting farmer, your Meeting's overseers, to bring you back?"

"Friend, thee disputes that thee has been the instrument of—?"

"I have been the instrument of your return. Judith, look around you. Your congregation desired you out of the clutches of the Randolphs before winter. They wished you comfortably set up at a widower's farm, and embroiled in mediating their latest petty debate."

Judith stopped, and widened her stance. She would not allow him to reduce the turmoil that was rending the fabric of her beliefs to petty debate. Even if he was from Boston, and didn't know better. "Has our Meeting treated thee unkindly, Friend?"

His smile was cold. "Not at all. You are experts in kindness. Killing kindness. I leave for Windover at first light." He turned to the house. "Good evening."

"Jordan, you cannot!"

He turned. " 'You'?" he repeated. "Did thee say 'you'? Am I now legion in number, like the Devil, Quakeress?"

"*Thou* cannot," she amended quickly. "By which I mean only that the coach has returned to Windover."

"I'm not taking the coach. I've bought a horse. A fast, stout Morgan. I hope the strength of her legs matches my purpose."

"But surely the Randolphs did not stipend enough money for—"

"The Devil take the Randolphs and their stipend! I no longer need their charity to care for my . . . my charge. Damnation! Will you take those blasted eyes off me, Judith Mercer?"

The scent, the one he shared with Ethan, permeated the warm Pennsylvania summer night. Judith stepped back. "Ethan will keep his word," she stated quietly. "He will not impede his own recovery. There is no purpose for thy fear."

She felt his fingers on her arm. It was so dark. They were alone, far from the house, with only stars for company. Was it her fear or his own she was feeling now?

"Judith, please forgive me," Dr. Foster said in a hoarse whisper. "I'm grateful for all you've done."

She raised her head. "What have I done, Jordan Foster?"

He smiled. "Thrown my ordered, solitary life into confusion."

"I must share that honor with thy charge at Windover."

"Will you share his life, when he asks that of you?"

"Friend Jordan, thou must not—"

"I know I must not! But I've crossed every other boundary. I know the kind of love Ethan has for you, Judith. It will not fade, or forget. Do not marry this farmer to seek out contentment, I warn you. One cold winter's night you will be sitting by the fire with your grandchildren all around. Then a story, a scent, a breath of Virginia air will cause a piercing at your heart as strong as the one you felt in our coach at parting."

Tears welled behind her eyes. How did he know? How did he know so exactly?

"Judith?" She heard her father's soft call, then saw his shawled form approaching them. She turned away from Jordan Foster's intense eyes.

"Ah, there. Thee is with our good doctor for company," Eli said, laughing. "Exactly what I told Prescott—'She's hardly stumbled into a wolves' den,' I told him! Poor Prescott is not used to thy wandering nature, Judith, or thy love for the heavens. Are they not a glorious manifestation of creation tonight? Do they not put thee in mind of our nights on board the *Standard*?"

Judith did not have to wait to become a grandmother to feel the stab.

Ethan caught the scent of a well-lathered horse. It was more ripe than the fastest of the Virginia post riders. Next came the metal clang of spurs. How did the rider get past the servants and his mother with spurs on? A deadweight landed on his chest. His eyes sprang open.

"Wake up. I haven't slept in the last thirty-six hours. You're not getting naptime today. Many happy returns of your day, three-and-twenty. Here are Judith Mercer's latest letters. Delivered."

The mud-splattered man had Jordan Foster's voice. Ethan glanced down at the leather packet lying on his chest, then at his mother, standing breathless and glowing with happiness in the doorway. She wore Betsy and Alice gripped to her skirts like ornaments. All were still dusted with Indian meal from the pudding portion of his birthday supper.

"Anything else I can do for you, you miserable Randolph brat?" Jordan demanded.

Ethan felt his own slow grin enraging the doctor further. "Yes," he answered. "Stay the winter. Help me to walk."

16

Ethan saw the children first, waving red, white, and blue handkerchiefs from the dock. The river schooner pitched, sending Anne Randolph into his arms. Ethan widened his stance, maintaining balance for both of them.

Jordan Foster frowned. "Use your walking stick."

"On land, perhaps," Ethan conceded, catching the chestnut stick with one hand. "But the sea is my home, *n'est-ce pas*?"

"Speak English, you confounded brat," Jordan Foster replied.

Anne Randolph giggled against Ethan's shoulder. She was leaning on him, he realized. And she was the lightest of burdens. When had she gotten so light? Would she someday float away? Foolish notion. "Our bickering disturbs my mother, sir," he said.

The doctor flushed. "Mrs. Randolph, I had no wish—"

"Ethan's teasing you, Jordan."

Their welcoming party was still searching for them along the schooner's deck. Impatient, Ethan let out a shrill whistle. His sister cocked her head, lifting her baby higher.

When they found Ethan, his nieces' colors flurried faster. But his sister's handkerchief fell from her hand.

"Sally?" Ethan whispered.

"She'll be all right, darling." His mother squeezed his arm.

"She looks away from us. What's wrong with her, Mother?"

"Nothing," she soothed.

Disembarking, he was astonished by the difference in his nieces since they'd gone home at Christmas. It was only early spring and each appeared inches taller. The baby squirmed until Sally set her down between her sisters. Charlotte took faltering steps toward him.

Ethan dropped to his good knee. "*Incroyable!* Little Gull, have we learned to walk together?" he asked as she toddled into his arms. Her faltering steps were much like his own had been, buoyed by his doctor's skill, his nieces' confidence, his mother's love.

Ethan was so absorbed by the baby's changing beauty, he didn't notice the tears staining his sister's cheeks until he stood.

"Why, Sally, what's the matter?"

"Matter? Matter? You're . . . so tall!"

"I have gained a few inches on you since last we danced, sister dear," he conceded with a smile. "Mother has been teaching me the latest steps, Sally. I can—"

"Poor Judith!" she wailed now.

"Poor?"

"I knew of your progress through our letters, and look at me—a fountain overflowing! You are very cruel, not to have told her."

"But I asked your advice. You wrote that you thought it would be a fine surprise."

"That was before I s-saw you!"

He placed his hat on little Alice's head. "I'm going to help them disembark my horse. *Petites jeunes filles,*" he instructed his charges firmly, "have your mother talking sense before I return."

"Oui, mon oncle." Both sisters gave him a smart salute.

Weeping women. Ethan would never understand them. He attached the lead rope to Lark's bridle. Even his horse was female, and touchy after the schooner trip upriver to Richmond. He breathed into her flaring nostrils, then clucked soothing words at her ear. He led her slowly through the cobblestone path where the women and Dr. Foster waited beside the coach.

Ethan was depending on his sister. Sally must keep his fragile mother from changing her mind about allowing him to travel on to Pennsylvania. He had no wish to fight her, too.

It had been hard enough doing battle with his father, although Winthrop the second and his own stupidity had helped Ethan in winning the old man's blessing.

He should have known better than to be lured into the barn loft when he was barely walking, Ethan realized now. Why weren't his defenses up against his brother's false comradeship, the smell of bourbon on his breath, his clothes? Did he want to believe so badly that Winthrop actually had what he'd offered—something Ethan needed to court Judith?

It was only once up in the barn loft, trapped, that he saw what his brother thought he needed, a leering look at Phoebe and Paris as they climbed to their secret trysting place. When Ethan called out, his brother had locked his arm behind his back and slammed his head into the floor.

The lovers weren't running, as Ethan had hoped they would be at his warning, but staring in silence at him under his brother's hold.

"Let them go," Ethan demanded between his teeth.

"Go? Where do you think you are, little brother? Gentle Windover, with Mother giving you dancing lessons and the great bull protecting you? This is my place, where my people do as they're bid."

"Phoebe is—"

"Of Windover, yes. But Phoebe is being very naughty, fornicating with my coachman, without permission. Shall I whip her soundly before I send her home? Or shall I order they continue so you'll know what to do with that icy Quaker for whom you have such fondness?"

"No."

"No? What's to be done, then, now that you've spoiled my little gift? Ah, perhaps you'd like a more direct approach, man of action that you are? Shall I leave you with Phoebe, now that my Paris has begun to unwrap her for you?"

"Yes."

Ethan felt his brother's knee grind into his back. "Yes, what? from our most polite and grateful hero?"

"Yes, please." Ethan spat onto the floorboards.

His brother finally released his arm. "Paris, remove my brother's boots. He would like to sleep with your wife."

The man's eyes burned hatred for both of them, Ethan surmised, as he approached. But he followed his master's orders. His brother threw his boots into the hay below. "Now, let's leave them some privacy, shall we?"

Paris gave a moment's hesitation, during which a small sob, a plea, escaped Phoebe. Then he climbed down the ladder, followed by Winthrop, chuckling. "Yes, this will work even better."

Ethan stood slowly, then stared after them from the loft, ignoring his throbbing head and arm, his crippled stance, so consumed by his anger that he even forgot about Phoebe's presence until she clutched his arm.

"We are married sir, Paris and me—the preacher from Southampton wed us, and I know it was wrong but we asked permission three times over and, Master Ethan, my daddy tells us you be a different sort than your brothers and, oh, please, don't do this, sir!"

He looked down at her tear-stained face, stunned. "Do?" he whispered.

She bowed her head, clutching at her homespun gown. Cowering, he finally realized. Good God. Brave, sprightly Phoebe was cowering. Finally the words Jordan Foster had used to ease his own terror came to him. "Phoebe. I wouldn't hurt you for the world," he said. "Let's go home."

His father had ranted at him that night behind the closed door of his study. "Keep your hands off Aaron's children! There are plenty of the others willing—"

"Willing?"

"Of course willing, privileged to be favored by you, though the children will be as stained black as—"

"As Aaron?"

"Damnation, you know? And you still—"

"Took my niece? No, Father. Your source for that information is incorrect." He turned to the harvest gatherers in the old tapestry and folded his arms.

"I—I see. I thought the story preposterous, of course, after all that devotion to Miss Mercer and your preaching to us with those absurd notions about servants. But, what in hell went on at your brother's? If Winthrop didn't have to pull you off her, how did your face . . . Ethan Blair, you can barely stand!" he accused.

"I'm tired, that's all. Might I go?"

"Yes. I think you'd best go to Pennsylvania and fetch your lady home, son."

That moment was as close to the difficult old man as he'd ever remembered feeling, Ethan thought as his eyes now swept the busy city's streets. Richmond—Virginia's capital, home to ten thousand. He was here. His sister's house. No father, no brothers. First step to Judith. He grinned, realizing that he, like his brother-in-law Barton, was now rich in dancing women. They would help him win the one who didn't dance.

* * *

Alice fit the cushioned stool under his leg as Betsy pulled off the boot. It was their ritual from the winter, after Jordan Foster's cage came off his leg. Ethan welcomed the feel of the small ministering hands, but didn't like being without Aaron's boots. He would have worn them to bed, if they'd let him.

His mother had instructed him well in social graces over the winter at Windover. Tonight she had nodded to him from across the room if she'd taught him the dance, so it was safe to ask a lady. None refused him. Dancing had been so important to him when a child. Now he was pleased to have managed not to step on any glittering slippers in the course of the evening.

But he'd needed the walking stick on Richmond's hills, and between the dances. The walking stick made him a cripple still. Walking sticks were going out of fashion. Old men and lawyers, politicians, and a few pompous merchants still used them to traverse city streets. Younger men walked with a sprightly, free American air that Ethan envied.

Ethan was paying for the dancing, his brother-in-law's tour of his surveyor's office and city streets. Pain rode from his knee to his hip as he reached over to kiss his fresh-faced nieces good-night before Anne and Sally led them away upstairs. Jordan Foster saw the pain, Ethan knew, from his frown. He'd seen many versions of that frown over the course of his stay at Windover. But the doctor said nothing as he handed him a steaming cup of tea. Perhaps distraction would save him from a scolding. And he knew the subject that had the best chance.

"My mother is different here, isn't she, Dr. Foster?"

"How?"

"Happy, free. Even her walk is different. Taller, more sure, less cowering."

"Cowering?"

"To my brothers, my father. Was it always this way, sir? Back in the time you were in your position at Windover, was she this way then?"

"Drink your tea."

"Mother should visit Sally more often, don't you think?"

"I think you should take some laudanum." He brought a small vial from his waistcoat pocket.

"Why?"

"To kill the pain."

"Pain, sir?"

"Ethan," Jordan Foster warned.

Ethan stared at the half-empty vial. "Laudanum. Source: opium. Flower, poppy. China."

"That's right."

"What else does it kill, Dr. Foster? Confusion? Doubt? Will? Laudanum enslaves, I think."

"I am not in the slave trade!"

"I was not saying that. My English is not clear."

"It's clear enough." The doctor's hand touched his shoulder. "You have known laudanum addicts while on board the *Standard*?"

"Two of our surgeon's assistants." Ethan put his cup on its saucer. "One killed the first mate in an argument, the other threw himself overboard." He returned the cup of tea to the doctor's hands. It felt too heavy to hold. What was this weakness? "The pain. It's my own fault, I walked too far with Barton, I danced too long."

"True enough."

"So it has a purpose, this pain."

"You're not a Quaker yet."

"Eli and Judith would never give me laudanum."

"What would they do?"

"I don't know," he admitted.

Ethan watched the doctor shake his head, replace the vial to his pocket. *He finds me such a sorry student,* he thought, *how can I convince him otherwise? Quaker purpose. Not these dulled senses.* He put the teacup on the small table, closed his eyes. He felt the man's hands on his brow. Soothing, like Fayette's hands.

"Dr. Foster?" he whispered.

"What troubles you besides the leg?"

"My father rips the sewing from my hands, calls it woman's work. He stuffs my head with numbers, plantation accounts that I can't make come out any differently—owing, unprofitable. Tired land, not tobacco land anymore, why can't he see that?"

"Numbers. Everything is still numbers to that man," the doctor said bitterly.

"My brothers breed slaves on their plantations instead, then sell them to the cotton and rice and indigo plantations farther south. This must not happen at Windover. To Aaron, to his family, not to any under our care. I promised. But what can I do? Only a third son, an afterthought, returned from the dead, with no place."

"Rest from it all now. Until Midwatch. Then find your bed."

The pain was allowing it, yes. "Where are my boots?"

"Here. Beside your chair."

The boots were his freedom, they and the walking stick with the brass lion handle that Micah had made for him. Micah had forged a fine double-blade knife, too, which Aaron had sewn into a pouch in his right boot. It stayed, invisibly sheathed against his calf. Fayette had already taught him how to use a knife with accuracy and skill.

The doctor eased him out of his coat as if he were a child falling asleep by the fire. Even his questions were leveling under the glassy surface of a becalmed sea.

"I feel better," Ethan whispered, as the doctor drew up the green coverlet to his shoulder. "See? Your listening, your touch was enough to relieve the worst of the pain."

"Along with the laudanum I put in your tea."

Even the surge of anger didn't reach the glassy surface. "Bloody hell," Ethan managed a soft curse. "Not right."

"I know what's best."

"You should have asked me."

"It was only a few drops. You barely finished half a cup. Do you think it's easy, watching you in pain?"

"Not respectful."

He was furious, but so tired. He turned his face to the wall. The doctor's silent footfalls left the room.

Deeper in the night the beast came, red, writhing, after Judith. She screamed. Wild, unearthly. The knife. Where was it? He woke, gasping, his mouth dry. Damned laudanum.

He rose, pulled on his boots, walked to the room's bookshelves. He leaned on one, running his fingers fondly over leather-spined histories of the Greek and Roman worlds. Outside, all was silent. The city had lost its busy voice. He must forgive Jordan Foster, Ethan thought. Slipping the laudanum into his tea was not a great transgression, in light of all the man had done on his behalf.

The doctor had been more patient than Ethan believed possible, and had talked of his Edinburgh schooling, and his work among the Indians, and in the war. He had even endured his father's constant reminders that his start in life had been funded by Randolph money. Fayette had taught him to be a more generous friend. Had Jordan Foster become his friend, then? Is that why he fretted so over his feelings? Ethan's thoughts scattered at the sound of screaming. He raised his head, startled. Judith. No. Not Judith's screams. A baby's.

His sister's town house was so compact he didn't have to walk far to a small sitting room that faced the street. Sally paced before the windows. When he called her from the doorway, she started, still unused to seeing him on his feet.

"I'd hoped she'd not wake you."

"It's Midwatch. I was awake. What's wrong with Charlotte?"

"I know it sounds like she's in a ring of the Inferno, but she's cutting a tooth, that's all."

"Cutting?"

"A new one is breaking through."

"I see. Might I hold her?"

"Yes. I'll fetch some more clove oil from the kitchen for her gums."

Charlotte fisted her hands and screamed as he watched the flying train of his sister's gown.

"Little Gull, Little Gull," he called as he lifted her over his shoulder, "this will not do. Your poor mother looks so tired!"

The baby answered with what sounded like an eruption. Then came an abrupt silence that rang in his ears. Ethan walked to a banister-backed chair and placed his youngest niece in his lap. To his astonishment, her mood seemed transformed. She cooed and took his finger into her mouth. Ethan felt her swollen gums, and rubbed.

Soon his sister stood breathless in the doorway. "What French sorcery is this?" she demanded.

He smiled. "She likes the taste of a new-flavored finger maybe, and perhaps—Ow! *Sacre-bleu!*"

Sally laughed. "She does have three other teeth, brother!" she warned, taking the baby into her arms before settling into the sea green sofa. Charlotte nuzzled fitfully at her mother's loosely laced nightgown. Sally satisfied the baby on her breast in seconds.

Ethan watched in wonder. "Doesn't she bite you, Sally?"

"Your little gull cannot bite and suck at the same time," she explained, "for which I thank the heavens! But she didn't want any part of me before you took her. Oh, Ethan, there is the answer, on your shirt."

He looked at the white stain and grinned. "She belched."

"She did more than that!"

He shrugged. "I have smelled worse. Fayette used to douse me in clove oil to make me presentable for visits with Judith on the *Standard*. May I?" he asked, pointing to the corked bottle she'd set on a nearby table.

Sally laughed. "Be my guest."

He rubbed his shoulder with the oil. The sour odor was replaced with a scent that filled his being with a longing that even the beauty of his sister and her child could not dispel.

"You've been cheerful about duties no unmarried man endures," Sally said softly.

"In training to leave that miserable state, maybe."

"Oh?" Ethan loved the interest that broke through even his sister's fatigue. "And I imagine you've devoured the writings of William Penn and George Fox you asked me to send to Windover."

Ethan brought the chair closer to his sister and leaned as far forward as it would allow. "Sally, none of the Quaker writings you sent speaks toward courtship rituals."

His sister's light brows lifted in surprise. "I shouldn't think so, being religious tracts."

"But does not passion have the ability to transform both lovers to a higher plane?"

"Is that Monsieur Fayette's teaching?"

He shrugged. "Sally? I need guidance."

She touched his face. "Perhaps you should talk to Barton."

"I have talked with your husband. All afternoon. About the best routes west and north and east to the sea. And he gave me maps, and the wonderful leather coat he used when he was my age and a post rider. He's a most excellent man, Sally."

His sister shook her head. "He has also been a wonderful husband. A kind and considerate lover."

"I know. You both glow with your happiness. I desire that for Judith and me. But I am not entirely—what did Judith call it?—an innocent."

"Why, Ethan . . . while a prisoner?"

"I was not a prisoner. I was a ghost, in Fayette's shadow. That's how I survived. And when I was of age, he purchased for me the favors of a woman."

"You mean, a—?"

"Yes."

Sally stared into his soul. "She broke your heart," she whispered. "Oh, Ethan, this woman broke your heart."

The French could have used his sister's services as a spy, Ethan thought ruefully. "She made too much of me, perhaps. But Clarisse showed me things, things she said would please women I loved."

"And?"

"Should I have not, Sally? Should I have not kissed Judith, or touched her in those places?"

"Have you and Judith . . . ?"

"No, no. But how can she long for something she's never experienced? Fayette said I had to steal a piece of her soul at every parting, so she would not forget me."

Sally smiled. "Some give adornments, a ring."

He frowned. "Sally. Judith does not wear rings."

"Did she receive these affections? Did she return them?"

"Oh, yes. And she is very strong. But a little frightened of her own strength, I think."

"My."

" 'My'? Your what?"

"I'm a little astonished."

"Sally, I love this woman more than my life. Help me to win her. How will it be when I go to Pennsylvania? I touch the ink of her letters and taste her mouth again. How will it be when I see her?"

"I think you are not the only thief of souls."

"She has mine, of course. How could it be otherwise?"

"How, indeed." His sister remained quiet for a full minute. Ethan was patient. It was always wise to be patient with women, Fayette had instructed him. Finally, Sally smiled. "Follow Judith's lead in Pennsylvania, among the Quakers, not Monsieur Fayette's. It will require some restraint, I think, from both of you."

"Yes. Yes, of course, you're right."

"Unclench your teeth, brother dear."

He laughed. Quietly, to keep from waking her sleeping child.

"As for her father and community," his sister continued, "you must be a good guest among them, Ethan, watching for ways to show them you are a worthy suitor."

"But will none of that matter if I am not a Quaker?"

"Since your conversion is not likely, it's your only chance."

"What?" he teased. "You don't see me as a Child of the Light?"

"I see you as incapable of untruthfulness, brother. Even in the pursuit of your heart's desire. Evasion," she said, yawning, "now that's another matter. You are also a crafty Frenchman."

Sally was falling asleep there, on the sofa, with her child in her arms. "I'm sorry, darling boy," she murmured. "Such a long day."

Ethan went to the chest in the hallway and drew out a soft coverlet. He placed it over his sister and her child, then banked the room's fire. Small things. But he had never done such things. *I could care for a woman and child, couldn't I, Sally?*

His sister smiled in her sleep.

"That's not my trunk," Ethan protested.

"Oh, there were a few more shirts that wouldn't fit in the smaller one," his mother explained.

"The smaller one was bigger than I desired, *madame,*" he told her sternly. How could a woman who was so light not understand his need to remain unencumbered, movable?

"If you have room in your saddlebags for those maps, and that dreadful coat of Barton's, you can have the coachman carry this trunk."

Ethan wondered if he would ever get beyond the city limits of Richmond. The good-byes at Sally's house had been bad enough. They'd gone on so long that he, his mother, and Jordan Foster had barely reached the overland coach's origination point on time. He had already had a devil of a time convincing the driver that it had been arranged that Lark would ride in the coach's wake for the entire journey, in order to give Ethan his own transportation to Prescott Lyman's farm.

Ethan would have preferred a ship. But his mother had refused any mention of his going out on the open sea, even the coastal waterway. Now this trunk business.

"There is some yardage I couldn't resist when Sally took me shopping yesterday, too, darling," his mother confessed with a nervous smile. "Cambric. Isn't it a pretty shade of rose? Please tender it to Judith for me? It will make such a lovely, a lovely . . ."

When he saw her tears, Ethan forgot his anger and folded his mother in his arms.

"In the North," she sobbed out, "people are not so friendly, so hospitable as in this country. They care only for business, for money, in the North. They will cut your throat!"

"Why, Mother," he said, looking over her shoulder, "you slander our esteemed Bostonian friend."

"It's he who told me these things!"

Dr. Foster held up his hands defensively. "Not about throat-cutting," he protested, "not a thing about throat-cutting!"

"Ethan, I understand why you don't wish to take our coach and six," Anne Randolph continued. "But if you would only take a servant—"

"We've discussed this many times. How would it be, coming to court at a hearty Quaker farm household, unable to take care of myself without a servant?"

"It would be expected."

"It would be pitiful, Mother."

She nodded, slowly pulling out of his arms. "Pitiful," she affirmed, smiling, though her tears continued to flow. "Forgive me. I was determined not to do this."

"I'll write to you. Every day."

"I know, my darling."

She straightened his cravat with shaking fingers. "Boys are supposed to squander their mother's love," she whispered, "not to return it tenfold."

"Squandering the only woman's love that is free? That would be very foolish, no?"

She laughed. "Poor Judith! She will be helpless."

Anne Randolph finally released him and leaned into the doctor's hold at her waist. Anchored. *Don't float away, Mother. Stay with him.* How handsome a couple they made. His mother should marry the doctor someday, Ethan decided. Theirs would be a love match between old and trusted friends. It would not be based on property or ambition the way her childhood marriage to his father had been. The habitual sadness in Jordan Foster's eyes would disappear. His mother would never cower again. She would gain more substance, and so not drift away.

He couldn't wait to tell Judith his discovery. Jordan Foster and his mother loved each other, he was sure of it. Ethan took a step toward the waiting coach.

"Use your walking stick," Anne Randolph called. "After dusk. Don't forget."

Ethan sighed, and turned to the doctor. "Well?" he challenged. "Speak up. My mother's stealing your admonitions now."

"Win your heart's desire," Jordan Foster said quietly.

"And if I cannot?"

"Steal her away."

"What?"

"You heard me, brat. Now be off, before your mother floods the streets of Richmond."

17

Ethan finished making camp along one of Barton Gibson's routes though the wilderness. He was too excited by that accomplishment to yet think about sleep. Lark whickered softly.

"No complaints," he told his mare. "You've gotten me into this."

It wasn't strictly true. But his horse's suffering was the catalyst for his decision to leave the coach road and travel to Pennsylvania on his own. Lark had begun their journey hale and hearty, but was soon suffering in the dust behind the coach's wheels. That was not fair, was it? Especially when Ethan had the warm coat and excellent maps drawn by the best surveyor in the Commonwealth, and the burning need to present himself to the Quakers simply, something his family did not fully understand.

He was cataloging the reasons for his decision, Ethan realized, as if any had the power to stop him. He was free, he reminded himself, a free American. Of age, not a child, except in his lack of experience on land. That had only presented itself as a problem when he had to send the blasted trunk somewhere, and could not think of a place safe from his family's knowledge. So he sent it to the edge of the world, where his last sea-born duty still lay.

Ethan detected a sound on the wind. Human, angry. Was there a camp near to his? Or a farmstead? He would not be able to sleep until he knew, so he hastily finished the letter to his mother. *Your obedient*— No, best make it, *Your loving son, E. Randolph,* he decided. Of that sentiment he was sure. He stored the letter in his traveling writing desk.

When he stood, his leg buckled. He recovered, yanked up his walking stick from where its lion's eyes were intent on the fire. "After dusk, yes, Mother," Ethan muttered as he trudged through a stand of trees toward the light of another campfire.

Around the fire two men held a third down. Ethan entered the circle of light. "May I assist—"

Only when the two men turned did he realize his mistake. Their expressions were far from companionable. Ethan's peripheral vision told him the campsite had been sacked. And the man lying beneath the two was deathly still.

Ethan whispered, *"Merde."*

A man with blood on his hands stood. *"Vous parlez français?"*

Ethan widened his stance. *"Oui. Pourquoi pas, mon ami?"*

He repeated his offer to help in French and in feigned innocence, while trying to get a better look at the still one. The two men spoke to each other in their native language.

"Don't, François! We were not born to this. Listen, listen to him. His accent, it's our own!"

"Yours, maybe."

"He's a countryman!"

"So?"

Ethan began thinking in French, to make the words come faster. "Is this true? What country? La Rochelle, the finest seaport in all of France?"

Ethan saw the glint in the second man's hand. A knife. Ethan's own was tucked inside the case Aaron had made in his right-footed boot. *Try the sharpness of your wits first,* Fayette had taught him.

Both men left their prey and descended on Ethan. He recognized the longing in the bearded, friendlier one's eyes. "La Rochelle?" he asked. "Incredible! When were you there last?"

The one called François shoved him silent. "Your name?" he demanded of Ethan.

"Maupin."

"What?"

"Washington Lafayette Maupin."

The man laughed. "A French-American Alliance baby. Look at him—about twenty! Born during our bloody Terror, I think."

Ethan tried to project wounded dignity. "You find my name amusing?"

"We meant no offense, my friend," the bearded one said. "Tell me. In La Rochelle, are the towers still standing?"

"First let me attend your injured friend," Ethan said, seeing the legs of the downed man stirring. "Perhaps I might— God's blood," he whispered suddenly, in English, recognizing the traveling clothes. "Jordan."

"You know this man?"

"It's my . . . my cousin. My American cousin."

He went down on his good knee, forgetting any notion of his self-protection among the thieves. He pulled the black cloth from the physician's face.

Jordan's throat was cut, there, below his beard's line. Ethan forced his fingers to probe the wound. Bloody, but not deep. Not yet deep enough, was it? The doctor's hand took his sleeve. Ethan felt the same warmth as the one that comforted him at their first meeting.

"Watch your back, brat," Jordan Foster whispered.

Ethan spun around. "Countrymen!" he called out to the advancing thieves in Fayette's French, "I am overwhelmed with gratitude!"

"You are?"

"Of course! What can I do to repay you for caring for my foolhardy kinsman after his run-in with thieves? You are Good Samaritans worthy of the famous hospitality and graciousness of the cobbled streets of La Rochelle!"

"I'm from Marans," the sour François muttered.

"A beautiful village! Along the canal, is it not?"

The thief still looked suspicious. "Are you Catholic or Huguenot?" he demanded now.

Ethan's head spun. One affiliation meant brother, the other enemy, and he had no idea which would yield which response, so he resorted to the truth. "A heathen Deist, I fear," he apologized.

"Deist. Alliance baby," François muttered, but the threat was gone from his voice. "Your cousin was only being threatened. The knife slipped. If he had kept still—"

"Until our rescue," the other thief finished quickly.

"I will advise him," Ethan assured them, "just as you say, for his next encounter with highwaymen." He hoped he looked even more guileless than he felt. "Please do not trouble yourselves further. I am armed, and have a horse who will break the bones of men unwise enough to cross me. She's beyond those trees. I need only whistle—"

His fingers went to his mouth as the thieves put up their hands.

"We'll be on our way, then."

"Must you go? At least allow me to pay you a reward for your service to my family."

"Urgent, quite urgent," they repeated, almost together, ignoring his silver dollars and grabbing their packs. "We wish your cousin a full recovery, *monsieur!*"

Ethan watched the pair disappear into the night as he replaced the coins to his pocket. Jordan Foster nudged him with his foot. His voice was weak. "What in hell was that all about?"

"A Frenchman's honor overriding his desperation." Ethan gave a shrill whistle and kicked dirt on the sputtering campfire.

"What are you doing?"

"Offering my hospitality. I'd advise you to take it."

He helped the older man to his feet just as Lark found them.

"I don't need . . . I'm able—" The doctor protested as Ethan hoisted him onto the barebacked horse.

"No, you are not. And I cannot carry you."

"Get my bag."

"Yes, sir." Ethan ground his teeth together.

"And use your stick, goddamnit."

Ethan found his camp untouched. He eased Jordan Foster from Lark's back then gave him his own place by the fire. The doctor allowed him to look under the black cloth at his throat.

"It has stopped bleeding," Ethan told him.

"Good."

"What are you doing in these woods?"

"Trying to make camp. Until I was overcome by two brutes who appear to be great friends of yours."

"You were following me," Ethan corrected. "At my mother's behest."

"I was on my way to Philadelphia, to visit my brother-in-law." Ethan did not hide his skepticism.

"He's been begging me to come for years!" the doctor insisted, now avoiding the younger man's eyes. "The timing of the visit was your mother's idea, yes," he finally admitted.

Ethan growled. "Look at you. She will never let either of us out of her sight if she learns of this."

"The scar will fade. If you sew it correctly."

Ethan felt the color drain from his face. "I? I cannot—"

"What's the matter? Can you only spout remedies and pontificate on your Quaker botanical cures? Treat my neck like one of your ship's sails, my ligature like your Judith's hair."

Ethan felt cold, suddenly. He wasn't ready, not for this.

"Imagine," Jordan Foster said more kindly. "You have a good head for imagining. I've been to a barber. My shave got too close, that's all."

"But you don't shave."

"Imagine!" Jordan yelled, then took a pained breath and spoke more softly. "You checked the wound when I was on the ground?"

"Yes, sir." A spasm started in Ethan's right-hand fingers.

"Then you know there's no threat to— Stop that!"

The twitching stopped.

The physician resumed. "What's beyond, Ethan?"

"Beyond?"

"Beyond the muscle wall. I can't ask you in French, man!" He breathed out. "Come now," he tried again. "From the back to front, what's in there?"

"Spine. The spine."

"Yes, yes. Go on."

"The pharynx—throat. Next the esophagus."

"Its common name?"

"Gullet."

"Yes. Purpose?"

"Digestion."

"Correct. Now tell me the respiratory apparatus."

"Trachea—windpipe. It continues downward from the larynx."

"Undamaged, isn't it?"

"I don't know. It's so dark."

"Ethan, it's undamaged, or I would be having trouble breathing, wouldn't I?"

"Oh. Yes, that's right."

"Now"—he raised his head to give Ethan a full view of his injury—"what do you have here?"

He was in pain, Ethan could see it. *Think. Think through your own distress,* he told himself. "Oblique wound of the neck. Four inches long, sir. Some muscle damage."

"And it needs—?" the physician prompted.

"Cleansing of coagulated blood and foreign bodies. Suturing. Adhesive plaster. Bandaging."

"Good. You have water. Decent firelight. Everything else you need is in my bag."

The physician remained silent as Ethan brought forth the oil, needle, waxed shoemaker's thread, plaster, and gauze bandaging.

Dr. Foster's pale lips compressed into a firm line. "Ligatures, about a half-inch apart. Can you tie a square knot?"

"You are asking this of a sailor?" Ethan used his haughtiest tone, to make his teacher laugh. It did not.

"Begin," Jordan Foster commanded.

Where was his humor? Perhaps the physician had spent too much time in Scotland, Ethan reasoned. The Scottish seamen he'd known on board the *Standard* were always the most sober.

Jordan Foster remained still, his eyes open, staring at the stars, as Ethan pulled the thread through the broken skin of his wound and tied each ligature with a double knot. Ethan would remind him of his own stillness, he decided, the next time the man wished to put laudanum in his tea. As he wiped the needle in the oil-soaked gauze, the physician swallowed hard.

"Almost finished," Ethan whispered.

"Yes. Good."

The pain was there, in his voice. Spilling out the corners of his eyes. But Jordan Foster spoke as taskmaster again while Ethan fitted the strips of adhesive plaster on either side of the stitches. "You will have to remove them tomorrow or the next day. Why?"

"To try to avoid the stage of inflammation."

"And if the wound becomes inflamed?"

Ethan tried to turn his expression wicked. "Then the world is turned upside down. I get to play your keeper. As such I'll get you drunk with spirits, or laudanum. Get to hear all your secrets, no?"

Finally, a smile burst across Jordan Foster's mouth, though it disappeared almost as quickly as it came. "At last, some humor," Ethan said, winding the bandage around the physician's throat.

Jordan frowned. "And I suppose it humored you to offer those scoundrels money?"

"It's what they wanted, I thought."

"Of course it's what they wanted. They're thieves!"

"Desperate. But not real thieves, I think."

"Ethan?"

"Yes, sir?"

"What if they come back?"

"They will not get a second chance. I will kill them."

"What?"

"I have a knife."

"The Frenchman, on your ship. He taught you how to use it."

"His name was Maupin. Or Fayette. Yes, he taught me. I spent many hours alone. I was small and crippled, easy prey." Ethan cocked an eyebrow in rueful response to the doctor's sympathetic expression. "And very handsome, yes?"

The doctor pressed his arm. "Ethan, none of the sailors ever—?"

"No. Fayette protected me. Some assumed I was his lover, I think. I was not. He was a woman's man only, as I am, so our great beauty was wasted on each other, yes?"

The doctor sneered. "Peacock."

Ethan sneered back. "Nursemaid."

"Maupin was reckless," the doctor said. "It cost him his life."

"What are you saying?"

"That night you were discovered, captured. Climbing the masts in a storm at his age!"

"Following a full-grown man at yours, sir! Fayette was also reckless when first he took my weight over his shoulder after the lashing. That is why I am here to plague you now. What afflicts you besides that wound? Are you angry that his language saved us both? Fayette was the bravest of men. His final action— "

"Almost cost you your life."

"You know nothing of it! Nothing! *Rien du tout!*" Ethan turned away from the physician, pulled both his legs in tight against his chest. His breathing went ragged.

"Ethan."

Ethan buried his head in his arms.

"Son, it's not good for your knee to— "

"Leave me alone!"

The gaping silence hovered between them.

"You heard my envy speaking."

Ethan brought his head up. "Envy?"

"When we all thought you dead, Maupin raised you. Splendidly."

Ethan turned. "What?"

"You heard. Don't humiliate me further."

"I remain unfinished, Dr. Foster," Ethan whispered.

"Unfinished?"

"If Judith will have me as her husband, I will need a trade. Will you take me on as your apprentice? We don't need much, Judith and Eli and I. We have simple tastes."

"But Ethan, your family—"

"I am not my family's heir. Too much has happened to me. I will never be a gentleman. I will never be a slaveholder. But I want a family of my own. One like yours was, with music and kindness to strangers. One like Sally's. I need a trade to accomplish this. I need you, Dr. Foster."

The physician looked away and bit his knuckled finger. This was a curse, Ethan remembered. Where? In Italy? Is that what the physician thought him, a curse? Jordan Foster faced him again. His dark eyes looked almost pupil-less. They stayed on Ethan without wavering.

"My name is Jordan, except before our patients. Then only, am I Dr. Foster to you, understand?"

Ethan smiled. "Yes, sir."

"Winning Judith will not be easy, I warn you, even with my promise of a trade and a roof over your heads."

"I know that. But once I do, perhaps I'll give you to my mother after all."

"What?"

"I may be unschooled ignorant, but I'm not blind, Jordan. And I am Mother's favorite. She won't marry again without my approval. So, when the time comes, you'll have to come to me for permission to seek her hand."

"You arrogant—"

"This is not a good start to your courtship. Or your healing. As your surgeon, I must insist you calm yourself."

"I'll tell your mother of your disobedience, I swear I will!"

"Not without the details of our adventure tonight. I suggest you rest while I take the first watch." Ethan found the post rider's coat and drew it up to Jordan Foster's shoulders.

"You are your mother's child, Ethan. Don't distress her."

"What? I should have let those cutthroats hack through the rest of your miserable . . . Wait. Jordan. Cutthroat. She knew it. As she bid me farewell. Do you remember? My mother knew one of us was going to get his throat cut."

The physician looked stunned for a brief moment. He shook it off like a chill. "She was frightened, that's all."

"No. That's not all. She has visions. My mother has visions, as I do! Perhaps you're right. Perhaps I *am* her child."

"You don't get them from your father," Jordan Foster murmured.

"What do you know of my father?" Ethan asked him quietly.

"Everything."

"Did she ever love him?" he barely whispered.

Why was it so important he know this, Ethan wondered, as he scanned the trees around their camp, instead of looking at the doctor, whom he feared would laugh at the question. Was it his arrogance, this need to be what Martha called him, a product of love? Or was it a simple desire to see Anne Randolph's eyes unveiled, unburdened, happy again?

Ethan finally turned away from his vigilant watch across the darkness. His physician-turned-patient's eyes were closed, his breathing easy and at peace.

Ethan shook his head. Foolish. Why did he think Jordan Foster had the answers to everything?

18

Ethan dismounted, leaned against the saddle until the stiffness left his right leg. He looked around at two dozen carts and carriages, and half as many horses. He'd come upon a gathering at the sprawling farmhouse. What kind of gathering? he wondered as he stroked Lark's withers. Was this even the right place? He heard a door behind him open. Soft, slippered steps sounded on the farmhouse's flagstone walk. They were followed by skipping.

"Beecher! What has thee brought us today?"

When Ethan turned, the girl stopped short. She was older than Betsy, but not yet a full-grown woman. The boy peeking out at her hip matched Ethan's eldest niece in size. Both fit Judith's descriptions of the Lyman children.

"Thee is not Beecher," the girl said.

"No. Is this Prescott Lyman's farm?"

"It is."

Ethan reached for his hat, then remembered as he touched the rim. Stupid, that was the first thing Judith taught him about Quakers. No hats-off to them. He finished removing it, and wiped his brow with his sleeve as if that had been his original intent.

He didn't like the hat; it reminded him of the civilian style the army wore. He preferred the black japanned straw hats he'd worn while a midshipman aboard the *Ida Lee*. But of course his mother would have none of them. He left the hat on the stone shelf of the well. The boy approached his mount.

"She's a fine horse," he offered.

Ethan grinned. "And gentle. Lark's her name. I have been riding her hard since we left Philadelphia."

"Thee must rest her, Friend. And replenish thyself," the girl said. Ruth Lyman. How old? Fourteen, Judith had written. She was staring at him. Why? Was he so mud-spattered he repulsed her?

Ethan nodded his thanks as she pulled up the bucket of cool water. He took a long swallow from the ladle she offered.

Her little brother came closer and reached up to Lark's neck. Ethan lifted him higher, without thinking, the way he did his nieces. A look of fear sparked the girl's expression, but the boy laughed and rubbed Lark's ears vigorously.

"Ah, this she loves!" Ethan approved.

The boy cocked his head. "Thy speech is strange, Friend."

"Hugh!" the girl chastised him.

"From what country does thee come?" the boy continued as Ethan set him back on his feet.

"The country of Virginia."

"Virginia? Where Judith's letters come! Did thee bring more letters?"

"Yes. And packages enough to fill two saddlebags. For Mercers and Lymans."

"Packages! I am Hugh Lyman. Does anything bear my name?"

"I remember it distinctly."

"And thee did carry these things all the way from Virginia?"

"I have."

"Does thee hear him, Ruth? Now the Randolphs have hired their own post rider to bring us presents!" He tugged at Ethan's leather coat. "The crippled boy our Judith delivered from the hands of the British is himself coming to visit," he proclaimed proudly.

"Is that so?"

"Hugh, the post rider has no interest—"

"We have seen his coach and six, when it brought our Judith and the doctor," her brother continued. "It had marvelous fast and sleek horses, like thine own. I keep watch for that coach. Father is not happy. It's planting time. We must make room for the crippled boy and his servants, all besides getting the crops in. He is very spoiled, Father says, and will be very demanding on our Judith."

"I hope that will not be so."

Ethan cast a longing glance toward the farmhouse. *Let me show them differently,* he pleaded silently.

"I'll see if Judith can be called forth from Meeting to see thy bounty," Ruth Lyman offered.

"Meeting? It's not Sunday."

He'd planned carefully not to come on Sunday. Did Quakers gather on other days as well? Was the farmhouse full of them?

"This is a special session. Judith Mercer has been asked to serve as mediator in disputes between the followers of Elias Hicks and those who insist on a defined creed and imposed authority."

"Quakers are in dispute with each other?" Ethan asked.

"I fear so, yes. Most of us here follow Brother Hicks and serving our Inner Light. But the Meeting for Suffering is very powerful."

Who were these people who shone a beacon of peace to the outside world but fought among themselves and treasured suffering?

"Something troubles thee, Friend?"

Ethan stared at Ruth Lyman. Brown, braided hair pinned close to her head, like Judith's. He opened his mouth, but all his thoughts were coming in French.

"Thee is not used to the company of Friends?"

Ethan's eyes darted over the carriages. "Not so many at once," he finally stammered.

She smiled. "We are not so dreadful, Friend post rider from the country of Virginia! Be at thy ease."

But Ethan had come to steal Judith from these people, so her words brought cold comfort.

Once the girl slipped inside the white clapboard farmhouse, Ethan yanked off the leather coat. It slipped through his shaking hands. The boy caught it, then laid it on the low stone wall.

Ethan heard Fayette's voice inside his head. *Do something normal, to return your balance. See to your horse.* Ethan pulled the double-blade knife from his boot. The child stepped back abruptly.

"Hoofpick, Hugh," Ethan assured him as he lifted Lark's front right foot and went about his task.

"Th-those are fine boots."

Ethan smiled. "My brother made them." He moved to the next hoof. His young companion ventured closer.

"I've never seen a knife come out of a boot."

"No?"

"Or such a knife."

Ethan looked up from his work. "Would you like to finish this one?" He offered the walnut handle.

Hugh's eyes widened. "I would."

Ethan held Lark's leg steady as the boy picked the hoof clean. Yes, this was returning his balance, Ethan realized. "Good work," he complimented the child.

"Thy knife is so light."

"Yes," Ethan said with pride. "Thrown, it flies."

He recovered the knife and walked to Lark's hind legs.

"My sister Ruth admires thee," the boy said, following him.

Ethan turned. "I'm witless today. She is very kind."

"She lets Beecher fetch his own water." Hugh rolled his eyes the way Betsy did when she caught Ethan sighing over a letter from Judith.

Ethan chuckled. "You would make an excellent partner for my niece, I think, Hugh."

"Thy niece? A girl?" He sounded dubious.

"Well, yes."

"Does she take pleasure in fishing?"

Ethan cleaned the third hoof, carefully directing the point of his knife. "She does."

"And is she able to skim stones?"

"Seven on one fling."

"Thee saw it, post rider? Seven?"

"Saw it?" He released the last hoof and patted Lark's hind quarters. "I taught her. I've done nine. To give her a goal."

The boy looked toward the house. "They'll be keeping Judith at Meeting for a time yet, post rider. We should walk thy poor sweating mount to the creek to finish her grooming."

"Do you think so?" Ethan asked, one horseman to another, as he wiped the blade of his knife with his oiled handkerchief.

"Follow me," the boy directed.

The creekside sported crocus plants. A field of wild strawberries was starting to sprout. The wild strawberries were being picked when Ethan left Virginia. Traveling north was like traveling through time as well as distance. He would experience two springs this year. The thought pleased him immensely, a welcome distraction from his own nervousness.

Ethan tied a slip knot in Lark's lead rope and circled a small limb of poplar with it. There were less poplar, more laurel and white birch, since he'd crossed the border into Pennsylvania. He must ask Eli Mercer why that was. He brought two grooming brushes from his saddlebags. Hugh Lyman reached for one. Ethan smiled, handing it over.

"I'm in your debt, Hugh."

"Not after thee rode here, all the way from Virginia! Why is thy boot heel higher on the right?"

"Because that leg is shorter than the other."

"Oh." Hugh brushed the horse's flanks, thoughtfully stealing glances at Ethan's movements. "Did thy knife slip once?"

Ethan threw back his head and laughed. "No, *petit frère*."

"What does that mean?"

"Little brother."

"In what language?"

"French."

"Do Virginians speak French?"

Ethan ruffled the boy's flax-colored hair. "This one does."

Judith sat in the garden. She was supposed to be meditating on the best way to bring the factions inside together, but she pulled Ethan's latest letter from her skirt's deep pocket instead.

"Peace. Oh, Ethan, I need some peace," she whispered.

Reading the letter achieved that purpose, refreshing her mind in the process. He was coming, as maddeningly free as the letter was of details. She wanted to tell him how seeing her brethren embroiled in ever-deepening controversy overwhelmed her spirit. Could she cocoon herself and Ethan in serenity when her Meeting sparked conflict all around them?

He would doubt his welcome, she was sure of it, despite Prescott Lyman's promise that his home would accommodate—what did he call Ethan?—her "hapless sailor on his ill-timed visit." She wished her father had not accepted this man's hospitality. She wished she were anywhere but this place that daily reminded her of her blighted childhood home.

Judith heard the footsteps behind her. She returned the letter to her skirt's pocket. Trapped, Judith realized suddenly, looking upon the faces of the angry, expectant men. Trapped, among Quakers, her own people? It was worse than being caught like a fly in amber under Captain Willis's gaze, because it was so unexpected. She wished she could return to her own Philadelphia Meeting. Prescott Lyman stepped forward.

"We continue. Thee has found refreshment, Judith?"

Ruth's blue skirts wove their way among the elders' browns. "The Virginia postman waits, Father. To deliver his letters and goods."

Prescott Lyman frowned. "Tell him to leave them and go."

"But he has rode this day from Philadelphia, and his horse is very tired and I've thought to offer—"

"I would speak with this man, and see to his comfort," Judith declared, rising, leaving them all staring after her.

Ethan and Hugh watched the stone skip.

"Four . . . five . . . six only!" Hugh proclaimed. "And that was thy third try, post rider."

Ethan grunted. "It must be that Pennsylvania water is more dense, perhaps more magnetically charged than that of Virginia."

Lark whinnied.

"See?" The little boy laughed. "Thy horse knows it's only thy arm needs charging!"

"*Et tu,* Lark?" Ethan asked.

"Your horse understands French?"

"That was Latin."

Hugh shook his head, laughing. "I'll find thee a flatter stone, Friend," he promised.

Ethan stared into the still-pool part of the creek. He went down on his good knee and felt his face. Clean-shaven; he'd managed that much this morning in Philadelphia. But he was smeared with mud to such a degree he might have Judith, too, calling him "post rider." He pulled his long shirt out from his trousers and dipped its tail into the water. But wiping his face only smeared the mud further. He plunged his head into the pool and scrubbed the mud off with his hands.

Hugh laughed as a spray of water flew off Ethan's hair. Footsteps, a regiment of footsteps sounded on the flagstones behind where the boy stood. Ethan heard Judith's voice over his frantic heart's pounding.

"Packages?" she was saying. "I care not for packages, Ruth. What I'm wanting is—" She stopped in the shade of a giant oak as he turned. "—Ethan."

He rose to his feet, nodded. "Judith," he said.

Her hand reached instinctively for the oak's support.

Not the tree, Judith, he directed the thought at her. *Not the tree. Me. I can hold you now.* She stepped forward as if called. So many people around them. Was he dressed plain enough, enough like them? But he did not note their clothes or expressions except for the tall man with sunken cheeks who was standing beside Ruth.

"This man isn't Ethan Randolph," the man said, as if saying it could make it true.

Judith's eyes filled with tears. *Laugh, Judith,* Ethan thought. *Don't cry, laugh. I'm well, I'm here.*

She approached, lifting her hands gracefully from her sides, like the ladies who'd approached him to dance at his sister's house. Beautiful hands. Strong; blue veins. Why hadn't he remembered what beautiful hands Judith had? He wanted to sweep her up in his arms, but thought of his sister's warnings. He kept his eyes on Judith Mercer's hands, waiting for her lead.

"My," she whispered.

His fingers twitched with the nearness of her. "I asked Sally if I should tell you how well I've mended over the winter." That anxious, adolescent voice slipped out of him. Once out, he couldn't stop it. "She thought bringing you my newly achieved ability to walk would be a fine surprise. That is, until she saw me herself. She changed her mind on it, there at the dock, in Richmond. But it was too late then, you see, for I rode here more quickly than a letter could be posted and— You're not crying, are you, Judith?"

She shook her head. Then she finally completed her arc, took his hands in hers, and squeezed. Ethan felt drops dripping from his hair into his shirt and neckerchiefs. "I should have waited for thee here, by the creek," she whispered. "Thee can never stray far from the water."

Her voice faltered. Ethan held her hands tighter. He stroked her palms gently with his thumbs.

"It's good we are blessed by a roaring flow this year, then," her father said, rushing through the throng of men. "Welcome, our dear Washington, to Harmony Springs Meeting."

19

The Africans from the hold of the *Standard* shook him awake, instead of easing him to sleep. Ethan rose from his bed in the kitchen loft, careful not to disturb Hugh beside him. He pulled on his boots, then his trousers. He stuffed his long shirt into them. He did not bother with braces, but reached for his waistcoat; that would provide enough warmth against the early spring Pennsylvania night air, he decided. He wasn't going to Meeting. He didn't have to think about the impropriety of a woman seeing any trace of his underwear. A soft grunt escaped him. People on land wore entirely too many clothes.

He navigated his way around the cornmeal and buckwheat barrels, the wool and flax wheels. He climbed down the narrow stairs to the kitchen. Its hearth embers still glowed warm. It smelled like Martha's kitchen: sweet and yeast combatting the spit-turn grease of various meats. This had been another woman's kitchen, the children's mother, a Quaker widow who'd left Prescott Lyman her children and her farm.

Ethan stepped into the bracing chill of the March air. His ears opened to the night songs of the sheep and fowl. He frowned at the silver buttons of his vest. The Quaker men's buttons were wood or bone. He hadn't thought of enough details when he sought to dress like them. He left the buttons undone. Tonight he needn't think about his shortcomings.

Like bringing Martha's molasses candy for the children. Prescott Lyman handed the sack back to him, grimly stating that he could not let the children indulge in sweets made by slave labor. When Ethan explained that Martha was his friend, the farmer only stared him down. What did these Northerners know of his life? Ethan thought, still angry at those cold eyes, at the disappointed obedience of the widow's children.

The tattered, unearthly rags of the *Standard*'s people were impatient with his stick-assisted stride over the uneven ground. Had they been dead so long they forgot how difficult it was to navigate over land?

Ethan wondered. He felt their amusement as they floated toward the grove of fruit trees. Even ghosts laughed at him.

Ethan turned away from the farmhouse and Judith, sleeping somewhere in the confusing maze of a dwelling. Another time and place, he would have hunted her out, good guest be damned.

The stiff wall of propriety stood between them, invisible but as real as the partition that came up between the sexes once their silent Sunday Meeting broke up into men's and women's business. Their days were segregated, too, the men in the field fixing worm fences and plowing for corn, the women in the house and herb gardens.

Ethan missed Judith sitting beside his bed, their intimate meals, their time on the quilt under the warm Virginia sun. He'd kissed her there, and felt the strength of her passion. Why did they have to pretend none of this happened?

She was happy he'd come, wasn't she? He wasn't even sure of that anymore. Was he only a complication on this new life she was forging for herself and her father? Would things go the way of his worst fears?

That the big-boned farmer coveted Judith, of this he was certain. Jordan had seen it, had warned him. This thing that drove Prescott Lyman, it was not what Ethan felt for Judith—it was not love. But would Judith accept his land, his children, himself? Would Judith marry Prescott Lyman? Is that why he disliked his host so?

The ghostly Africans' images disappeared in the farm's most remote orchard. Ethan listened, but heard only the scurrying of a raccoon family, the bat wings sifting through the night. There. Above the trees, the *Standard*'s slaves left the earth itself. They drifted skyward, their rags sparkling. Ethan looked up. Bereft, landed.

Follow, they told him.

Impossible.

Follow, they insisted.

He found the tallest tree of the orchard, placed his walking stick at its base, and began his climb. From its height he would be guided by his friends as the heavens curved over him like a bowl. He would find Ursa Major's dipper spilled empty, but still pointing toward Polaris on the tail of Ursa Minor. Perhaps there, in the stars, he would find what the people wanted of him.

"Judith?" Ruth called from the bed beside her.

"Yes?"

"Thee was wonderful at Meeting."

"Not I."

"Thy Light, then. And the wisdom within. But Father says it will not keep the split within the Society of Friends from coming, the split between those who seek to remain a peculiar people, apart from a cruel and corrupt world, and those who would give public testimony, and so influence our country, and the earth."

"Where my words lead is not my concern, Ruth. My concern is only to follow, to speak as I'm directed."

"Thee needs to care for thy father now, here among us, my stepfather says. Does that make him a follower of Brother Hicks?"

"Even Brother Hicks charges us to follow our Inner Light, Ruth."

"Thee feel drawn to lead a life with us?"

"I cannot yet speak on that subject."

"When thee spoke at Meeting, I began to understand why thee is so treasured among us."

Judith thought of her treasure—the first sight of Ethan Randolph, standing there at the creek, in his plain clothes, so like the Ethan of her vision at Windover. At Meeting she'd felt his discomfort give way to serenity, even from her place on the women's side. His deep stillness, how Quaker-like it was. Her heart began again to leap with hope. She couldn't contain it in that small place beneath her bosom. If Ethan could become a convinced Friend, what was impossible? Surely the Quakers who believed in helping the slaves escape to freedom in Canada and those who formed societies to send all the black people back to Africa could find some common ground?

She'd stood and spoken out, the words direct from her heart. It was her first testimony since she'd returned. She'd spoken of the past days of trials and persecution. Another such time was upon them. They must face outward, stand firm in an unjust world, without losing the quiet tone of their Inner Light. They must take the best parts of both philosophies, and live them.

"Judith? Will Friend Ethan remain among us?"

"I couldn't say, Ruth."

"I know he is worldly, and owns slaves. But he's not like other visitors at Meeting from the outside, who suffer it or snicker behind their hands at us. Ethan dresses plain and visits with Hugh and me at school and helps thy father mix his remedies."

"He is a good guest."

"I think thee and Father are too hard on him!"

"Too hard?"

"I think there is great turmoil in his heart."

"Has he spoken to thee of—?"

"No. These are my own musings."

"Sleep now, Ruth."

Judith breathed out. Why did Ruth, why did most of the Quakers, treat her as if she was a sage with answers to all their questions? Was she only noticing it now, twenty years since she first spoke out as a minister at Meeting? Now that she desperately wanted to be recognized not for her wisdom but for her humanity?

Judith couldn't wait until the girl was soundly sleeping. Tonight she would add to the guide lights. Ethan was a good guest, she thought ruefully, but she herself was not. Prescott Lyman knew nothing of the planned exodus, because of his view on public testimony, and his opposition to breaking the laws of men. But she did. The Quakers who had planned it had come to her, as if she could give them permission to help the runaways. And she had given the permission, had agreed to add hers to the lights pointing north. She didn't ask Prescott Lyman for his land as beacon site. She would confess her part if he found out. But she must follow her own Light. She rose from her bed.

"Where is thee going, Judith?"

"To the privy."

"It's cold. The chamberpot is here beside us."

"It is not so cold."

"Take thy shawl."

"I will, little mother," Judith said, kissing the girl's cheek.

"I do wish to be a mother, Judith! Do you think it's wrong?"

"No. It's a desire I've had since I watched my own mother nurse the young ones."

"Be our mother, Judith. I will share my babies with thee."

Judith left her shawl hanging on its peg beside the front door as she rushed outside. She ran along the flagstone walk. Was she too late? Would she fail to heed the slave people of the *Standard*'s directive to remember their descendants' flight toward freedom?

Judith was breathing hard when she reached the orchard. Something gold shone, even in the quarter moon's light, from its place propped against the trunk of the old apple tree. She brought her tin lantern closer. It was Ethan's walking stick. A white-sleeved hand sprang down before her eyes.

"Come climbing, Judith."

She looked up and saw Ethan's face, like a dark angel's among the budding leaves. She laughed. "I don't know how, love."

The endearment slipped out, like a Virginia memory.

"Of course you know," Ethan said impatiently.

"I never climbed trees."

"Why not? Sally did."

"Thy sister is extraordinary."

She felt his frown. "Kilt up your skirts, like when you feed the ducks. I'll keep you steady, I promise."

"Ethan—"

"No promises, of course. I'm sorry. Come up, Judith. The sight will be worth it."

"Sight?"

"View of the stars! The county around!"

The lights, Judith realized. This was her chance to see the lights. To add her own. And to put Ethan into the same position of danger she'd chosen for herself. But what if he were sent here, tonight, by God? He'd been sent before. He'd had visions, had known the slaves in the *Standard*'s hold, too. Still, she hesitated.

"Judith," he cajoled, "where is my brave shipboard companion?"

She tucked her nightgown's hem into her high-waisted sash.

"There, good," Ethan approved as he pulled her up into the tree. It smelled faintly of its coming apple blossoms. He was coatless. She'd seen him coatless many times, of course. But not here, and not since his outward appearance had changed so profoundly. Judith took hold of his rounded arm muscles as he helped her climb higher. She trusted those arms; they were still the strongest part of him.

They faced each other in the cleft of the tree's trunk. She felt the bark's texture through her slippers as she breathed Ethan's scent—leather, iron, seed corn—through the fine, soft cotton of his shirt. Quaker men wore linen or linsey-woolsey shirts, not expensive slave-labor cotton. She would never tell him, he was trying so hard to honor them. None but Hugh would see his shirt, up in their kitchen-loft sleeping quarters. Hugh and herself, now.

"What have you brought?" he asked.

"My lantern."

"Let me take it. We'll add your light to those of the heavens."

He thought the lantern was a thing of fancy. Good.

"Are you cold, Judith?"

"A little."

At first she feared he'd send her down to the ground again. But he found another way to warm her. He yanked off his waistcoat and dressed her in it, down to the last silver button. It felt like an embrace, and her arms were still free, unhampered by the constraints of a shawl. A most useful garment. Why didn't women wear them?

Judith stared at the outline of Ethan's chest through his shirt. It was not like his brothers', or what his father's broadness was in the dining-room portrait at Windover. It was lean and sleek, emanating sinewy strength. It belonged to a wildcat who dwelled in these Pennsylvania trees before the Quaker farmers came.

"Come higher," he urged, suddenly disappearing among the branches with her lantern.

Judith looked down at her bare legs, exposed below her knees. The night air swept through her gown's skirt. It felt delicious. She could do this. She could climb higher. Wiping her sweating palms against the vest, she followed his footfalls.

In the top branches, Ethan turned, smiled. "Here we are again, like on the spring night we met. Fellow night owls."

"On the quarterdeck," she finished, breathless, sitting back on a curving limb.

"Not so low as the quarterdeck now," Ethan said. "Look at the stars—they're all around, without horizon."

She smiled. "Where does that place us?"

"Watch!"

His eyes were too bright, his imagination had flared too hot, had invaded too far into what was real, what was safe. Judith reached for him, but he scrambled farther out on the limb.

"Ethan, don't—"

"Shhh."

He stood slowly. He walked out on a branch not wide enough for both his feet. He had to place one behind the other, like an acrobat she'd chanced to see in a London street fair once. He kept his weaker right behind the left. The branch quivered under his weight. Judith sensed his surprise. He did not yet see himself as he was, a grown man, full of grace and power. Not small, but compacted in his sleek cat's frame. Not crippled, but miraculously mended. Not ugly, but almost unbearably beautiful.

Judith tried to send him her vision of him, to make him understand the danger, to bring him back. But he only walked out more boldly. His shirt flared. She saw his initials embroidered on the hem.

Ethan swung her lantern in a graceful arc, adding it to the ones that shone from neighboring Quaker farms, pointing north. He was doing exactly what she'd been asked to do at the appointed hour. But he was not looking at the guiding pattern below, but at other lights. The ones that studded the blue-black sky.

"Fayette!" he called, laughing, into the night full of stars. "*Regardez!* Now I am master of the mizzenmast!"

He will fall now, Judith thought, through the new green branches, past the old limbs, to the cold ground. The way Fayette had fallen.

The lantern slipped from his hand. She heard the tin facing crushed to the ground below, its light extinguished.

Ethan turned, stared at her, the mirth in his eyes weighted with sorrow. "I miss him, Judith," he said, as if admitting a terrible secret.

"So do I," she whispered, offering her hand.

He took it. His was cool, dry, with a faint tingle about it. She pressed it to her cheek, her neck, then lower, against her heart. It warmed there, at last. He kissed her temple.

"Would you care to tell me who we were signaling and for what purpose, Judith Mercer?"

Judith's mouth closed in a firm line. "No."

He would not know everything, this bright-minded man-child with too much pride, she decided.

He shrugged indifferently. Judith followed him down from the tree, though less nimbly, so that when she reached the soft moss around the tree's roots, he was gone. She called out his name, whipped by her anger.

She heard his walking stick sifting over the spring ground to locate her lantern. Beside her again, he put the battered tin into her hands. She stared at it.

"It's not so bad. I can hammer it back," he offered, "first thing, at morning's light."

"This was not the cause of my distress."

"No?" His voice was curious, teasing.

"No. I only direct it at the lantern, at you and your acrobatics. My distress is with myself tonight. I am caught in a cleft place, Ethan. Friends are not supposed to engage in subterfuge—anything that could not bear the light of day."

"Well, it's a good thing the fall of night is upon us, yes?"

"I ask thy forgiveness, Ethan Randolph."

"Forgiveness? Did we do something wrong?"

"No! Not wrong! I—apologize for my anger."

Another of his sweet, perplexed looks.

"And my ungovernable temper!"

He grinned. "I don't think it's yet spent itself, *ma chère*."

He was no Quaker convert. The adventurer, Prescott Lyman had called him. The third son of aristocratic Virginia planters is often the adventurer. His family was indulging him in his Quaker adventure. She must have been mad to entertain the notion of telling him what he'd done from the top of the tree. He'd help form the string of guiding lights of an exodus of runaway slaves, perhaps from one of his insufferable brothers' plantations. What would he have thought of that?

Judith tucked the lantern under her arm and walked blindly in the direction of the house. She heard his strong, three-step gait stumble. By the time she'd turned, he was directly behind her.

"Thee is so different now, Ethan," slipped out.

His laughing countenance disappeared. "Why? Because I can walk? Because I can keep up with you? Almost," he amended.

"No."

"Did you like me better helpless, Judith?"

Before she could answer, Judith felt the child's scream send a wave of shock through them both.

20

Throwing his walking stick beside the kitchen's back stairs, Ethan grabbed the rafters, propelling himself to the loft. Judith followed, praying the child had had a nightmare, but knowing he had not.

Blood spurted from Hugh's nose and chin as his arms swung out wildly. A scurrying, there in the dark, shifting shadow. "Ethan!" the boy cried out. "Don't let it at Judith!"

The rat was poised beside Judith's skirts. It leaped. Ethan reached to his boot top, threw. His knife entered the rat's belly in midair. The creature thudded against the buckwheat barrel, then fell lifeless to the floorboards.

She stared at it in stunned silence.

"Did thee see, Judith?" Hugh proclaimed. "Did thee see that?"

The rat's death throes had been so brief that it was already still, under the straight-blade dagger. She felt the cold sweat run down her back. Ethan's knife became the weapon that had lodged in her mother twenty years ago. Judith fought the purple spots bursting before her eyes.

Ethan caught her arm, pulled her close. "It's over," he told her.

"Yes," she answered, sounding vague, even to herself.

"We must help Hugh now, Judith."

She nodded.

He pressed his warm lips against her cold ones. Better. He drew out a folded handkerchief from his waistcoat, the one now buttoned up over her nightgown. Warm. Would she die without his warmth? Judith wondered, still caught in the horror of that night. His eyes were steady, vigilant. She needed them. He took her shaking hand and led her to the boy in the bed.

"Head back, Hugh," he instructed gently, staunching the blood flowing from the boy's nose.

"Is the rat all dead?" Hugh asked.

"All dead."

"Could I see him all dead? With thy fine knife stuck in him?"

"Later." Ethan turned to Judith. "I'll help him downstairs. Fetch your father," he instructed.

Judith reached the stairs as Ethan's strong arms lifted the boy from his blood-spattered sheets.

"Why did you kiss our Judith, Ethan?" she heard Hugh ask.

"Because she needed kissing. Head back."

The night air finally cleared Judith's mind. *Duty.* Not these thoughts of her mother's wounds, testimony to Esther Mercer's efforts to save the little ones. *Duty.* To Hugh, not the little ones, so still, asking no questions about kissing. Judith's lungs were bursting when she returned, her father close behind.

Hugh sat on the kitchen table by a bright lamp, regaling his sister and stepfather with the story of his rescue. Prescott, his hands caught behind his back in a white-knuckled grip, watched as Ruth daubed Ethan's water-soaked handkerchief on the boy's wounds.

Judith realized that neither Ethan nor she had thought to call Prescott Lyman; only Eli and his remedies. As if they were Hugh's family, not he. It was a vanity. It was presumptuous, prideful. Where was Ethan?

She smiled at the little boy. "Well, my valiant protector looks sprightly," she observed.

"Keeping still has been his greatest trial," Ruth said, peeved.

Ethan descended the back stairs with the bloodied sheets and a brown paper package, his eyes focused on its contents with a grim, set look. Prescott Lyman had shoved him away from Hugh's care, Judith thought, had given him cleaning duty.

"Ethan says Monsieur Fayette taught him how to throw a knife when he was on the high seas!" Hugh announced. "But he says ship rats were not so big!"

Eli smiled. "Indeed?" He handed a small medicinal envelope to his attending sister. "If thou will place a mustard plaster, Ruth, Judith and I must visit with our rat catcher and the remains."

Judith followed her father to the hearth. Ethan opened the paper wider to reveal the brown rat. It had small ears and coarse fur. Ethan turned the animal with the blade of his gleaming knife, then, without a word of warning, neatly eviscerated it from its neck, through the wound in its belly, to the base of its tail. He used the knife's blade to spread the skin aside.

"Healthy?" he asked her father.

Eli inspected. "Appears so, son."

A smile relieved some of the worry from Ethan's features. "But why would a fat, healthy rat attack Hugh like that, Eli?"

"He could smell, but not get into the stored provisions, perhaps."

Behind them, Hugh cleared his throat. "Stay still," his sister insisted.

"I cannot." He pushed her hand away. "I must tell you all. Help me, Judith."

Judith approached. For the first time since his ordeal began, the boy was crying. She took his hand. "What is it, Hugh?"

He stared at their clasped hands. "I found the molasses candy which Ruth and I were forbidden to eat. In thy saddlebags, under our bed, Ethan," he said in a small, repentant voice. "I ate two pieces while thee was gone out tonight. The rat smelled it on me, I'm sure. Do not worry. He was not rabid. I am heartily sorry, Ethan, Father."

Ethan laughed out his relief. "The candy. Yes, drawn to the candy. He must have thought he'd found a great molasses swamp in you!" He caught up Judith's free hand and pressed it to his cheek. She opened her fingers, glided them down the plane of his face.

Prescott Lyman frowned. "There are ladies present," he said. "Perhaps thee would clothe thyself now, Friend?"

Ethan looked down at his flowing shirt, opened nearly to his breastbone. His relieved elation turn into chagrin. He released her, turned, and mounted the stairs.

"He tries so hard to honor us, Prescott." Eli voiced the words in Judith's angry heart in a kinder tone than she could have used.

Their host lifted Ethan's bloodied knife from the hearth. "Friends, this is not for hunting or butchering. This is a weapon."

"Used with care, I'm sure," her father countered.

Prescott Lyman's eyes returned to the rat. "And precision. How well do you know this man, Judith Mercer?" he demanded. "Must I be concerned about placing him in the same sleeping space as my son?"

Judith felt her anger. "The very notion of thy concern is unwarranted."

Her father placed his hand on her arm. "I am grateful our young Washington intervened between that sweet-loving rodent and the possibility of more suffering for Hugh."

Their host granted them a smile that reminded Judith of many he'd bestowed on Ethan. *He thinks my father indulges me,* she realized. *In what—my Virginia adventure?*

"Eli, thou calls Ethan Randolph by a name he used aboard ship a year ago. That man must bear little resemblance to this one."

"His essence remains. Fired by his suffering, informed by his past, now that his veil of memory has lifted."

Judith watched the hostility in Prescott Lyman. He had been kind to them. Perhaps too kind, between the cabin he'd had built for Eli and his solicitude in following her every household suggestion. It had pleased her, this home and its lovely children, in her own country. But it had put her in mind of her own farm, before that night. She had accepted too much, she realized.

Ethan descended the back stairs, dressed in a coat she hadn't seen before, of dark blue wool. Plain, but not Quaker-like. A double cravat and a vest of silk-brocaded silver stripes covered every trace of linens underneath, though the scent of starch told her he'd changed his shirt also. He was hatless, his long hair combed back from the peak at his brow. He said nothing, but wrapped the rat's body in its brown paper and headed for the door.

Hugh left his sister's side and tugged at his arm. "Ethan? Where does thee go?"

"To bury the rat, Hugh."

"Will others come to our bed, to the loft?"

The dark petulance left Ethan's face as he crouched beside the boy. "Not if Grayneck beds down with us. She'll keep the rats away."

"But Grayneck likes the kitchen."

"Then we must convince her that our quarters are better."

"How?"

The shared-secret smile. For Hugh, this time, Judith thought, with a stab of envy. "How?" Ethan echoed the boy. "Why, with the benefits that come with changing her mind."

"What are they? When shall we do this?"

Ethan touched the cheek beside the plastered chin.

"Tomorrow," he promised.

"After school?"

"Yes."

Ethan stood. Ruth Lyman stopped him again before he reached the door. "I fear thy fine handkerchief may be ruined, Friend Ethan."

Judith heard Hugh's exasperated sigh. But Ethan remained patient, though the brown paper sagged under its bloody burden. "I have many more," he assured the girl. "My mother thinks a proper gentleman must always have three or four on his person. So she packed a dozen for me." Ethan rolled his eyes in Hugh's direction.

Hugh laughed. "Is thy mother kind and beautiful, Ethan? Like Judith?" he asked.

"Yes."

"I wish our Judith was my mother."

"I know, Hugh," Ethan whispered, before hastening through the doorway and into the night.

Judith felt misery descend on her shoulders. Ethan, her Ethan, after ten years on the open sea, had understood what she, on her own home ground, had not. God surely had a sense of humor akin to Fayette's. Her father took her hand, held it in his comforting warmth. Why did she not see the growing expectations of these dear children? Judith understood burdens. How could a family that had offered to relieve so many succeed in making her feel so weighted?

"Judith, Eli," Prescott Lyman proclaimed suddenly, pulling her out of her thoughts. "I have the answer!"

"Answer, Friend Prescott?"

Prescott Lyman shook as if palsied. "I am being called upon by these children that God put under my care. I am humbled by their wisdom. It brings no anger, no resentment. Praise God, it makes me as happy as a child!" A chortled giggle escaped him. "Blessed moment!"

Judith linked arms with her father before he offered the farmer a hand.

"Speak thy heart, Friend," Eli said quietly.

"I have not welcomed this man who has brought joy and protection to my household and family!" he proclaimed, looking at the door. "Should I do it now? Eli, Judith?"

Judith stepped back, she was so startled by the change in Prescott's usual slow and deliberate demeanor. Even Hugh and Ruth clung to each other.

Prescott Lyman broke from her father's grasp, then turned. He took Judith's hands, the way Ethan had done, when first he came. The energy she'd felt then now reversed itself. She was so weakened she could barely stand.

"Judith, will thee place my poor nipped chick back under his covers?"

"Yes, of course," she breathed out.

He released her. "I shall do as I am bid by my Inner Light. I shall return his weapon, and help our new chick recover his wounded dignity this night! I shall follow my heart!"

"The ground is hard still."

Ethan recognized the voice. He kept his eyes on his task. "Yes."

"Not like in Virginia."

Ethan grunted, hoping that would pass as a response. He wished Prescott Lyman would leave him to complete the task alone.

"Thee has chosen the wrong instrument, Friend. I'll break the earth with my spade. Then thy work will not be so difficult."

Ethan looked up, saw the spade at the ready in the man's hands. He threw Eli's gardening tool down. "I can't even dig a hole properly?" he muttered.

"Ethan, Ethan, where could thee have learned how? The Atlantic? On a plantation where a gentleman never soils his hands with labor?"

Prescott Lyman's tone was patient, as Eli's was when they worked with the plants and seedlings. Still, he did not trust it. Ethan picked up his shovel. "I'm sorry, sir. No, not 'sir,' but Friend."

"I have not thanked thee for bringing thy youth and life to my too-sober household."

"Life?"

"I've had a revelation, a vision. Has Judith instructed thee in this? Does thee know the nature of revelations?"

"Yes."

"I must follow mine. I've let my own distrust interfere with welcoming thee with the full measure of my heart. I've poisoned myself to thee, Ethan, because of the love I hold for her."

Ethan put his back into his task of hauling away the dirt Prescott Lyman was breaking into clumps. He didn't want to speak to the Quaker farmer about Judith. Not while in his best suit of clothes, the Virginia planter's spoiled third son, digging a grave for a dead rat.

Prescott Lyman went on. "Tonight I finally saw in her eyes what I had feared. She has chosen thee."

Hole. Deep enough? Rat, get the rat in the hole. Ethan did so without ceremony. Blood smeared his palm. Wary. Be wary of this man.

"Ethan, does thee understand my meaning?"

"I don't know."

"Come now, we are both grown men. Thy intentions toward her are honorable, of course?"

"Yes. Yes, of course."

"And thy presence here, thy plain clothes, thy attendance at First and Fifth Day Meetings, they proclaim thy interest in our way of life. Could thee embrace our ways, Ethan Randolph?"

It was none of this man's business, Ethan thought angrily, what he could or couldn't do. He shoved dirt in the hole.

"Do not distress thyself over thy conflicted heart. There is time. Judith has told us of thy difficulties with accepting thy family's decadence now that our ways have touched thy life."

Decadence? Had Judith called his family decadent?

"She needs time as well, Ethan. Does thee understand?"

"Time?"

"I do not mean to offend, but at what age did thy mother marry?"

"My mother? She was fourteen."

"Fourteen. Yes. Common in Southern planter families. We do not follow such customs here, where we seek helpmeets, not . . ."

Ethan's gaze met his. "Not what?"

The man's open mouth closed. Missing teeth. In the back. Some of the holders' teeth were like that on board the *Standard*. Food deficiencies. Past hardship. His would be that way, if it weren't for the limes, for Fayette's care. Who was this man?

"What is it you call my mother, sir?" he demanded now.

"I do not seek to judge thy family. Only to explain mine. Understand that."

What Ethan did not understand was this sudden jerk in the conversation. What did his mother's early marriage have to do with him? He was not a child. Neither was Judith.

"Thee is so young, so ardent, impatient. And not yet convinced. We do not take converts lightly, Ethan Randolph. Convinced Quaker are the strongest of us all. I am one of them. Brought to Meeting by my wife, the mother of Ruth and Hugh, when my own heart was blackened."

"Blackened?"

"As black as the countenance of thy father's bondsmen. But my dear wife, she was a woman of Light, like Judith. She helped me find another way. Thou must study well, with us, in our family, to be as strong as I am."

Ethan wished to be nothing like this man towering his farmer's strength over him. "I follow my Light. I have my own. Judith says I do."

Prescott Lyman's brow descended with impatience. "Thee will need it in the years ahead." he proclaimed. "Thee must protect her!"

Ethan's eyes met those of the Quaker's. Fierce eyes.

"I will protect her," he said quietly.

"Forgive me." The older man rubbed at his temples. Strong fingers, that left strange purple blotches there. "She has become very dear to me. Thee is not the man I would have chosen for her. But I will accept her choice, if thee becomes one of us."

They finished filling in the hole together, and pounded down the small mound of dirt. Then Prescott Lyman took Ethan's shoulder. It was not something he did often, touch anyone, Ethan surmised. "I invite thee into my household, Ethan Randolph, as my own treasured son."

Ethan stared at his host. He had a father. An imperfect one, one he'd often wished were not his relation at all, but Ethan wanted no part of this man. "That's very generous of you," he finally said, resorting to Fayette's insistence on politeness.

"It may appear so. But it's selfish. Judith takes such delight in thee. I wish to see that delight every day, secure under my own roof. What better way to achieve it than to bestow three instead of two children as my marriage gifts!"

"Children, marriage?"

"Come, come! Thee must know of our plans! Of her father already secure in his own home on my property? I understand Judith, Ethan. I know what kind of marriage to make with her. I respect and will abide by her disinterest in the life of the body. But she was born to be a mother. And what her celibate nature has not provided, I can. I will give her three children, two of whom will give her more infants to fill her arms, in due time, will they not?"

"What?"

"Thee may begin thy courting tomorrow. And may ask my daughter to marry on the day she turns sixteen—less than two years away. Do not look so defeated. It is not such a long time! In the meantime live here, learn our ways, become convinced. Wean thyself of that unhappy life that has scarred thy unfortunate youth."

Prescott Lyman smiled. He was not used to smiling, Ethan thought. It looked strange.

"There," Prescott exhorted anew. "We have buried all the evil between us, have we not? As thy past life will be buried through thy diligence, thy hard work among us. There will be perfection in this house, however corrupt the outside world rages around us. See it! See it with me, son!"

The high moon made a halo of light appear around Prescott Lyman's wiry gray strands of hair. Ethan couldn't find his voice, in any language.

The farmer's unnatural smile finally faded. "I have been riding on the happiness of my own Light, I fear. Thee needs not give me thy thoughts on this now, of course. Think on it. Rest well with thy doting little brother tucked under thy protective arm."

21

Ethan threw himself into solitary fence-mending as if his life de-pended on keeping cranky geese penned. At noon dinner he took his place at the long table with the hired men. Judith felt his head one of the times she glided by the table with her pitcher. A mother's gesture. He wanted to tell her what he thought of her mother's gestures, but bolted from the table to avoid the temptation. Stares at his back. He didn't care. He was tired of being polite.

When he met Hugh after the boy's schooling, he felt the day's tensions finally easing. Hugh stared up at his horse.

"Thee has never brought Lark before, Ethan."

"Special service to the wounded."

Hugh's fingers hovered at his scabbed chin. "It made for a good story today—the rat, thy knife, that throw."

"I'm happy to amuse your friends," Ethan said dryly, offering a hand to haul the boy onto the saddle. He slipped up easily, like Betsy. When did boys and girls begin to change, separate? Ethan wondered. And why?

"Where are we going?" Hugh asked.

"Courting."

"Courting? Courting who?"

"Grayneck."

"But she's up at the house."

"We'll be bringing her a present."

"Oh." He eyed the bucket swinging from the saddle. "We're going fishing!"

"You're a bright-minded boy, Hugh."

"Thee has hooks?"

"Don't need them."

"Chubs and suckers take the hook, Ethan."

"Grayneck has more delicate tastes, I think."

"For what?"

"Minnows."

"Minnows? They're so small. How are we going to catch minnows?"

"With handkerchiefs."

Ethan loved the look of incredulity that rendered the boy speechless. Short journey completed, Hugh tied his strapped books to the saddle. He ran ahead of Ethan to the mossy banks of the creek.

Ethan dismounted, watching Hugh's flying run. He'd run like that, as a boy. *Stop it,* he told the self-pity threatening to join the host of ugly thoughts plaguing his mind today. He could still follow energetic boys to fishing holes, walk screaming babies quiet.

"Over here!" Hugh called, wading into the water. "They're scooping out their nests!"

Ethan showed Hugh how to lay their handkerchiefs on the bottom, weighting the edges with little stones. The minnows formed a school over them. Ethan quickly gathered one catch up in his handkerchief net and emptied it into the bucket.

"How did thee learn that?" the boy asked as the bucket's water swarmed with silvery wisps.

"From Aubrey. We used to court the house cats. So that they would protect baby cradles from invasion by field mice and snakes."

"At Windover? But where were the mothers?"

"Serving in the big house. Or the fields. Aubrey's mama Martha had charge of all the babies, there at the cookhouse. But sometimes she was called away, too. The babies needed the cats on guard. We kept them feasting on minnows, so they'd take pride in their work. It will be the same with Grayneck. She'll protect us, if we can win her up to our quarters with these."

They secured the bucket and mounted Lark.

"Martha—she's the one who gave Judith the book of instructions on how to make good things to eat?"

"That's right."

"She's wife to Aaron, who made thy boots. And mother of Elwood, who tends crops and Aubrey who died, and the smithy who made thy knife . . ." He thought a moment, "Micah."

"And Phoebe, a born schoolmistress, and Tempest, who dances like the storm she was named for, and Milly, who already makes bell fritters as good as her mama's."

"Elwood, Aubrey, Micah. Phoebe, Tempest, Milly," he recited.

"Very good, Hugh. You're getting to know my family."

"Thy family? But they are Negro slaves."

"True enough."

"And thee, their master?"

"No. Only the son of their master. I was far away when I was supposed to be learning about masters and slaves, so I remain ignorant. But I think I would have been a very poor student even so."

"Friends are taught that no one is a slave."

"We share that conviction, Hugh."

"Will thee become a Friend, Ethan? So that we can be brothers?"

The reins suddenly felt heavy in Ethan's hands. He was Judith's lover in Virginia. Must he become her son here in Pennsylvania? Would she ask that of him? Could he honor the request? He must. Didn't Fayette charge him to love her in the form she chose?

He eased the boy down from the saddle. "We should scout up Grayneck now," he said, his voice hoarse.

Hugh looked up at him with guileless eyes. "Thy friends at Windover—thee does not make them sound like Negro people at all."

"What should Negro people sound like?"

"I'm not sure. But they wouldn't be able to teach a white person about cooking or fishing with handkerchiefs."

"Why not?"

"They wallow in ignorance and despair, Father says. It was a terrible sin to bring them here, and we must work to send them all back to Africa."

"Back to Africa?"

"Yes. Father belongs to a society that would buy them a country in Africa and send them back to it."

"But they're Americans!" Ethan spoke his astonishment. "We might as well send ourselves back to England and Scotland and Ireland and France and Germany and—"

Judith stood in the back doorway and called their names. Her voice scrambled all but sweet, tormented thoughts from Ethan's mind. He handed the bucket to Hugh.

"Ask her if she can spare some custard cups. I'll rub down Lark, then fetch the cat."

"Stay, Ethan. Look, our Judith waits for us. Perhaps she needs kissing again."

Ethan pulled the horse in the opposite direction.

But there was no escaping her once he entered the kitchen with Grayneck under his arm. Her floury fingers were on Hugh's shoulders. Baking day, Ethan remembered. Three of the neighbor women were around the hearth, too, besides Ruth, whom he wished to see even less than Judith. The Quaker women were instructing them both, he realized now, in housewifery. Wisps of Judith's hair curled at her temples.

"Ethan," she greeted him softly, "a scarf might prove—"

More mothering. He frowned. "I'm inside now."

One of her hands left Hugh's shoulder and rested at her hip. His gruffness was annoying her. Good. "Perhaps thee would explain thy need for these custard cups?"

Ethan snatched them from her hands. "To catch the cat," he began, putting a cup at her feet as he released Grayneck. Brown calfskin slippers, floured too. How had she managed to flour her slippers? The tip of one skimmed the other. Like a kiss.

"Who'll chase the rats," he continued as Hugh poured a portion of their minnows into the cup. Ethan climbed several stairway steps, setting down the second cup midway. "Who roam in the loft," He set down the last cup beside the loft's bed. "Where Hugh sleeps," he finished his variation of a verse he'd learned as a child. Being Quakers, they hadn't heard the verse, and so thought him more clever than he was. The women hid smiles behind their hands. Except for Ruth, whose smile was open, admiring, infatuated. Why had he not seen *that* before?

Grayneck, full now, ignored their last offering and climbed into Ethan's arms instead, licking at his fish-scented fingers. The women giggled softly, there, around the curve of the stairway. How beautiful women were, Ethan thought. How had he lived without them so long?

Judith left their company. She knelt beside his bags, drawing out one of his shirts. She swirled it in a graceful oval on the floor. Then she eased Grayneck from Ethan's arms and nested her in the fine cotton folds. Her hand reached to Ethan's shoulder. "Come down. Taste some pie," she urged. She used him for balance as she stood. A simple gesture, welcomed because it acknowledged his new strength. But something else went through her fingertips as she touched him. A scent.

Hugh followed the women down the stairs. Ethan stayed there on the floor, listening to their fading footsteps, their sprightly tones. He shook his head, swearing softly in his second language. Lemons, he finally realized—the source of his arousal. Judith wore her shipboard scent there in her fingers. She smelled of lemons.

* * *

Judith cleared the stray hair from her forehead with the back of her hand as Ethan appeared, a streak of brown and forest green before the side Dutch door slammed.

"What humor has gotten hold of that man today?" she wondered aloud. A scarf hung from a peg by the door. She took it up, looked back at the women. "He doesn't understand the cold we get here still," she said, "once the sun goes down."

They shook their heads in sympathy, as if his visit was a burden on her. She didn't care. She didn't care about anything except seizing this chance to be alone with him.

How could he move so fast, this man who couldn't run, who was not using the stick as he'd promised his mother? She passed the herb garden and the henhouse, following his trodden grass path. There. He stood by a willow. Judith called his name.

His back stiffened before he entered the sweeping curtain of the willow's spring shoots. He stayed very still there. What was this game? She ducked into his confine and held out the scarf. He turned before it could touch his back.

"Ethan, thee must—"

"*Zut alors,* woman! I am not cold!"

She believed him. He looked fevered. But she resisted the urge to touch his forehead, his eyes were so fierce.

A breeze stirred the willow branches so three tendrils blew softly across her cheek. Delicate, exquisite, she thought, closing her eyes. It gave her the tranquility she needed to speak her heart.

"Ethan, what disturbs thee today?"

His fine brows slanted, he swallowed. Judith waited.

"The lemons," he said, finally.

"Lemons?"

"No, not the lemons, of course not the lemons. It's you. And the lemons. With the lemons. By way of the lemons." He growled, sighed, looked away.

She'd followed Martha's recipe for the lemon custard pie. To please him. To give him a taste of his home. Was that so terrible, trying to please this independent Virginian with laughing eyes and winning ways who was daily slipping out of her hands, away from her ministering gestures that he had accepted so freely aboard ship and in Virginia?

"Judith," he tried again. "I have failed."

"Failed? How?"

"I cannot do this."

"What?"

Judith felt a dread circle her heart. He was about to tell her of changed circumstances, his family's discouragement, their differences. He was about to break her heart. Why did he look as if his own heart was breaking? She must lead him. *Thy life's purpose, Judith. Lead.*

She smiled. "Come now. Is it so terrible, what thou must tell me? I climbed your tree last night, Captain of the Mizzenmast," she reminded him.

"I frightened you, up there. I'm sorry."

"Done." She bowed her head. Were they about to be undone? She strangled the scarf between her hands. "Tell me. Please," she whispered, "tell me now. I am not as strong as I look."

He took a long breath. "I am not like you. I am not a Quaker. I don't talk to God."

"Don't talk to God, Ethan. Talk to me."

"I cannot return your love in any form you desire. I have failed him. I have failed Fayette, because I cannot . . . *Je regrette, mais*—"

"Ethan!" she shouted. "In English!"

"I cannot be your child, Judith."

She tilted her head. "What?"

"What?" he echoed. "Was that not English?"

"What does thee mean, impossible man!"

"Last night, Prescott Lyman gave me permission to court Ruth."

"You . . . desire Ruth?"

"No! But if you marry him, I will then become your son, he says, through the marriage, and so be in his family. But I have a mother already, Judith. I have too many mothers!"

"Too many . . ."

"My desire is to be your husband!"

"My. Oh, my."

"Don't start with your 'mys' like Sally!" he railed. "I tried to follow her advice—no touch, no word, no kisses. Follow, follow, honor my hosts. Find out what it means, marriage to me, in your religion. But I can't even get to being seen as your suitor. *Sacre-bleu,* Judith, how much can a man endure?"

She laughed out her astonishment. He closed in. Furious, she realized, as he snatched the scarf from her hands. He roped her close with it before stopping her mouth with his own. It was an assault, it was rude. She didn't care. She drank his deep, probing kiss, wishing she'd peeled the lemons days before, if he liked the scent so well.

He stopped abruptly. "Judith, are you not angry?"

She shook her head, breathless.

"You were not laughing at me?"

"No! At myself, the great reader of hearts. I misread thine, in thinking thee came to Pennsylvania to return my pirated soul."

"Return? Do you think me a witless fool, *madame*?" One hand anchored at her waist, her real one, not the artificially high one of her gown and apron. "Judith. Listen to me. I cannot offer what this farmer has. But Jordan Foster has agreed to take me on. Choose me and you choose a physician's apprentice. We will have small rooms in Jordan's home. But with a garden, for your father."

"My father?" she whispered, her love flowering another blossom.

"Of course your father, our family." He leaned down, kissed the curve of her face. "Judith, what little I have will be yours. And I will love you all my life, whether you'll have me or no."

He was warm. Much too warm for his coat. He might sicken, wearing it. Judith lifted it off his shoulders. It fell to the ground at their feet, the scarf following, unwhirling like a dance from his hands. Did this man do anything without grace?

"I don't understand how Prescott Lyman sees you," he whispered against the strands of hair that had escaped her cap. "But I desire you whole, my sweet, strong Judith, I delight in you whole."

She drank in his leather and cinnamon and minnow scent, before he lifted her there, against the willow's trunk. Her feet dangled, suspended. He was not the tallest of men, but he was that tall, her Ethan. That strong.

He teased her with tiny kisses at her ear, then down her neckline. "If you will have me, I will take you down," he confided between them. "The first time we join our bodies will be like this, within the sound of water. And the world around will turn red and bursting with delight. This I promise you, Judith Mercer."

Judith felt invaded by the rush of his words. As his fingers gently danced down her spine, curved out along her breech, she welcomed him closer, closer even than he'd been on the quilt at Windover. She loved the glide of his tongue, the low snarl of his desire. She called his name softly against the head of dark waves pressed to her pounding heart. Something burst inside her with the sound. Burst open. Yes, she knew that feeling. She stroked the mane back from his brow, feeling satiated, languid. Sweet ear. She must have a taste. Her tongue swiped the lobe. "Mmmm. Honeysuckle," she remembered that part of the taste of him, from the quilt at Windover. He must have been working among the honeysuckle shoots. She tasted again.

He growled. "*Dieu,* Judith, don't do that."

"It pleases thee not?"

"It pleases me too much."

"I wish to please thee too much."

There. Again it started. His palms at her hips, this time, circling. She parted her legs and felt his heat glide over her skirts and contend with sweet insistence against her thigh. Once, twice. Surges of his young, vital desire, leaving her wet, wanting the further intimacy these things he was doing promised. He muttered in garbled French. Beautiful, as beautiful as endearments, were his blasphemies.

He released her with a gentle, exquisite kiss, and set her on the ground again. As her feet landed, he braced his elbows against the willow's bark. He forced his body back, though it remained hovering close as he found his voice.

"You'll . . . consider marrying me, then?" he asked.

She nodded, laughing, hiding her face in his chest. "I will."

His thumb traced her hairline. "Then I must speak with your father." He kissed her. "Today." Deeper. "Now." He picked up his coat, took a step away, then threw the garment over his arm, and crushed her against the tree again, assailing her already swollen lips with fresh kisses.

He growled with mock menace before he kissed into the palm of her hand. "Finish your pies," he said. "But no more lemons until the wedding, yes, Judith?"

With the last rustle of his footsteps, Judith felt herself glide along the willow's trunk to the ground. She touched her tender bottom lip, felt the slight, glowing rash his afternoon beard had made along her neck. And down farther. My.

Ethan Blair Randolph loved her. He was not a rich Virginia dilettante. He'd come, respectful of her people, armed with his apprenticeship, the promise of a trade—all of which he'd said he'd do. And with one thing he'd never promised, his own mobility. Why did it all seem like such a miracle? Because, she realized, she had never believed it. She had never believed that Judith Mercer was worthy of such happiness. But here it was, offered by this wondrous man, after all the years alone.

Her breasts tingled, as if he were still pressing that beautiful tapestried vest against her homespun. She hugged herself, unashamed of the curves of her shoulder, her breasts, that her lover found so beautiful. He never lied. She was beautiful, then.

Physician. Of course, Ethan would transform those sailmender's hands into those of a physician. Her father would have a garden. Judith's hand glided down to her middle. And, perhaps, a legacy. Did she dare wonder if she could have a child to mend her father's heart, to give her sweet young husband joy? Was that a true vision of her Inner Light?

22

"Ah, Ethan!" Eli Mercer welcomed him. "Thee has tasted Ju-dith's bounty already!"

Ethan felt a blush starting to flame his face.

"No colorful excuses now, the scent is all over thee!"

Judith's father steadied the tulip poplar seedling next to its stake. He laughed, shaking his head. "It is not an offense to me, son, to be a young man, hungry for her delights."

The blush reached his scalp now. Eli Mercer continued his work. Did Judith inherit her serenity from him? Ethan wondered. He'd felt the core of hers when he'd kissed her. It helped him feel rooted, even as the heated blood was pulsing in his veins.

Her father's serenity had its own life too, infused by his lively curiosity. Was he another interesting oddity to this gentle, generous man? Ethan wondered. Eli looked up from his task.

"Loan me thy finger, will thee, son?"

Ethan crouched beside the small tree, his gift, which had weathered its journey from Virginia and now thrived under the botanist's care. Eli looped the string around Ethan's finger as he held the stake.

"I have written your suggestions on liming the soil to my mother to convey to Elwood," Ethan told Judith's father. "He is already noting good results in turning the tobacco soil to food crops."

"And the lad's health?"

"Much improved."

"This speaks well for thee, Ethan, this concern for thy father's bondsmen. Out now, please."

"Out?"

"Thy finger?"

"Oh." Ethan pulled his finger from the knot.

"Why, thy hands resemble Jordan Foster's," Eli observed.

Ethan smiled, pleased. "I am his apprentice, after all." He remembered when he'd said similar words about Fayette.

"Thee has been fortunate in thy teachers. Now, sit, sit. A grand place here at sunset, is it not?"

"Yes."

"How pleasing that thee joins me in observing its glory. I hope this shady vale becomes a place where one comes to strengthen the soul, once I am gone. Is it presumptuous? To think I might leave this earth better than before I came?"

"You've done that already. You've left Judith."

"Why, Ethan, what a splendid thing to say."

"I love Judith, Eli." He pulled apart a crackled leaf from the autumn before. "I would marry with her, if she'll have me."

The botanist stood. He began gathering his tools.

Ethan raised his head. "Did you hear me? Do you understand?"

Eli stopped. "Does thee think when age is in, wit is out?"

"That's Shakespeare," Ethan realized with a shock.

"Your gift of his book of sonnets was not my first introduction to the poet. I spent some years disowned by my Meeting. In that time forayed into decidedly secular literature."

"You were disowned?"

"When I was thy age, the revolution was raging. I became what was later termed a Fighting Quaker."

"Eli. You fought in the revolution?"

"Is it hard to imagine such a thing?"

"Yes."

"Always the truth from thee." Eli Mercer chuckled, shaking his head. "Thee will have to rely on that fine imagination to picture me, then, Valley Forge to Yorktown. Afterward, I expressed my remorse, was forgiven. Then I married Esther—"

"Esther," Ethan breathed.

"Has Judith never told thee her mother's name?"

"Never anything of her childhood. You once said it was marred, remember?"

The old man winced, as Judith did sometimes when Ethan sensed a memory he'd summoned pained her. "It is time, past time to tell thee why, my dear Washington. Thy generous heart will not find it difficult to forgive her omission. Judith was our firstborn, followed by two boys and two little girls."

"Brothers, sisters." Ethan felt his heart expand as he imagined smaller Judiths, and two Hughs to teach fishing. Where were they? Where were these children?

"Yes. Until a Tory soldier I'd fought made his way down from Canada one night, years later. He'd had a farm close by ours, Ethan. He was ruined by the war. Like most of the Loyalists, he lost his land, afterward. He emigrated to Canada, where his family died of sickness, hardship. The night he returned, with the remnants of the men who'd been under his command . . . Well, thee can see I was the most likely target."

"Target? Why? How?"

"I'd bought his acres. I was prosperous following the war. Even after I'd freed my bond servants to demonstrate my new piety to the members of my Meeting."

"Eli," Ethan called, as if he wished to be shaken out of a dream, "what happened?"

Eli Mercer's face lost all of the humor Ethan thought lived there. He looked, for the first time, old. "If I'd been home earlier that night, I alone might have borne the rage. Perhaps then they wouldn't have suffered so."

Ethan felt an iron claw clutch his insides. "Suffered? Did Judith suffer?"

"She suffered worst of all, son. For she walked in on the blood, the stilled bodies of her brothers and sisters—executed with military dispatch. And my wife, less . . . clean, for she'd fought her murderers for the children's lives. My future, my family, gone. Only I was left, hanging in the chimney, still kicking at the walls, though my life was swiftly taking its leave. Judith, my little Judith, she climbed those stone walls. Imagine that, a wee girl of twelve? She cut me down."

Ethan felt the blood drain from his tingling fingers. His head dropped into his hands.

"Down. That's right—between thy knees, child," Eli soothed, rubbing the back of Ethan's neck with his cool, soil-dampened fingers. "Forgive me. I didn't imagine thee could endure all thee has, to go frail at our story."

Ethan lifted his head, blinked away the last of the purple spots impatiently. "Where are these men?" he demanded.

"They were pursued by the authorities, of course. They took a stand. All but one was killed. He disappeared, despite repeated inquiries on both sides of the Canadian border."

"I will find him, the one left. I will kill him."

"My dear Ethan, there has been too much killing already. Begun by my sin. Does thee not see the spiral?"

"I see danger."

"Danger? After all these years?"

"You did not lose your future, Eli Mercer. You had Judith. You are not safe. She is not safe."

"Ethan, listen. Sit beside me. Please."

Ethan hardly realized he was standing in his agitation, tense and wary from the prickly air around them. When he sat, Eli Mercer's hand took a hold on his shoulder.

"I have felt this way, on occasion. Most recently, since we returned to our country from England. Perhaps it contributed to my illness, the foreboding, the worry for Judith. I do not wish to drive it into thee, my dear boy."

"Tell me the rest," Ethan demanded. "Tell me everything."

"Judith was my life, after," Eli began quietly. "She is still. Her hair went white within a year, and she began receiving her visions. She began speaking out at Meeting, too, then was moved to her missions. It's been a glorious time, Ethan. That's why I was spared, I think, to help her in her ministry.

"I thought we would continue the way we had, in the twenty years since that terrible night. Until our homecoming on board the *Standard*. I felt a shifting then, a change in her starting. Before meeting thee, she was becoming a Light, a cool blue spirit. To me, perhaps even to herself. Now I see the part of her she's kept submerged."

"She has her Light still," Ethan protested.

The older man's grasp on Ethan's shoulder warmed. "Yes. And purpose, missions. As does thee, and us all. But, Ethan, Judith missed her childhood. She was robbed of her youth, her frolicsome time, by that night. She began to understand that as she ministered to thee, who suffered too, so young—"

"So I, the bitter reminder, should now go away?"

"No, no, my dear Washington. Thee does not perceive my meaning! Listen. Thee has been robbed as well. And survived, whole, a fine Child of thy Light. Parts of thy memory were cut away, weren't they? Judith knew to stay until thee was restored. She did stay at Windover for thee, didn't she?"

"Yes."

"It's thy turn to minister to her need. That is how I see it."

Ethan tried to hide his smile behind a look of imperious scorn. "Eli Mercer, are you saying I have some obligation toward this woman?"

"I'm saying plodding, calculating Prescott Lyman wishes to marry a sister spirit who will help him raise his deceased helpmeet's children.

He is not interested in a woman. Thee has never seen her as anything but that emerging woman who is my glorious Judith."

"Eli, should she have me, the Meeting will not approve of our marriage, will it? She will be shunned?"

"Sat upon."

"Sat—?"

"It means 'disowned.' Gently, of course."

"Forever?"

"Until she says she is sorry, and leaves thee." He grinned. "A route is open to her return. Always. Now the prospect of this possibility might keep thee on thy toes as her helpmeet, yes?"

Was it possible? Ethan wondered. Was Judith's father teasing him? Did he have Eli Mercer's approval of his courtship?

"If Judith's Light tells her to choose me as her husband, but she will be disowned for doing so, how can she follow her Light and remain a Quaker, too?"

"Puzzling, isn't it?"

Ethan ran his hand through his hair. "It eats itself."

"Just so! Know this. The Inner Light is the final arbiter."

"She will remain a Quaker, though the Meeting disowns her?"

"My daughter will know what she is. She will always know, don't fear for her in that, son." His face sobered. "Ethan, a split in our Society is coming, I fear. Over what to do about slavery, over public testimony. If the Meeting isn't all of her life, the way it has been these many years, if she's standing outside, a friend of the Friends, with thee—it might not destroy her so. I know this: My daughter must follow her Light. Perhaps her next mission is herself."

Yes. There was no doubt. This gentle man with scars of his own would not stand in their way.

"Plant the rest of your trees, Eli," Ethan commanded. "You'll have to do your best with a smaller plot in a town physician's garden."

The man's eyes lit. "Does thee mean, I might be welcome—?"

"Judith will have enough changes—putting up with me, and that bad-tempered Boston physician, and closer living in town. You will join us there, won't you?"

Eli frowned. "Closer living? I have kept my botanicals alive in rooftop gardens in the foul London air, child," he protested, feigning insult. "Make thyself useful, landlocked sailor. Fetch me some water, so I can leave this place better than I found it."

Ethan fought the urge to salute Eli Mercer, before he took the proffered buckets. A soldier in the Revolution, his Quaker father-in-law had been. Like the uncle Ethan was named for. He wanted to hear more about that. And how had Eli Mercer managed to free his slaves and remain prosperous? Ethan desired to do the same for Windover. He would, someday, to keep his wife from regretting the Quaker price of loving him, and for the sheer pleasure of watching his brother Aaron's children walking unbowed.

Once he'd filled the buckets at the well, Ethan swung them in an arch over his head to see if all of the water would stay inside. A child's game. He was going to become a husband. He should be showing Eli he was a worthy son-in-law, not dallying as he climbed the hill.

He pictured Judith's father laughing at his concern, and calling his play an experiment in scientific method, perfectly sound and useful. The image was interrupted suddenly by an unnamed terror. He heard a garbled cry. The buckets dropped from his grip. "Eli!" he answered it, before he forced his feet forward in a faltering gait that was as close as he could come to running.

Eli Mercer was almost in the same place Ethan had left him—close by the young Virginia tulip poplar tree, which was down, its delicate trunk broken, its stakes pulled out, the dark, rich earth scattered. Judith's father clutched one of the stakes. His fingernails scratched frantically on the wood's surface. Writing. Ethan looked there, at glyphs whose meaning he didn't understand. Then he followed along the arm. Red. So much blood. Everywhere.

He dropped to his knees, coming down too hard on the bad one. He needed to feel the pain, he was going numb with his terror. He reached into the carnage, pulling torn clothes, pale skin together. No good. None of it was doing any good. Chest. Opened at the breastbone. Spouting blood overwhelmed his efforts. His eyes clouded with tears.

Not time. Not time yet for grief, he told himself. *Tend.* There was life yet, and senses. Eyes, ears, tortured breathing. Eli had struggled hard to defend himself. His would not be the dispatched death of his little ones.

Ethan lifted Eli's head into his lap. Blood spilled out of his already-full red mouth, the start of the assault, and why his cry was so drowned. The blood soaked into Ethan's waistcoat, but the change in position made no difference in the man's breathing. That was almost done, only wafting the hairs of his nose slightly.

Ethan bent closer. He swallowed down his grief as he loosened the dying man's cravat. Eli's eyes recognized him, or perhaps his hands. Could he still hear?

"I will love her always," Ethan whispered. "And protect her. Always, Eli."

The last breath to leave Eli Mercer's body was a sigh.

Ethan looked around the garden he was carving from this neglected corner of Prescott Lyman's land. Decimated, in this golden twilight. The fear of hurting Judith's father gone, he buried his head against the ripped chest, the way he'd wanted to retreat into Fayette. He rocked, partly to assure himself that he was alive amid the slaughter. Tears mixed with blood and grime on his face. He felt comfort there, on the back of his neck, exactly where Eli had massaged when he'd gone faint.

"Eli, your dread was no illusion," Ethan whispered.

He heard Judith's lilting call to her father. Close. Ethan lay Eli on his side in the grass. He eased off his coat and placed it over the bloody face. The turkey vultures would go for those moist places first. He remembered seeing them pecking away the eyes of dead animals at Windover. He pried the stake that Eli had used to defend himself from his freezing grip. It was important. He didn't know how, but it was important. He shoved it into his waistcoat as he rose unsteadily to his feet.

Judith was at the end of the path to her father's cabin when he reached her. Her eyes went wide with alarm.

"Ethan! Dear God. What has happened?"

"Happened . . ." he repeated tonelessly, stupidly.

"You're hurt."

Of course, the blood. "No." He shook his head, dragging the words out as if English was not his first language. "Not me."

"Where's my father?" she demanded.

"Stay here," he urged gently.

"Let go."

"No. Stay!"

She screamed. "Ethan, let go of me!" So strong. She fought, jabbing with her elbows, kicking him off balance with calfskin slippers. She bit him hard on the shoulder—a bony part, so he worried more for her teeth than any harm she was doing him. *Hold. If you lose her, you will never get her back,* rang through his head. Others were coming in response to her screams. No matter. Hold on to her.

The blood and sweat between them finally helped her slip out of his grasp, turn. He reached for her waist. Missed. She stumbled farther away. But she had to lift her skirts to run. He leaped out and caught her then, bringing them both down on the dirt path.

"Judith," he summoned her frantic eyes as he pinned her to the ground with his greater weight, "Eli—"

"No!"

"There was nothing else I could do."

She screamed for her father like a lost child. Kicked. Ethan felt the weapon Eli had used against his attacker enter his own side. He ignored the pain and held her there below him.

Other hands pried his fingers back. Two of them cracked under the weight of hobnailed boots. The pain finally forced the blue skirts to slip from his grasp. He fought back the multitude of hands, fists, heavy farmers' bodies. Their boots struck. He protected his side, fearing they would kick the stake in farther, and his own blood would obscure what Eli Mercer had worked so hard to scratch into the wood in his last moments alive.

"Stop!" Judith's fiery command finally halted the assault.

Ethan rose to his elbow in the billowing silence. He coughed the dust and blood from his throat, then stared up at Judith. She seemed tall again, as when they were on board the *Standard*. Too tall to fit so well under his heart.

Her remaining strength left her face as their eyes met. She swayed, like that night she'd raised the bone cup to toast Fayette. But this time she did not fall. She widened her stance, then turned and ran toward the body of her father.

"Catch her, you damn fools," Ethan barked at the Quaker farmers.

They did not. He blasphemed in both his languages as he struggled to his good knee. The last kick cut under his jaw so hard he felt his teeth sever a piece of his tongue before he fell senseless, even to Judith's screams as she discovered her father's body.

23

The scent of cold iron sapped Ethan's strength. Where was he? Why had they put him here? For how long? Where was Judith?

A soft crooning started. It reminded him of the rhythmic cadences of the people in the hold of the *Standard*. He opened his eyes. The ragged shadow was bigger than those faint images. And more dense. The crooning stopped.

"Evening," he heard the greeting through the void.

"G—" Ethan choked, his sore tongue too big for his mouth.

"Touched fellow, I be Atlas. Only one they caught tonight. My woman, my two little girls, still follow the lights."

"Lights?"

"Leadin' north. On the end of the sky's drinking gourd."

"T-to Polaris."

"What be that?"

"The North Star." He swallowed painfully. "Runaways?"

The big shadow came closer. "Now, I don't knows much, but you seem possessed of a good enough mind to me, cousin."

"Thank you."

Ethan sat up slowly against the wall. His side ached, where he'd packed mud against the puncture the wooden stake had made. His right hand hurt. The sound of chains echoed. Chained. Like the slaves on the *Standard*. He was chained. Had he become one of the slaves, somehow? He wasn't brave enough, not for that. He fought panic. The deep, companionable voice, so normal, so calm. He had to hear it again. "And now, Atlas?" he managed to croak out.

"Now? Why, they bring me back to Mary's land, I expect. Whip me good. But not enough to harm me much. I'm a strong worker, and it be planting time."

Ethan tried to move closer, but the pain made him groan.

"What be your trouble, cousin?"

"Fingers," Ethan remembered.

He felt a wince of sympathy, through the dark. "Gone or broke?"

"Broken, I think."

"How many?"

"Two."

"Two? Why, that ain't nothin'. Keep them still and Atlas, he hunt you up some splinting, wrap you up something fine."

Ethan listened as the man foraged freely. Atlas was not chained. Where was this place? Rats. Did he hear rats? No knife to keep them back. "Will they hunt your family?" Ethan asked into the darkness.

"Some, I expect. But Sully and the little gals gonna make it this time." Ethan heard a ripping. Cloth; loose weave. "My brother's got a farm, a mule in this Canada. The English up there won't give us folk back, I hear."

Ethan closed his eyes. "I'm sure you're right."

"Gives me your hand, real slow like," the voice commanded. "Atlas fix you, if'n you stay real still, and don't bite or holler."

Ethan cupped his good hand under the aching, damaged one and sent them toward the voice. Atlas crooned his comforting melody as he set the bones, then splinted and tied the strips of cloth. "Better?"

"Much better. Thank you."

"You got schoolin', don't you, brother?"

"Some."

"They don't like schoolin'. Hide it. Not much meat on you, either. And young to be in so much trouble they got you chained."

"I'm three-and-twenty," Ethan protested.

The man chuckled.

Ethan lowered his voice. "Will you try to run away again, Atlas?"

"Soon's I heal. 'Course, I could try now. Ain't no hounds. The bounty men, they up and left, mostly. Be only one slave catcher, and he be fond of his corn liquor. But I gives all bribe barter to my Sully, 'fore we parted."

Ethan glanced down at his vest. He yanked off the buttons with his good hand, then thrust his fist out, opened it. "Here."

"What you got, brother?"

"Buttons. Silver. Take them. Godspeed."

Ethan heard Atlas examine his gift. "Now what fine gentleman did you steal that waistcoat off, crazy boy?"

"I didn't steal it!"

Atlas moved closer. "Sweet Jesus. You's . . ." His voice trailed off in shock. Ethan didn't know what had gone wrong between them. But he wasn't a thief. Except of Judith. If he could get out, he'd steal her away from the pious Quakers who'd chained him in this place.

His companion snatched hold of his good hand. He yanked back Ethan's sleeve, baring his wrist, then returned the hand, slowly. "Why," Atlas whispered in awe, "be you a white man?"

"Yes."

"You—don't smell white."

"Oh? How do whites smell?"

"Like they eats, full of pork fat. You smell like you eats nigger greens and corn and . . . and you's chained, and sharing space with me without a howl of complaint."

"Why should I complain? You're the best company I've had in weeks," Ethan said gruffly.

"Why, the Lord in His mercy protect you, sir! When the bossman says you's touched, not to come close, not to speak to you on account you'd bite off my ear as soon as look at me, I knew then I was in for a treat, a good story to tell, but . . ." Ethan watched the glints of silver as

Atlas tossed the buttons up and caught them again. "Now I done got myself the key to salvation besides!" he concluded, jubilant.

Ethan enjoyed the sound of the man's deep laughter in this harsh, suffering place. A massive hand patted his shoulder.

"Rest yourself now. But find your worth 'fore they eats you whole, young one," he advised.

The eight-fingered slave was gone with the morning. Ethan wondered if he'd dreamed the man until he looked down at his own fingers, splinted between a spoon and broken pencil stub, and resting on his waistcoat. All the buttons of which were still missing.

"Open this door," the familiar voice demanded.

"Now, sir, the prisoner beat a dozen Quakers senseless! He—"

"Open it. Now."

"As you say, sir."

Ethan tried to close his torn shirt, hide the iron cuffs that shackled him to the wall. Pointless.

Jordan Foster crouched beside him. He steadied his cool, clean hand on Ethan's forehead. His thumb traced around his bruised jaw, his split lip.

"Open," he instructed.

Ethan obliged.

"Christ in Heaven," Jordan muttered, seeing his raw-edged tongue. "Any teeth broken? Loosened?"

"No, sir."

They seemed like a miracle, the physician's hands. Ethan had wanted his own to become like them, hadn't he?

"I can't tend him properly," Jordan Foster insisted to the man beside him. "Remove the shackles."

"Not me, sir, he'd strangle me soon as—"

"Give me the key, then, damn you!"

"It's your neck, sir."

"Leave!" Jordan shouted.

The man was only too glad to scurry out, though Ethan didn't remember doing him any harm. Silence then.

"Do you think I'm mad, too, Jordan?"

"No, son."

"They took my boots. Tell them to give me back my boots, will you?"

"I have done that."

"Thank you."

The doctor released the shackle from his damaged right hand. "What in the name of Heaven did you splint yourself with?"

"Not me. Atlas. He used what he could find."

"Atlas?"

"He's gone now."

"I see." Jordan exhaled, opening the cloth ties.

"Leave it be. Please."

"Suppose you let me judge, this once?"

Ethan clenched his jaw. "Yes, sir."

The doctor continued taking apart Atlas's work. "Don't know when to let go, do you?"

"Of Judith? No, sir."

"Two simple fractures of phalanges. Both set well. Should cramp your writing for a little while, brat."

Ethan grinned through the clench in his already aching jaw. "I'm ambidextrous," he ground out.

Jordan Foster shook his head. "I should have guessed. Maupin would see to that."

"You don't know half my talents."

"I'm sure I don't." He resplinted, then wrapped the damaged fingers in the fresh gauze from his bag. "Adequate, for now," he conceded.

Ethan took his hand back, resting it under his trousers' left brace. "I could have told you that. Before the torture," he groused.

To his surprise, Jordan Foster smiled. "Let me see your side now, there's a good fellow," he said gently.

"She didn't mean it. She didn't know I had the stake there."

"Stake?"

"A wooden stake. It was next to the little tree. Eli was holding it when I found him. Where is it now? It's important."

"Lie still."

"I made a mud paste with the dirt of the floor and rainwater that puddled from a leak. I haven't been fevered."

"Hush now, magpie." The corners of the physician's mouth turned up. There. He was in a better mood.

"Jordan. Don't tell my mother."

"Too late. She'll be coming. So will your brothers."

"Merde."

"Watch what's left of your profane tongue. The magistrates are just outside."

"What do they want?"

"Let me finish cleaning you up before they're treated to the sight of you."

"Judith wouldn't mind. She's seen me worse. Does Judith have the stake? Does she understand the marks her father made? Where's Judith?"

The doctor looked uneasy. "Let's dispense with that shirt."

The blood had soaked through the weave, and dried brown. Only traces of his own; it was mostly Eli's blood. It had comforted him, alone in the darkness, with the cold iron. When Dr. Foster helped him remove the shirt, he suddenly felt as he did without Fayette's coat—lost.

"Jordan?"

"What is it, son?"

"They don't believe in grief, the Quakers."

"I know."

"I did not wish Judith to see Eli that way. That's why I held her back, though she fought like an avenging angel. Was it disrespectful, presumptuous of me, to hold her back?"

"Protective," he said kindly. "It was protective." He pulled a new shirt over Ethan's head. One that smelled of lavender and fires, ink, gaslamps, brick. Of a city. Philadelphia. Where he'd gone to visit his wife's brother, wasn't that it? There was so little he knew of this man.

"When will they let me out of here?"

"Let you out?"

"Yes. They misunderstood, the Quakers who beat me. They thought I was hurting Judith, yes? Isn't that why they put me here? And hasn't she explained?"

"Ethan, Judith hasn't spoken. Not a word."

"She hasn't? Who sent for you?"

"A child, I think, from the handwriting on the note."

"Hugh," Ethan realized. "He found your name, your brother-in-law's dwelling in Philadelphia listed among my things. Clever boy."

"Ethan, do you know where you are?"

"Some sort of holding place. When first I came to myself, they were taking my boots off. You know I can't walk without my boots, and I couldn't make them understand—"

"Ethan, listen to me. This is a jail cell. You're being held on suspicion of murder."

"What?"

"Eli Mercer was killed with your knife. The Quakers think you were trying to kill Judith, too."

24

Ethan turned his attention to the grim, whitewashed ceiling of the small cell. Of course, that's what it was, a cell. Murderer.

"They'll hang me, then?" he asked Jordan Foster.

"No, of course not. If it even goes to trial, we'll—"

"Trials don't matter. The truth doesn't matter. Like on board the *Standard*."

"This isn't the *Standard*. You have friends, an influential family. They're coming. We won't let anything happen to you."

Ethan tried to push the image of Eli Mercer's corpse from his mind. Straight, bloody line—an evisceration, like the rat. That's how the murderer wanted it to look, not fully realizing Eli Mercer's own strength, his love of life. Everyone in Harmony Springs Meeting knew how Ethan had opened the rat, thanks to Hugh's storytelling. Everyone.

"That's what he wants. A trial. Attention on me."

"Who? What who wants?"

"The one who killed Eli."

"Did you see him?"

"No." Ethan tried to swallow around the strangling grief lodged in his throat. "Did you bring any drinking water?" he managed to whisper.

"Yes."

Once he'd emptied the crockery cup, Jordan Foster began to scrub at the grime on his face. Without complaint. Was the doctor even enjoying the task? Ethan looked at the muddy water in his basin.

"Small wonder he thought I was black."

"Who did?"

"Atlas. We had a most enjoyable conversation, while he thought I was black."

"If you're having such a good time, perhaps you should stay the season." The doctor frowned. "Ethan, listen to me. There were known to be renegade slaves roving this area for days. Perhaps—?"

"Atlas. Judith's lights, her nervousness. Of course, it makes sense now."

"What makes sense?"

"From the apple tree's branches, Judith and I watched lights of neighboring farms, pointing north. Added our own. We were engaging in subterfuge, she said. So that's what she meant. The slaves got north, then—all but Atlas?"

"Your friend slipped away, too, just after dawn, though no one can figure how. Damnation! You were supposed to be courting Judith, not assisting runaways to Canada!"

Ethan smiled, though it irritated the crack in his bottom lip. "Perhaps it was part of my courting duty. She hadn't told me yet."

"Good." Jordan Foster helped him back into his waistcoat. "You still don't know anything, remember. What the devil happened to your buttons?"

Ethan winced. "I don't think you want to hear about that."

The doctor threw up his hands.

"No runaway killed Eli Mercer, Jordan. Eli would have helped any, as Judith was doing."

"Perhaps it was a panicked attack. An accident. It's happened."

Ethan remembered Eli's wounds. "It was calculated," he said. "We are all distractions. Jordan, Eli was a Fighting Quaker."

"What has that got to do with—?"

"After the Revolution, a Loyalist band killed his wife, all his children but Judith. He must have known this was coming, and that I needed to know. Someone was listening. One of these Quakers is no Quaker. He's a Loyalist."

"But, Ethan, that war was—"

"Not forgotten. Not forgiven. Not by him. The one who killed Eli, opening him up, slashing his heart's artery. Making him watch his own life's blood draining . . ."

The grief again, physical, choking. He leaned over the doctor's arm, heaving against his sleeve, then into his handkerchief. Jordan Foster made quiet, worried sounds, until it ended. Ethan rested his throbbing head against the doctor's chest.

"Clear. You drank the water too fast, that's all. No blood. Easy, son. Breathe easy now."

Ethan's good hand clenched the physician's sleeve. "Jordan, I have to get out of here."

"You will."

"Stay close to Judith."

"Her people won't allow that."

"Go around them. Go to Hugh. He'll show you where she is.

Promise me. You are not a Quaker. I can ask that of you, a promise. Jordan, keep her safe, until I can get away."

"You must not think of escape."

Ethan grinned at the doctor's worried face. "Do you not envision me outrunning them?"

He was expecting to be chided, but the physician sighed. "Thank God," he murmured.

" 'Thank God'? Is that what you say as I draw you into yet another disturbance of your valued peace?"

Ethan thought he saw the sheen of unshed tears in the man's dark eyes. "It's only—" Dr. Foster whispered. "Ethan, after hearing of Judith, I thought, What would I do if you, too, were . . . not yourself?"

"Go to her, Jordan. They are webbing her in that cocoon of piety. She is Judith still. We will weather this, she and I, and come out on the other side of it stronger. Will you tell her this for me?"

She didn't know how long she'd been sitting in the austere, whitewashed room. She had trouble keeping track of time. Except for day and night, it all ran together.

Nothing was required of her anymore, that was part of it. Not cooking, cleaning, gardening. Not even feeding the fowl. How were the chickens and ducks and geese doing without her? Someone would feed them, they were worth something. What was she worth?

Where had Ethan gone? He could have told wonderful stories, so that no one would be sad, or grieve for her father. Prescott thought it best she not attend the sitting. He said she wasn't well enough. But she didn't feel sick, just empty.

Prescott said Ethan would never return. He watched her face when he said it. And he said it every day. She hadn't heard her own voice in so long. Why did Prescott bother her daily? Did he think she would speak? There was no longer any need. To speak, to pray, to seek the Light in herself or others. She was not a Quaker. She had no name, was no one's daughter. She'd loved a dancing tree-dweller, once. That would fade. She would fade, if she sat here, very still. She would fade, and then disappear.

Thunder, rain. They made it hard to be still, to stay away from the window. Wet rose petals. Too early for roses. From where had that scent come? She walked to the single, small window of her room. Far below stood a woman. Did the woman not have the sense to get herself out of the rain?

She walked down the stairs. The doors opened before her, forming a path through the maze of the widow's added-on farmhouse. Who was doing that? The little one, the boy. She was fond of him. Hugh—he was leading the way, then hiding from her. It was a pleasant, silent game. The boy understood, better than his stepfather, her need for silence. But his path led to the rain, the flash of lightning, the sad, stung eyes of the rose-scented woman.

She walked outside, holding out her hands, the way she used to do with hurting people, before she'd begun to fade. The woman took them, giving her more substance.

"Judith, please."

She was still here, then?

"He needs you." She had small children, this woman. One was a baby she'd allowed Judith to hold, to dream over.

"Who?" Her voice. Was it her voice?

"Ethan. He needs you to speak at the hearing tomorrow."

"I will, then."

"How long have you been subject to fits, Mr. Randolph?"

"Fits?"

"Come, come, we possess all the sworn statements that came with your release from the British frigate *Standard*." The magistrate slammed the portfolio of documents on the long chestnut table. "The chief medical officer claims you were not only lame and subject to powerful seizures, but that you attempted suicide when only moments away from freedom. We have the documents."

"Consider the source of those documents!" Jordan Foster shouted.

The questioner spun around. "Will you deny Ethan Randolph's return to that unbalanced state after a fall from his horse?"

"He was not unbalanced. Never unbalanced."

"You were his physician through the second series of seizures."

"They were caused by a fever."

"*Brain* fever."

"Brought on by injuries sustained by the fall! I explained it to you, as did his mother, his sister, his brothers. It was the fall, and the elevated temperature of his body. His mind is sound."

"Sound? One of those injuries was to the head. It affected his very memory. Do you deny that, Dr. Foster?"

"I don't know what restored his memory. No one could say with certainty."

"Just so. Little is known about the workings of the mind."

Watching their exchange reminded Ethan of the battle off Trafalgar.

He didn't want to go back there, so he detached himself from the bombardment and let his eyes sweep the town meeting-chamber. Still no Judith. Sally, her hair and clothes dripping wet, had visited his cell in the dead of the night to tell him Judith had spoken at last. A few words, a promise to attend today's session.

He should not have hoped for it.

The hearing's population was nearly evenly divided between the sober cloth of the Quakers and the Virginia finery of his family and their nervous, hired lawyers. The paneled room had grace but little ornament. It dated from when the Quakers ruled the entire colony of Pennsylvania, Ethan thought. Their best time, the time of their reasoned experiment, Fayette had called it. They had pulled themselves out of the running of Pennsylvania since, and held no offices. What would Fayette think of these Quaker observers, sitting uncomfortably in the high-backed benches? He was already guilty, in their sight. They were searching his eyes for the *why*.

A few strangers sat in the room, too. Those had been sent from Washington, perhaps from Dolley Madison herself. They were men "of no little influence," his brothers had said, as if they were part of a gambling game, like the ones they'd tried to draw him into on their plantations. This was all some kind of a game, like chess, or craps, whist. Or Trafalgar. He felt as powerless as he had strapped to the gratings on board the *Standard*. He'd worked so hard not to feel that powerless again. What had happened?

Ethan shifted his gaze past Winthrop and Clayton to his mother. Anne Randolph patted Jordan Foster's hand. How beautiful she was. Both were striking in their courage.

Ethan looked among the Quakers for . . . what, the hundredth time? There: Judith entered their midst with Prescott Lyman, who held her arm in a tight vise. Her gown was dyed with indigo. It reminded Ethan of the sea at midnight. But she was so pale. And her eyes. There was something wrong with her. Something very wrong.

". . . Mr. Randolph, do we take your silence as refusal of our request?" the middle magistrate, Seymour Hess, asked quietly.

Stay engaged. Don't let them hang you for stupidity. "I'm sorry," he whispered. "The question?"

"Would you show us your wrists, so we can determine if the *Standard*'s surgeon's sworn remarks are fabrications?"

"They are not."

He stood, yanked off his coat impatiently, and began pulling up his shirtsleeve. "It is here, see?" he informed all three gray men in a clear tone as he held out his wrist with its single scar. "It was a sharp knife with an ivory handle. I know how to put knives to use, as you gentlemen have already ascertained. I could have had it over within minutes."

His mother stifled a cry.

Damn you. Ethan willed his curse to burn into the magistrate's heart. "What interests you?" he asked impatiently. "Why I began or why I stopped?"

"Begin with why you would think of such a thing," his inquisitor said.

He shoved his coat back on and sat. "The captain met with me before we came ashore at Norfolk. He put the knife in my hands. He said if I did not kill myself, he would slander the love Henri Maupin and I held for Judith Mercer. He would call it carnal knowledge."

"And you believed he would have?"

"Yes."

"Why? Was there any truth to—"

"This was not about truth. I had been powerless for ten years on board the *Standard*. I had only Maupin for protection, and now he was dead. I had watched my shipmates set the noose high after an absurd treason trial wherein Captain Willis had been both judge and jury. My place was less than esteemed."

Silence. The air crackled with it. What did it mean?

"And what convinced you to cease opening your veins, Mr. Randolph?" Seymour Hess asked softly.

Ethan heard the distant echo of annoyed African clicking cadences. "Voices," he whispered.

"Voices?"

He looked at Judith. "The clear voices of conscience. Not to allow them to win. Not to compound the wrongs done me."

The magistrate on the right, the most dangerous one, spoke in his condescending tone. "Why, Mr. Randolph, now that a certain lady is in our midst, your notions sound quite Quaker-like."

"Do they? I believe the early Quakers were also considered lunatics by the local magistrates. You hanged three of them in Boston, did you not? One a woman?"

"That—that was over a century ago," he sputtered. "And Pennsylvania is hardly Massachusetts!"

Ethan shrugged indifferently. "Please forgive me. I am not so well traveled on land. North of the Mason-and-Dixon line, the states and commonwealths run together for me."

The magistrate stood in his anger. "Do you mock this Inquiry?"

Ethan sat taller. "Will you mock my parents by telling them they spawned a murderer?"

Jordan Foster winced. Ethan's mother squeezed his hand. They were comforting each other, he realized. Sally's face was glistening with tears. But Judith's glassy eyes had not found him yet. *Damnation.* Teasing the pompous magistrates about Boston heretics. He should have a care with the grim set of his humor. He knew better. Fayette had taught him better. He had caused his family enough pain.

"Tell us what happened the day Eli Mercer was killed, Ethan Randolph." The middle magistrate's voice had turned hard, unyielding, as he stood. Seymour Hess was the tallest of the three, Ethan observed, trying to distract himself from the distinct possibility that he'd lost the only one who was even listening to him.

"I'd visited him, while he was planting the poplar tree."

"The one from Virginia? Your gift?"

"Yes."

"What was the purpose of this visit?"

"I told him I wished to marry Judith."

"Judith Mercer, his daughter?"

"Yes."

"Are you familiar with the consequences of a Quaker considering marriage outside the sect?"

"Yes."

"And they are?"

"Disownment."

"So you went to Judith Mercer's father, to tell him you wished to become a convinced Quaker."

"No, sir."

"Then you went, knowing you would receive his refusal to allow this marriage?"

"No."

"Explain yourself, sir."

"I had hope that he could guide me on that part of it. If there were exceptions made. Eli is my friend."

"*Was,* Mr. Randolph. *Was* your friend. He's dead."

"I know he's dead! I watched him die!"

"Yes. So you claim. An unfortunate discovery, of a deed done while you were fetching water in buckets never found. Moments sooner and you might have prevented it, isn't that what you said?"

"Yes."

Ethan felt unbearably burdened by the magistrate's tone. But there was no escape. "And a tree stake containing a dying man's last message has disappeared, too," he continued. "We have all your statements on record. Now we wish to explore your meeting with Eli Mercer. Your talk. What made you hope that he would give this proposed marriage his blessing? Your family's wealth and position? Did you think you could buy his permission?"

"No."

The left-flank magistrate cast a disgusted glance toward the federal men. "You planned to use your status in the city of Washington as a naval hero of the late war and a favorite of Mrs. Madison?"

"Of course not."

"What, then, sir?" Hess asked. Quietly. Perhaps he'd not lost the man's attention yet.

"My love for Judith," Ethan said, looking at his hands, the crooked bend of one healing finger.

Right-flank now. "This love of yours, it wasn't enough, was it? And so it turned to anger when that Quaker gentleman refused your suit, however kindly. Eli Mercer had always been good to you. He had saved your life. Why did you let your rage blind you?"

"What?"

"The rage, man! The rage you felt at his refusal!"

"I felt no rage."

"Why not?"

"He didn't refuse me."

"Do you expect the men of this panel, do you expect these decent members of the Quaker Harmony Springs Community, to believe—"

Ethan stood. "I have no expectations, sir. Only an obligation. To speak the truth. I have spoken it. Now either charge me with this crime or allow me to go home. I am sick to death of this."

Without being dismissed, he left the stand and returned to his place on the bench between Sally and his mother. Sally squeezed his arm and pressed her cheek into his shoulder. "The states run together, indeed! What a reflection on me, your geography teacher!" she said, her voice dancing between tears and laughter.

His mother slipped her hand over his shaking one. It was cool, steady. He closed his eyes. The middle magistrate spoke toward the Quaker section of the room—to Prescott Lyman.

"May we ask the identity and health of the lady who has seated herself at your side, sir?"

Judith stood. "I'm Judith Mercer. And I'm able to respond for myself," she said in the familiar, clear voice.

She walked to the stand Ethan had stalked away from, and sat. So pale, Ethan thought again.

"Our sincere condolences, Miss Mercer, and appreciation for your appearance at this hearing. Have you understood Mr. Randolph's answers to our questions?"

"I have," she said.

The left magistrate stood. "Do you wish to press charges against the prisoner in the matter of the aftermath of your father's—"

"No."

"But the assault on your person following—"

"A mistaken impression. I am firm in the belief that Ethan attempted to spare me from viewing the condition of my father's body."

"Miss Mercer, several have stated that Mr. Randolph held you on the ground. By force."

"He was . . . adamant, as was I."

"Did he say, 'There was nothing else I could do'?"

"Yes."

"How did you take his meaning?"

"That he had attempted to help, to treat my father's injuries."

"Are you sure of this?"

"I'm sure, sir."

Sir? Ethan thought, confused. Why was she calling the magistrate "sir"? And where were her *"thees"* and *"thys"*? The right-flank magistrate stood, circled her chair. "How long have you known Ethan Randolph, Miss Mercer?"

"Since the fifth of April, eighteen hundred and fifteen."

"A year, then."

"Yes."

"Your reputation precedes you. Your good works on behalf of the unjustly persecuted are known within and without your community. Your word is honored and trusted here, Miss Mercer. Now, you and your father helped secure Ethan Randolph's release from HMF *Standard,* did you not?"

"We did."

"Further, you guided this young man's reunion with his family, and his recovery of both body and memory in the year that's followed. Is that a proper rendering of the facts?"

"Yes."

"Now, Miss Mercer, were you aware of Ethan Randolph's intentions on the day of your father's death?"

"I was."

Ethan sensed his surprise. "How did you know these intentions?" the magistrate questioned.

"Ethan had made them known to me first."

"I . . . I see." A disturbed reaction. Why? Ethan wondered. Did no one believe any part of his own testimony? Was Judith's confirmation such a shock? The man coughed. "Then you sent him to your father?"

"No. He sought my father on his own."

"Immediately?"

"I was given to understand that."

"He was agitated?"

"Excited, perhaps."

"By your refusal."

"I did not refuse him."

He pointed to Ethan. "You agreed to marry this man?"

"I agreed to consider his suit."

"Agreed to consider. Of course. You were alone with him, knew the workings of his intemperate mind. That was wise."

"Ethan is not—"

"Do you have any doubt as to what your father might have answered to Mr. Randolph's request for your hand in marriage?"

"No," she mouthed, too silently to hear.

"Miss Mercer?" the magistrate prompted.

Ethan saw the pain enter Judith's eyes. He began to comprehend what she was doing to her father's memory as a forgiven Fighting Quaker, and to her own life among them as she spoke. *Wait, Judith, there must be some other way.* But there was not. She'd stepped across the threshold, as always, with her courage leading her. He felt the tears welling up behind his eyes. *I didn't mean for this, Judith,* he tried to tell her.

"Miss Mercer?" left-flank persisted.

Her lower lip quivered. "I have no doubt," she said, louder.

"Based on your father's love, his protection, his devout Quaker standing in your Meeting, will you now assert your belief that Ethan Randolph's version of that meeting's outcome was a lie?"

She locked her eyes on Ethan's for the first time since she'd entered the room. The open wound of her grief was not enough to induce him to look away. "Here, Judith," his sister whispered, lending more strength to Ethan's efforts. "The truth is here."

The magistrate pointed at Ethan again. "Miss Mercer, will you confirm this man's statement a ludicrous lie?" he pressed.

"I cannot," Judith whispered.

"Why can you not?"

"Ethan does not lie."

"His freedom, his very life is at stake, Miss Mercer. Consider that he has powerful motivation! Will you at least entertain the notion—"

"No. He does not lie."

"He is no Quaker, without need of oaths," the magistrate persisted. "Look at him closer. Let the scales fall from your eyes. He was steeped in your father's blood, woman, and acting like a madman. Despite your hopes, your dreams for Ethan Randolph, you must know what he meant by 'There was nothing else I could do'!"

Ethan bolted to his feet. "Leave her alone! God damn you all!" he shouted, lunging for the magistrate's throat.

25

Ethan's cell looked vastly different now. Before his family had ex-erted its influence, he had been considerably less comfortable. The shackles were gone, though the iron rings in the brick wall remained. The gaunt space was eased by a roped featherbed, a desk. A washbasin and pitcher stood on its stand, the chamberpot tucked away within its cabinet. What cabinetmaker had fashioned it? Ethan wondered. The same one who'd built Eli's coffin? He searched the darkening sky he could see through the high window. No stars. "Why couldn't I have run faster, Eli?" he whispered.

—*What's done cannot be undone. This line of thinking serves no purpose,* Fayette's voice admonished inside his head.

What would happen to Judith? Would the Quakers drive her out, because she had brought her Light to the hearing? Her goodness was palpable. The magistrates had to consider her words before charging him with her father's murder. She had cast the first shadings of doubt in their minds, not him playing the imperious Randolph, and certainly not his outburst of temper.

The proceedings had come to an end soon after his brothers pulled him back from the harassing magistrate. The Quakers had hustled Judith off in the opposite direction, cocooning her again. He would not allow that. It was dimming her Light. How soon before it would go out? He would die before he allowed that.

How could he think about allowing or not allowing anything, here in this cell? *Out.* He must steal Judith and escape them all. He scanned the room. The bedsheet could serve another purpose. A fork from his next meal could become a weapon. *Stop.* A little more patience, his sister had urged. He was even losing faith in his women. *"Consider the possibility,"* his mother had said in her soothing tone, *"that these people will behave honorably."* A hard thing to imagine. He wondered again if his years at sea had made him too wild to be landed.

Read. Escape that way, for now, into fine-tuned poetry, a galloping tale. Ethan searched among the spines of the books his sister had provided. He opened the pages of Plutarch to see Betsy's colorful chalk drawing of his first steps. The jubilant circle of women stood around a jelly-jointed scarecrow. He closed the book and sat on the edge of his bed, surrendering his head to his hands.

Sally had brought only her nursling to Pennsylvania with her, but never to the hearings, or his cell. Of course, she shouldn't. Despite its rudimentary comforts, this was still a keep, with all the despair and poison of its former inhabitants. Not a place for Charlotte. But he missed his gull.

When the cell's door opened and he saw the ashen paleness of Sally's face, Ethan thought he'd never see any of her children again.

He stood, took his sister's arm. She leaned on him heavily until he sat her down on the bed. Tears. Ethan knelt at her side.

"They've charged me, then?" he whispered.

"Worse," she barely managed to say.

"Worse? What could be worse?"

"They . . ." was as far as she got before she fell to weeping again.

Ethan yanked out a handkerchief and blotted her tears.

"Sally, why did you come alone?"

"Mama and Jordan went for a walk. They charged me to wait. Out there." She gestured at the cell's door. "To wait, and compose myself. You, shut away, alone in this place, and me, just on the other side of the door—I couldn't bear it, Ethan! I wanted to sit with you, until they returned. I thought I could be g-good, you know?"

He gave her his handkerchief and perched himself on the small stool at her feet. "You are good. You're the best sister a worthless, no-account, can't-keep-himself-out-of-trouble idiot could ask for! But you must stop crying, or my poor niece will miss her dinner."

Sally looked down at her milk-soaked bodice, and began wailing anew. His attempts at humoring women were having the opposite effect lately.

"Sarah Ellen!" Anne Randolph summoned, behind them. "What are you doing to your brother?"

Ethan turned, astonished. "Mother, Sally's not—"

"You!" she scoffed. "You have no sense! And she has less! How have I deserved such children?" She faced her daughter, her graceful hands fisted at her waist. "What have you told him?"

"N-nothing, Mama."

"Good. Now stop this caterwauling, we have very little time!"

"Time for what?" Ethan asked Jordan Foster, swaddled in neckerchiefs and looking less astonished at his mother's behavior.

"To get you out," the doctor said quietly.

"Out? They're not pressing charges?"

"No."

"So I can go home?"

Her mother's cautionary look strangled Sally's sob in her throat.

"Not home, darling," Anne Randolph said softly. "Not just now." Ethan saw tears flooding her light eyes. *Sacre-bleu,* not both of them, he thought. He turned to the doctor again.

"What has happened, sir?"

"A bargain. Your brothers promised the good magistrates to keep you locked up at Windover for the rest of your life—in return for their judgment of insufficient evidence. They're making clandestine arrangements now, to spirit you to Virginia under the cover of darkness and before word of the ruling gets out."

Ethan stared straight ahead. His visitors went out of focus.

"Ethan?" Sally called him back.

"They'll make me the mad brother in the attic."

"Exactly," Jordan Foster confirmed. "The ruling is accomplished, the dealing done. But your mother won what we needed—time."

"Time?"

"From Winthrop and Clayton, time to explain all to you. They're not imagining you'll take it well. I've promised to drug you into submission for your transfer to the coach."

Ethan looked up. "Why?"

"So it will be easier for us to pass."

"Pass?"

"We are almost the same height and coloring." He yanked off his hat, began unswaddling his scarfs. "We will exchange clothes here, now, and both keep our heads down, and hope they are their usual unobservant selves long enough to give you a start. Perhaps until the first carriage stop at the inn to get Charlotte and our baggage."

Ethan stared at him. "You've shaved your beard," he realized.

"Easier than you growing one. We've brought you blackening soot."

Rude, to stare. Stop it.

"What's the matter with you?" his friend demanded.

"N-nothing," he stammered. Jordan Foster was a more handsome man, without his beard. That pleased his mother, he thought, from his quick glance at her lustrous eyes. He felt himself grinning at the doctor, despite his own predicament. "It's—"

"It's what? What?"

"Delightful to see you, Jordan."

"Bloody hell. Off with your britches, pest."

"You can't have my boots. I need my—"

"No one wants your boots!" The doctor ran his hand through his dark hair and calmed down. "Come. It's time for you to shed another skin, Ethan," he said with a sudden, flashing smile. "You can do it again. My stout Morgan mare is outside. She'll take you far, if you treat her well. Use your compass and the stars."

Ethan nodded, though he was struggling to keep up with the surgeon's tight, clipped speech.

"Go east, my darling," Anne Randolph urged. "Somewhere remote. For a little while."

"Toward the ocean," Sally offered quietly.

Her mother nodded. "Yes, toward, but not one foot on any manner of ship, no sailing the open sea, do you hear me?"

"Yes." Ethan touched the careworn beauty of Anne Randolph's face. "Your brother's name. May I have it?"

"Of course. You've had it always."

Jordan Foster came between them, a knife in his hand. A fine knife, almost as fine as the one Micah had made for him. He leaned down and placed it in the pouch Aaron had fashioned in his boot. "Establish contact with Sally through the post in a fortnight. We will meet soon after, apprentice."

"You'd still consider—"

"There is no 'consider.'" The doctor reached into his vest, drew out a leather wallet, and emptied it of currency. He put it into Ethan's hands. "We have an agreement, remember? Here is an advance on your first earnings. You have two weeks' time to get your affairs in order and be ready to join me, Mr. Blair. I will do the same. The city of our practice must be big enough to support another doctor. What is Richmond's current population, Sally?"

"Ten thousand," she answered promptly, his student again.

"Richmond might suit us, I think."

The women's hands linked, squeezed. Ethan looked into beautiful, beaming faces. His chaotic world was coming together again by way of this impossibly generous man who had transformed himself into his twin. He must say something, be polite.

"At the hearing—I'm sorry about the remark against Boston, Dr. Foster," he tried.

Jordan smiled. "Think nothing of it. We hanged witches, too, you know, besides the three Quakers."

Ethan did not feel as strange in the doctor's clothes as he'd imagined. The blue coat fitted larger across his shoulders, but his legs were longer than the dark-striped trousers' cut by an inch or two. That astonished him. He'd never imagined himself taller than Jordan Foster, but here was proof. The women ripped the seams and pulled the fine worsted wool to hide the heels of his specially made boots. He kept the doctor's loose white scarf high and his broad-brimmed hat low over his more abundant hair. His mother lowered the lamplight in the already dim cell.

When they came for their prisoner, Ethan looked at only parts of his brothers: Winthrop's shoulder, Clayton's hands, to keep track of where they were. His mother and sister kept pulling him into their circle to assist them with the stumbling figure in his clothes.

Winthrop let out a disgusted snort, pushing Ethan aside and hauling Jordan Foster over his shoulder. Ethan's breath caught in his throat, but he had enough wits left to snatch up the fallen hat. Winthrop deposited his burden next to Sally in the shade-drawn coach.

Both women distracted Winthrop with slaps and protests as Ethan quickly covered Dr. Foster's balding spot with his hat. Winthrop slipped backward out the coach door.

"We have him now," Anne Randolph stated impatiently. "Go ride outside with the coachman, both of you," she demanded of her elder sons. "Go with God, Dr. Foster," she said more softly, squeezing Ethan's shoulder, and giving it a slight, indiscernible push. His last view inside the coach was of his sister's swollen, tear-stained face. She, too, was mouthing *"Go."*

"Well, I think our wild cub has gained a few pounds in captivity!" Ethan heard Winthrop tell Clayton. He turned away, his face burning from the note of triumph in his brother's voice. He felt Clayton's hand on his back as he reached for the reins of Dr. Foster's Morgan mare. He froze.

"Listen, sir. I know you've grown fond of the boy. This was a terrible business. But the only way, believe me. He will not be mistreated. I give you my word on it, Doctor."

Ethan bowed his head, burying his chin deep in Jordan Foster's collar. He would never trust his brothers' word again.

"Are you sure you won't join us?"

Ethan nodded.

"Mother has the rest of your concoction? Just in case he should become fractious on the way home?"

Ethan gritted his teeth, nodded again.

"Good. He's gotten very strong, working among our niggers and these damned Quaker farmers. You saw him go after the magistrate! This is best. We won't forget your help, Doctor."

Ethan counted his brother's fading footfalls before he mounted. Behind him, the coach and six began its journey. He cast a quick glance east, but once sure his mother and sister could no longer see him, he pulled the reins north. Toward Harmony Springs.

Judith felt jolted awake when her head hit Mary Waldman's shoulder. The woman looked disgusted. Judith had embarrassed herself. This had never happened before. Why couldn't she keep her mind focused? She was tired all the time. The tea would help, Prescott had told her, but though she drank and drank, it didn't even quench her thirst.

She had slept so long after her appearance at Ethan's hearing that it was becoming part of the dream that had been most of her life since her father's death. Had Ethan reached the magistrate's throat, as Prescott claimed? It was not proper to feel magnificent over his burning, protective anger, but Judith did, without remorse. She was feeling the pulse of his indignation now. It was helping her to wake up. That and the commotion at the doorway.

Shouts. Her people rarely shouted. Why was this happening? And why were they shouting at Dr. Foster, standing in the aisle? He removed his hat. Chestnut hair tumbled past his collar. Too long. No gray. A shadowy, smudged beard. Not Dr. Foster. It was Ethan.

His eyes found her.

"Judith Mercer," he called in a fine, declaiming voice, "I have come, with your father's approval. Will you have me for your husband?"

She looked at the hand he offered her, there, across the room. A flood of memories cut through the hazy thicket of her mind. Leather thimbles, three drops of blood, the strands of her hair becoming the means to raise his sails. She saw the hands grasp the coat of the doctor on the dark night of his fall, demanding the chance at his mobility. Then those hands were lost in the softness of Hugh's gray cat, whom she'd wished to be at the moment he stroked her. Finally, she saw those beautiful hands vainly trying to staunch the flow of her father's blood, his hot tears dropping, mixing with the red.

Now those hands desired hers, after everything that had passed between them. They trembled a little as her silence wore on. He was used to silence, as she was. It was not the silence that caused his shaking. *He's afraid,* Judith realized. Afraid, standing here, in the midst of these people who believed him to be a murderer.

—Of course he's afraid. Brave people are not senseless ones, Judith, her father admonished. *—Now. Answer the boy.*

She stood slowly, then stepped forward. "I am charged to love thee, Ethan Randolph," she said, "by the Light which dwells within my breast. I take thee as my helpmeet, with no law but love between us."

She placed her hand within the strong, fine palm. Judith looked up. The sweat on his brow glistened like morning dew as he smiled.

She reached for her cape hanging from a peg on the wall. Another hand grasped her wrist, twisted.

"Thee chooses death, Judith Mercer," Prescott Lyman warned.

"I listen to my Voice," she said quietly.

"Thy Voice!" he said, his own echoing with scorn. "It was drowned silent by this murderer's purpose!"

"No."

"Release your hand or I will cut it off," Ethan said with a steely sureness. She saw the gleam of metal in his hand and felt afflicted with deep revulsion. No more. No more knives.

Prescott Lyman complied, but his eyes grew more inflamed once he'd lost contact with her. "Nothing! Take nothing!" he shouted at Judith. "I would have thee naked before us in thy shame!"

She heard the shocked murmurs of those at Meeting. She felt the searing heat of Ethan's anger.

"I need nothing," she said, taking her lover's arm. The door was so far away. She must keep walking, she told herself, though each step was like one taken in a nightmare, impossibly heavy. But she must reach the door, so they could all see this was her will.

Outside, the wind blew at her face and her knees gave way. She felt Ethan's steady grip below her ribs as he leaned over her.

"Laudanum," he said, his disgust tempered by sorrow. For her. He was not all anger. The sorrow was a gift from his heart. It overwhelmed her. No, she must stay alert, or she would slow him down. They would catch him. He wrapped her in his coat and lifted her onto the horse's saddle. Once he'd mounted behind her, he gently eased her left leg over. She whimpered in surprise.

"You must ride astride, Judith," he said, "so I might keep you steady."

She bit her lip and nodded.

"That's good," he encouraged. "Now anchor your feet between my calves and the horse."

"Like this?"

"Perfect," he said, when she knew she'd done it in a far-less-than-perfect fashion. Voices rose behind them. Judith felt his body lean over to protect hers. He urged the horse to a full gallop.

They remained on roads and traveling trails throughout the night, some so overgrown it seemed Ethan's horse forged them. Judith tried to stay alert. But once he was sure that none were at their heels, he slowed their pace and encouraged her to rest, steadying her with a grip on his trousers' braces. She dozed fitfully against his chest as he clucked soothing sounds that he'd used while tending animals and children. Were they for her or his horse? It didn't matter, she loved the sounds and the steady beat of his heart. As dawn was breaking, they picked a trail through bush before stopping at a small stream.

When Ethan eased her down, Judith collapsed in the tall spring grass. He dismounted and was beside her in an instant.

"Stiff. My legs are just stiff," she protested, leaning on his shoulder to rise. "Don't, Ethan. I can—"

"Hush."

He lifted her high and walked a steady gait that astonished her. Under the new leaves of a sycamore he finally set her down. He folded her gown's skirt, then her petticoats back. She winced under his hands' gentle touch on her legs.

"They are coming back? You feel the prickling?" he asked.

She nodded.

"Good. Keep moving them, yes?"

"Yes."

He kissed her cheek shyly, before standing, walking to his saddlebags, then the creek nearby. He returned with a small basin filled with cool water. He dipped his handkerchief into it and, ignoring his own mud-spattered state, gently bathed her face and hands. Judith couldn't remember the last time anyone had done that for her. She felt her senses coming alive again under his touch.

"Ethan?"

"Yes, love?"

"Where are we?"

He wiped the last line of mud from her forehead. "I'm about to have a look around." He disappeared above her, into the limbs of the sycamore.

"No acrobatics!" she admonished.

His laughter sounded like music.

When he dropped down at her side again, his face was flushed with exertion and happiness. "I got a good view of the land around, Judith. Appears to me no one's following. And there's a town in sight. With a steeple. I think it would be safe to—"

"Ethan, why are you wearing Dr. Foster's clothes?" she asked. "And riding his horse?"

His face pinched, dissolving a measure of its happiness. "I had to run away."

She touched his hand. "Did the magistrates decide to accuse?"

"And ignore your testimony? No. They released me. Jordan took my place so I could escape my brothers."

"Why?"

"They won my freedom by promising to keep me a life prisoner at Windover."

She traced the line of bitterness around his mouth.

"You and Dr. Foster—you deceived your own brothers?"

There. She'd coaxed a half-smile from him. "Jordan almost played his part too well."

"What do you mean?"

"He stumbled like a drunken man. Winthrop carried him to the coach over his shoulder."

"No! And still thought it was thee?"

"I suppose so. I was busy listening to Clayton's pious rationalizations, said to keep his own precious soul feeling clean about the abduction."

Judith hid her giggle behind her hand. "Ethan, thee must not speak so!"

"Why must I not? They are insufferable, unmanly cowards! Done in, now. Oh, I'd give the next three tobacco crops to see the look on their faces when they discover they've captured Jordan Foster!"

They were both laughing now. Judith didn't know which felt better—her own laughter, or listening to his.

"Oh, but Sally! And your poor mother!" she realized suddenly.

"Poor? Triumphant, you mean. It was Mother's idea. And it worked, imagine that!" The dark eyes turned serious again. "I cannot go home, Judith. And I cannot remain here in Pennsylvania."

"We cannot," she amended quietly.

He smiled slowly. "It's true, then," he whispered. "You did marry me, there in your Meeting House?"

"Yes."

"Well, I'd best be about the business of marrying you back."

Their noses were almost touching. "Ethan," she confided to him, to the air of wild spring beauty around them, "I'm afraid."

"So am I," he whispered softly. "You've chosen a renegade, Judith. In my own family, and with your people until I can prove myself innocent of your father's murder."

"How?" she whispered.

"By finding this murderer of your family."

"My family?"

"Yes. Eli told me the story. Of your climb up the chimney, my strong, brave wife."

She began to tremble. He took her arms. "Are you afraid of me, Judith?" he asked, searching her eyes.

"Not of you. For you."

"I see." He smiled. "That's allowed. In moderation."

She touched his face. "Thank you. For coming for me, Ethan."

"I hope you do not regret your decision, *ma chère,* even if we manage to stay clear of both factions looking for us, I have only the slightest prospects."

She rested her fingers in his windblown hair and stroked his sooty jaw with her thumb. "Your prospects indeed," she whispered. "What about mine? I don't have so much as a cloak to keep out the cold."

"I do not have a name," he countered sadly.

"That's how I found you. And I loved you then."

"Did you? You did not only pity that scrawny, crippled sailor?"

"Who knew the constellations, who sewed better than I? And stole a piece of my soul I've now given him forever."

"Judith," he said in a gruff whisper, "I don't believe it yet."

He held her close, kissing her temple. She shivered with happiness, though he must have thought it was with cold. "Let's get you covered. And we must gain that paper."

"Paper?"

"One that says we're married. Who will give us one of those? The church down there?"

"I don't think so. Churches mean banns and ceremony, and—" She felt cold and sick, just thinking about another religion, one with precepts and doctrine and no Inner Light. Ethan took her hand.

"Of course. We've had our church wedding, such as it was."

"At knifepoint?" she realized.

"Well, yes. But I would not have threatened had he not held you so! Prescott Lyman never had you to lose, did he, Judith?"

"No, love."

"Good. We need the legal paper. From whom would we get that?"

"The justice of the peace, I believe. Do you think it safe?"

"If any discover we've been here, they'll know only that, not where we're going."

"Where *are* we going?"

"You see?" He laughed, standing, then pulling her to her feet. "They won't even be able to drag that out of you!"

"It's her people against it?" the tall, lean matron at Ethan's side asked.

"Yes," he admitted, because he was afraid to lie to a woman who reminded him so much of his sister. "How did you know?"

"Couples dressed as you, hard-traveled strangers, with no baggage, they usually come in the middle of the night, not in the light of day. But they're always eloping on account of they're underage, or their folks are dead set against it."

"We're not underage."

The woman laughed. "If I'd thought you were, my husband would have sent you home with a lecture ringing in your ears a while ago."

Would this woman say, if someone asked, that Judith was lucid, clear-eyed, with enough of the vestiges of the laudanum gone when they wed? Would the paper stand, bind them, allow no man, no court, no Elder, to pull them asunder?

He tried to concentrate on the scene in the adjoining room of the comfortable house on the edge of Pelhamtown, Pennsylvania. There, in the hearth room, Judith was surrounded by the woman's four small daughters, each contributing spring flowers to the wreath for her hair. White larkspur mingled with huckleberry and lavender.

The fifth child, a boy, had run to fetch their father, the justice, who was presently helping a neighbor to mend a fence. Or was he bringing the magistrates down on them?

Ethan felt his heart pound harder, felt a twitch start, beside his eye. Christ, stop that. The smallest child climbed into Judith's lap to place a dandelion beneath her chin. A born mother. Prescott Lyman was right about that. Another worry. Could he give her a child? Or was he sterile like his brothers?

"Why, you're afraid she'll refuse you, even now," the woman said.

He nodded. Of course he was worried about that. Would Judith, now clear-eyed, say yes to him? Mrs. Curtis offered him a small glass filled with a ruby-colored liquid.

"I usually leave this to my husband, later. But you'd best swallow it now, young man. Good," she purred as he obeyed. "Ease your mind, Mr. Randolph. We've yet to lose a bridegroom."

The door opened and a man whose head skimmed the rafters of the room entered. He was aproned and muddy and had the most open, congenial expression Ethan had ever seen.

"In good time." The woman complimented the son who'd fetched his father. "Mr. Curtis," she summoned the man, "put on your robes of office. Roger, accompany our Mr. Randolph on his shopping rounds while the wee girls and I complete his bride's finery."

She wiggled the third finger of her left hand to remind Ethan of the wedding ring she'd encouraged him to purchase before she pushed him toward her son. Ethan glanced back at Judith. Her beaming smile made him finally realize they'd come to the right place.

"He scarcely wants you out of his sight, as if you'd disappear!"

Judith looked down at her hands and thought about how close she'd come to doing just that. An involuntary shudder shook her frame.

"You don't desire to disappear on him, do you?"

"Oh, no!"

"Good. We like your man. He's very handsome, isn't he, girls?"

Her daughters agreed with vigorous nods and giggles.

"Do you think so?" Judith asked, realizing she was indulging herself in vanity. But if she couldn't do it this day, when could she? "I mean, I've always seen him so, but others, when he was sick, and what with his lameness . . ."

"Lameness? What lameness, dear?"

"You didn't notice?"

"Notice what?"

"Of course his boots help."

"Now, what woman with any eye for beauty would be looking at the boots of that fine-formed man?"

Judith felt a flush ride up her neck and burst at her cheeks. The tips of her fingers pulsed with longing to touch her fine-formed man.

"Not that physical beauty is the basis for lasting attachment, of course," Mrs. Curtis continued as she scrubbed the last vestiges of their wild ride from Judith's indigo skirt. "And it's his attachment to you touches my heart, and makes him all the more comely, if I might be allowed to say so. But you're both as nervous and fretful as wrens over a nest! Shall I put on a pot of tea as we—"

Judith felt a sudden wave of nausea. "No tea," she whispered.

"Why, my dear, you've gone quite pale. When have you last eaten?"

Judith pulled Ethan's damp handkerchief from her pocket. She held it over her mouth, retching. Nothing came of it but an overwhelming dizziness.

When she opened her eyes again, her feet were raised on the sofa. One of the cherub children was fanning her face. Mrs. Curtis dabbed her forehead. What had happened? Had she fainted?

"Better?" the matron whispered.

"Yes."

"Good. Now, don't raise your head, but see if you can get a little of this plain porridge down. Will you try?"

The woman held a tiny, steaming baby's spoon to Judith's lips. She didn't even need to open her mouth very wide to pull in the warm, smooth oats.

"There, your color's returning. Your poor hovering man might get an 'I will' out of you yet today!"

"Is Ethan returned?"

"Not yet. But the girls have finished your garland, and my husband's as clean as can be expected, so we've done our part here."

"You've been very kind."

The woman touched Judith's forehead. "How many months gone are you, little wren?"

"Gone?"

Judith followed the woman's glance at her middle and felt a fresh flush at her cheeks. "I'm not . . . gone. I mean, it's not possible. Ethan and I—we haven't you see . . ."

"Oh, I beg your pardon. It's common, with hasty marriages. And with you being ill—I'm sorry. I should have known. He told me it's your people against the marriage. The girl's family usually isn't, if she's in that way, and the father's as willing as he seems."

Judith felt the tears sting her eyes. "I have no family. But my father loved Ethan like a son. Once he died, my people couldn't accept. One of them made me tired all the time, with laudanum in my tea, so I was confused, and couldn't go to Ethan myself. I'm still sick from it, and a burden. When he needed me, when they held him prisoner, I couldn't go, until it was almost too late!"

"What happened?"

"He came for me. After they'd beaten him. He braved them all to hold out his hand and come for me." The woman and her children's rapt faces almost overwhelmed her again. She leaned back in the pillows.

"That's the best story!" the oldest girl intoned quietly.

Her next younger sister skipped in from her station at the parlor window. "Put on your garland, miss," she called out. "They come. And your man has the prettiest sea green cape over his arm! And oh, Mama, look, he's leading Mr. DuBois's white mare Two Hearts!"

"I suspect Two Hearts is this lady's mare now, Katie."

The ceremony with its swearing was almost too strange for Judith to bear at first. But when she watched Ethan repeat the words after the justice, in his unique, French-accented Virginia cadence, she lost herself in him, in the sound, ignoring sense. Even the scar Ethan had received at the time of his fall off Cavalier looked like another benevolent track of mud on her distracted, nervous, beautiful bridegroom's face as he pledged his troth.

When the justice asked for the ring, his son held out three silver bands in his palm. Ethan looked at her apologetically. "This will help seal everything, this and the paper," he said quietly. "You don't have to wear it, Judith."

She nodded, trusting him. Ethan tried one, then another ring on her finger. Both slipped on too easily. The third was a perfect fit, Judith thought, though she'd never worn a ring before.

Then it was her turn. The sounds came, first in syllables, then words, then phrases. It was not so bad, with the gentle justice's patience, with Ethan's eyes steady on her face.

Then, silence. Familiar, rich silence.

"You may kiss her if you'd like, son."

Ethan blinked, looking to Judith as if he'd just been yanked from the ocean's depths. "May I?" he asked her politely.

Judith glanced over the room's occupants. Hope filled Mrs. Curtis's and her female children's eyes. It overruled the single son's sour-faced vote. She nodded her permission for their first public kiss.

Ethan leaned down, touched her lips with his, pressed further. Her lips parted and she tasted warm wine and felt a gentle, teasing pull of promise. It left her tingling long after the little girls showered them with creamy yellow narcissus blossoms. Their kiss was still causing her hand to shake as she entered her name in its place on the marriage certificate.

Once the ink was sanded, Ethan folded the document carefully and placed it in her hands.

"Deep in your pocket, Judith. For any who would try to pull us apart, in the world men have made, not the one we will make together.

Mon dieu," he whispered, suddenly, as he glanced out the parlor window.

"Ethan? What—?"

He grabbed her hand. "Are all fees paid?" he asked, running past the smiling justice as he poured wine.

"Yes, but won't you and your wife—"

"We cannot, we regret . . . *Allons-y* . . . Judith?" he begged as his English gave way, but his feet did not.

She yanked her new hooded cape from the chair beside the scullery door. "Thank you, for all your kindnesses, good-bye!" was all she could manage before her new husband swept her onto the white mare.

She didn't care if it was her disappointed suitor or her bridegroom's greedy older brothers behind them. Judith Mercer wanted only to emerge on the other side of her past with Ethan.

3

Ethan Blair

26

Judith watched Ethan shed his coat, vest, and even his beloved boots as he sprinted across the sandy dunes. Without boots he was hobbled, but seemed blissfully unaware of it until he fell. Even then he waved off her assistance and coursed on.

When he entered the Atlantic's pounding surf, he stood still at last. So still that the waves buried his feet in their shifting sands, evening him out again on his mismatched legs.

Judith gathered his clothing and boots as she walked. She set them on an outgrowth of rock, warm from the late-afternoon sun. Then she removed her own slippers, ruined again though he'd patched them twice for her. She kilted up her frayed indigo skirts and stepped into the foamy surf. Just as she didn't think he'd noticed her presence beside him, he turned. His beautiful eyes were shadowed dark with exhaustion, reminding her of Washington on that first night on board the *Standard*. He took up her hand, pressed it to his face. *Yes*, she thought. Even his several days' growth of beard was like Washington's.

"The sea's at our backs now, Judith," he said, above the waves. "I spoke with the lighthouse keepers. We can rest awhile here, in a shelter all our own. Would that please you?"

She nodded, blinking back tears, before pulling him down to her mouth and tasting her husband there in his home, the sea.

They had been three days and nights on back roads and trails, avoiding her persistent former suitor and his five-man tracking party. They'd never stopped for more than a few hours to rest the horses, to scan Barton Gibson's maps and blue-chalked post rider's routes, to sleep lightly, propped up against each other.

They'd bought their provisions—eggs, bread, a little cheese—from free black farmers as they traveled. The families knew from their eyes that they were running. Judith spoke for them, as her husband feared his accent would turn them away from a slaveowner's son. None turned them away, as poor as they themselves were.

Was it truly over? How had he found this place? Found? It was as if he'd been driven to it. The tide was coming in. Ethan lifted her above the spray. Their kisses deepened as his hand rode down her hip, flaring its long, strong fingers, massaging. Judith's memories of their harrowing journey began to fade with the power of their passion. His beard scraped her face. He was everywhere, eliciting first tiny, then deeper gasps. Judith felt the wetness between her legs. Not from the waves, they were not that high. She thought he might take her down there in the surf. Could she hold her breath as long as he?

"Mr. Blair!" They heard the cry from the shore. "The key!"

Ethan eased Judith back to her feet with a stream of indiscernible French, and took her hand. But by the time they'd reached the lighthouse keeper, who was standing beside the rock that held Ethan's boots, stockings, and coat, her ardent young husband was smiling affably.

"This is Judith, Del. My wife—Mrs. Blair," he amended.

"I figured as much, sir," the man said with a laugh as he touched his cap. He was about fifty, and his face was lined in what appeared to be a perpetual squint. "Seems my own missus was right. 'Go and rescue that poor bride from his sea madness, Del,' says she. 'And tell himself he'd best treat her better than these worn-down horses while I'm his landlady!' So there it is, message delivered, along with the cabin's key and here—my Ida's six-egg pound cake to keep you both from starvation's door until morning."

Del put the wrapped cake into Judith's arms and handed the key to Ethan. "Storm's coming. A nor'easter," the lighthouse keeper informed them. "As I could see you were busy observing for yourselves just now," he added, a grin widening his weather-beaten squint. "There's plenty of firewood. It might last the length of your hideaway from those doting relatives who wouldn't leave you in peace!"

Judith watched the lightkeeper trudge across the sand toward the tower house as her husband leaned against the rock and pulled on his boots.

"Doting relatives? Ethan, what did you tell them?" she demanded.

"The truth," he said. She frowned. "In a more lighthearted vein, perhaps. I *am* a Blair, Judith," he insisted, standing, "and I asked my mother if I might use the name."

She nodded. "We're Blairs, then, of course."

He buttoned Jordan Foster's vest over his shirt. "Not yet."

"Not yet?"

"Marriage needs consummation," he explained with a studiously indifferent shrug.

Judith tried to affect a pout. "Cake first," she challenged.

His eyes went playfully menacing. "No cake."

"Ethan—" she warned, backing away from him. "I'm very hungry."

"So am I."

She giggled, covering her mouth like the silly, lighthearted girl she was, for the first time in her life.

"Do you suppose our landlady can see us from there?" he asked, tracking her steps.

Judith's eyes shifted quickly up the hill to the lighthouse and pier, then back. "It's possible."

"Good." He caught the cake in the web of his coat and slung her over his shoulder. Judith clung to their bag of foraged possessions, laughing as he brought them over the last of the dunes, then into the piney woods.

His playful voice changed when he stopped. "Judith, look," he summoned in an awestruck whisper, as he returned her to her feet.

She turned, still laughing. Before them stood a weathered cabin among a grove of gnarled cedars. Through the roar of the pounding surf in the distance, Judith felt a profound peace about the place.

Ethan mounted the wide porch steps. He put the key in the door's padlock and opened it. Inside was well-chinked and cozy. The large single room was a home.

Judith spun around, running delighted hands over a red woven tablecloth, blue-fringed shawl, two whale-oil lamps, and the featherbed on a bolster frame. All under the peaked, open rafter roof. After their hunted days, each new discovery felt like a luxurious miracle.

She wondered if she was being frivolous, until she realized her castaway husband was doing the same. Ethan opened chests containing pillows, quilts, candles, food staples, and crockery ware. His fingers traced everything as if it would disappear. "Del said they use this cabin when their children's families visit, as well as an emergency shelter when the need arises. But I didn't expect—"

"Oh, Ethan, it's beautiful here."

"Yes."

"You know this place, these people, don't you?"

"What do you mean?"

"You've been here before."

"No." He turned away from her. His eyes focused on a child's spotted gray rocking horse by the fireplace. His fingers skimmed its black mane as he glanced up at her. He opened his mouth twice, but seemed to think better of speaking. "A storm is coming; we'd best settle ourselves in," he finally declared.

As he brought a bucket to the rain barrel outside, Judith set out basins and pitchers on the two nightstands. She removed her battered wedding wreath from the bag and draped it over a chairback, then put logs and kindling in the hearth.

Ethan returned. Together they worked the tinder to flame.

"Good fire." He complimented her shyly. Judith moved close. He continued to stare into the flames. "Before we, that is to say . . ."

"Become consummated?" she offered.

"Yes. Exactly, just so. We must talk about—" His eyes darted in her direction at last. "Why, Judith, what has happened to you?" he asked, tracing the slight rash along her jaw.

She felt herself coloring. "You . . . happened," she explained. "Remember? In the waves?"

His hand went to his prickly beard.

"Oh, I'm sorry. That was thoughtless, I beg your pardon."

"I don't mind, my darling."

"I'll shave. Yes. Now. I'm sorry," he said again, backing away.

Judith set the kettle on the hearth. Soon its water warmed both basins. He lit the lamp and placed it close by their two washstands. Judith slipped out of her indigo gown, placed it on the chair beside the bed, and wrapped the blue shawl across her shoulders. She pressed a damp linen towel to her face and peeked above it.

Ethan's opened shirt looked as it did when he was on the treetop in Pennsylvania. How Judith envied his ease of manner, even as her heart was pounding at the intimacy of washing herself beside him. He steadied the blade of his fine knife with his thumb and drew it over the offending whiskers, hidden under soap foam. Long strokes, smooth, graceful. He shaved much differently than her father had. Her breasts began a pleasant tingle.

"Don't you require a mirror?" she heard herself asking.

"Fayette taught me to do without. Though sometimes he liked to play the barber himself."

"I shaved prisoners at Dartmoor, the ones who had injuries to their hands. They were so grateful over such a small kindness," she remembered.

"Ange venérable," he whispered.

"What does that mean?"

"Angel. I call you angel. This offends you?"

"No."

He kissed her cheek. Soap bubbles clung. The tingling intensified. He seemed to know what was happening, there insidc her, and retreated to his basin.

When he'd finished, he turned to her. She had barely rinsed her face, and felt a trickle of water easing down her neck. His eyes followed its route until it disappeared. Judith ached for his touch.

"I'll bank the fire." He slid past her, engaging in the task.

Was this purposeful, what he was doing? Teasing her, like a child, but with a man's skill. Then mysterious, unaccountable shyness. As she knelt on the hearth rug, he finally looked into her eyes.

"Judith," he began, "there is a subject I've tried to push from my mind. But here, now, I find I cannot."

His eyes skimmed the spotted horse. Dread encircled Judith's heart.

"Children," she whispered.

"Yes. Prescott Lyman, when we buried the rat, he called you a born mother, Judith. That was the only thing that ever bothered me. He could give you Ruth and Hugh, and we, the two of us, might never have a child, because—" She watched him fight the constriction in his throat. "Because—"

"Of me," they finished together.

Their expressions of amazement must have looked mirrored, Judith thought later.

"You?" Ethan asked.

"Yes, of course, you think I'm too old!"

He looked baffled.

"Don't you?" she demanded.

"No! Why would I think that?"

"Because I am three-and-thirty and have never— Ethan, because of the years between us!"

"They are nothing! Sally is older than you are. And my mother, when she gave me life, was older. Silly woman. I fear my own inability, not yours!"

"But, Ethan," she glanced down between his muscled thighs and fought her blush, "you are hardly—"

"It's not from want of desire. Judith, neither of my brothers has children. My father blames their wives, but I don't believe it is they who are responsible. No matter how disagreeable Hester and Clara are, they wish their estate secure as much as their husbands do. I think it is Winthrop and Clayton who are . . . unable."

"Why do you think this?"

"My brothers pride themselves on following my father into his biblical world of wives and concubines and issue. But Judith, they have none, not a hint of an heir from any of their legitimate or conquested breeding in their slave quarters. I think it must be them. Does my speaking of these things offend you?" he asked suddenly.

"No."

"Good. That's good. Well, I am their brother, so that same inability might be bred in me. It would hardly be fair to you not to know my doubts, would it?"

"Ethan—" Judith fought back a smile. "—you are also brother to Sally, who has issue."

"But Sally's a woman."

"What arrogance! Is she less related to you because of her sex?"

"No."

"She is closer to your age than your brothers are. Perhaps something has afflicted them, made them unable. Nothing has harmed her. Nor you, perhaps, as her brother born after her."

"That sounds . . . sensible."

"Oh? Is that not why you chose an ancient wife, Ethan Blair? Her wizened good sense?"

Judith rejoiced as the buoyant noise sounded off the hearthstone. She'd gotten a small laugh out of him. It made her feel bold, powerful. That and his own annoyed, Fayette-influenced words. *Silly woman,* she told herself in that voice. The years between them were nothing to him! Why should they bother her, then?

"Oh, Ethan, we love each other. Let's leave the rest to God."

"God." He said the word as if recalling a distant, unpleasant relative.

Judith smiled. "Yes, God, heathen. And even God cannot help us unless we go about the business of consummating this marriage!"

As the wind howled, Judith could still hear waves pounding as her sweet, unburdened husband moved close in that stealthful, tantalizing way she loved.

"Business, is it, Judith Mercer? My love for you?" As she opened her mouth to his kiss, she felt his fingers do what they had never dared before: They pulled a pin from her hair. She heard the tiny, sifting sound of it reaching the hearthstone. Others followed, more and more quickly. It was as if he'd spent their courtship memorizing where each was placed. When her braids descended, he stopped.

"Still, if God does not favor us—"

"We'll do what we've always planned. We'll steal one of Sally's," she assured him, before fisting his shirt in her hands and stopping any further speech with a kiss of her own.

Ethan unbraided his new wife's hair slowly, dusting her face and neck with kisses as he worked. The sound of her breathing was ever-changing: now a low hum, then a catch, then a soft, giggling purr. Finally, he was free to glory in her strands unbound. He parted the moon-colored waterfall and bared the shoulder beneath, nuzzling deep.

He loved the feel of her strong fingers coursing through his scalp as he brought her down under him.

Suddenly, the fire flamed high in the hearth and an insistent voice began badgering him in clipped French.

—Get off her, you brute! You think a woman wants her back crushed into a stone floor her first time?

He lifted her into his arms. She kissed behind his ear. Gratefully? Were they her thoughts he'd heard? Did she think him a brute? He tripped on his discarded vest, then lurched forward, unbalanced.

The voice again. Laughing. Judith Mercer did not speak French. Or have so wicked a laugh.

He felt his face grow crimson. *Get out. Go away,* he told the voice as he placed his wife on the bed. Judith clutched at her shawl's folds. Her eyes went wide. "Are you angry with me, Ethan?"

He climbed onto the bed beside her. "No. Oh, love, no." He began a trail of kisses down her wonderfully salty arm, nuzzling aside the shawl, grateful to her shift's loose, thin weave.

Judith released the shawl. As it drifted to rest around her hips, her chameleon eyes lost their traces of blue and flashed silver. Like his veins igniting. He pulled down the covers behind her. Cold. That was good. He needed that cold as she pulled the ties between her breasts. He traced their contours slowly with his shaven cheek, then with soft pulls of his tongue, mouth. Her fingers danced along his back. Her voice pealed like a bell before she fell back into the pillows.

Ethan could barely stand to look at her in the languorous glow of her *petit mort. Sacre-bleu,* his beautiful wife lying like that, and he still had his boots on.

The left came off easily. With the right, he was too impatient. He emitted a small cry of frustration.

Judith sat up like a shot. "Ethan, are you hurt?"

"No."

—Oui! Imbécile!

Ethan sighed. "Yes," he amended.

Judith smoothed the hair back from his forehead with shaking fingers. "I have been so demanding, not thinking of you, your leg." Her voice became suddenly low, dusky, as he pulled one of her ministering fingers into his mouth. "It is very difficult to think at all when you do these things, husband."

He kissed the tip of her smallest finger. "Shall I stop?"

"Only long enough for me to complete ridding you of my rivals, your boots."

He laughed, which seemed to raise her breasts even higher beneath the thin muslin. Judith went to her task as he tried to calm his breathing. But her hips were very fine, too. As was the curve of her backside. There was no part of her not beautiful. She turned.

"Better?" she asked.

"Worse."

"Your leg?"

"My hunger. My delight in you."

She smiled shyly. Her hand touched his damaged leg, exquisitely caressing through the trousers. "You've been bearing all the rigors of the journey to this place, this wondrous place you've found for us." She stroked higher, his thigh. "Ethan, I am so ignorant. Tell me what I might—"

"That is excellent fine, Judith," he gasped.

She looked down. "Oh. Oh, I see."

—*Yes,* the voice approved. —*You know this woman. Her need to feel useful. And she is untouched. She is giving you this gift of her, untouched. Be worthy, and clever. This first time, above you. But do not shock her.*

Ethan lifted his wife's caressing hand, kissed into the palm. "I fear my leg's not strong enough, as you say, Judith, with the rigors of the journey, for me to . . . to lord over you as your husband tonight."

"It's not?"

No. Wrong. Tears. Where's the damned voice now? Ethan wanted to cry out in his frustration. "Judith, don't cry. There is another way."

"Another way?"

"Astride, we could accomplish our duty."

Judith wiped her tears with the back of her hand. "Astride? As on Two Hearts?"

"Yes! . . . Well," he reconsidered, "not exactly." He snorted almost like her horse did, making her eyes widen, then soften in amusement. "Only if it pleases you, of course," he assured her.

She pushed him back gently against the bolster. "The sight, the touch, the scent of you pleases me, Ethan Blair," she murmured, slipping astride him as easily as she'd come to mount Two Hearts over their days of running. "They have, always."

He grinned. "Scent? Even the clove oil?"

She giggled softly, her hair sifting across his shoulder. "The clove oil, especially."

Her shift's hem reared back, revealing the creamy smoothness of her legs to midthigh. He spread his hands over the planes, feeling the contours, pushing her linen's billows higher.

Her nervous fingers slipped under his shirt, found the buttons of his bulging trousers.

"Miss Mercer," he contended, kicking them free there, under the warming sheets, the quilt, "I'm shocked."

"You will become my husband this night," she promised.

—There, good. Now. Be patient. Allow her to take you.

Ethan sat higher in the pillows, and brought down her shift's right sleeve slowly. She whimpered when the action freed a breast. He stroked the clothed nipple with his finger, gently suckled the other.

"Yes," Judith gasped, her perfect thighs dancing against his sides. Harder. She sang out a clear, haunting note and collapsed on his chest, languid again. Women's rushes. Where do they find all that strength? he wondered, laughing, kissing her drooping eyelids.

She smiled wide. Ethan reached under her shift, brought her thighs closer to where the impatient part of him waited.

"Ethan?" she whispered against his ear. "I feel this wild ache, this longing."

"Here?" His fingers found the mound of hair between her legs.

"Oh, yes," she sighed.

He explored further. Wet. That was good, it meant she wanted him, did it not? "Tell me," he whispered, suddenly feeling his own inexperience, even as his hardness strained beneath her. It had been five years since the night with Clarisse. What did he know about anything? He had only spent three hours with the woman, isn't that what Fayette himself had—

—It was enough.

Judith took part of him in her hands. Her hold increased his ardor. "Ethan, you're so . . ."

"Desirous of you," he tried to help.

"Yes, that. But your skin here, it's so soft, like a newborn's," she said with wonder, caressing him there, innocently, without realizing her touch was driving him to distraction. No, not yet. Not there, in her hand.

"Judith, please. When you're ready—" He tried to talk further, but his voice became guttural surges. He thought he would die from the intensity of his need. But he stayed there, below her, and waited.

Judith rose to her knees, then eased herself, with exquisite slowness, down. Slippery, delicious, glorious. Her blood trickled between his thighs. Bride blood. It pooled in the folds of his nightshirt beneath them. Had he hurt her? Ethan reached his hands to her face, cupped it between them.

"Are you well, Judith?" he whispered.

"Very well, husband."

She never lied. Ethan smiled. His hands wove through the folds of her shirt, took her hips. He lifted her, then gently set her down on him again. Once, twice. "Does that please you?"

"Oh, yes," she said, bowing her head, splaying his chest with her moonlit hair as the wind of the storm joined the waves' music outside.

She came forward, anchoring her hands at his shoulders, and began to move all on her own. He groaned deeply, delighted by her ability to give him pulsing squeezes as he lay buried there between her thighs. More notes rose from that beautiful white throat. What had he ever done to be granted these gifts from this woman?

The pulses came faster, more insistent. He answered them with thrusts of his own; what did she call them—wild longings? Soon he only had the power to hold her waist between his hands and hope for the best, which, he thought later when his wife lay collapsed in his arms, might have been good enough for this, their first completion of intimacy.

The rain's relentless beat was dying. —*Vigilance. Protect her,* the voice advised gently.

"Vigilance," he repeated, remembering from that night long ago how soundly he would sleep now. They could steal Judith if he slept that well. Steal her away forever, those relentless horsemen. Their Quaker pursuers, Eli's assassin, and his own brothers merged into a single force in Ethan's mind. He felt sweat line his brow. They would not be content, none of them. Not while Eli's blood beat through Judith Mercer's veins. They would always be following, until he killed them. Was this a vision of truth or the effects of his own exhaustion? he wondered, even as he sat up, ripped the fabric from the hem of his long shirt.

Judith murmured in sleepy protest as he anchored her to his wrist. He placed feathery kisses on her fingers as he finished his work, then eased back in the pillows. She settled herself against his heart, content.

—*Good,* the voice finally approved. *Now, you may sleep.*

The voice was attached to someone walking away from him, there, on the backs of his eyelids. He called. The figure continued, faster. He ran, lunged, fell on his face in the briny water of the *Standard*'s hold. His hand had only managed to grasp the edge of Clarisse's gold tapestry shawl.

Judith stretched, luxuriating in the featherbed and her husband's heat against her back. The wind still howled outside the shuttered windows of the cabin, but the rain had stopped. Ethan shifted, murmuring. *"Toujours. Allons danser."*

She turned. *Danser.* Dance? Was he dancing there behind the audaciously lashed lids? She decided she must study French, if her singularly handsome husband insisted on dreaming in the language.

In the distance, the waves of the Atlantic crashed against the rocky breakwall—the water over stone her husband had promised her at their first joining. How had he known?

Judith felt tears welling behind her eyes as his peaceful, even breathing wafted against her neck. She must stop this or it would wake him, and he needed his sleep. They must look after each other, they were a family now. Judith grabbed a fold of her shirt to press against her running nose. His hand followed behind the motion, like a marionette's. What had caused that?

Judith lifted the quilt. Ethan shifted, growling. He was naked under the covers. But the last she'd remembered he'd left his shirt on. Why had he removed it? The blood, of course. His shirt had caught her bride blood. It was now set out on the bench, facing the newly banked fire. Washed gleaming white again. She must have slept very soundly not to have heard him do all that. Judith shook her head.

"Night owl," she chided.

"Hmmmn?" He tucked her closer.

Now her hand was the marionette's, pulled to him. Judith saw the soft muslin bond linking their wrists. She stared at the fabric's initials, then at his drying shirt's ripped hem. "Ethan," she called softly, "my dearest love, why have you tied us together?"

"Joined," he murmured. "None asunder."

"I see," she whispered, kissing his cheek. She heard the sound of heavy boots on the porch outside. Her breath caught, panicked, in her throat.

27

Ethan's eyes shot open. He leaned over the bedside and lifted the knife from inside his boot. He cut their bond with one upward stroke. Judith stopped her mouth when his fierce eyes told her to keep still. He sank silently beneath the covers and emerged with his trousers on and reaching for his boots.

Judith watched her husband's long strides to the door. He lifted the latch and disappeared onto the porch.

No sound came but that of the relentless ocean. Then voices, laughter. Ethan's voice, and that of Del Burnett, the lighthouse keeper. Relief made Judith melt into the contours of the featherbed.

"Judith," Ethan summoned, standing above her. There was no sign of the knife, only a large steaming soup tureen between his hands. The remnant of their muslin link dangled from his wrist. "You'll have to eat this chowder, or I'll catch all hell from Queen Ida."

Judith laughed. "You must have frightened Del half to death."

He shrugged and placed the soup on the table. "I think he was more shocked by the two of us sleeping until noon."

"I have never slept until noon in my life!" she proclaimed.

Ethan grinned. "Behold," he announced, before opening the window's shutter. The sun was high, even through the dense mist outside. The sight of her husband's back covered with a gnarl of scars suddenly made Judith wish to weep, before he yanked his shirt over his head, then distracted her by climbing on the bed and showering her shoulders and neck with kisses. His shirt smelled wonderfully fresh and tinged with—What was that scent?

"The chowder's hot," he urged softly. "Let's eat."

She traced a line from his cheekbone to his chin. "And then?"

"Dessert. We go back to bed."

"Mr. Blair! In the afternoon?"

"And I get to yank the shift off *you* this time, wife."

"I did no such thing to you!"

He looked down his nose at her. "After your bridal modesty, I'd hardly expect you to admit it," he teased, rising, tucking his shirt into his trousers.

"Ethan, I did not take thy shirt in the night."

"Of course not." He sniffed like a haughty Frenchman. "Nor wash it nor set it out to dry by the fire? Why, your very basin betrays . . . *sacrebleu,*" he whispered suddenly, his stance crippling a little as he stood before her nightstand.

"What is it?"

"A piece of weaving, that's all," he said softly, the humor gone from his voice.

"Let me see?"

He brought her the basin, which had been washed clean of her blood. Left at the bottom was a triangular edge of shimmering tapestry cloth. He sat beside her on the bed, watching as she lifted the remnant. Judith felt its woven gold threads warm her cheek.

"How beautiful it is. And it smells like your shirt."

"Hyacinth."

"Yes, exactly, hyacinth!"

He bowed his head, but she could see him biting down hard on his lip. "I'll be back directly," he whispered, and then this man who'd bound himself to her all night disappeared into the mist outside.

Not far, he mustn't go far from Judith, he told himself as his legs took longer strides. He wanted to watch for the mist to lift, for herons and egrets. But he couldn't push the woman from his mind. Or the memory of her brilliant shawl, of her hyacinth scent filling the dank hold of the *Standard*. Clarisse had not lied to him, Fayette had. She had not married a merchant; she had died.

The ground grew wetter. His boot caught in the switchgrass growing at the spring tideline. It brought him down. Fayette caught him, becoming the trunk and low limbs of the wax myrtle tree. Ethan looked past its branches, skyward. The mist was lifting. He closed his eyes and felt the sun warm his eyelids, drying the tracks of his salty tears.

"What are you doing out here, wallowing in the mud?" Ida Burnett demanded, standing over him, her plaid skirts flying, a basket of clams at her ample hip.

Ethan scrambled to his feet. "I—wanted to gather some marsh flowers for my wife, for our table, before we feasted on your chowder, Mrs. Burnett. The sedge is in bloom by now, isn't it? And the reed still purple?"

She frowned. "Too much salt here, for either."

"Oh? Well, I suppose I'm lost, then."

She sighed. "Can you see the cabin through the pine?"

"Yes. Thank you."

She turned, shaking her head, causing a breeze herself with the straw picture hat tied over her frilly white cap. Ethan had lost all hope of winning this woman over when she turned back to him.

"Mr. Blair!"

He almost saluted. *"Madame?"*

"The wax myrtle's in bloom just above you, if you've a mind to climb. Looks pretty bunched with the black needlerush, which you'll find up toward the cabin. You'll need something to get back in your wife's good graces once she sees those clothes."

"I appreciate your suggestions, Mrs. Burnett," he said, bowing low.

"Bridegrooms," she muttered, but hid her face in the shadow of her enormous hat before she turned and continued on her way. Had he amused her, at least?

Judith took the needlerush and myrtle blossoms from his arms. She searched his eyes. Their suffering was replaced by a vigilant glow.

"Ethan, you look like someone lit a candle inside you."

He grinned. "There, then. How do you like it?"

"I? Like what?"

"Your own medicine, this Inner Light. It's daunting, yes?"

She turned, arranging the flowers in a bowl on the table.

"Judith," he asked her quietly, "what has happened to your '*thees*' and '*thous*'?"

"I am a friend of Friends now, I think, my darling."

He smiled. "That's what Eli said you might choose."

Her hands stilled. "Did he? Did he truly?"

"I never lie." He teased her with her own testimony about him.

"And when he said this . . . my father did not sound disappointed?"

"In you?" He stood taller. " 'Judith will know what she is,' he said, exactly like that."

"Without your accent."

"What accent?"

She covered her mouth as the giggle escaped.

"No," he admonished her softly, "don't hide, *ma chère,* ever." He descended like a clear-eyed hawk and kissed once, twice. Again, deeper. Tasting.

"You've eaten!" he accused her suddenly. "While I was lost in the swamp!"

She backed away. "I'm sorry. I was so hungry. And worried about you, and it smelled so—"

"This is very rude. And must be punished."

"Punished?" She saw the gleam in his eyes and laughed. "Ethan Blair, I will never get used to thy teasing!"

He swooped her into his arms and headed for the bed, loosening her gowns as he went.

"You must eat—" she protested mildly.

"It's Judith Mercer's bounty that interests me now," he assured her. She sank in the featherbed under his kisses. He started on her bodice ties as she groped for his trousers' buttons.

Judith reached up, taking in the daylight vision of his torso through the fine weave of his shirt. She ran her hands over his narrow hips. Between them, the sign of his hunger for her was apparent. And larger than she remembered from deep in the shrouded night.

"Your leg feels better today, does it?" she asked shyly.

He closed his eyes. With a force of his will, Judith thought, he eased his breathing into a more regular pattern. "Last night. Would you like to start that way now, my love?" he whispered tenderly at her ear. "Above me?"

"Yes. Please."

"Everything you do pleases me, Judith," he promised as she climbed astride him.

She let the softness of him glide along her inner thigh. With the delight of anticipation born of their night together, she placed him inside her. She moved, whimpered, then cried out until she felt she would die of happiness.

But it was not like the night before, at her fulfillment. He was still hard inside her. What did that mean? she wondered. Had she done something wrong?

He slid his arm around her back and brought her beneath him, reversing their positions. She reached up, touched his face, remembering their time on the quilt at Windover, trusting that he would never hurt her.

"My," she murmured, "you are quite . . . well."

"Nay, Judith. I am a desperate man, fevered with love of this woman, my wife."

His words, his gentle prodding. What was happening? "Too much," she murmured.

He stopped, there above her.

"Between us," she explained. "Too much . . . cloth," came out of her like a growl. He grinned, yanking his shirt over his head. The sight of him ignited another spark of desire within her. He was approaching, circling that desire slowly, with craft and assurance, like a thief of souls. She grabbed his shoulders, welcoming him inside her.

"Yes," he encouraged her at the ear. "Oh, my darling, yes." He moved more insistently. Judith grabbed wildly for the bed's bolster so that she would not take flight without him.

"Ethan!"

"Here. I'm here, love."

"Kiss me!"

He obeyed, giving her a different mooring—his mouth, his tongue, and fine, strong teeth. Her fingers dug into his scalp, his ridged back. It shocked her, at first, until she saw the sparks in his eyes, heard his guttural urges to continue. Every part of her struggled to stay below his deep, assertive plunges at her core.

Then came the last, the warm wetness before he diminished inside her, and fell gently onto her steaming body. He made a despairing sound of surrender before his head bowed to her shoulder.

His breathing evened. "Too soon?" he asked.

"No, no," she assured him, stroking back his wet hair. "It was perfect."

"I love you, Judith," he whispered gruffly.

Judith felt the twitch beside his eye with the sensitive skin above her bared, still-tingling breast. It made her think of his fever convulsions. What had she done? He must eat. But though she now felt she could move a mountain, he was falling asleep, there beneath her heart. How different men were.

When she tried to slip out of bed, he caught her hand.

"Stay close."

"I will. Rest, love."

He did not sleep in a tight, small place, the way she'd trained herself to do after being a guest in half of so many hosting families' beds, Judith realized. Although Washington had curled himself in his hammock, this man she'd married slept stretched out, his body's form distinct and powerful.

Judith felt herself grow wet again at the sight of him, shrouded only in the bed's sheet. She fought the urge to wake him, to ask him if they could start all over again.

She pulled a light blanket to his waist. *Vanity, Judith,* she scolded herself, *and selfish, to have enjoyed this bliss while your husband was yet to break a nightly fast that had stretched past noon.* Well, he'd started it, hadn't he?

She spun away from the bed. Useful, do something useful. She picked up the haphazard trail of their discarded clothes. She examined his ripped shirt, cast off so fast a button had flown across the room. She found the tin that held sewing supplies, and quickly threaded a needle. Behind her, her young husband shifted, breathed out a wistful sigh. She longed for his touch at her breasts, and between her legs.

The porch, she admonished herself—and fled.

There, Judith shielded her eyes with her hand, taking hold of the post. She waved to her stout landlady, then fingered the long, loose braid that fell to her waist. It was as far as Judith Mercer, of the intricate braids beneath her cap, had gotten dressing her hair on this first morning of her consummated marriage. No, afternoon. She wore no shifts beneath her indigo gowns. But Queen Ida couldn't see that, could she? *Burnett,* she reminded herself as the woman's jaunty step approached. Not Queen Ida. Burnett.

"Mrs. Blair," the woman announced tersely.

"Good day to you, Mrs. Burnett. My husband and I thank you for the chowder."

"Sit down, sit down. I wouldn't have stopped at all if it wasn't for you looking like one of my own daughters, and maybe thinking me rude if I did not." She looked over the task in Judith's lap. "He's ripped his shirt besides muddying his clothes in the marsh, has he?"

"The hem's a little frayed," was all Judith would admit.

The big woman sat on the bench beside her. "A good, strong seam," she observed.

"Ethan taught it to me," Judith blurted out her pride in him.

"He doesn't sew!"

"Better than I. He mended the sails—"

"Knew it! My Del knew he was a seaman from the wide-stance walk on him, but I knew it from the eyes!"

"He was, yes."

"Navy, or merchant marine?"

Judith prayed for guidance in her silence.

"In the war, was he, little one? Del says his back's horrible scarred, the likes of which he's only seen on slaves."

"I—don't mind them." Stitch. Lock. Stitch. Judith felt a trickle of sweat at the small of her back. No more questions, please.

"Your trunk's in order, I hope?"

"Trunk?"

"Just beside you, child. Del left it this morning." Judith stared at the fine, leather-bound trunk poised at the end of the porch. So Ethan did know where they were going, and had sent a trunk. "Must admit, we were puzzled by it," Ida Burnett continued, keeping a watchful eye on her, "all the way from a Virginia coachstop keeper, transport paid, no explanation with it. Where is your husband now?"

"Asleep."

"Asleep? Does he sleep around the clock?"

"We had a very wearying ride." The image of Ethan above her, his face suffused with delight as she moved, squeezed his thigh—that ride invaded her mind, not their journey here. "Yesterday, the days before . . . wearying," she finished quickly as her cheeks flared red.

"The escape from your doting relatives."

"Escape, yes. I would ask thee in . . . but my husband needs his rest so desperately now, I think."

Thee. Had she said "thee"? Had Ida noticed?

"Ah. Desperate is he, this bridegroom who beds you till noon, pulls his knife on my poor husband, then roams about fetching flowers in the mist?"

"Ethan didn't mean—"

"He fetches something else to you as well, I'll warrant, before he takes to his napping."

Judith hid her hands within the folds of his shirt as she felt the fresh flush at her cheeks.

Ida Burnett laughed. "Ah, the men. It takes everything out of the poor creatures, don't it?"

"Does it? Have I . . . Oh, Mrs. Burnett, have I hurt him?"

The large woman threw back her head and laughed. "Lord love us, little one! Don't you be thinking you're doing him any harm! Didn't your mother tell you the ways of them?"

"I lost her early, and never thought I'd marry. My knowledge is so limited," Judith shook her head, and felt the warmth of Queen Ida's fish-scented fingers against her cheek. "But I do wish to be a good wife in all ways. I love him so much!"

"Aye, I've gathered that. Is your sea-crazed husband treating you well in return?"

"Oh yes," she proclaimed fiercely, "Ethan is the best of men. You'll see. You will not regret your kindness to us, Mrs. Burnett!"

"Well. Your horses are not so bad off as first they looked. And my Del knows human nature better than me. So I trusted his judgment, though you're confusing, the two of you. I thought your man a mite touched when first you came in with the storm, that is, after I got over his look."

"Look?"

"How old is your husband, Mrs. Blair?"

"Three-and-twenty."

"Yes." The word came out of her like a sigh before she turned no-nonsense again. "He yanked you out of the plain folk with that fearsome weapon of his, didn't he?"

"I came freely, Mrs. Burnett."

"Ida. Ida and Del. We are friends of the Friends here."

"We are Judith and Ethan only. And pleased to be among you."

The gruff woman rose and wound her way over the dunes without ceremony. Judith discovered a wrapped loaf of oatmeal-scented bread on the porch's step. The door behind her cracked open.

"She's gone?"

"Yes."

"If we're going to have our first proper, roof-over-our-heads meal together, you'd best give me my shirt."

Judith tried to smile away the catch in her throat she felt at the sight of her tousle-haired husband leaning against the doorway. She faced him at the threshold. "I'm bereft of undergarments, myself," she announced.

"Here."

He handed her the snowy-white shift casually draped over his arm. It was clean, dry, without a trace of bloodstain. And scented sweetly of hyacinths, just as his was.

He snatched his shirt from her hands and reentered the house. "Good seam," he conceded.

28

Ethan watched the sand for signs of life below. He was good at clamming, even Ida said so. And it kept him away from Del and his sons urging him on to the Atlantic. Why did his mother send him to the shore with a promise not to set foot on a vessel? Was there any way around it? Stop. It was ridiculous, to feel deprived here.

He heard Judith's laughter behind him as she rode Two Hearts across the dunes. How she and his bride gift had taken to each other. Dr. Foster's horse was still wary of him after their wild journey. But they were all less skittish these days. The trail to them had certainly gone cold. Surely Prescott Lyman had gone back to his farm, his family, his widower's life. And the arrangement the magistrates made with Ethan's brothers had been a private one. Officially, there were no charges against him in Eli's death. Suspicions would remain, of course. Most of Judith's people thought she'd married her father's murderer. All but the murderer himself.

After their first two weeks with the lightkeepers, Ethan had sent the letter to his sister in Richmond as Dr. Foster had instructed. Judith began sewing a gown for herself from his mother's gift of rose-colored cambric and one of his shirts, refashioned. It lay across the foot of their bed, almost complete, yet there had not come a reply. Sometimes that made him feel cast adrift, here at the edge of the world.

There: a small hole in the shape of a key. The clam sign Ida had schooled him to find. He dug with the double-pronged instrument she'd bestowed on him once he'd demonstrated his interest. Now she teased him about his newfound skill. "If that physician loses his patience with you, Mr. Blair, you may return and clam for Del and me."

Sometimes Ethan sensed the ghost of remembrance between himself and the lightkeepers. Their kind eyes would drift sad then, and he would turn away, in case it was the look of him that caused it.

The scrape of shell. Ethan dug deeper, then pried the clam loose.

"That's enough to carry back between us," Judith said.

He looked up. The bright sun was blocked by one of Ida's hats, shielding both Judith and him in its shade. On the grassy ridge behind her, their horses grazed with only loose rope halters assigning them to human masters. Judith's skirts were drawn up over her waistband from her barebacked ride. After three weeks, the indigo was fading, but her petticoats seemed whiter.

They both dressed for the weather instead of any notion of convention. Ethan had packed Jordan Foster's clothes in the bottom of his trunk and wore his own. But he'd gone coatless for days. He wished for an even stronger nor'easter than the one that had blown them to this place, one that would separate their little home from the mainland. Then they would need no clothes at all.

"What are you grinning at?" Judith demanded.

He stood, hitching slightly as his right knee protested the action's swiftness. "That hat. I'm hoping it won't fly you away."

The mirth in her eyes darkened with mischief. "You'll keep me grounded, will you not, husband?"

He caught her waist. "Grounded, yes."

She opened her mouth under his kisses. The taste of her did what it always did. Yes. There were very few layers between them. And his need was so urgent.

"These clams," he said at her ear, "they'll keep in the shade."

"But there's no—"

"Your hat's shade," he said, pulling free the tie, sailing the hat backward. It missed its bucket of clams target by three feet. They didn't notice.

Easy. Slow down. No more tears, stitches, patches in their clothing, he told himself. Judith's deft fingers were helping keep her gown intact this time. They unlatched his way to her as they reached the tall grass. He didn't deserve this woman, her beauty, the power of her lovemaking. But feeling undeserving had never stopped him from pursuing his heart's desire, not as a Randolph or Fayette's Washington. It would not as a Blair.

The grass shielded them completely once they were on their knees, teasing themselves with nips, kisses, licks at sun-burnished, gloriously salty skin.

"Marsh maiden," he whispered as she went down beneath him. The grasses flattened like a halo around her white braid, her indigo-lavender skirts.

"Not a maiden any longer," she whispered hot, dusky, without a hint of regret.

He felt her fingers weave through his hair as he gently suckled her breasts. Her back arched, she urged him on. Now, if he could find her through the petticoats. One, two. Bless you, Judith, only two today. Wet, ready. Inside. There. The rich, red promise of her. Whispers at her ear as he toiled at his favorite labor. Where would it take him this time? Love words, phrases in two languages, punctuated by her demands for translations, his inability to think of them.

Her skittering laughter burst forth, sea-siren music. His imagination turned her a glistening green, there below him. It webbed the fingers that explored his thighs. She was beautiful green. What was he, this time? Not a man with a stiff, aching leg. One who could fly. As high as the sun itself. Then swoop down, capture this astonishing creature. Deep moans told him she was ready for his deepest plunges, the wildest flight of his imaginings. She welcomed him with a high-pitched wail as he crashed like Icarus into her sea. Then Judith's arms drew him close, though he was wet with the sweat of his effort. Fingered again, she combed the hair back from his brow.

"Sweet Ethan," she whispered at his ear.

Yes. He would touch a thousand suns to die such deaths.

Through his contented drowsiness he sensed their horses approaching, restless and frightened. He opened his eyes. The sun was gone, the sky no longer blue. Thunder. Drops of rain on their upturned faces. Judith slipped out of his arms. She closed the portals of her clothing, then spun away, chasing her hat as a gust of wind blew it toward the sea. She tied it to her waistband. Ethan yanked on his trousers. He placed her cloak over her shoulders.

"Lightning. This is not good," he said quietly. "Come. We must bring the horses to shelter."

"But the clams, Ethan."

"They will keep. Mind me, woman, I'm a lowlander."

He hoisted her aboard Two Hearts, pleased by the sure grip of her thighs, her instinctive command of the white mare. He called Dr. Foster's horse and mounted. The rain pelted Judith's skirts. She raised her hood around her head. They rode a steady gallop across the dunes and toward the lighthouse.

The horses stabled, they found the house and grounds deserted, though the tower's reflector oil-lamps were lit and shining against the encroaching darkness of the sudden storm. At the pier, Ethan saw four horsemen approaching two huddled figures on the edge of the dock. "Judith. Is that . . . ?"

"Del. He's protecting Ida from those men."

"Yes. That's how I see it too." He grasped her hand.

They had not seen any but Ida and Del and their sons for so long. Was that why the hard-faced intruders looked barely human? One, the leader, pointed a tobacco-stained finger.

"Who in hell are they?"

Del raised his head defiantly. "Our guests. They have nothing to do with this."

Out on the ocean a vessel struggled against the sudden storm. That was the source of their argument. It was overloaded, Ethan could see that. The single mast was down, both sails flying in shredded tatters.

"For the love of God," Del said, "allow me to sound the alarm!"

"And let your nest of abolitionists take flight in the warning? Stay where you are. I've got everything I need now, including the constable in attendance."

"Mr. White—" Ida appealed to the one who didn't smell of bourbon.

"Sea's too rough to send out a boat, anyway, Miss Burnett," he said, without looking at her.

Scrambling to keep the vessel afloat were eight people. A family, Ethan thought, from their differing sizes.

"Dear God," Judith whispered beside him.

The small boat disappeared behind a swell. It came into view again, accompanied by high-pitched screaming. Ethan counted only seven aboard now. A dark head bobbed above the waves nearby. Gleaming streaks swarmed around it.

"There's one for the sharks," an amused voice intoned behind them. "Them in the boat won't leave him. They'll all go down."

Ethan had promised his mother to stay off boats, but not out of the sea itself. He pulled off his left boot, then his right. Judith's strong grip took his arms. "No!"

"They're not sharks, Judith, they're dolphins. They're trying to help. I'm a good swimmer. I can hardly do less, can I?"

She nodded, but whether it was in acceptance or despair, he couldn't tell. Tears streaked down cheeks already wet with rain. He pulled off his vest and placed it and his boots in her arms. "I follow my light, Judith Mercer," he whispered at her ear. He kissed her, then dived off the pier.

When he felt the cold Atlantic's assault, he wondered if it was such a good idea to tell her that. If he died, would she ever trust her own Light again?

His head broke the surface, closer to the distressed sloop than he'd thought possible. The smooth, strong strokes Aubrey'd taught him returned, making him feel powerful in the water. An illusion, Ethan realized, when a wall of water plunged him under the depths.

He opened his eyes to the flash of silver. The dolphin was about his own size and not nearly as bothered by the churning sea. The animal nodded its head twice, almost playfully. Ethan grasped the dorsal fin. It was smooth, but he could hold on. How many times had he imagined what was happening now?

There: a shadowy figure descending, lifeless, below them. Ethan remembered Judith's tear-stained face. He released the dolphin and grabbed. He caught cloth, closed his fist around it, and kicked for the surface.

Water. Only water, no light. How deep had he gone? He couldn't keep his breath locked inside. He expelled it. Slowly, until panic set in. Then it gushed in great bubbles. There was nothing to replace it but water.

He sent a message out toward the returning flash of silver. He had not told Judith who to go to if he should die, he explained. He had not told her so much of what he stored in his heart. He must not die now. His grip began to quake. —*No. Not let go,* came the command. The dolphin's smooth coldness. Under him. Rising. Speaking? Propel. —*Kick.* Legs kick, rise.

Ethan's head cleared the surface. He gasped and coughed and breathed air. Behind him he heard the calling voices, saw the boat. And he could see the shore. He lifted his burden higher above the waves. Homespun shirt. A head. A boy. Still, lifeless. No, not lifeless. Harry, Aubrey, Fayette, Clarisse, Eli. No more death. Ethan swam as if both their lives depended on it.

The boat followed. The storm past its peak, the forks of lightning receded eastward out to sea. Judith stood in the water at the shore. Everything would be all right now.

Above the waves, Ethan held a boy of twelve or thirteen, Judith guessed as she waited, shivering. He'd need help once his feet were on the ground, this wondrous swimmer who could not walk without his boots. The wave buffed her back, but she recovered her stance. She caught one of the boy's arms. Together they dragged him to the shore.

Ethan shifted the gray figure gently to his side. If there had been panic beneath the waves there was no sign of it left. The boy's face was beautiful, serene. The men rushed forward.

"This one's dead," the first announced.

Another man spit in the sand. "Risked your neck for a dead nigger, you bleeding idiot," he informed Ethan, then followed the others who were pulling the sloop ashore and counting their remaining captives. Judith heard the hesitant step of the sad-eyed constable.

Ethan ignored them all. He gently prodded the still form.

They were soon surrounded by women's high wails, men's searing, silent grief. Behind them were the slave catchers, knowing only that they'd gotten seven out of eight. Judith wanted Ethan away from them all. He was pale and shaking and his eyes frightened her. She called.

Nothing. She touched his sleeve. He pushed her away.

He crawled around the boy. Quickly, the way he used to scramble about below the decks of the *Standard*, before he could walk. Completing his circle, he squatted beside the still figure. They were all watching him now.

"Aubrey!" he summoned. "Breathe!"

The heel of his left hand shot out. It thumped the boy hard between his shoulder blades.

Judith thought the resulting sound was the mother's shock. But it had burst from the boy himself. A cough. Another. Then a green wad projected onto the sand. Flickering eyelids. Movement. "Good Lord," Del said behind her.

The woman surged forward, but Ethan stayed her hand. They all watched as the boy vomited, then took in great gulps of air. He pulled himself to his knees, then finally looked up at them, blinking.

Ethan released the woman. He tried to stand, but forgot his boots were not on his feet. He fell. For the first time, Judith smiled at the sound of one of his soft French blasphemies as she covered him with her cloak and took his head in her lap. His teeth were so white against blue lips. Behind them, the clang of the metal chains.

"I'm shaking?" he stammered.

"A little."

"It's the cold, yes, Judith?"

"The cold."

"Not the fits?" he whispered.

"No, love."

"They'll think me mad, lock me up, with those chains. Not the fits again?"

"No. The cold, that's all," she pressed him close, praying it was the truth.

He closed his eyes. Judith could feel him trying to will himself warm. But even his soft groan of frustration shuddered. Del appeared on his other side and together they brought him to his feet.

"You'll be right as the rain once warmed, clamdigger," he assured them both. "Come. Lean on me."

Inside the lightkeeper's house Ethan breathed in Queen Ida's clam-and-strudel scent as she peeled back the blanket and rubbed his arms as if they were tinder to start her hearthfire.

"Need more meat on you, bridegroom. It's no wonder you can't handle the cold!" she admonished, making him smile. She threw a pair of her husband's light trousers and a shirt from the basket at her hip. How kind this gruff woman was, even in the midst of her own adversity, he thought.

And her eyes told him she was guilty as charged. Del and Ida Burnett had been keeping more than the light, and the men with the iron chains were out to see them destroyed for it. A worried glance passed between Ethan and Judith as he pulled on Del's trousers and she helped him with the leather braces. Judith knew. Wasn't his wife a lawbreaker too? And he himself had given the silver buttons away to the eight-fingered Atlas.

"Damnation," the head slave catcher said, suddenly pumping Ethan's hand. "You can have the full reward on that young buck, sir! I ain't never seen anything like what you done to yank him back from the—"

Ethan stood. "Reward? What are you talking about?" he demanded. "These are my people, sir."

"What?"

"Seek your runaways elsewhere. Martha and Aaron and their children are my father's seasoned house servants," he said in his most imperious Virginia accent. He faced the huddled family. "You all were sent up the coastal waterway by my relatives, weren't you?" He turned to the constable and slave catchers. "My family does not think my wife and I can survive our simple seaside holiday without being tended! I warned you to be on watch for them, did I not, Del, Ida?"

"You did indeed sir," Ida said quickly.

"When I get ahold of my brothers, I will wring their necks for putting valuable property in danger!"

Judith took his fisted hand in her gentle grasp. "Now, husband," she soothed, "calm yourself."

He stood. "What do you think, Aaron? Can the mast be repaired?"

The oldest male of the boatmen bowed. "We'll fix her, master, we'll set all aright, you be at your ease 'bout that!"

The woman beside him pulled the drying cloth from the hearth and began to rub it gingerly against Judith's scalp. "Leave the men talkin' 'bout that wicked sloop like she was a child, missus," she chimed. "Let Martha look after your own self now!"

Judith smiled at the kindness, then looked to Ethan as if wondering if she should have ignored it, the way Clara and Hester ignored the slaves at Windover. Ethan grinned, no help at all.

The head slave catcher's eyes narrowed. "And your name, sir?"

"Washington. Henry Washington. My wife, Judith."

The uneasy constable came forward. "Washington, sir? Virginia Washingtons? Related to—?"

"We want no preferential treatment because of our name, of course, Constable. We are, as Del said, residing here humbly as their guests."

The man stepped back. "Of course." He turned to the slave catchers. "He went into the water after his own property. He's not daft. That makes sense."

Ethan hoped only Judith heard the grinding of his teeth. He raised his head. "I would appreciate your leave to get my wife and servants settled before a higher toll is taken on my father's estate."

Constable White squared his shoulders. He faced the head slave catcher. "I believe you are mistaken in this hunt, Mr. Stone."

"Where's proof—like their papers sayin' that these niggers are not runaways but his daddy's blasted house servants?" Stone demanded.

"Out there," Ethan replied tersely, pointing with his chin toward the ocean. "I have heard of such things happening in the North—of loyal traveling servants being ruthlessly hounded, captured, sold to new, unscrupulous masters. But here? Here, south of the Mason-and-Dixon line? I am appalled, sir!"

"Easy, Mr. Washington," the constable said. "No one's going to—"

One of the clanging men glared at Judith. "Now, this patched-together woman don't look like any damned plantation mistress!"

Ethan stepped between them. "I am only a third son, but you will speak more respectfully in the presence of my wife, sir!" he demanded. The four black men quickly flanked him, even the recovering boy. The woman and girls surrounded Judith.

"You and your men will leave these people to their recovery. You are banned from this property until further notice, Mr. Stone!" the constable stormed, finally standing at his full height.

"It's these lightkeepers are the lawbreakers! You cannot—"

"I have so ordered! Take your complaint up to the magistrate!"

"Merde. Magistrates again," Ethan whispered.

Once the intruders had gone, Judith felt that the hearth room was infused with triumph and a celebration held down from giddy heights by a cautious hope. She watched with pride as Ethan listened intently at the boy's back as he breathed.

"Sounds good, sir?" his mother asked.

"Better than this bruise looks." He lifted the boy's shirt higher and winced. "I'm sorry I hit you so hard. What is your name?"

"Whatsoever you say it is, sir."

Ethan smiled. "Free people choose their own names."

The boy cocked his head. There were gold glints in his tightly curled hair. "Who was Aubrey, Doctor?"

"I'm not nearly a doctor."

"But Miss Ida, she say—"

"Queen Ida's the most skillful deceiver in these parts, I'd wager."

The large woman spun around, fisting her hands at her waist. "You'd prefer to live on in song and story as the Almighty Himself maybe, with the power to bring back the dead?"

"I—" Ethan stammered under her ferocious tone.

She turned her attention to the boy and his mother. "He's only just a doctor, like I said, one who knew there was a wad of seaweed in the child's throat," she explained softly, reserving her flinty tone for when she glanced back at Ethan. "And I'm no grand dissembler. Lost my title to you this night, 'Henry Washington'! What tales you can weave of whole cloth!"

"Judith!" he commanded. "Tell this confounded woman I never lie!"

Judith smiled. "Ethan is in need of spectacles, perhaps, concerning the identity of these travelers." She eased herself under his arm, turning him back to the boy on the bed, who was rubbing his eyes in exhaustion. "Ethan," she chided softly, "answer this child."

"I forgot the question."

She shook her head. "Aubrey was my husband's friend," she said. "He taught him how to swim."

The boy raised shining eyes to Ethan. "He taught you right good."

"Yes."

"He be dead now?"

Ethan bowed his head. Judith hugged him close. The boy smiled, and held up his hands, as if he were offering them something.

"My old master, he likes them Roman folks. Named me for one: Octavius—Gus. But I'm right taken to this name you hit me with, sir. I'll be Aubrey in the cold country, the one that will not send us back, if'n you gives me leave of his name, Doctor."

"Hush, child," his mother admonished him softly.

Ethan looked into the boy's eyes. "I'll tell Aubrey's parents there's a new freeman in Canada with his name," he whispered, then turned abruptly from the bedside. He walked past the girl stirring fresh chowder on the hearthfire and out the door.

Judith followed. The wind picked up the red skirts of the gown Ida Burnett had bestowed on her, billowing the excess material. Ethan sat below her on the porch steps. It was time, for some unburdening. Before the dolphins took him below the waves again.

"Aubrey was my nephew, Judith. My kinsman."

"Ethan."

"Aaron is my father's son, his oldest son, by a slavewoman named Hagar, who wore a red cardinal feather, here." He pressed his finger to the knot of Dr. Foster's fading red stitches at his temple.

She took his hand down gently, kissed the scar. Why did she do that?

"You . . . don't think me blighted?"

Her brows slanted in amusement, in that way he loved.

"Blighted?"

"For coming from such people? Who would hold slaves, who would make a woman . . . Then own his own son?"

"Aaron is a fine man, who is also related to your father, husband."

"Yes, but—"

"And I am married to a fine man. I thank his parents for their part in his existence."

It was taking her less and less time to disarm him, Ethan realized, smiling. "I share kinship with slaves, Judith."

She shook her head. "Only you would take that view of it, Ethan Blair," she told him. "Not that they share your blood, but that you share theirs."

He didn't understand the difference, but her words sparked another thought. "Perhaps that's why they sang to me, the slaves in the hold of the *Standard*. Perhaps that is why I must keep my vow to see Aaron and his family freed."

"You vowed—?"

"Yes. Before I left for Pennsylvania. I have no idea how, of course. Only the burning need. It's worse, now."

"Oh, Ethan."

He shrugged. "Not much of a Randolph, am I?"

She held his face between her long, seamstress fingers. "I think you would feel the same if you were Hagar's son, or Eli Mercer's, or Maupin's," she said. "And I take a measureless pride in my husband."

She kissed him then, and he returned her sweet generosity, before easing himself comfortably against her skirts.

"This Inner Light business, Judith. It's dangerous sometimes, isn't it?" he whispered, watching for the rise of the moon.

She rested her hand at his shoulder. "Yes, love."

"Not that I regret today—who could? I used to dream of swimming with the dolphins who followed behind the *Standard*, remember?"

"I remember."

"And today, I did." He stared into the sky as the fast-moving clouds cleared their view of the constellations. "And . . . I think I talked with one, Judith."

"My."

"Not talked exactly, of course, but I heard—here, inside my head. He reminded me to kick. Are you laughing?"

"No, Ethan."

He squeezed her hand and leaned his head deeper in her voluminous borrowed skirts. "Judith. If, sometime, anything should happen . . ."

"Nothing will happen."

"Judith, listen. If the convulsions come over me again—"

"They did not, it was the cold!"

He sat up, brought her hand to the curve of his face before trying again. "But, should they," he insisted quietly, "or should my brothers, or any manner of local, commonwealth, state, or federal officials ever achieve their dearest wish to lock me away from you—"

"Ethan," she pleaded, "don't, please. I can't bear this."

"Oh, you've borne much worse, love," he reminded her, stroking her tear tracks gently with his thumbs. "Judith. The thought of having you and Eli caring about what happened to me kept me alive after Fayette on the *Standard*. Did I ever tell you that?"

She shook her head.

"No. Exactly. I have been remiss. Out there in the water today, all I could think about were the things I've yet to tell you. Things like—Judith, you gave your father to me. And I, who thought that fathers were cold and distant and demanding . . . well, suddenly this wondrous man was calling me 'son.' . . . I'm not doing this in the right way."

"It's right," she assured him, though she was still crying, not celebrating, as he imagined the Quaker manner of grief to be. He kissed their twinned fingers.

"Jordan will be that for you, Judith. And my sister is your sister. And Mother, yours. We have a family, you and I. Promise me you'll stay with them if the need proves—"

"Yes, yes." She pressed cold fingers to his lips and nodded.

"Done, then." He pulled out his ever-present handkerchief. "Now, now, no more of this, or Dr. Blair will give you a proper blow and make your poor back as bruised as that of my hapless patient in there."

He leaned close, his tongue taking a playful swipe at her earlobe. "You are so delicious I will argue even with my Inner Light toward remaining out of trouble."

"Oh, Ethan." She hugged him hard enough to bring a spasm to his still-aching lungs.

"Silly woman," he said gruffly, easing her grip.

Ida and Del stood over them suddenly, their affable demeanor gone, and purpose overcoming even the grief in their eyes. What had he done now? Ethan wondered, then realized immediately it was what he hadn't yet done that was causing this.

"We almost lost you." Ida said.

"I—" He looked to her husband. But Del was holding firm, too. Well, why shouldn't he?

"It is time for all deception between us to cease. We know the look of runaways," he said.

"And that you served with our Harry aboard the *Ida Lee*," Ida whispered.

"How?" Ethan breathed out.

"Your hand, child," Del explained. "The letter we posted for you to Richmond was in the same strong, steady hand that wrote our boy's letters home from the sea. Did you think we would forget your skill in getting his thoughts on your own fine paper, Midshipman R.? Or sharing your oilskin packets to house the letters, so that now we have something left of him?"

Ethan felt Judith squeeze his hand. "On Mrs. Madison's list. Burnett, of course," she whispered. "H. Burnett; age: eleven years."

Ethan looked away from the couple's penetrating gaze. This was more difficult than he'd imagined. "I'm sorry," he whispered. "I'm so sorry. He was at my post, you see, when the cannons fired."

"He was killed when the British boarded you?"

"Yes."

"He didn't drown, then?" Ida asked.

"No, *madame.*"

"That's a good thing."

"Good?"

"He was only afraid of drowning."

"Were you with him, when—?" Del asked in a choked whisper.

"Yes, sir. I held him, his hand here, against my heart, until pulled away. It wasn't long in coming, the death. It had grace. And a terrible beauty."

Del Burnett took his wife under his shoulder and shook Ethan's hand. "You and your fine lady honor our household, sir."

"No. No, I don't. But we were in such desperate need, Judith and I. And Harry said his family would never turn me away if ever I came to this place, on the shore of Maryland, where his parents kept the light."

Ida reached into her apron pocket. She drew out a letter sealed with his sister's stamp. "There *is* a physician in Richmond, isn't there, dissembler?" she asked Ethan quietly.

"Yes."

"This came today." She handed him the missive. Ethan broke the seal and scanned the contents.

"He's sent for you, then?" Del asked.

"Yes. But I think the Washingtons must repair their sloop and send their servants to sea again before the Blairs return to Richmond. If you might suffer the lot of us a little while longer."

"Such a little while, Midshipman R. and your beautiful bride." The woman brought the edge of her apron to her eyes. Queen Ida, Ethan realized, was crying. Perhaps that was the strangest event of the day.

29

"Where are your things?" Jordan Foster asked as they stood in the small vestibule of the two-storied house on Charles Street. Judith clung to Ethan's arm. What was required of an apprentice doctor's wife? she wondered. She couldn't even cook a proper meal. And she and her ardent lover were so far from the shore and its freedoms.

"This is all," he said. "Judith's reticule. My saddlebags."

"Oh, I see."

Ethan glanced back at where their horses stood off the main thoroughfare of the busy street. "You have stables?"

"No. I keep Lark at livery. It's just down the street."

"Ah." Ethan nodded. "Has she been much trouble?"

"She's served me well. I have a wide circuit of patients."

"Already?"

"Your sister's beat the drum."

Ethan smiled. "She would. Will you come outside? To see your horse? We call her Morgan, for the breed, because I do not know her name. Judith's mare is Two Hearts, and they've been good companions. Do you think we can keep them stalled together? Is it very expensive, boarding them out?" He glanced over the doctor's shoulder. "This is a fine house. As fine as your place in Norfolk, isn't it? I do not have my bearings. Does Sally live far? When do you think we might—"

The doctor took Ethan's arm, abruptly stopping his flow of words. "You're staying?" he asked in a strained whisper.

The two men stared at each other for what seemed to Judith an eternity.

"Is that not our agreement, sir?" Ethan asked quietly.

"Yes."

"Seulement change d'avis?"

"What?"

Ethan blinked. "Pardon. I ask if you have changed your mind."

"No!"

"Good." He grinned in a way that made him look very young. "If you had, I'd owe you money I no longer have." Judith felt his hand squeeze hers as he sobered his expression. "Give me a chance, Jordan. I know that I talk too much, but I listen well too, especially when I'm not frighted to the bone."

"Frighted? What has you frighted, son?"

"You, standing here on your doorstep, looking at us as if we are strangers! Dr. Foster, Judith and I, we require little—a place by your fire. It will not be so bad. We won't give you cause to regret your generosity. I will work very hard. And Judith is worth a dozen of me, you know that! She'll—"

The doctor looked out at the slice of Virginia sky. Judith felt Ethan's hand grow cold.

"Mon dieu," he whispered. "It's something else. Something's happened. To my mother? Sally? One of the little ones?"

"No, no, no. Everyone is well."

"What is wrong, then, sir?"

Jordan Foster's eyes searched theirs again, as if they had the answer. "You're staying? Here? With me?"

"Yes!"

The sad-eyed man finally smiled. "Well. Well, then. Allow me to welcome you. Come in, come in. Welcome home, Judith, Ethan. Home, yes. Welcome home."

Judith stepped out of her husband's hold, and took the physician's hands. She kissed his cheek. "How good that word sounds to us, does it not, Ethan?"

She turned to see him scowl.

"Well, Candide?" the doctor prompted. "Where is your chattering tongue when your wife calls upon it? Are you happy to have come here to cultivate your own garden, or shall we cast you out to sea again?"

Judith laughed. "Oh, Jordan, don't give him that choice! We'll lose him forever!"

Ethan's scowl deepened. "I'm going out to talk with the horses," he announced, and turned on his heel. "They make sense."

"Your walking stick," the physician directed, fetching it from beside the door.

Ethan growled, snatching the doctor's offering. He propped it on his shoulder and walked toward the horses, muttering.

Inside, Dr. Foster took Judith's cloak and bonnet. "I'll put a tea on. And there's a cake around here somewhere, some kind of cake a neighbor brought over yesterday. Poppyseed, I think. Judith, your gown."

It was a simple, high-waisted garment worn over one of Ethan's shirts, one she'd refashioned to more feminine lines by sewing tucks in the generous sleeves. She'd tied ribbons along her arms, too, as she'd seen women do to make gentle puffs. It would not do to look patched-together in Richmond. She must not bring shame upon her husband. Had she? "My gown, sir?" she whispered.

"It's lovely," he said.

Judith smiled. "Anne Randolph gave me the cambric."

"I remember. She said it would enhance your coloring. It does." He swung the kettle over the small fire in the hearth. Judith surveyed the large room where the doctor probably saw patients. She recognized most of the furniture from his home in Norfolk, and was struck again by his sacrifice for their sake. She wished he would sit.

"Are you well, Judith?"

"Now, yes."

"I—I didn't know."

"Didn't know?" she asked, patting the place by her side.

He sat. His eyes implored hers. For what? she wondered. "We were so concerned about his freedom, you see," he finally said. "I should have known he'd not leave that place without you. I would have provided better—two horses, more money, had I known."

She laughed. "Jordan, you were our lifeline!"

"Was I?"

"Of course! Your hesitation stems from what I sense, then? You believed it was we who might change our minds about your offer of a home and Ethan's apprenticeship?"

"Of course! I failed him."

"How?"

"He asked me to look after you, when he was in prison. I should have known what they were doing to confuse you, to make you consider the possibility that Ethan was capable of. . . . I'm a physician!" he exploded, standing, rubbing his forehead. "Ethan knew. Webbed—he kept telling me that your mind was webbed, that you would be yourself again once we got you away. Why didn't I listen?"

Judith felt overwhelmed by the burden of his remorse. He stared into the small fire.

"Jordan, sit beside me again," she invited. "Please."

He did, but his eyes did not leave the fire. "After I left the coach party—was thrown off, actually—I came back. By then you and he were gone, and Prescott Lyman following. I didn't think you had a chance against his trackers—you doused with laudanum, Ethan barely landed on those new legs . . ."

"Who told you? About the laudanum?"

"Hugh. He didn't know what it was, of course, but he led me to it."

"Poor child. He and Ruth, they are blameless in this. They only wanted a mother."

He shook his head. "The trail went cold soon after you were out of Pennsylvania. For the trackers. For me, following them. I would have gone mad, I think, were it not for Anne and Sally. There was nothing to be done but prepare this home, they convinced me."

"No. I think they did not convince you."

He smiled ruefully. "Well, they succeeded in keeping me busy with the move upriver. When we received Ethan's letter, I still couldn't believe you would come, that you'd desire to stay. Judith, please forgive me. I should have listened, from the beginning. He had to steal you himself."

"He didn't steal me. He offered his hand. I took it. Freely. Under no influence but my Light."

"Does he hate me now?"

"Hate you? All he can speak about is your bravery, your sacrifice. We are astonished by your generosity."

He finally turned to her. "Truly?"

She tried to look stern. "Have you known me to be an idle flatterer?" she demanded.

"Even without your '*thees*'? Even married to a Deist and dressed in rose cambric? No."

"And now. Is it true what I feel? That Ethan and I are not burdens? That you believe our presence is your own good fortune?"

He bowed his head. "I suppose I will get used to it. Not being able to hide anything from you, Judith Mercer."

She touched his hand. "Jordan, Ethan so desires to follow your path into healing. He learns quickly, as a child learns, with no fears that anything is beyond his ability. You have Sally's word and Fayette's and your own experience with him to assure you of that. His own sufferings have made him kind and patient and compassionate, and—"

"You don't have to market me your husband, Mrs. Blair."

She removed her hand to her lap. "Perhaps I must confess my own shortcomings, then." She bit her lower lip. "Jordan Foster, I have never kept household accounts, nor churned butter, nor made cheese, and I am a failing, miserable cook!"

Judith stared at her hands. She felt the doctor's frown.

"Well, how do you propose to contribute to this household?"

Judith raised her head. "I'm a good seamstress. I can take in sewing, and cut my silhouettes. And if there's a garden plot . . ."

His frown deepened. "There is. It's in ruin."

"I'll bring it back! I know about soil restoration. It will be flourishing, come spring. And I'll have all my father's medicinals growing in window gardens within weeks, you'll see!"

The physician shook his head. "Judith, Judith." He said her name fondly, she realized. He was such a different, less stern man when out of Ethan's sight. Why was that? "I have kept my own accounts for many years. And my work here has been largely on a barter basis. That should make both your perceived inadequacies disappear."

"How?"

"Few numbers will trouble either of us. If your husband and I manage to help our patients remain healthy, there will be an abundance of meals, smoked meat, fresh fish, and even a few delicacies to adorn our table. There will be no starving here."

She noticed the steam vapors behind the doctor's head. "The water's boiling," she told him.

"There, see? You can cook!"

Judith laughed, the last vestiges of trouble dissolving from her heart.

"I am so glad you married him," Jordan whispered.

"He married me back. There was equal courage in that."

Judith opened the wardrobe door and found handsome inlaid-wood compartments and spaces too generous for their needs, as they'd given Ethan's trunk and most of its contents to the runaway family there on the shore of Maryland. She began emptying her reticule. Two of the compartments were already filled. Anne Randolph had sent another dozen sheer cotton shirts up the river for Ethan. In the other an Oriental shawl of delicate, rich burgundy cashmere waited for her. She pulled it out, draped its soft folds over her shoulders. Though Ethan's sad, elegant mother had never done more than squeeze her hand, Judith felt encircled in her arms.

Her husband turned from his place at the window. "It suits you," he said quietly. He looked out over the busy streets of Richmond again. His eyes darted with the activity. He had never lived in a city, Judith realized, only on the sea and at Windover. She would help him get used to it. Jordan Foster had provided much more than a place by his fire. They had their own fire, their own gabled rooms in the house's second story.

"I like it up here," Ethan declared, "by the stars."

Judith smiled.

"Small windows, though."

"Ethan Blair, are you complaining?"

"No. There are so many people out there, Judith. And everyone moves so fast! I'm glad for this height. And the wall that places them on that side of us."

Judith walked past their cherrywood sleigh bed to her brave, but not fearless, husband. She embraced his middle, resting her face against the silk backing of his waistcoat.

"I feel safe," she whispered, "here in these rooms, in this house where my husband will discover the healing in his hands."

He turned, took her arms. "If ever you do not feel safe, you'll tell me, yes? You'll not listen to pedantic Reason declaring it makes no sense. You'll listen to your Light, and tell me?"

"Yes," she said, slipping her hands past the opened buttons of his waistcoat, and hugging him close.

"Welcome home, Judith," he whispered into her hair.

"Welcome home, beloved," she answered, raising her face to his descending mouth.

Their door swung open. "Perfect, they're kissing! Throw!"

Judith felt Ethan's heart accelerate. He shoved her head down and turned his back to the assault. But she had already seen their attackers. "Rice!" she called to him, laughing. "Ethan, there's no danger—it's rice."

His hold on her loosened. "Rice?"

Betsy giggled. "For the bride, the bridegroom—for showers of happiness. Didn't the Frenchman teach you, Uncle?" Betsy called.

Judith opened her arms to welcome Sally and Barton Gibson's family. Ethan was already stooping to catch his youngest niece.

"Put the seabirds in mine, too!" Alice clamored, thrusting the cut black silhouette back at him again.

"Alice!" Barton Gibson scolded his middle daughter.

"I'm sorry, Father. I mean, if you please, Uncle Ethan."

Ethan laughed. "This is a child who knows what it is she wants, yes?"

"You're sensing a family resemblance?" Sally asked.

"Exactly." He drew the child in question up onto his lap. They studied the silhouette he'd cut of Del and Ida's lighthouse together. "Now, Alice, show me where the birds should appear."

Judith swept by and ran her fingers through his unruly hair, drawing it off his brow. He caught her hand, kissed into its palm. Judith thought of the first time he'd done that, on board the *Standard*. It was the first of so many gifts. And now her captive sailor had given her what she never thought she would have again—a family.

"Was Ethan a willful child, then, Sally?" she asked.

"Oh, something chronic! Winthrop and Clayton could not make him skip to their tunes at all!"

Ethan frowned. "They had bullying tunes," he muttered. Betsy's arm slipped around his shoulder protectively.

"If Ethan caught something up in his mind," Sally continued, "and it captured his fancy, he would see it to conclusion. Once I suggested trying one of the experimentations you'd taught us, Jordan."

The doctor's head came up from his study of the lighthouse silhouette. "You remembered my experimentations?"

"Remembered? When Ethan found our record book, he insisted we do each one of them all over again. Which was the best, Ethan?"

He grinned. "Flight."

"Oh, yes! We sent a toy up in a hot-air balloon, Judith."

"You didn't!"

Ethan frowned. "It was not a toy. It was my dearest friend. I went to sea with Androcles."

Judith realized that Jordan Foster leaned in closely as the brother and sister talked of their childhood. His eyes brightened. Judith saw glimpses of him as a younger man, eagerly sharing his love of learning with the older Randolph children. Later, as Ethan drew his sister up to dance to her husband's hornpipe tune, those eyes brightened further. When his nieces insisted she try, Ethan favored her with a bridal waltz. It was not difficult, because his arms remained around her and her steps followed his. This was dancing, then? No, this was the waltz, that many believed scandalous. Barton's music slowed, went wistful. Judith was even able to relax enough to catch the spark from her partner's eyes and wish they could continue this dance even closer. She blushed hotly, seeing Sally's nod of understanding. When Barton finished his tune, Jordan Foster put his hand on Ethan's shoulder.

"Our rounds begin at dawn, apprentice," he warned, then bade each of them good night before leaving their small upstairs sitting room and climbing down the winding stairs.

Sally's fingers drummed against her flush lips. "We've overstayed, Barton," she announced. "But perhaps Jordan will forgive us this once. Girls, gather your things while I wrap the baby." She kissed Ethan's brow. "To bed. He's worried about you."

"Worried?" Ethan laughed. "About getting a full day's labor, perhaps."

"No, Ethan. About you." She looked to Judith. "I don't envy you your place between these two, my sweet new sister," she said.

30

Ethan trailed behind the doctor, who followed the maidservant. Low ceilings of the half-timbered house made them all stoop. Finally, the bedroom, cluttered with shelves lined in lace. And crockery. Not useful crockery, like Judith's bowls, plates, and serving dishes, but crockery dogs. Ornaments, with no purpose. Judith would be mystified in a room like this, Ethan decided. He was mystified. He smiled. Was she making him a common-sense Quaker already?

The maid propped the pillows behind the head of a frail woman. Warming her lap was a small spaniel who was not yet represented in the crockery gallery, but destined to follow his predecessors, Ethan thought. The animal stared hard at Jordan.

"Good afternoon, Mrs. Willard," he said.

"What's kept you?" The woman's querulous voice contrasted with her appearance. "It's past tea. I've sung your praises to my own detriment. You've got too many patients now to care promptly for me."

"It has been a busy day."

"Leave us," she instructed her maid, but watched the tilt of the girl's head as she passed Ethan. "Well," the old woman demanded then, "who is that shadow that sparks Nancy's eyes?"

The doctor turned. "May I introduce—"

"Come into the light, man! Closer! Why Jordan Foster, he's—"

"My new assistant, Mrs. Willard. Ethan Blair."

"Blair, Blair? And what is wrong with you, young man, that you are not called by your father's name?"

Ethan halted midstep. His smile froze. *"Madame? Je ne connais-pas—"*

"French! Jordan, you rogue, he's French?" The spaniel in her lap cowered. "I'll have no revolutionary touch me!"

"He's as American as you or I, Mrs. Willard. You've frightened him, that's all. Ethan, speak English."

But he couldn't speak at all. Ethan felt the doctor's hand on his shoulder. The woman continued shouting.

"*I've* frightened *him*? Bloody revolutionary!"

"Look at him, woman, he's but three-and-twenty! How could he have guillotined your relatives before he was born?"

Jordan looked exasperated. The dog began a high-pitched whine. Ethan wished he could help, but fear was still caught in his throat. He felt his life in Richmond unraveling. How did this woman know he was using his mother's name? What else did she know of him? *Listen,* he told himself. That was most of doctoring, listening.

Mrs. Willard stroked the dog silent. She turned to Jordan. "Why did you not school him in Edinburgh, like yourself? What could he learn from Frenchmen?"

Jordan Foster's thumb and fourth finger pressed his temples between them. "Mrs. Willard, you have misunderstood."

"I am fourscore-and-ten. I understand perfectly well about youthful indiscretions! It's hardly a terrible punishment that this one has come under your wing at last, is it? Now that the work of raising him to manhood is done and you have need of an associate? Come closer, young man."

Ethan obeyed the woman surrounded by even more white lace than that which choked her shelves. Her dog bared his teeth.

"Closer," she insisted.

He released the handles of the doctor's bag and stooped until he was below her gaze. Her light eyes peered down at him from the mountain of pillows. He held his hand out under the dog's jaw, the way he had with the animals at Windover, and those meant for slaughter on board the *Standard*.

The dog licked his palm. The woman shouted as if Ethan were hard of hearing, as well as French. "Do you understand me?"

"Yes, *madame*."

"You are very fortunate. Other fathers would not give a second thought to children conceived as heedlessly as you were."

That was it, Ethan finally realized. She'd seen their common coloring. She thought him Jordan's son. Illegitimate son, conceived without design in France. That was all. Relief flooded him. He almost laughed, but willed his mouth, if not his eyes, sober. "I feel fortunate indeed, *madame*."

Her curious, Cupid's-bow lips set in an aged face pursed, almost sweetly. "Good, good," she approved.

"Mrs. Willard, this is insufferable!" Jordan Foster proclaimed.

Not even he himself had ever made his master this angry.

"You don't have to get choleric over it all these years later, Jordan," his patient chastised. "It's commendable, what you now seek to rectify." She returned her attention to Ethan. "I don't like being bled or purged, young one."

"Oh, neither do I."

She raised her scant eyebrows in surprise, then smiled. "There, then. An agreement between us. Now tell me about this new salve."

Ethan opened the doctor's bag, offered the jar. "It's more the old salve touched by my wife, *madame*. She grows medicinals on our windowsills."

"Wife. You have taken a wife?"

"Yes."

"American?"

"Judith's from Pennsylvania."

"And you are faithful to your Judith?"

"Yes, *madame*."

"This is very good. It shows you can overcome your unfortunate heritage. You'll have a chance here, young man, in America."

"I have heard such things. And I am grateful for the opportunity Dr. Foster has afforded me."

She patted the side of his head as she took his offering. "He's got your becoming modesty, Jordan, to make up for that rakish look about the eyes," she said, opening the jar. "You must remain true to your wife, Ethan Foster. She is cursed in her marriage."

"Cursed, *madame*?"

"Foolish women fall in love with men like you on sight."

"But, Mrs. Willard, my wife is the most wise person of my acquaintance."

"And she fell, the same as the rest." She sniffed at the jar's contents. "Like your mother did, for that one." Her dismissive wave turned into a grasp at the air. "Where are you going, Jordan Foster? Attend me!"

The doctor turned slowly in the bedroom doorway. Ethan could not bear the look in his eyes. He tried to think past his own hurt, to come out of the world the woman had created, to what was real. This man had had children, once. "Mrs. Willard, perhaps your words remind Dr. Foster of his true son, the one he lost."

"Lost? Lost? Well, now you're found, can he not see that?" she demanded loudly. "Jordan, this child cannot help his circumstances. Give him your name! Where are you going? Examine my throat!"

Ethan smiled uneasily. "I believe it's improving, Mrs. Willard," he suggested.

Her chin braced a girlish pout as she stroked her dog's back. "Don't the old have any privileges?" she fretted. "May we not be allowed to speak the truth without consequence?" Ethan stared at the doorway, where the servant Nancy made a helpless gesture. "Are you angry with me, too, young one?" Mrs. Willard asked in a smaller voice.

"No, *madame,*" Ethan assured her.

"Will you examine my throat, then?" she asked, offering a palsied finger's dose of Judith's salve.

"Of course." He took it. "I am honored by your trust." His hands smeared the fresh-scented salve as he checked under her jawline for swellings. There were none. Jordan had allowed him to do this for others, before. He'd allowed what Ethan did next. While Nancy held the lamp close, he placed the flat stick against the woman's tongue and peered into her mouth and down her throat.

"The congestion is almost gone."

She noticed his trembling hands and smiled. "Your wife has blended a sweet mint into that horrible concoction, has she not, young Dr. Foster?"

Nancy hid her smile. Ethan knelt, pressed the old woman's hands between his, gently. He felt her bones through paper-thin skin, fragile as twigs on a dead tree. "Yes, wintergreen. My Judith is the best of our household, Mrs. Willard. Dr. Foster is its head. I am apprentice only. Not doctor, not Foster. I am my mother's son. Hers alone, yes?"

What was wrong with his own throat? Ethan thought irritably, swallowing past the obstruction, the twinge of loneliness.

Mrs. Willard's pinked lips smiled, almost kindly. "Someday your wife Judith's children will teach you differently," she said.

The cook had shoved a meat pie in his hands and a manservant had spiraled him out the front door with Jordan's bag under his arm. Ethan walked down three steps and sat. Now what was he supposed to do? Where had Jordan gone—to their next patient? But even in his anger, how could he have left this one? It was against everything he'd taught Ethan about a doctor's responsibilities.

Was this a test? Ethan looked out over the busy street. He had no idea where he was. That was it. That was the nature of the test, to see if he could get himself to the next listed patients on his own, he decided. Wasn't Jordan always complaining about his sense of direction, better suited to the sea?

Ethan lifted his head, sniffed the air. Through the man-made city smells came the scent of the James. Mostly fresh water here, so far from the Atlantic, but water, he could smell it. He was on Richmond's south side. There. He knew that much. A broad, busy street on the south side. The list of Jordan's next three patients was in the bag.

It was an ordinary day with ordinary rounds, on foot, to three more people who only needed fresh jars of Judith's salve. He would be providing delivery, listening to progress through ailments, not much more. Yes. That's why the doctor had abandoned him.

Jordan Foster was a rude man. They raised rude men in Boston, he would tell Sally on their next visit. She would slant her brows in sympathy and laugh, easing his troubled mind about remaining the physician's student.

Ethan placed the pie on the flat bottom of the bag. He wished he could go home to Judith. He pictured her in the back of their house, sewing her strong seams, or tending the garden. He would creep up behind her, to see her fine eyes fire before he kissed her. She'd scold him, reminding him that they lived close to their neighbors in a city now, and that Mrs. Atwater was likely watching them from her window above. But if he'd sparked Judith well enough by then, she'd leave her work and go upstairs with him.

Yesterday, they hadn't reached the bed. They'd loved each other against the curving wall of the stairwell, in that square the sun warmed from the window above. How wonderful she had felt, her strong legs wrapped around him as he'd entered her.

Had he pleased her well enough in return? She'd laughed—that high-pitched musical tone at first, the one that reminded him of the bells at St. Martin's, the Catholic church down near the docks. Then, as he pressed closer, deeper, her laughter had turned guttural and not religious at all. Did he dare think of Judith as being, even for a moment, not religious at all? Did he dare think a woman who spoke with God might love him forever?

Today would be different, better. Today he would coax her gently, then carry her upstairs, onto the bed. He would praise those strong legs, her laughter, and her sweet nature as he watched her sea-change eyes for what pleased her, and when. He would love her until the light faded. Then they would rise, eat all the pie, and leave Jordan with gruel and greens for supper.

Ethan shook the images from his head. The sun was lowering in the sky. His bad leg had already begun to ache. He looked down at the doctor's efficiently checked-off list. Where in hell was Easton Street?

31

Judith finished crushing the black walnuts. Now she had only to sweep the big room before her reward to herself: an hour working in the garden, pulling the last of the summer's weeds and putting the soil to bed for the winter, as her father used to call it. Today she would ease the jonquil and tulip bulbs in along the brick walkway Ethan had repaired, too. It meandered a little, like he did if he didn't use his stick after sunset, but even that made it more dear to her. Come spring, when Jordan saw the bright colors along the walk, she was sure he would not be angry that flowers had joined her medicinals and herbs.

At the sound of the furtive knock, Judith laid her sewing on the chair and went to the door. She hoped it wasn't a patient; she hadn't yet swept the floor.

A girl of about fifteen stood in the doorway. Her clothing was poor but neat, except for a streak of mud. Her hands had disappeared in the folds of her ragged shawl.

"Good afternoon," Judith greeted her. "Are you in need?"

"I am, missus," the girl said.

"Would you come in?"

The girl took a swift glance at the corner of Charles and Court Streets and ducked under Judith's arm through the doorway. Judith closed the door and turned, smiling. "My husband and Dr. Foster are visiting patients this afternoon. Might I—"

"Ain't sick, missus."

"No?"

"Maybe I could do a chore for you? Haul water, sweep?"

"Ah, I see. Mrs. Atwater sent you over to help me?"

"That's it, missus!" she exclaimed. "And I'm plenty strong, and neat when nobody's knocking me into ditches!"

"What is your name?" Judith asked her gently.

"Odette."

"Odette, I appreciate my neighbor's concern, but I'm afraid we don't hire out help here. You're the third she has sent over."

"Please let me stay a little while! The captain and Miss Atwater says you be kind and good, and they are both gone away and I must get off the street!" Odette exclaimed suddenly.

Judith waited until the girl's breathing eased before she smiled. "Would you have a slice of Mrs. Atwater's blueberry cake with me, Odette? She sent over so much this morning that she must have known you were coming."

"Did you hear me Missus Doctor?" The girl pulled her chained hands out of her ragged shawl's folds. "I be a runaway!"

"Not from me, I hope. I'm Judith."

Three hard raps at the front door sent the girl to her feet. Judith held out her hand. After only a second's hesitation, Odette took hold. Judith led her into Dr. Foster's room and quickly lifted his bedding. "As still as you can manage, Odette," she whispered. The girl climbed in and Judith laid the bed over her form, then repositioned the pillows.

She left the room as the front door opened. Two men—one with shoulders hunched up to his ears, the other portly and brandishing a whip—stood in the doorway. As fearsome as they looked, the line of eight chained human beings beyond them was what made Judith's knees feel weak. It was not the first slave coffle she had seen in the city of Richmond, but it was the most miserable.

The hunched man touched the rim of his wide hat. "We're traveling through to load at the docks, when we lost us a runaway. Ragged mulatto gal slave, muddied up some. Real crafty bitch, she is."

Judith said the first words that entered her mind. "There are no slaves here."

The man cocked his head as far as he could, considering the shortness of his neck. "You sure? She might of broke in on you, missus, ready to do you harm. Best let us—"

"I'm sure."

"Still, my man better see to your safety. Daniels!" He called the portly man forward. Daniels headed straight for Jordan's bedroom.

"That's most kind of you, sir, to put yourself and your valuable charges at risk on my behalf, especially since Dr. Foster has put the house under quarantine."

"Quarantine? Bloody hell! Against what?"

She lowered her voice and tapped her lip. "Have you heard of the black vomit?"

"Yellow fever? Here? Daniels, get out of that doorway! Let's get these niggers we got left toward the dock!"

Once they left, Judith barred the front door before rushing to the doctor's bedroom. She lifted the bedding from a breathless Odette, who looked around the spare, tidy room, speechless.

"Yellow fever done visited this house, Miss Judith?"

Judith smiled. "No, dear. I merely asked if he'd heard of it, did I not? I was going to tell him we were under quarantine only to foul-mouthed slave catchers at present."

By the time Ethan had completed his rounds, the pie had made room for two pints of fennel vinegar, a half dozen turnips, and a bottle of the barrelmaker's best cherry brandy. He'd found all three patients, and they had welcomed him, even without Jordan.

Home was less than a half-hour's walk away when the liveryman's stable boy Tim grabbed his sleeve. There was a tall, barrel-chested man beside him.

"This be him?" the man asked the boy gruffly.

"Aye, sir, Ethan Blair, the physician's assistant."

Ethan tensed, but the rough-looking man took off his hat. "Suppose you could bring him home, Mr. Blair?" he asked quietly.

"Who, sir?"

"Your master. Mine thinks he'll come to no good end if he swallows another pint of ale."

"Ale?"

"Atop all that corn whiskey."

"Where?"

"The Duchess of Gloucester."

"Who?"

"The Duchess ain't a 'who,' sir. She's a 'where.' A tavern. My master keeps her. I'm Curry. Curry Post, the rabble rouster there."

Ethan offered the doctor's bag to the boy. "Would you carry this to Judith, Tim? Tell her Dr. Foster and I will be home directly?"

"I will, sir."

Ethan searched through his vest for a coin, but found none. He'd left the house without money again, something Jordan chided him for often. "There's a piece of pie at the bottom for you," he offered.

"No need, Mr. Blair. Your lady poulticed my burn with her sassafras Monday week, and didn't ask a thing for it. I'll deliver your bag and message."

Tim disappeared beyond the lamppost. Ethan was already falling behind the tavernkeeper's servant.

The big man looked back, puzzled. "You ailing?"

"Just slow."

"An injury?"

"Yes."

His eyes found Ethan's elevated right boot. "War?"

How he hated questions. "Yes."

"Army, was it? I had a nephew with Andy Jackson at New Orleans."

"I was at sea."

"The sea? Good Lord, it's lucky you are to be back at all!"

"How far is it to the tavern, Mr. Post?"

The rouster grinned. "New to town, are you, lowlander?"

"Yes."

"Must be, not knowing the Duchess. Just around this bend. Your master can hold neither strong drink nor his crafty Boston tongue in an argument. He's playing the Devil, and has both the Federalists and all manner of Democratic Republicans at his throat."

Throat—Jordan had had enough damage done to his throat. Ethan quickened his step, though it caused pain to ride up his hip. Jordan Foster, drunk and brawling. This man, with his questions, besides picking up the Tidewater Virginian in his speech. What part of any test was this?

The tavern's sign was a Renaissance heraldry design of crosses and jewel-toned squares and circles. Ethan followed Curry Post into a backroom stale from lack of air and too much arguing. Behind the shelved Dutch door that led to the supply of spirits, a man Ethan judged to be the tavern master kept a careful watch. Jordan Foster was presiding over a discussion whose combined venom, he seemed blissfully unaware, was directed at him. Curry Post plowed through to its midst.

"Now, gentlemen," he announced, spinning around to catch Ethan's shoulders in a gruff embrace. "Do you know the doctor's assistant? This here's Ethan Blair, young veteran of that late conflict which kept us free to argue as Americans! Mr. Blair fought on the high seas so your miserable hides are safe for himself and the doctor to poke at in peacetime."

Jordan turned slowly, his red-rimmed eyes fired hostile.

"Dr. Foster," Ethan addressed him formally, as he was instructed to do in public, "my wife is waiting supper."

"A hero indeed," Jordan Foster proclaimed, as if Ethan had not spoken. "Battles, scars! Tell them about it, Mr. Blair."

Ethan stared at him.

"Look how silent, how modest! You will never find him in here, telling lies about his exploits, not this one!"

"That's not good for my business, Mr. Blair," the tavernkeeper chided affably, wiping a glass while maintaining his vigilant eyes on the room.

"Come here, Ethan," the doctor invited. He poured two glasses from a quarter-full bottle. "You like bourbon, don't you?"

"No."

"What, a Virginian, without a taste for bourbon?" He thrust the glass into Ethan's hand. "I forget . . . you aren't wholly Virginian, are you? But we must drink! To what, hero? To whom? Your mother? That French beauty plying her trade? On the streets of Paris, Marseille? La Rochelle, perhaps? Come, come, you know! You've played it all out in that head. Where was I the hapless victim of her wiles?"

Ethan dropped the glass. It shattered. The scent of bourbon reminded him of his brothers' houses, of slave breeding, of corn gone bad, rotten. "Stop this," he warned.

"Why? Isn't it what you seek? To be rechristened yet again, bastard son of a French whore, made doctor by my grace?" Jordan Foster picked up his own glass and flung its contents in Ethan's face.

"There," he pronounced. "You are he."

32

Ethan felt the splash of bourbon with a shock. His eyes stung, clouding his vision. He thought of Harry Burnett as he lay writhing in pain on the deck of the *Ida Lee*. This was what it felt like, burning a face off, to become another. He was dimly aware of someone offering him a pair of gloves. What for? A duel. Jordan Foster had insulted his mother. Here in a tavern, a public place. He was Ethan Randolph, a Tidewater Virginian, was he not? Had he no honor?

"Don't," his new friend, the one who had waited for him when he was out of step, counseled from his other side. "He's blind, mean drunk, your master is," Curry Post said. "Listen to me. He don't have no sense about him just now, Mr. Blair."

Ethan walked out of reach of the gloves. Slowly, he offered the doctor his hand. "Let's go home," he said quietly.

The physician staggered, then rose to his full height. "You can't find your way around this city until your stars come out," he said.

"They're out."

The belligerence was fading fast from the doctor's face, replaced by something sad and lost that Ethan didn't understand.

"It's dark?"

"Yes."

"She'll be waiting, won't she, our Judith?"

"Yes, sir."

"We must go, then."

He grabbed his bottle of bourbon, took a step, then stumbled. Ethan took hold of his forearms. Jordan looked around.

"Caught me, 'fore I hit the boards. Did you see, gentlemen? Could I ask for a better apprentice?"

Curry Post walked them to the back door and into the stable yard. "I'll ask if I can get away—" he began.

"It's not far. I can manage," Ethan said with more confidence than he felt. "Thank you for all your help."

"Mr. Blair?" He looked behind them. Ethan saw a curtain waft at a window. Curry came closer. "If you would, sir, some advisement?"

"Yes?"

"My Ellen. She's in the first three months yet and feels poorly."

"Tired?"

"Aye, and sick."

"What does the midwife say?"

"Won't go to her this time. On account of we lost two already in the first three month. No midwifes, no doctors, she says. But she's sick, Mr. Blair."

"Is she keeping down her food?"

"Naught but bread, a little porridge, tea."

"Judith flavors a blood tonic with wild sarsaparilla. I'll send over a bottle in the morning. Where?"

"Here, sir. Out back."

Ethan scanned the noisy tavern. "Take her for daily walks, Mr. Post. By the water."

"I'm only just Curry, sir."

"If I'm Ethan. Thank you for your help. And your own advice."

"You had a mighty pull toward pistols at dawn, did you not, low-lander? You'd best promise me you'll not pitch that Yankee firebrand down a well if'n he becomes too burdensome."

Ethan grinned at the thought. "We're both rousters for our masters tonight, are we not?"

Curry Post looked over Jordan Foster's crumpled form, frowning. "Mine works me hard, but he don't scorn my family."

Ethan smiled sadly. "Well, mine doesn't work me all that hard. Take good care of your wife, Curry."

"Aye, sir. I will."

"Small meals," the doctor murmured, slipping down Ethan's side. "Tell him."

Ethan bolstered his burden higher. "She should eat small meals, too," he called to Curry Post.

"Small meals. Aye. Thank you, doctors."

They had only reached the first corner before Jordan Foster's knees buckled and he slid into the gutter.

Ethan knelt beside him.

"Don't throw me down the well," the doctor beseeched quietly.

Ethan snorted. "River's closer. How well do you tread water, Jordan Foster?"

"Can't swim a stroke."

"Now, that's a shame."

He brought the man to his feet, tucked his bottle into his trousers, then bent the lifeless form over his shoulder. It was easier for a while not to struggle with the drag on his side, but soon Ethan regretted his words of assurance to Curry Post. His leg shouldn't feel this badly, even after the long day, and this extra weight. His boot must need a new heel. How much would that cost? Could he shave it down as neatly, as carefully as Aaron had, to fit his walking gait? Ethan felt a deep longing for Windover's trees, its sea breezes. He heard a rustling, saw muddied slippers. He looked up.

Judith stood before him, her head and shoulders wrapped in his mother's bride gift, the cashmere shawl, her face glowing—with what, her Inner Light?

"Almost home," she assured him. Together, they eased the doctor onto his feet and brought him over the remaining streets.

In the physician's small bedroom, they worked silently to get him undressed. It was a comfortable silence, even as Jordan Foster growled as they placed him between the sheets. He would feel much worse tomorrow. Ethan found pleasure in the thought. He would never be as good a person as his wife was, he thought ruefully.

He pulled up the light blanket, then glanced at the portraits of the dulcimer woman, the two children. *What are we to do with this man?* he asked the woman silently, before leaving the room behind his wife.

Soon Judith had the hearth table candlelit. The meat pie was covered with cloth, Judith's greens and fresh peas sprinkled with the fennel vinegar.

"Tim said most of this bounty you earned yourself today, husband," she said brightly, as if he'd not brought a debauched man home, and didn't reek of a distillery himself.

Ethan shrugged. "My hungry look," he replied.

What had the old woman called his look? Rakish. He wouldn't know the first thing about looking rakish. She was seeing Fayette, not him. He was small and crippled, was he not? Not handsome, not a man women loved on sight. Ethan stared at Judith's linens spread over the doctor's table, at her useful crockery. Did the doctor hate him now? Would they lose their home?

"Will you sit, eat?" Judith asked, gently slipping his damp coat from his shoulders.

"I cannot."

"Ethan?"

"My leg," he finally admitted. It was now a red, ugly pain, high, where it attached to his hip.

"Oh, Ethan. Lie by the hearth, love," she urged, taking his hand, leading him to the doctor's sofa, then lifting his leg so gently it didn't hurt any worse. He took her hand.

"Too much walking, that's all."

"And weight."

"It wasn't far, the tavern. The Duchess of somewhere—somewhere English—it's called. A servant there, Curry Post, his wife needs some of your sarsaparilla tonic, Judith. Tomorrow. Will you remind me?"

"Of course," she said, leaning over, kissing his throbbing temple. What was the use trying to hide anything from her? He rested his head in his hand, breathing through the pain. "Ethan?" she called softly. "Shall I bring your supper?"

"No. Sit here beside me. That's what I need."

She stepped out of her muddied slippers—very muddy—where had she been before she'd met them, the docks? Why? The puzzlement made his head swim until she cosseted close, warming him. "What happened?" she finally asked.

"Jordan went to the tavern late this afternoon, drank to excess. I brought him home."

"I know that much from Tim," she chided him gently. "Ethan, what happened between you this time?"

He told her. Everything. Calmly. With barely any of the catches of anger, grief, frustration he felt. She listened, her serene face bathed in the room's deep shadows. When he finished, she rose to her knees, facing him. Her thumbs coursed an arching massage along his cheekbones, his tight jaw, his tense brow. Her touch turned gentle as she swept around the scar from his fall, and the old, white ones, from the cannon-fire burns. He breathed deeply.

"Walnuts," he said. "Black walnuts."

"I've been chopping them. For the headache tonic. Better?"

"Infinitely."

"And now I'm going to make us a tea."

She rose, walked to the hearth. Only a few feet away. Still, it came, unbidden: *Don't leave me.* The aching need of a child abandoned. Ridiculous. It angered him. But with her warmth gone, Ethan felt bereft.

"Judith?" he finally called.

She turned. "Yes, love?"

"Why was it so painful to be taken for his son?"

She left her preparations and rushed to his side, taking his head beneath her heart. She held him there, the way Sally had held him his first day at Windover. Judith's arms went from warm to glowing. He was within the circle of Light of this woman who talked with God, he realized. He wanted to stay there forever. "That wasn't the cause of his pain," she whispered into his hair. "He loves us."

"You, perhaps. Who could not love you? It that what it is? Jealousy? Because he desires you and you are my wife?"

"He does not love me in that way, Ethan."

"Are you sure?"

"I'm sure. You and I are becoming his family. Your Mrs. Willard saw. I think he's afraid of that. Perhaps because he's lost one family—his little ones, a boy and a girl, along with his wife, remember?"

"The children. The dulcimer woman he didn't know enough to love."

"Yes."

"He tries to drive us away with this public insult to my mother?"

"Perhaps."

"Judith, for a moment, a moment only, I . . ."

"What, love?"

"I wanted to kill him."

She swept his hair back nervously. "You have a right to your anger. But you did not act on it."

He felt her lips form a smile, there against his cheek. "We are this difficult man's orphans now, yes?" She swept his mane back from his brow again, playfully. "Though you come more encumbered than I."

"Encumbered?"

"With an entourage of doting women and families both slave and free also claiming your heart," she explained.

A groan rose from the doctor's bedroom.

"He'd best hope his orphans don't abandon him before this night is out."

"Oh, Ethan, what can we do? I know nothing about remedies for what ails him."

"How is our honey supply?"

"We have plenty."

"We'll need it." He rose, limped for the cupboard. "And eggs, soft-boiled," he continued, as he drew out a small pot, "but not until tomorrow. I suppose we'll have to beg a couple from Mrs. Atwater." He rummaged her gracefully set table for a teaspoon. "Oh, and a few ounces of that damned bourbon. I wish we could wring it out of my coat."

"We don't have any bourbon!"

"Jordan's bottle," he remembered. "It must have dropped when you came upon us."

"I'll find it." Judith lifted her shawl from its peg, and wrapped it around her, turning. "Ethan, how do you know this treatment?"

"I grew up holding Fayette's head after shore leaves. It's made your husband a sober man, Mrs. Blair."

She frowned. "Something else I owe that scoundrel?"

He caught her waist at the door. "I fear as much, *ma chère*," he whispered, bending over her white neck, nuzzling her scarf aside so he could plant soft kisses along her collarbone. He reveled in the smoothness of her skin, the catches in her breathing. Salt air. Tar. Yes, she'd been to the riverfront. Why? He pulled the drawstring of her chemise and nuzzled lower.

"You are feeling better, I think, husband." she purred.

His hands stroked down her side and cupped her bottom. "You have my complete cure within your power, *madame*."

She giggled deliciously and he felt the hot rise in his loins. They were so close she felt it too, he knew from the way her eyes widened. He closed in on her ripe mouth.

Another groan erupted from the bedroom.

"The bourbon," she whispered, dancing her fingers along his pouting lower lip.

He sighed, releasing her, swinging open the door. *"Sacre-bleu!"*

The woman in the threshold held up the missing bottle. "Ethan Blair." Anne Randolph arched one fine brow. "Since when does the sight of your mother promote one of your colorful blasphemies?"

33

"It *was* a blasphemy, wasn't it?" Anne Randolph demanded.

"The mildest cant, Mother," Ethan said, before snatching the bourbon bottle from her hand.

Judith's sharp eyes warned him of the neighbors' lights. They pulled Anne Randolph inside the doorway, then caught her in their embrace. "You two are as bad as your sister and her subterfuge. I waited until dark as she instructed."

Ethan caught sight of another figure on the street. Aaron returned from paying the coachman and arrived at the doorstep with his long-gaited stride. Ethan pulled the bondsman inside. His eyes drank in the sight of his mother and Aaron as if they'd disappear. "The table is set, supper warm, see?" he proclaimed. "Judith must have known you were coming, there's so much food tonight, yes, Judith?"

The groan. Reminding him of their circumstances.

His mother started. "Ethan, you have a patient here?"

He looked down at the bottle, honey pot, and spoon in his hand. "Yes."

"Jordan trusts you already to care for this unfortunate, son?"

"Uh, yes."

His mother's eyes lit with purpose. "Perhaps we might help?"

"No, no! It's not a difficult treatment, but requires some patience and duration. Like Martha's rice pudding, yes, Aaron?"

"If'n you say so, sir."

Judith tugged at her shawl's fringe. Nervous, too, he thought as he backed his way toward the bedroom. "Please sit," he implored. "I'll be out directly." He felt badly, leaving them to Judith, but he needed time to think. Quiet time.

Jordan Foster was neither cooperative nor a quiet patient. Soon Ethan had smeared them both with honey. Before Jordan fell back on the bed with the proper dosage inside him, he'd thrown Ethan to the floorboards. Ethan had barely scrambled to his feet before his mother appeared in the thrown-open doorway. Anne Randolph walked to the bed, where the doctor breathed out a snore.

"Good God," she whispered. "His throat!"

Ethan frowned at the physician's opened collar. "That's an old wound. I didn't do him any lasting harm, he always snores that loud."

"You cut him, Ethan?"

"No. I closed the wound. He bade me do it!"

"When?"

"Mama—"

"When?" she demanded.

"Last spring," he said softly, "on the way to Pennsylvania. When you sent him to follow me. Stop looking at me like that; it's you who foresaw it, *madame!* The thieves are long gone. He's healed."

She nodded, though the color had not returned to her face. "And now? What ails him now?"

Ethan gave up all title to subterfuge. "He's drunk."

His mother considered the sprawled body. Ethan raked his hand through his hair, which solidified its unruliness in honey.

"When is the next dosage?" she asked.

"In twenty minutes."

"I'll render that," she resolved.

"But—"

She looked at his smeared vest pointedly. "Could I do worse?"

"Mother, listen—"

"No, you listen to me, young man! I helped one hundred and twenty-eight souls through the epidemic of seventeen hundred and ninety-two. Surely I can perform a procedure as simple as making rice pudding. Aaron?" she summoned the man standing beside Judith in the doorway.

"You did, Miss Anne, you sure enough did!" he confirmed, smiling.

Ethan sighed. "Six teaspoons of the honey," he instructed. "In twenty minutes' time. The same again twenty minutes after that. Let him sleep, keeping the bottle of that damned corn whiskey in sight, and giving him a drink from it if he wakes asking for it. After three hours, another cycle: three doses of six teaspoons of honey, repeated at intervals of twenty minutes. In the morning, more honey, and a soft-boiled egg at breakfast and midday."

Anne Randolph smiled. "I'll be gone back to your sister's house by first light. Barton must bring me home by noon, as he's off on another of his expeditions soon. You'll have to feed our patient the eggs yourself. Judith and I will sit with Dr. Foster now. Go. Attend to your own needs. Leave us to visit together as we see to your unpleasant predicament."

"*My* predicament!"

" 'Your,' in the good Quaker plural, my love. I do not absolve Jordan in this folly, of course. Do not clench your teeth at me, Ethan Blair! There, that's better. Now, if you can kiss your lady and me without soiling us, you may do so, and be gone."

Ethan knew better than to argue with her further. He approached, standing between his mother and his wife. Most of his anger dissolved. How he'd missed this woman in all her iron delicacy. He reached down, kissed Anne Randolph's cheek. "Welcome to our home, Mother," he said.

"An interesting welcome." Her caustic tone, her frown, were belied by eyes bright with life. Jordan Foster was inches away, with his mother's vibrant presence lost on him. Ethan took pleasure in that.

He immediately faced the disapproval of that pleasure from Judith's fathoms-cold stare. He could hide nothing from his wife, he thought again, as the flush of shame sped up his neck. Judith's eyes warmed with pardon, and something else. Passion. He reached down, blocking his mother's view, and kissed his wife full on the mouth. The blush coursed from his face to hers as he tracked his fingers over a terrain starting from her cheek and ending where her chemise was still unlaced between her breasts. He broke away, leaving her breathless. Leaving himself worse. Would his mother see?

"Ethan," she declaimed, too concerned with his wife's appearance to notice him at all, "get out! You've left poor Judith quite besmeared."

"Poor Judith," he muttered, as he pulled an ever-present handkerchief from his waistcoat and threw it at the lady in question.

Aaron shook his head when Ethan limped into the hearth room. "As I thought. You ain't been taking good enough care of that new leg."

Ethan growled. "It's letting me know that."

"Take the warning, young one," his kinsman advised, pouring heated water into a basin. Aaron laid an absorbent cloth over his arm before he brought the steaming basin to the sofa. He'd found everything needed. Ethan took the cloth, dipped it in the water. He washed the sticky honey off his hands, face, and clothes.

When Ethan finished, Aaron bent to retrieve the bowl. "Leave it, sit. Please, Aaron, you are our guest. Visit." He motioned to a straight-backed chair, but Aaron quickly took the three-legged stool that Judith used when she warmed herself by the oven on baking day. Ethan sighed, but accepted his choice. "How is Martha?" he asked, sitting on the sofa. "How are your children? My father? The harvest?"

The big man's hands reached out. "Would you give me that boot, sir? Long as you're going to badger me, I may as well keep busy."

"You're tired, Aaron? My badgering can wait. Sleep. Take the sofa. No, our bed upstairs. I'll show you—" He'd risen halfway before Aaron had him back in the sofa's depths.

"Is it city life or your doctorin' or you been drinkin' that brew you's doused in that's made you take leave of your senses?"

"I am in full possession of what little senses I have," he insisted. "We are not at Windover. This is my house. Well, Jordan's. He's from Boston. Do you think he would approve of you sitting like a faithful dog at my feet?"

"I ain't—"

"No, he would not! You are my elder brother, Aaron, my guest here. I was a sailor. I can sleep anywhere."

"So can I, sir."

Bested again. "All right," Ethan conceded, remembering him crouched in the fireplace at Windover. "So can you." The big man's hand rested at his shoulder.

"I brought me some leather, so I'll get to work." Aaron pointed to the arm of the sofa with his chin. "You, sir, keep that leg high, an' be a dutiful son to Miss Anne."

Ethan propped his foot where Aaron indicated. He heard the murmured voices of the women talking. Though their words were indistinct, he recognized Judith's powerful, musical tones contrasting with his mother's rounded speech. Aaron examined his right boot carefully. Ethan watched, content in the silence between them.

"You patchin' up folks real fine here, your sister and the little ones say, Ethan."

There. At last, "master" and "sir" gave way to his name. Aaron had given him permission to go to their secret place, to regard him as his brother. Was putting something useful to do into those big hands the key? Ethan smiled.

"My sister, my nieces told you of our success?"

"They done that, yes."

"Did you expect anything different from them?"

"No. Didn't expect you to be no one but the man I knows, neither." He frowned at the boot's worn-down heel. "Sure wish I had my bench. But I'll see what I can do."

Ethan turned toward the bedroom doorway. "They won't be able to control him. We have to be ready to help soon, Aaron."

"Oh, child. There be a few things you don't know 'bout your mama."

"And my father? How is it he allowed you both to travel upriver?"

"Miss Anne got other business."

"Business?"

"Trading."

"I don't understand."

"Early frosts killin' off the tobacco, wheat, the seed corn. Your brothers, in past times, they would send their people to help out at the old place in times like these. But they irated at your mama."

"Since she helped Jordan and me to trick them in Pennsylvania?"

"That be the truth of it. Well, now, your mama needs to raise some cash, as everything going ragged, clothes to tempers."

"My father's temper?"

"Oh, old master only peeved you ain't come back."

"Does he know why?"

"Well, he got a scrambled notion of events up in Pennsylvania, I think. On account your brothers keep painting themselves the great heroes, pulling you from the North. You be the bad one, slippin' out of their grasp, not comin' home, disappearin' with your lady in tow. Now, old master, he like that part, you towing Miss Judith, mind. Your brothers, they sure your sister knows where in the wide world you off to now. That's why she send for Mr. Barton to bring us in the dead of the night for visits. I gots to fetch Miss Anne back by dawn, like in a fairy tale."

"What is she selling, to raise the cash?"

"Bride gifts."

"Bride gifts?"

"Yes. Nothing you would even know, she's had them packed up so long already."

"I wish I could help."

"You and Mr. Jordan and Miss Judith, you got your own city row to hoe, sir. Your mama, she keeping us all from want's door, like she always done, don't fret yourself."

Ethan looked at the closed bedroom door. "Aaron. It's past time. They're not calling us."

"Maybe them ladies don't need us, young one. You'd best get yourself used to thinking in that direction."

"A treatment for overindulgence at the drink, this honey remedy," Anne Randolph observed.

Judith nodded, wondering if she would ever feel comfortable in the presence of Ethan's beautiful mother.

"He learned that medical knowledge while at sea, I'll wager."

"Yes," Judith whispered.

"Drunkenness! Has he subjected you to it often?"

"Oh, no!"

"A recent madness."

"Yes, a madness. Dr. Foster's. But not Ethan's!"

"Just because he's the one left standing does not excuse my son's erratic stance, his deception, his behaving like a Randolph man!"

Judith set her mouth in a firm line. "He carried Dr. Foster home from the tavern, straining his leg, hence his stance. My husband does not indulge in spirits to excess. You misjudge him, Mrs. Randolph."

Anne Randolph blinked, then regained her composure quickly. Her soft tone astonished Judith. " 'Mrs. Randolph' will not do. What did you call your mother?" she asked.

"Mam," Judith breathed out. " 'They call thee Mam, thy little lambs,' my father used to tell her."

"And now my Ethan has that woman's stalwart lamb coming to his defense. Judith, would you consider calling me Mother? Or Mama, as Ethan does when he's not angry with me?"

Judith stared at her lap. She nodded.

"Good. Now, in return, I promise to open my mind to possibilities besides the obvious ones of my hasty judgment. Tell me what happened."

When she did, Judith noticed Anne Randolph's eyes change with each sentence. Ethan had spoken eloquently of his mother's veils. Judith realized she was watching a full spectrum.

When she had finished, Anne Randolph sat back in her chair and closed the lids over those enigmatic eyes. As she opened them, a new woman emerged. She took the elegant silver watch tucked into her waistband and stared at its numerals. "It's past time. If you'll pour, my new daughter, I'll shove the honey down this recalcitrant's throat."

She placed the palm of her hand on the sleeping man's shoulder and shook him with a direct, no-nonsense strength Judith didn't think the mistress of Windover possessed. Dr. Foster opened his eyes. He stared hard, confused.

"You're going to take your remedy without any bother, aren't you, Jordan?" Anne Randolph asked.

He continued staring at her mutely as Judith poured the honey onto the spoon. He obeyed each command to swallow.

"Now close your eyes," Ethan's mother said softly after the last.

He reached out. She took his hand. "I've destroyed everything, haven't I, Annie?" he whispered.

"Nonsense," she whispered, stroking the hair back from his brow.

34

Ethan sat stiffly in the chair by Jordan Foster's bed, relieving Ju-dith of the duty. The doctor's color had returned early that afternoon. As had his temper, Judith had warned him. Jordan complained about the egg portion of his remedy, but had eaten. Ethan began drifting off to sleep himself, his head in his hand.

"Did you deliver the jalap remedy to Mr. Hill?" sat him up again.

"Yes, sir."

"And check the Collins baby's fever?"

"No sign of one. Third straight day."

"So you gave Mr. Collins a bill for services rendered?"

Had him. *Damnation,* Ethan thought. "No, sir. I forgot it was the last visit."

"Forgot! With what are we supposed to pay the rent? Your card tricks? Are you afraid the money might turn to dust in your hands?"

"You may be right, sir."

"What is that supposed to mean?"

Ethan took a deep breath. "I am sorry about what happened at the tavern, Dr. Foster," he began formally.

"I'm coming out of a dead drunk without so much as a headache, and *you're* sorry?"

"Yes. I wish I could take your son's place, instead of being the cause of your pain at his loss."

Jordan looked away quickly, scanning the spartan room. His focus riveted on the portraits of his wife and children. "Ethan," he breathed out. "Oh, God, Ethan. What am I doing, all over again?"

"I don't understand, sir."

Jordan Foster finally looked away from his lost family and at his apprentice. Ethan was shocked to see tears in his eyes. "She played her dulcimer for you, you said? In your dream?" he whispered.

"Yes, sir."

"I burned everything. There's not a trace of any of them. Why did Maggie play for you?"

"I don't try to understand the gifts of the women, Dr. Foster. But perhaps you loved her better than you remember."

"Ethan, forgive me."

He smiled. "There's nothing to—"

"Please."

"Yes. Of course. I do, sir," he said. How could this man who'd twice given him his life be asking this? But he must stop his infernal questioning, as Fayette would say, and be gracious.

"Let's start again. Agreed?"

"Agreed," Ethan said cautiously.

"Did you manage all right today?" Dr. Foster asked.

"Yes. It was a light visiting schedule. And I had my compass. Mrs. Willard is asking for you."

"That intrusive old—"

"She needs us, Jordan. She needs both of us."

"Her plight finally got you calling me by my Christian name again. For that I'm grateful. Nothing more. I don't know where you find the patience with her."

"She reminds me of my father."

"Your father?"

"When I came home, he took Judith for my light skirt mistress. I wanted to . . . to snap him in two, shamed by even the possibility of having such a doddering old imbecile for a father. When my memory of my life in his house returned, I realized something else."

"What?"

"That I was never what he expected, either."

"What do you mean?"

"He was the grand architect of our family. He still is, even as his life's work is disintegrating around him. Everyone had a place in his scheme, followed his preordained destiny. He had his heir in Winthrop, his churchman in Clayton, and beautiful Sally to ornament his house. I was a surprise, an afterthought, with no place."

"Were you very unhappy?"

"No. I was my mother's child, and Sally's. What man could complain under those women's care? I tried too hard, that's all. To gain my father's affection. I took my position on the *Ida Lee* to help multiply his fortune, and so to find a place in his heart. I was too young to understand. The objects of his affection have never been people, have they?"

"Not—not in my experience."

"Even people were to him possessions, like Mrs. Willard's china dogs. I fear becoming him, Jordan."

"That's not possible."

"My hands grow cold and sweat when I handle money, when I figure accounts, when I lose control of my anger. I love that Judith cannot master cooking, and so I do not have the scent of roasting meat about me, as he always does."

"Ethan."

"You will not cast me into an asylum for these things, Jordan?"

"I have no great fondness for spit-turned meat, myself."

"Truly?"

"Truly."

"You must tell our Judith this," Ethan urged, "she frets on it."

"I will. Judith endures quite enough for our sake already."

"My mother will be reminding us both of that when she visits again, I expect."

"Your mother? She's in Richmond?"

"You don't remember her dousing you with honey last night?"

"You doused me! I knocked you down over it, damn it all!"

"That's when she threw me out and took over your care."

"No. No, she did not."

Ethan shrugged. "Ask Judith. She never lies."

Jordan grabbed his apprentice's waistcoat. "How will she ever forgive me for my miserable state?"

"I did. And my mother's more generous than I am where you're concerned, I suspect."

"Don't start that nonsense again. Ethan, help me. Intercede, please. Tell her I haven't failed you, or she'll hate me."

"You haven't failed me. And my mother will never hate you. She found her strength in that time with you, I think."

"What time?"

"I only know the stories. It was before my birth. The time of the sickness. You remember, don't you?"

"Of course I remember."

"That's good. It wouldn't do to have a principal player in a family legend to be forgetting his place."

"Hang it all, where's Judith?" Jordan Foster suddenly stormed.

Ethan blinked. "Am I talking too much?" he asked.

"Yes," the doctor answered dismissively. "Where's Judith?"

"Gone to bring the tavern rouster's wife some tonic."

"Since when is this woman our patient?"

"Last night. You don't remember talking with her worried husband, either, do you? No wonder drink does not appeal to me. I've had enough of my own memory problems without inviting new ones. But do you see what a fine physician you are now? You draw new patients in, even while inebriated."

The tavern was quiet, the noon diners having gone their way. Judith tried to imagine Ethan trudging street after street with Dr. Foster on his back while she brought Odette to the docks, dressed as a laundress to deliver a stack of Ethan's shirts to the *Opal.*

The sloop's captain, Mrs. Atwater's son, reminded her a little of Fayette. He had held her hand, praised her courage, promised her Odette would be safely delivered north with the others. To freedom.

She'd felt fired with purpose when she'd asked to be allowed to sew clothes for the runaways he collected along the James. And so pleased when he accepted. Why did she want to do more? People were already suspicious of her plain dress, her slips back to the *"thees"* and *"thys"* of a Quaker.

She had missed the fiery purpose of her missions, she admitted to herself. But now she had no Meeting to sponsor and support her efforts. She had only these two men who would put their hands in the fire for her. She must make sure they were not called upon to do so. She risked her husband's dream of becoming a physician. And she would put his life at risk, if ever he were called to defend her. But Odette was so brave—wasn't her obligation to help in some way?

If she told Ethan, he would understand that she must follow her Light, just as he had followed his own in the stormy Atlantic. But she must protect him from this, her small mission. And so, she now had a secret from her husband. A small secret.

She looked up at the jewel-colored sign.

"Judith Blair."

She turned. A woman stood in the shadow of the building, her long shawl fringed in green. Judith saw a shift in the shadows and felt the woman's deeper scrutiny. "It's you put the sassafras in the waiting-woman tonic?"

"Yes," she said, relieved the woman was no slaver.

"Who taught you that?"

"My father."

"A doctor?"

"He was a botanist."

"Herb doctor?"

"Yes."

"You bring this tonic to Ellen Post now?"

"I do."

"Where's your husband?"

"Caring for the doctor."

"The drunk one."

"He's sober today."

A short burst of laughter erupted, before the eyes turned serious again. "Hark at me now. Curry Post, he told your man about his ailing wife yesterday. Your man, Curry said, bespoke him thus: 'What does the midwife say?' he spoke."

"I did not hear the words, friend. But that sounds like Ethan."

"Does it now? They don't look to be stealing away the women from me, then, those new doctors?"

"No, Mother Ballard."

"You know me?"

"Thy questions, concern for Ellen Post, give you away."

"It is that, what you call it—concern. I had naught to do with the loss of the two before this."

"I'm sure you did your best. You're highly spoken of by all the mothers of our acquaintance. My tonic is very mildly doused, and of good flavor. Would you like to see a bottle?" Judith asked gently.

"I would."

Judith approached the alley between buildings, as much as she feared enclosed, shadowy places since her father's death. She handed the bottle to the midwife. Her hands shook.

"You 'feared of Mother Ballard?"

"No."

"Of the dark, then?"

"The dark, yes. Sometimes."

"Not when that husband casts about for you in the dark, I'll wager!"

Judith felt herself blushing.

"Closer. There. I can see for myself now something they say about you—that your hair does not come with age, but by the touch."

"Touch?"

"A terror. It's true, what else they tell? That your man stole you out of the plain folk, and married you all legal? Did the doctor's bastard son do that?"

Judith wondered at the swiftness of rumor.

"Did you marry Ethan Blair common or legal?" the woman persisted.

"Legal. Twice."

"Twice?" The woman laughed again in that breathless burst. "Think on it! There are wonders yet in this new world of Reason. Visit with Ellen Post. Then come to me." The midwife smiled and Judith got a glimpse of her ancient, earned beauty. "Your man will not learn everything from the schooled doctor. He chose well in you. Will you come, that I might get a better understanding of that tonic, and yourself? Are you brave enough for that?"

Judith wished to embrace her own family, after the sadness of Ellen Post's story, and the wonder of the midwife's pronouncement. She peeked into the doctor's bedroom, smiled at his sleeping form. She expected Ethan to be keeping vigil, but there was no sign of him on the first floor. She climbed the stairs to their rooms. His desk looked as if he'd been interrupted midletter. Beside his chair, his boots, newly refurbished and shining thanks to Aaron, were discarded.

She turned when she heard his high-pitched whistle, like the dolphins' greeting.

He sat in a corner by a rear gable window, the way he sometimes did in his quarters aboard the *Standard*.

"Ethan," she said, approaching, "what are you doing?"

"Hiding."

"From what?"

"Whom," he corrected her quietly, casting his glance above.

"Whom, then?"

"Mrs. Blair!" sounded a cheery voice from below.

Ethan groaned.

"Mrs. Blair?" it came again, "is that you I saw come in just now?"

"Meddlesome woman," Ethan muttered, "and her damned hens."

Judith sighed and approached the window so that her head and shoulders cleared the sill. She looked down over her garden.

"Yes, Mrs. Atwater, I'm home. Is your son off safely?"

"Himself and cargo both, bound for Philadelphia, thank you, dear. Now, you appear tired, sweet girl. After all you've been through, to need my good brown hens to come to aid the . . . indisposed member of your household this morning! Shame, I say."

"Dr. Foster, my husband, and I are most grateful for your eggs, Mrs. Atwater."

"Shall I visit, start a supper for you, poor dear, with no servants of your own by way of those two shiftless men?"

"No!" Ethan pleaded, taking hold of her ankle.

"I'm quite well, Mrs. Atwater," Judith tried, "and must be about my household duties."

"True," Ethan agreed, his voice suddenly low and amorous, his hands removing her slippers with exquisite deliberateness.

"You are so good, after those two behaved so badly yesterday. Common knowledge now, please do not attempt to defend them! How is Dr. Foster faring?"

"He improves." Judith felt her stockings gliding down her leg under Ethan's fingers.

"And your husband?"

Judith couldn't banish the breathless tremor from her voice as the ties of her first petticoat were urged free. "Husband?"

"Yes, your husband! I've been calling after him since you left. To chastise him soundly, and speak again on hiring a live-out girl to help you." Another petticoat gone. "No one answers!"

Ethan growled. His teeth bared against her thigh.

"Where is he?" Mrs. Atwater demanded. "Making his rounds?"

His tongue's caresses turned circular.

"Rounds, yes," Judith could barely breathe out.

"Well, I'm glad he feels well enough to be about."

"Oh, he feels very well."

Ethan stifled laughter, there, below her breasts. Unlaced. He'd unlaced her completely. She pushed down his head, now in danger of rising above the windowsill. Her daygown slipped off her shoulder, threatening scandal. But his clever hand reached up, caught the back seams, held them.

"I must go, Mrs. Atwater. My duties, you see—"

"No," Ethan growled low beneath her, "she does not see." Judith reached, even as the captain's mother finally granted her leave and pulled in the shutters harder than she'd intended.

Then Judith whirled about. The action left her wearing nothing but her shift and sent her husband sprawling. "Ethan Blair," she summoned in a whisper laced with fury, "you've made a wanton, deceitful woman of me!"

He rested back on his elbows, among her discarded gown and petticoats. "I heard no lies, Judith."

"Distracting truths, then!"

His finger traced the arch of her foot. "Distracting, yes. Artful truths."

Judith stepped out of his reach. Did he know anything about her activities the day before? No. He was teasing her. Her shift slipped off one shoulder.

Ethan's eyes lingered on the breast his wife's sudden movement exposed. Different. It looked different to him today, he realized. Darker.

"Stop that!" she demanded.

"What? Stop what?"

"Stop looking at me like a . . . a doctor!"

"But Judith, that life station is . . ."

She flung herself onto the discarded undergarments.

". . . my fondest . . ." He attempted to complete his thought, but she stopped any further words with her mouth over his. He felt her anger mount with her ardor until she tore her mouth from his.

"You did not think to work *these* buttons free, while you were removing me from my clothes?" she demanded, yanking his waistcoat closures so hard that two of them tore loose.

He grinned. "And miss this?"

Ethan was vaguely aware of the day's light growing dimmer. *Don't leave her there, on the floorboards,* he admonished himself. He was used to sleeping anywhere. Not she, not his gentle Judith. Gentle, even when she'd strafed his chest with her strong, accurate, seamstress fingers. At the height of her rushes, he'd felt their calluses, but never nails. He loved his wife's wildness.

But he must take better care of her. Wasn't it bad enough they hadn't reached the bed, again?

Now, her languid smile told him she didn't mind, for all her mock protest over the time and place of his seduction. He kissed her temple. She burrowed her back deeper against his shirt. Was she sleeping already? This was different. Her falling asleep before he did. Different, like her nipples, like the softer feel of her belly. Different, like . . . He nuzzled against her temple and breathed deeply. Yes, even her scent was softer, sweeter, more . . . what? Female? Could he ask Jordan about these things, or would the physician laugh at him?

Then, suddenly, she was crying, their nest of petticoats not enough to silence her tears, to hide shaking shoulders.

He turned her gently to him.

"Judith," he entreated. "Have I done something wrong?"

She smiled. "You've done something very right. We have." Her cheeks dimpled.

"Have we?"

"Yes. There is a child within me, Ethan," she announced.

"A child?"

He touched his own lips. Then he brought her close against his heart, so she wouldn't see it. The fear that rode on the heels of his joy. For the child of Judith Mercer's lineage. For the child's mother. Because of her father's long-ago service to the Revolution, because of the one Loyalist who had gotten away that night of their stand. The one who had come back and killed Eli Mercer. He would return, looking. For Judith, no longer celibate and without heirs. For their child. Neither would be safe from the one who'd killed her father.

Ethan waited quietly beside the tree in the park where he met Sally and the children every midweek afternoon. It was a tall poplar, its leaves turned red and gold on this shining autumn day. Poplars grew quickly. He wondered who had planted it, in the generation before his. Had his mother's brother, the uncle he was named for, ever seen it, ever stood in its shade?

His sister and her chicks entered the park's grounds. He slipped behind the tree as she found their meeting bench. She sat, and neatly divided the shortbread among her children. Even tiny Charlotte took a piece and quickly slipped off her mother's lap to join her sisters skating through the downed leaves. How fast children grow, too, like poplars, Ethan thought, watching, feeling suddenly shy, awkward.

They found him, and pulled him to their mother. Sally looked up. Knowing already, he thought. She must know. For he did not always stand mutely before her, grinning like an idiot, did he?

"What is it?" she asked. "Ethan, what has happened?"

He hadn't thought about how to tell her this thing, this marvelous thing she already knew. "Ethan?" she prompted again. "Is Judith well?"

"More than well. Come summer, your children might be safe from our pirate clutches, *madame*."

Sally sprang to her feet and let out a small squeal that reminded Ethan of the sound she used to make when he'd trod on her slippers during dance lessons.

He swung her high in his arms, drawing the looks of two passersby. His nieces giggled. That slowed the steps of an older couple, who gave them all a disapproving glance.

Sally kissed his cheek, then straightened his neckerchief. "You must not be so . . . so demonstrative in public places. Not without Judith beside you."

"Why not?" She sat on the bench. He took his place beside her. "Why not, Sally?" he persisted.

"Sweet brother," she began finally, "I am a matron whose husband's profession keeps him away from home for weeks and months at a time.

I must be careful of my friendship with Dr. Foster's handsome assistant."

"But we are both married! You allow the girls to call me Uncle. Does that not make it clear that we are not lovers?"

His sister's hand reached for his face, then resettled in her lap. "It makes it more likely in the eyes of some," she explained quietly.

Ethan got that same sickening feeling that had marred the news of Judith's pregnancy—that the one who'd killed Eli would come to destroy her. But this foolishness, these rumors would help, wouldn't they? He removed his hat with a flourish, knelt before her, and kissed his sister's hand.

"Let them talk!" he proposed.

"But, Ethan—"

"Don't you see, Sally? If they think me your lover, they will never attach the name Randolph to mine, yes?"

She stood. Her black-and-white-striped skirts swooped around him. "And what about my name, brother dear? What about my good name?"

"Oh yes, of course." His head bowed. "I am odious, Sally. I don't know why you tolerate me at all."

His sister shooed her children away farther, then took a place on the bench beside him. "You are nothing of the sort. I should not be so sensitive to the opinions of persons who don't matter a whit. Barton is the only one who matters in this."

"And Judith. She would have to brave slander." Ethan shook his head. "I don't think these things through well at all. Actions to consequences."

"Oh, darling, Judith will laugh at any whispers, more heartily even than Barton. Especially now that she has a much more important duty to attend to." She touched the side of his face. His women were so brave, Ethan thought with pride.

"What did Jordan say about Judith's interesting condition?" Sally asked, her eyes beaming.

"We haven't yet told him."

"What? Ethan you must!"

"Before you? Before Mama?"

"Ethan Blair, the man is your dearest friend, is he not?"

"He is ashamed of me, I sometimes think."

"What nonsense!"

"He chides me for—what does he call them?—my flights of fancy. And my problems with remembering to collect the money for our services. What will he think, Sally? Will he rejoice in the prospect of another mouth to feed in his household?"

"You are misjudging him," she maintained. "Badly."

"Am I? Did Mama tell you how he got in his cups last night?"

"She did."

"And I'm misjudging him?"

"Yes. I'm sorry for your wounded heart, but yes, you are. Listen well to me, little brother. We must both concentrate on healing the rift between Jordan and Mother."

"Rift?"

"Mother left for home furious with him!"

"About last night?"

"Last night, your worn-down bootheel, your adventure with thieves that neither of us knew a thing about—"

"Nor did you have to! *Zut alors,* if our mother was not so dedicated to looking at men in their underwear, she'd remain blissfully ignorant of what does not concern her!"

Sally threw her head back and erupted in laughter. But her mood changed dramatically. "Ignorant? So that's how you'd like us better? Is this reward for our devotion? All men would be tyrants if they could. Even you!"

He patted her hand, as a few more couples slowed their walks. "Now, Sally," he whispered, "it appears as if we've had our first lover's quarrel."

She could not hide her smile behind her hand. "I should have drowned you while you were still smaller than I, pest!" she hissed.

"Impossible. I was born in the sack, remember? Not destined for drowning. You must devise another way to be rid of me, sister dear."

Sally's face softened with— What was it? A flight of fancy? It was a family trait, Ethan decided then, this tendency toward imagination. "A baby. I look forward to sharing motherhood with your sweet bride, Ethan," she whispered.

He smiled. "We have dreamed on this day forever, it seems. But neither of us dared hope for it."

"Why not?"

"Reasons you would find ridiculous, I think. But, behind them, I believe it is because of the ways our lives have gone thus far."

His sister's hand covered his, pressed. "True, neither of you has led a charmed existence, despite your remaining undrowned. But it is behind you, sweet boy. All behind you."

"No. No, it is not. Sally, the one who killed Eli—"

"The Loyalist."

"Yes, the Loyalist, when he discovers that Judith is carrying Eli's grandchild . . ." He put his head in his hand, fighting the dark pain behind his scar.

"Oh, Ethan, good God."

He lifted his head. "I must find him first, Sally. I think I must kill him."

35

The smell of the runaway carriage's horses that permeated his clothes since Ethan had grabbed their reins was quickly overcome by the scent of dying. Jordan Foster called for him. He gave up the reins and joined the doctor and their new patient, fallen there, on the cobblestones.

Ethan had witnessed dying before. Why did he feel a kind of madness coming over him—here among the scent, the weeping, the crowd of hushed, shocked faces?

Perhaps it was because this stranger was a woman. One who had been—moments before—alive, walking the streets of Richmond, part of his new life, where he did not believe Death could follow. Walking the streets of Richmond, with her package under her arm. They were still here: arm, package tucked under it, muddy, rain-drenched. He knelt beside the woman with the bright red hair—hair, arm, package, green gown—but he could not put the parts of her together.

Fayette had never allowed him to see anyone this bad on board the *Standard*. Sprinkle of freckles across the nose. But he'd held Eli Mercer in his death throes, hadn't he? And Harry Burnett. He could do this: *Put her together, be of comfort,* he told his freezing brain.

Jordan Foster knelt at the woman's feet, removing his coat. "Ethan!" the physician barked. "Give me your knife."

He pulled his weapon from its sheathed place in his boot smoothly, mechanically, grateful for Jordan's familiar, disgruntled tone. There, the knife into his master's hands, barely disturbing the woman's head on his lap. Head, nearly severed from its pale white neck. It didn't matter, the care he was taking. She could feel no pain.

—Ruined. Cream cakes I baked for my sister.

Ethan heard the woman's wistful voice, though it was impossible for her to speak. He heard her inside his head, where Clarisse, and the chained slaves, and Fayette sometimes spoke with him. Together. At last. She came together.

"We'll deliver," he assured her quietly.

The knife in Jordan's hand stilled at the ready.

—*Good. Deliver. Thank you.*

"She's dead, Ethan," the doctor barked. "Assist me."

The Richmond ladies who'd flocked out of their houses at the sound of the screaming horses brought forth their sheets. Ethan eased the woman into their care. He joined Jordan, trying to understand his clipped explanation of what he was about to do.

With a quick sweep of the knife, Jordan laid open the abdomen and uterus. His hands went inside. Ethan's mind didn't sharpen fully until he thrust the wriggling baby and placenta into his arms.

"Too small," the surgeon pronounced. "He'll die. Let me—"

"She," Ethan corrected him. "It's a girl."

"What does it matter? Ethan, what are you doing?"

"She's cold." He held his burden closer, unbuttoning his vest.

"That's not necessary. It's not a mercy. Hand it to me and I'll—"

"Not 'it,' *she*."

Ethan stopped listening to any but the mother's voice, as it returned to his head, asking him to keep his promise of delivery. He pulled his shirt out of his trousers, then tucked the tiny child, her cord and pulsing afterbirth, against his skin. He secured them in soft cotton folds and waistcoat. Then he rose unsteadily to his feet.

A large woman took his arm.

"Her sister?" he whispered.

"This way, sir," she led him.

The darkened room was full of women. It smelled of blood, as he did. A different kind, though—lifeblood. The sight of him brought tears to the woman lying on the bed. Her red hair matched her fallen sister's. He'd brought something besides confirmation of Death's visit. How could he convince her of that? He walked closer.

One of her attendants rose. "Get out!" she stormed.

He stood his ground, focused on the new mother. "This little one, she's cold, *madame*," he whispered. "And hungry. And so small. She needs you." The child responded to his voice, curling herself closer into the space beneath his heart.

The sister's hand flew to her mouth.

Another woman approached so quickly he saw only flashes of her white apron. She peered inside his waistcoat, gently unbuttoning. She called for her bag, for her stout linen thread. She tied off the baby's cord, cut it, then lifted her from Ethan's bloody pouch. Second birth, Ethan thought as he sat, exhausted and bereft, in a chair in the room's corner, feeling the placenta's weight cold against his gut. Watching the bustling skirts. Listening to the hushed tones, the sister's high-pitched welcome. Then, contented suckling. Outside the circle of welcome, Ethan waited. Because Fayette said it was always wise to be patient among women.

Finally, one approached. He saw the red-embroidered design on her apron clearly now. Rich, swirling, interconnected designs. She carried a crockery bowl under her arm. A handsome, blue-and-white-painted bowl. Color—so much color. It hurt his eyes. She reached inside his shirt, lifted out the afterbirth, his last anchor to the tiny child. Her voice was kind.

"Tree of life, see?"

He stared between her hands, at the blue-veined, red-jelly mass, saw the pattern she described growing out of the whitened cord. Yes, the sheltering branches of a tree. He nodded. The wonder of it brought tears to his eyes. She placed the afterbirth into her beautiful bowl. Frowning—thinking him stupid, most likely. It didn't matter. Many people over his lifetime had thought him without much sense. Perhaps they were right. What had he done to Judith? Would her feet slip underneath a carriage wheel, too? The woman set the bowl aside, and wiped her hands on her apron.

"Come with me."

She was the midwife, Ethan finally realized, Mother Ballard, who was afraid he and Jordan wanted to steal her patients. "No," he protested softly. "Take care of the baby."

"She's snug. Between auntmother and cousinbrother, born three days apart." She cocked her head. "Do you understand me, Frenchman?"

Ethan nodded.

"Small, but she has a chance, I'm thinking."

He bowed his head.

"Come," the woman urged again, taking his hand as if he were a child. She led him from the room.

"I should leave now, yes?"

She clucked her disapproval. "Abandon your tiny patient so soon? And when your lady wife comes with that tea of hers, do you wish her to see you looking like—"

"Motherwort."

"What do you say?"

"Judith's tea is motherwort."

"Ah, you know a little more than your knives and surgery, do you? You listen to the botanist's daughter?"

"I am not a fool, *madame.*"

"And did I once say you were, touchy Frenchman?"

"No."

The red on her bodice blurred. Or was there something in his eyes? The whitewashed corridor became suddenly too close. He must not fall. What would she think of him if he were to fall while on duty, at a patient's house? He felt a surge of strength from the midwife's hand.

She pulled him into the large hearth kitchen, where her strong hands began stripping off his mud- and blood-caked clothes.

"Come now, do you think there's anything you have that I've not seen—God in Heaven!" She fell away from his back. But she approached it again, even tracing the ridges with her fingertips.

"White scars. And in a smaller place than the breadth of you now," she observed. "This happened half your lifetime ago. A child bore these lashes."

"I was twelve. Small for my age."

"Interesting. Sit."

When he did, she scrubbed his face with a wet, lavender-scented cloth.

"What do you find interesting, Mother Ballard?" he asked, hoping to distract her enough to ease her touch, which was as forceful as Martha's when he'd come in from playing in the salt marsh. Surely she was not so hard on her babies.

"That the abuse did not turn you cruel. There. Most of it's off."

"Along with a layer of skin," he groused. "That I had no use for, I'm sure," he hastened to add when her scrubbing hand threatened again.

She snorted. "The leg, now."

"Madame?"

"I'm wanting a look at your bad leg, Doctor."

"My master's the doctor."

Amusement in her eyes. "And what are you, his slave?"

"Assistant."

She shook her head. "Learn to accept what the people call you. I am Mother Ballard since my sixteenth year, imagine that. You must not correct unimportant things. Now, off with those choice boots."

"I can't walk without them."

"No need to walk. Off. And the muddy britches as well—what's under them is not foreign to me either."

He did as she'd bade him, which won him a fine-woven blanket before she pushed him into a Windsor chair. She sat on a stool opposite and drew his right leg across her knees. It commanded her attention for full minutes of observation, poking, and prodding.

"He has skill, this surgeon. He did well by you," she finally pronounced.

"Yes."

"Your lady says you engage yourself in pursuits of the mind, Mr. Blair. Besides your doctoring and horsemanship. What are they?"

"I read. Make ship miniatures. Observe the stars."

"Do not let those delights go fallow. This leg will not hold you forever, even after the Boston surgeon's work. That's if you manage to dance around trouble long enough to reach your elder years, of course."

Ethan grinned. "It's fortunate that the stars shine for good and troublesome alike then, is it not, *madame*?"

Her frown deepened. Ethan despaired of ever being able to cause her to smile. "They say you whistled sharp, then calmed the carriage horses, before seeing Leah Prichard out of her life, catching her child, and not allowing Dr. Foster to stifle her life away."

Leah Prichard. The woman's name brought the image of the harrowing accident into his mind. Muted him again.

"I smell those horses, under the blood on your clothes," she continued. "A wild-with-fear smell."

"Perhaps my own."

"I think not. You don't have the sense to be afraid when you see need. Only now do your hands shake. See? I know the secret of rescuers."

"You come by this knowledge through experience, Mother Ballard?"

She smiled at last, allowing him a look at her full, shining beauty. "Yes, they say *that,* too, about you," she said, standing, turning on her heel.

"Wait," he called, taking a few uneven, stumbling steps before he gathered the blanket around his nakedness. "Who is it says what?"

But she'd disappeared around the corner. The feelings their conversation had distracted him from hit hard in her ringing, silent absence. The shaking in his hands intensified, spread. Were the fits coming over him, here in this stranger's house? Ethan leaned against the wall, commanding his racing heart to still, his uneven legs to hold him. Neither effort produced results. With a soft blasphemy, he sank to the cold stone floor.

Mother Ballard returned, clean shirt over her arm. She knelt beside him. As he tried to look away, she grabbed his jaw, poked wide his eyelids. They rebelled his will, too, finally spilling tears.

"Tell me, I am out of patience with you. Tell me now," she commanded.

"My wife's with child."

"I know that. Who do you think told her?"

"Don't let her die, Mother Ballard," he whispered his fear. "Don't let my Judith die."

Her insistent grip turned into a gentle hold on the curve of his face. "Fetch the young doctor a whiskey, Emma," she urged the shadow behind them.

A man's voice answered. "He doesn't drink spirits."

The midwife turned. "What does he do when life catches up with him, surgeon?"

Ethan scrambled to stand. Only their joint grip at his shoulder kept him down.

"Jordan," he called, forgetting formalities, "this lady—"

"What have you done to him?" Dr. Foster demanded.

Her hands fisted at her waist. "I? I, is it? Who nicked the cord of that infant with your knife, butcher?"

"I did my best! That's a seven-month child with no hope. But I had a healthy assistant before he stepped into this house you preside over, witch!"

"Jordan!" Ethan summoned, "I'll not have you—"

"Quiet!" his master barked, without redirecting his attention from the midwife. "Now, suppose you tell me what's wrong with him?"

"It's a simple case of new-father nerves, not that you'd know a simple malady if it visited you on angel wings."

"Can't even keep your gossip straight! He is not a father."

"Come summer he will be."

"Ethan, tell this woman she is being absurd! Judith is not . . ."

Ethan grinned, mirth winning over his fears and the awkward timing of his friend's discovery. "I cannot do that, sir."

"You mean, Ethan, Judith is—?"

"So she tells me. And I've yet to find my wife a liar."

It was the surgeon's turn to stagger. "Bless my soul. A child."

To Ethan's astonishment, he felt himself lifted into Jordan Foster's embrace.

"You can't smother this one back into the womb," the midwife observed tartly behind them.

36

She watched her husband in unfamiliar clothes, squatting beside their wardrobe. He'd not even mentioned what all of Richmond was proclaiming, his part in the afternoon's carriage tragedy.

"Judith, where are my shirts?" he called, yanking off the borrowed linsey-woolsey garment.

"If you insist on changing your linens daily," she stammered, "I shall have to boil shirts more often."

"I change them for you, wife!"

"Me?"

"Do not women prefer their lovers clean? Or was I instructed poorly in this regard?"

She touched his collarbone. He smelled of the horse he'd gentled—wild, but far from unpleasant. "You were not," she admitted.

"Well, then! They cannot all be in need of washing. Judith, my mother has fortified me with at least two dozen." He saw it, her guilt. His eyes narrowed. "You've given them away, haven't you?"

"I—"

"*Sacre-bleu!* You're wrapped a dozen dock urchins in softest cotton while I'm itching unto madness!"

Judith knelt beside him. "Oh, Ethan, forgive me! But the winter grows so cold, and . . ."

His laughter erased her worry. He opened another compartment in their wardrobe. "Behold," he commanded. "Mother's knitted at least a dozen scarfs more than I can use. Give all but one of those away, but no more of my underwear, yes? I am no hair-shirt penitential!"

"No," she agreed, moving closer beside him. She was doing more than clothing urchins, she was breaking the law, putting them all in jeopardy. She didn't deserve his trust. Ignoring the scarf bounty, Judith eased his boots off. There. He smiled as she worked to ease the strains of the day from his legs. Higher. What did his thighs feel like through the tight weave of butternut trousers? Like muscled silk, she decided. His hand touched her hair.

"Are you trying to seduce me, wife," he asked gruffly, fingers touching the pulsing vein at her throat, "into forgiveness of your theft?"

"It would be no attrition, to exchange what is heaven for my transgression."

"So, you advise against this?" Lips, warm, pliant, pressing kisses to new-bared skin. "And this?" His clever fingers, exploring tender places.

"Not while I have breath to answer you yea or . . . oh, Ethan, yes . . ."

Dr. Foster called from downstairs. Ethan stifled a groan. "He's not done with me. I don't suppose your good works will earn me any time out of Jordan's hell, will they?" She tried to cast him a stern look, but it dissolved as he kissed her again, saying, "I'll return soon."

"Do, sweet boy," she urged, as he again donned the rough-weave shirt with a wince of discomfort.

Ethan had harbored a motherless child with the warmth of his body this day, a godly thing. Surely Dr. Foster would not look harshly on his apprentice. How Judith wanted her husband's body close to her and their own tiny being in her dreamtime. And she could not require he wear that borrowed shirt when she had stolen so many of his own, could she? At the thought of him lying naked beside her, her blood raced. Did that make her a wanton? *Purpose, Judith.* She tried to chase the disturbing thought away. *Find some purpose.* She shut the drawer of their wardrobe.

Judith heard the beginnings of the argument downstairs as she turned down their bed.

"Where were you when I was performing that surgery?"

"Beside you, sir."

"Where was your mind? Away, off on one of your fanciful expeditions! Doctors cannot afford such extravagances, Ethan."

"I was listening."

"Not to me!"

"To her. To Mrs. Prichard."

"So. You're saying what that rabble says! That she wasn't dead. That I took your knife and murdered her."

"No, sir. I'm not saying that at all."

"Betrayal, from you? Damnation! The woman was dead!"

"Yes, sir."

"No sound came from her, do you hear me? She did not speak!"

"No, sir."

"So, what were you listening to?"

"I don't know how to—"

"There is far too much you don't know, Ethan."

"Yes, sir. Always will be, I suspect."

Judith reached the bottom of the stairs as the physician threw up his arms in frustration. Ethan sat on the sofa as Jordan stormed the room on his stronger legs. She felt her frame become ramrod-straight as she watched from the shadows.

"You defied me, Ethan."

"Yes, sir."

It was a statement of agreement, without remorse.

"Then you left the scene without permission, with our patient—"

"*My* patient, if I defied you."

There. There was her Ethan.

"Your patient? What are you now, *my* teacher?"

"No, sir."

"Why not? Why not set up your own practice, you arrogant brat? Do you know what they call you now?" Jordan Foster demanded.

"Who, sir?"

"You know very well who. Our patients, the neighbors, every horse trader you've advised, and woman or child you've charmed!"

"Ask Mrs. Atwater how charming I am. She thinks Judith is the most long-suffering wife since—"

"Ethan, that crone tried to buy you away from me."

"Mrs. Atwater?"

"No, that Ballard woman!"

"Well." Judith heard Ethan's sniff of indignation. "I hope you told her I am not for sale."

In spite of her anger, Judith stifled a giggle behind her hand as Jordan continued.

"She said you've learned enough of hacking limbs and cutting innards and dosing people with laudanum. She wants you and Judith to learn about birth, about life, now. Not just you, but Judith, too. She offered to pay me for your time away from my instruction! Do you hear? Both of you are now to follow her around to her superstitious patients, helping them push their children into the world! What do you think of that, Dr. Blair?"

Judith stepped forward, out of the shadows. "I think it's a good idea," she said quietly.

The physician's eyes avoided hers as she stood beside Ethan. "I'm sorry if we woke you, Judith."

"I was not asleep." She anchored her hand at her husband's shoulder. "And you have no childbearing women as patients, Jordan. Most trust their own womenfolk and the midwives. It would be an opportunity for us. As the battlefield was for you."

"Judith, Ethan and I need to discuss—"

"Mother Ballard's offer? When it was made to us both?"

"No. There will be no discussion on that matter. I expressly forbid it."

Ethan's hand covered hers. "Forgive me, Jordan," he said quietly, "but you are not in that position."

"What position do you hold, Ethan Blair?" came out of their benefactor with the intensity of a rapier's thrust, hard and cold.

"A voluntary one, sir, your assistant. And you have no hold over my wife whatsoever."

"No assistant of mine will talk with creatures of the air while we perform surgery!"

"*Zut alors!* They are real! Mrs. Prichard, Fayette, Clarisse, the slaves in the hold, your own generous wife and children—they live here!" Ethan's fingers thumped against the scar on his head, which had now gone crimson in his agitation. "Does that make me a madman? Then that is what I am. There is nothing I can do about it! *Rien du tout!*"

Judith watched the doctor's eyes soften with remorse. But it was too late. Ethan's own had steeled. It was almost as if they had exchanged places. Jordan Foster exhaled a sigh. Of what? she wondered. Pity? Her anger surged. Her visionary husband needed no one's pity.

"Judith, please leave us to discuss this matter—"

"Judith is my partner in this and everything," Ethan interrupted. "And we both need her here, I think, sir."

"Toward what purpose?"

"To see it remains a discussion and not an exercise in futility."

"It already is that. You'll go where your capricious head leads, as always! Well, you will not take Judith with you, not this time. Not in her delicate state, I will not have it!"

Dr. Foster turned away from them.

Judith remembered back to Dartmoor Prison when a guard, bent on beating an inmate, was prevented by the Light coming through her. She offered a quick prayer.

"Jordan Foster!" she called.

He turned around.

"My state is wondrous and healthy, not delicate. All his life my husband has been guided by women's hands, including my own through the knowledge passed on to me from my father. You have allowed it. Mother Ballard is a healer. She has knowledge we require. Ethan and I value her offer of guidance. Our respect, our love for you, does not diminish with this. Trust us, sir. Please. We need you both."

"You need nothing! Nothing but the power of those eyes, that voice, Judith Mercer," he accused. "They stop mere mortals in their tracks."

Judith felt her knees buckle. The body of her young husband, even off balance, took over. She felt his arms help sit her down beside him. She felt his gentle kiss above her brow. "You are right, of course, Jordan," he agreed with his master. "Still, it humors this lady to abide here with us." He grinned. "Now, can we deny our Judith her amusement?"

She thought it was the sound of her nuzzling against his borrowed rough, linsey-woolsey shirt that caused the noise at first. A noise like the swarm of bees. But when she felt him tense, she knew it a bigger sound, approaching their door.

"You see? You see what you have brought down on us?" the doctor shouted from his place at the window.

"If I have brought it down, I will contend with it now. If you would take Judith upstairs, sir—"

"No!" She fought his attempts to hand her to the physician. "Ethan, you must not go out there."

He had her elbows firmly. His calmness permeated her distress. "This is a misunderstanding. Stay with Dr. Foster. I will call you if I tangle things further," he said quietly, touching the side of her face, the coldness of his fingers the only sign of his fear.

"Will you?" she demanded.

"Mais oui," he assured her. "You, Judith, are our hidden ace."

"Ace?"

He smiled at her ignorance of the expression, of his card tricks.

The doctor stepped between them. "If you think you're—"

Ethan matched his stance. "I don't think, remember?" he shot back, his anger erupting in a clean, white flame. "But I am a Virginian, like them. You and Judith are outsiders. I have the best chance. Now, for God's sake, Jordan, hold on to my wife!"

He pushed her into the stunned doctor's arms and walked out the door.

Judith recognized few in a sea of faces—angry, shouting. "Get the knife! Search! Search for other bodies!"

It subsided into murmurs as they caught sight of her in the doorway with Dr. Foster's hand at her shoulder. The gathering crowd of men were doing something they would not do, were their women among them. Judith sensed it in her bones. Now her presence quieted them, touched them with shame. Could her presence do all that? Is that why even Jordan Foster respected it, and was not pulling her inside? One of the men stepped forward.

"It's very late, Constable Warren," Ethan addressed him. "My wife needs her rest."

"Aye, sir. But I have a request for a search of your premises, regarding a certain incident on High Street today."

"I see. You have a warrant, of course."

"Well, no."

"As this is America, you will need one to enter our house, search, or seize property."

"Mr. Blair, it would be better for you—"

"It would be better for you, sir, if you were to obey the laws you are sworn to uphold."

"Was she dead?" someone shouted. "Was my Leah dead before you butchers took your knives to her?"

Judith didn't see the large man himself until Ethan walked down the steps and into the crowd. The hush allowed her to hear every soft-spoken word her husband spoke. "She was, Mr. Prichard. Dr. Foster and I are heartfelt sorry for your loss."

"They made me look," he said quietly. "Identify. She still smelled like flour, vanilla."

"Have you seen your daughter, sir?" Ethan asked.

"Sophie? She's with the miller's wife."

"Not Sophie. Your new daughter, sir."

"No. They say she'll die, too, the baby."

"She has a pretty mouth."

"Does she?"

"I think she would be glad for your company."

"You doctors. You did your best by my Leah?"

"By your new daughter, Mr. Prichard. Your wife, it was she did her best by us."

The man pulled his hat off slowly, held it between hands that could snap her husband's bones. "It's late. The women at her sister's, Doctor—they'll let me in now, you think, to visit the child?"

"I'm sure they will, sir."

"I'd best go there, then. Thank you." He shook Ethan's hand, moved on to Dr. Foster's, then bowed in Judith's direction. "Very sorry for the disturbance, missus. We'll leave you to your rest now."

"God keep you and your family, Mr. Prichard," Judith said.

The crowd followed the grieving father down the street, leaving only the constable and his two deputies.

"Will there be anything else, Mr. Warren?" Dr. Foster asked as Judith felt herself being shifted back into Ethan's care. "The night grows cold, and Mrs. Blair is without her shawl."

"As the complaint was brought by William Prichard, no, sir. We'll take our leave of you this night."

Judith felt the men close in on either side of her as they watched the authorities turn the corner. They stood together in hushed silence, Judith warmed by her sentinels, in no need of a shawl.

"Well," Jordan Foster finally breathed out.

"I remembered, this time," Ethan said softly. "Condolences first. Yes?"

To Judith's astonishment, the doctor smiled at his assistant. "Will you forgive an old man's envy? His grasping for family?" he whispered.

She reached out her hand from the haven of her husband's arms. "There is no need to grasp, Jordan," she assured him. "We are here."

"And you are not old," Ethan sniffed. "I will not give my mother away to an old man."

37

Ethan placed his smallest finger in the baby's palm. The grip was immediate. "How fine and strong you've become, Miss Prichard," he complimented, eliciting a gurgle from his patient and a pull at his coat from her sister.

"I squeeze better than Katie, Dr. Blair!"

Ethan turned from his examination. "Indeed? Then I must have a care to loan you a stronger finger, Sophie." He stopped beside the child as Judith reswaddled her baby sister and returned her to the woman sitting with Mother Ballard at the fireside.

The children's aunt did not hover so close as she did in the early days of the tiny child's life. None of the grieving household was wary now. All treated Ethan and Judith like family members.

Mother Ballard approached Judith as she opened her book to write their observations. She watched Judith's sweeping hand. "Bold lettering the Quakers teach," she said.

Judith felt her face flush with color as she realized her writing had changed under the influence of Ethan's own notations. His exuberance over his new profession came through his fingers, his bold strokes, the graceful arcs of his *y*'s and *s*'s. She was supposed to be the more grounded. But how could she not take flight with him as this miracle child thrived?

"Its flourishes are acquired," Judith admitted quietly.

"Interesting."

Mother Ballard had teased her since first the occasional "thee" and "thou" flew off her tongue.

Sophie Prichard stared intently at Ethan's hands.

"Why, Dr. Blair, one finger's crooked! Did Katie do that?"

He smiled. "No."

The midwife glanced down. "The bone was broken, once. The one beside it, too. Crushed, I'd say. Wouldn't you, troublefinder?"

Judith heard Ethan's fingers breaking again under the Quaker farmer's thick-heeled boots. Did the midwife see the slight twitch now, beside his right eye? Ethan touched the little girl's bright hair. "You are very observant, Sophie. Perhaps Mother Ballard will apprentice you once she gives up on teaching me."

"Will I be able to make babies who look like ugly little monkeys turn into Katies, too, then?"

"It is your aunt's care, your cousin's generosity in sharing his mother with Katie, and your family's love, that have done that."

"And you, scooping our Katie up after Mama died, keeping her warm until she could lie with Aunt Addy." Sophie frowned. "Don't you know the story?"

"I play only a small role in it. But we are kindred spirits, your sister and I. I, too, was born early and had a brave sister to help me thrive."

"I rock the cradle every afternoon!" Sophia exclaimed.

Ethan nodded solemnly. "Cradle rocking, did you hear, Judith? Are you writing it in our learning book?"

"Even as it's said, husband."

"I don't remember anything unless Judith writes it down," he confided to the child.

Judith stole a look at Mother Ballard. Had her curiosity about his finger been distracted by her approval of his modesty? The midwife stood over her shoulder, nodding, as Judith corked her bottle of chestnut ink and sanded her last notation. She'd never commented on what either of them wrote. People said the midwife could neither read nor write herself. Perhaps that's why she'd had taken them on, Judith realized, though she'd at first thought it only a small part of their bargain. Was this the first time her years of experience were being set down in writing?

She didn't care why the midwife had agreed to apprentice them, Judith loved this new part of their lives. Throughout the winter they followed Mother Ballard on her morning visits to the waiting women and new mothers and children. She only wished Dr. Foster was not so disturbed by it.

As they stood together outside, ready to go their separate ways for the remaining hours of the day, Ethan glanced up at the sky. "I'm late again," he said. "I hope Jordan hasn't left without me."

Judith handed him the pouch of red clover petals. "He'll wait when he finds we're low on Mr. Chase's remedy. I'll be home soon. Mother Ballard and I have only a few more man-shy patients to visit."

"That is good news." He touched her cheek, there in the doorway. "You'll remember to drink your horehound tea?"

"Mother Ballard starts brewing if I so much as smile crooked."

"I've told her that's all the warning you'll ever give."

"Traitor!"

He closed the door and held her close. She felt his shuddering sigh. Judith ran her finger over the line of worry at his brow. "Ethan, Ethan, my small sickness is a sign of the child planting firm, Mother Ballard says."

"But Jordan thinks—"

"We are both well acquainted with Dr. Foster's opinions, which go to great reaches to contradict our midwife's."

Ethan smiled. "They do, don't they?"

"Now, rescue him from the clutches of Mrs. Willard."

"Mrs. Willard *and* a late start? Perhaps I should allow him to continue on his own. Shall I take Two Hearts riding by the falls upriver today?"

"No, Ethan, you must not!"

"I am speaking in jest. . . . Judith?" He summoned her out of the vision of him falling, his call silenced by the sound of the rushing water. "Judith, what is it?"

She looked down, saw her hands gripping his sleeve. "You live with a woman without humor, Ethan Blair," she whispered.

"No." He grinned. "Merely another one who wishes me away from water. My seafaring days are done, then, wife?"

She bowed her head. "Be off," she whispered.

He leaned down and kissed her, there on the doorstep and in plain sight. She opened her mouth, welcoming his tongue's tender probe, though the kiss probably now added fuel of confusion to those Richmond citizens who still believed he was bedding every neglected wife, widow, and chambermaid who sighed down on him from their windows.

Judith returned to find him on a step halfway up the stairs to their rooms, in the afternoon square of sunshine from the landing window. Seeing him sent a bold rush of excitement through her, as it ignited the memory of them loving each other there, on another afternoon. She wondered if their baby started then, a gift of the sun and the love this man bore her. But now he looked dejected and mournful. A letter bearing Anne Randolph's seal dangled from his long fingers.

Judith placed her basket down silently and climbed to his side.

"What is it, love?" she asked.

"My father is dying, Judith. They want me to come home."

She felt an icy grip around her heart. "Who asks this of you?"

"My mother. My sister writes, too, see? She thinks her Christmas visit started this confinement."

"Poor Sally! How?"

"She is not so good a dissembler as Mother. He became convinced that she and her children were too cheerful, that they'd seen me. He demanded to know my whereabouts, badgering her so mercilessly she fled the room. He followed in a rush, tripped on one of Charlotte's blocks, and cracked his skull."

"Oh, Ethan."

"Now he raves—cursing, howling. Terrorizing them all. Demanding I be hauled in for my share of his final damnation, no doubt."

Judith fought her panic at the thought of Ethan returning downriver to Windover. She saw his brothers again shoving her away, telling her he was now theirs, in this family that eats its young. No. Anne and Sally, Martha and Aaron and their mighty sons, would not allow it, would they? Women and bondsmen. *Be sensible, Judith,* she admonished herself. What power had they against his brothers?

"But, Ethan, after all your mother and Sally went through to keep you safe under your new name, they could not be asking this. Your brothers—"

"They have given her their word, my mother says, not to do me any harm. The letter is written in her hand. I know it as well as my own."

She kissed his temple. "We'll go, then."

" 'We'? But our patients—"

"—will have to endure without us for a little while."

* * *

Once they'd told him, Judith watched the now familiar sight of Jordan Foster storming around his assistant. "I cannot go with you!" he said again. "Not with three surgeries scheduled, and Mrs. Martin recovering from the—"

"We understand. We don't ask it of you."

"Do you understand how powerful your brothers are? Do you understand the risk? Ethan, think! What do you owe the man?"

"It is not a request I'd grant, had it not come through my mother. I can refuse her nothing. That you understand, sir—yes?"

The doctor shook his head. "I wonder if the first Ethan Blair was as stubborn as you are," he muttered.

Judith watched her young husband cock his head in bemused curiosity. "Do you think I am my Revolution uncle returned to earth, then?"

"Do not catch me in your heathen beliefs!"

"Spoken like a true Bostonian, sir."

"Thank you," the physician said in his icy tone.

"You're welcome"—returned with Ethan's habitual affability, and, as always, before Jordan's frown of displeasure had moved a fraction. Judith wondered if two such divergent men had ever loved each other as deeply as her husband and their benefactor.

The next morning's mist gathered around her as the three of them stood on the dock together. Judith could keep the cry from her clear voice as they bade the doctor good-bye. But she could not stem her tears' flow. How fine they looked together, and as similar as Mrs. Willard's father and son.

Though the physician had known Ethan less time than she herself had, Judith couldn't imagine any father doing more for them than this man had done over the last tumultuous two years. And this was the most difficult gift—letting Ethan go. The price was heavy on both men. Did Anne Randolph realize how much she was asking?

Ethan faced himself into the stiff breeze, which forced him to squint as he shook the doctor's hand. "You'll ride Lark and Morgan and Two Hearts?"

"Daily."

"And no name-calling in your arguments with Mother Ballard?"

"On my honor. Ethan, don't forget your life here."

"It is my only life. I am not so foolish as I look. Without you, Judith would still see me as a spoiled third son. I was him once."

"Never," Judith whispered. "You were never him."

"How would either of you know?" he accused. "Even my mother would assure you I was. Jordan, I know I am a long way from finished. I would oftentimes turn Fayette toward despair, as I now do to you. A snail, but a determined one. I will be a good doctor. I will be a good father to the child Judith so graciously bears. But that father must now be a good son to his mother and sister who depend on him."

Jordan Foster turned away from his student and stared down the river. "Write."

"Of course. Every day."

They were summoned aboard. Ethan took Judith's arm and turned toward the sloop.

"Call," Jordan Foster whispered.

He turned back. "Call, sir?"

"If you need me. Call. I will hear you."

Ethan smiled. "You have before, have you not, you Bostonian conjurer?"

"You must not tease him so," Judith reprimanded lightly as they settled on board the schooner. Her young husband's beautiful eyes were sad, distracted.

"Judith," he called softly as the salt sea breeze traveled up from the Atlantic.

"Yes, love?"

"Our bed, there at Dr. Foster's house. It is a Boston bed, is it not? Called a sleigh bed? Is that how Northern sleighs are curved, then?"

"They are, yes."

"And snow. It is lacy, wondrous, like our time in Richmond? Little miracles, when viewed closely? White spiderwebs, no two the same? Do they disappear against the heat of a finger? Is this what pieces of snow are, Judith?"

"Flakes. Snowflakes. Yes. That's exactly what they are."

"I have sometimes dreamed of flakes at the window, and of looking out over great heaps of snow and horses and laughing bells in our sleigh bed, then."

"Have you?"

"Yes. But how can that be? I have never seen these things."

Judith faced the wind, squinted, but there was no fooling him with his own tricks. He handed her a folded handkerchief from his waistcoat pocket. *"Mon dieu,"* he cursed softly. "Figure it with me, Judith. Do not cry. This is not a crying sort of puzzlement, is it?"

38

As the schooner *Opal* approached Windover's dock, Judith's arm wound through Ethan's. He drew her close, grateful for her warmth. Beside them, Captain Atwater frowned. "Don't allow the Randolphs to keep you long from home," he advised.

Home, yes. Richmond was home, despite this man's disagreeable mother. Even she had served her purpose, Jordan said, proving there was one woman in the world Ethan Blair could not charm. Not even an egg from one of her blasted chickens. She'd eyed his coins as if they were made of wood. Her son was eyeing him that way now, as if he were a fraud. How had he peaked this family's ire?

Judith smiled. "Might we expect assistance if we wish to break free, Captain?" she asked.

The merry lines around the man's eyes stilled. "You'll have it, Mrs. Blair. Your very own Captain Atwater is ever at your service, and a true friend of Friends."

Ethan watched Judith's eyes. What were they saying to each other behind the words, the big blond captain and his own wife?

"Oh, Ethan. Look." She squeezed his hand, distracting him.

Tin lanterns illuminated the dockside at Windover and lit a path to the big house. Aaron's strong bass voice led a song of pulsing sadness. More of his life as that boy Ethan Randolph invaded Ethan Blair's being. The worry came with it—that he would forget the new man he was becoming by the grace of Fayette and Jordan Foster, by the love of Judith Mercer. That, so far from the brutal slave coffles of Richmond, here—where his father's slaves were well treated—he would forget his promise to Aaron's family. And that he would forget things he needed to know to protect his wife and keep her beside him.

The slaves' song was about sailing. Sailing over Jordan. A river—in the Bible. Was the doctor named for that river? Ethan wondered. He hoped his mother would marry Jordan Foster once his father completed this last business of dying.

The song. The rich voices. Aaron's wide, surprised grin as he recognized them. These things, not any grand illumination view of the big house, made him feel as if he was home.

Ethan's eyes were so intrigued by the tiny shafts of light that laced through the webbing of Judith's shawl that he almost didn't catch her when she lost her footing on the dock.

She laughed that fine, spun-silver laugh of hers. "I'm only finding my land legs!" she chided as he lifted her into his arms.

"It's not far, just over the mud, to where the shell path begins. Please allow me, Judith. You are not half the weight of Jordan Foster, and smell much sweeter."

She leaned her head on his shoulder.

"When will it stop, this courtship? Do you not know you have me fast in your hold, Ethan Blair?" she confided at his ear.

"Nothing is fast."

She touched his cheek. "Well, I will not argue this notion, since it grants me such a sweet result." Her hand wove inside his waistcoat to find his trousers' brace. She held it in her strong, steady grip. That was fast, he realized, that grip she had on his heart. Aaron, after scanning his leg's ability to bear an extra burden, retreated, motioning Micah and Elwood back as well.

Ethan reluctantly set his wife back on her feet when they reached the path. He took her hand impulsively, and kissed into the palm.

"God keep you here at Windover, Judith Mercer," he whispered.

"And you, beloved," she returned his prayer, before taking his arm. Together, they faced the big house.

"How fares my father, Aaron?" Ethan asked as they walked.

"Poorly, I hears, sir."

"Hear? What do you say? And my mother? And Martha?"

"Got no say. We ain't none of us been allowed in the sickroom lately, sir."

"What?"

"By order of your brothers, sir." Ethan felt Judith's grip on his arm tighten.

"Where are my brothers?"

That question elicited a smile. "Off to the Harrison place for a game of cards, sir. Didn't think you'd be coming after dark, I expect. Posted their people on guard, though," he warned, opening the riverfront door of the big house, "and their doctor be inside."

They entered. "What doctor?"

"Mr. Evans, sir."

"Evans? Does he yet live?"

"White wig, black robes, purges, bleeding basin, and all."

"*Mon dieu,* are they trying to—?"

His alarm was spiked by his mother and sister's joint cry of protest from outside his father's door. Ethan's hand swept the curve of Judith's face.

"Yes, go," she encouraged, nodding, releasing him.

He took the stairs two at a time and arrived, pounding at the door, with Anne and Sally anchored at his coattails. He heard the inside lock released, peaking his anger higher. The bespectacled doctor opened the door, smelling of blood, looking smaller than Ethan remembered. No, it was he who was taller now.

The black-robed man pursed his lips. "How dare—"

"—you lock this door against my mother in her house, sir?" Ethan finished. He shoved his way past the physician and entered the foul-smelling room. Winthrop Randolph was buried in his bed, his head swaddled in lint and wrappings, his right arm exposed, purple, bleeding from a vein not yet collapsed from the doctor's attempts to drain him dry. Ethan did not want the women to see this.

"Sally," he directed gruffly, "open a window. Mother, would you fetch me your brightest lamp?"

The doctor roared his protest. "Jubal, Calvert!" he called to the servants who had tumbled into the room along with Ethan and the women. "Stop this madman bent on murder!"

When Ethan turned sharply, the doctor yanked in a startled breath, then held up the knife he'd been using to bleed Winthrop Randolph. Ethan grasped his wrist, shoved him against the wall. He directed the knife against the physician's own throat. The man's wig went askew.

"The third son," Ethan informed him quietly. "You've heard something of me lately, sir? That I'm very good with knives . . . but subject to fits?"

The man's frightened eyes searched for his brothers' servants. Ethan smiled, continuing. "If a fit should come over me in my present agitation, and this knife slip? Well, black can't testify against white, can they, Doctor? Before anything untoward should happen, I suggest you all return to my brother Winthrop, with my thanks for your efforts. Yes?"

"Yes," the grizzled man croaked out. Ethan relaxed his hold, recovering the knife from the doctor's deadened grip. Then he eased his stance, giving the man just enough room to slip past.

Ethan flung the knife on the table of instruments. "Your chamber of horrors will follow," he said to the retreating, black-winged form.

Judith stepped into the room. Stopped—by fear. How much had she seen? The look in her eyes. He'd seen that look before. He glanced down at his bloodied hands, afraid to touch her with them.

"Another window, Sally," Ethan directed, "my wife is not well."

His father's fingers grazed his. Ethan bent over, listening for the frail voice within the wheeze that was left of Winthrop Randolph's demanding bass.

"You've come back."

"Yes."

"I need you."

"I'm here, sir."

The gentle breeze from the windows cleared out the scent of death as Ethan worked, stopping the blood flowing from his father's arm. He sensed the brightness of the lamp, his sister's grief and guilt. He was working for Sally more than for the old man, he realized, as he removed the putrid wrappings from his father's head. She must not feel herself responsible for this. The swollen bruise had turned yellow. Where was Judith? Judith must help his sister not to blame herself.

His mother's fingers pressed his shoulder. "Aaron's brought her to your rooms to rest," she assured him as if he'd voiced his thoughts of her. "She'll understand better when she wakes, my darling."

He nodded. How could he ever expect his gentle Quaker wife to understand his family, to understand himself in one of his Randolph rages? Had Judith again seen him as a killer?

The glassy eyes of Winthrop Randolph entreated him. Ethan took the bloodless hand. It reminded him of Mrs. Willard's. He skimmed his thumb over the knuckle.

"You'll help me die, Ethan, if it's my time?"

"Of course. Even if it is not."

"Not? Will I recover?"

"You have recovered from all but the effects of your doctoring. Perhaps you can rescue yourself from Hell once more, you disagreeable old man."

A thin smile appeared. "Has my wife gotten her way at last? Are you made a doctor? Has she fostered you out to that scholar–turned–Scots–trained–physician?"

Ethan let out a string of French curses in response.

Winthrop Randolph grinned his satisfaction. "Oh, stop your fussing," he reprimanded. "You're safe. Think you your women are the only ones who can harbor a secret?"

Later, Anne Randolph stood over Ethan, her long fingers lacing through his hair. "Sally and I will look after him now. See to Judith. Go to bed."

He glanced into the night shrouded in clouds. "My brothers—"

"—are too drunk to find their way home from the Harrisons'. Sally and I will not leave him. If they return, we will send for you."

"All right, then," he agreed, rising unsteadily to his feet. He met his sister's shining eyes. "Don't worry," he tried to assure her, "it will take more than a child's toy to bring him down." She hugged him close, this woman who would always think too much of him, who would never harbor a suspicion. The spoiled boy in him wanted only her love. But he was not that boy. He was a man, who must face the woman in his bed with courage and understanding.

He tried to enter the darkened room silently, though his leg dragged behind a little. He looked down at the halo of soft white hair, to his wife's sleeping face. A little fuller, he thought, though whether it came from weeping or the child within her, he was too tired to try to ascertain. Should he lay down beside her? Would she scream at the touch of her father's murderer?

He would have had no such thoughts at the lightkeepers', or in Richmond. Only here. In this poisoned place. He was about to turn away when she shifted in her sleep, curling deeper into herself. Her blanket slid away, revealing her strong legs' beautiful, curving form through the white of her nightgown. Higher, her soft, bulging child-space. Cold—she might become cold, revealed that way. He would cover her, cover her only, then go, find another place to sleep. But when his hand reached her hip, she touched it.

"Is he dead?"

"No. I think he will survive this."

"Truly?"

"If he wishes to. And I think he does."

"That is a great blessing."

"Perhaps."

"Ethan."

There, that slight reprimand in her voice. "I cannot rejoice, *madame*. I have lived under this man."

"A child has. Not you."

"Open your eyes wider. I am that child, Judith Mercer."

She sat up slowly. Her arms, bare, white. As beautiful as the moon. "Ethan, forgive me. Please."

He shifted his gaze to the stray strands from her braid glistening against the pillow. "There is nothing to—"

"We both know there is."

"I drew no blood from the physician, *madame*. What you saw was my father's purged blood."

"I know. I know that now. Ethan. What I saw—thought I saw . . . It was because of the knife, the blood, harkened back . . . Ethan, it was momentary. Like a dream."

"Like a vision."

"Yes. Of the past. It does not have dominion over me now, husband. It will never again."

He did not believe her.

"We are not strangers to trouble, you and I," she continued. "But I am not used to it coming this way, from within a family. Help me to understand."

"I— Judith, I don't understand it myself."

She took his hand, the one that had held the knife to the doctor's throat, and brought it to her lips. "Then come to bed. Understanding can wait for the morning. Keep my back from the cold, sweet husband."

He slipped on his boots in the predawn light. He wanted to bring Judith some of Martha's corn pudding, flavored with honey, to ease her sickness, to make her feel treasured here, in his troubled childhood home. To thank her for receiving him into her ripe, powerful, changing body. He was deciding if he should offer her the pudding hot or cooled to lukewarm as he headed through the dining room toward Martha's kitchen. He wasn't alerted to the footsteps until it was too late.

His towering brother pinned him against the wall. Winthrop Randolph's mouth reeked of bourbon. When he spoke, Ethan saw that one of his canine teeth was broken, still inflamed. A recent altercation at the card tables. Still drunk and hurting besides. This would not be good.

"Bloody little tyrant! Who do you think you are?"

When he moved, Winthrop caught his right wrist in an iron grip and brought it up behind his back, making him gasp. But not cry out. He would never cry out, because that's what his brother wanted, more than anything.

"I am now in charge of my father's care," Ethan said evenly.

Winthrop laughed. "Self-appointed!"

"Appointed by my mother and sister, and called for by Father."

"You don't have to tell me that much! Stinking old man can't even be dignified in death! Yelling for you. Threatening. Making me promise to Mother that I will not lock you away where you belong!"

The grip on his wrist twisted. His coatsleeve ripped.

"Get your hands off me," Ethan said between his teeth.

Laughter. "Still the emperor, aren't you? All demands, no pleading."

Ethan raised his left elbow between them, dug it deep into his brother's gut. Surprised, Winthrop backed away. Ethan had not been ambidextrous before Fayette. He used his new freedom to cut his fist upward into his brother's jaw, slamming the mouth shut with a bone-jarring swiftness. Winthrop howled in fury before knocking him to the floor.

A shower of sparks burst through Ethan's head. His mouth hurt. He swallowed blood. But Winthrop did not look so well, either. Ethan gathered what comfort he could in that, before the insufferable Clara flew into the room to curse him and pull her husband away.

Aaron leaned over Ethan. Micah helped him stand. "Elwood," Ethan turned to Aaron's youngest son, "would you kindly ask your mother to bring Judith some of her corn pudding?"

"Pudding?" He looked up at his father, who nodded. "Yes, sir."

"Lukewarm," Ethan decided, finally.

"Straight off."

"And if Martha would brook no protest and feed her? Before Judith's head leaves the pillow? That way she won't be sick, I think."

"Done, sir."

"Thank you."

Ethan was glad his father had slept through the clamor downstairs. And it was easy enough to hide his damaged lip in the dim room as he urged his mother and sister to their needed rest on the sofa. But it was not long past daylight before the old man woke them bellowing, "Where's Ethan?"

Ethan raised his head from his Molière, a bad translation, which had him scribbling in the margins. "Here, sir."

"Not a dream? You, driving that bleeding fool out, letting in the air—life?"

"Not a dream."

The old man scowled, like his old self. "How long are you home?"

"Until you are well. Or dead."

"Disrespectful child! Were that Frenchman alive, I'd thrash him soundly! Are you married yet, rogue?"

"I am, sir."

The old man's eyes lit with interest. "To the sling-hipped Quakerwoman, with the mischief about her eyes?"

Ethan sighed. "Judith. Her name is Judith."

"Your brothers, they said you hunted her down like some wild Indian, there, among the Quakers. They say you killed her father, when he refused your suit."

"I didn't kill anyone."

"Then why were those accursed lawyers I hired to set you free so expensive?"

"I—"

"Never mind! Water under the bridge! Has your wife done her duty? Is she breeding yet?"

Ethan glanced up at his weary-eyed mother, whose look urged patience. "She is, yes."

"What? She is? She has told you this?"

"Yes."

"There, splendid! And not a trick of your brothers' silly wives to gain a trinket or two from me. Quakers don't lie! I told you she was a good choice, Ethan."

Ethan smiled at his ancient, impossible father and the florid color coming back to his cheeks. "She is that, yes," he agreed.

"She'll bring forth a great, lusty Randolph male from those hips."

Ethan growled, shifting.

"What in hell has happened?" his father demanded suddenly.

"Happened?"

"That cut by your mouth! Is your sister planting her deadly children's blocks under you now?"

Ethan cast a quick look as Sally bit her bottom lip in distress. He suppressed the urge to wring the old man's neck. "No, sir. I . . . fell."

"Fell—*fell*? You, the dancer? You did no such thing! Good God. Not a day returned to us. Which one of them went after you this time?"

His mother touched her husband's shoulder. "He's not saying."

"I *am* saying," Ethan insisted, "that I fell."

Winthrop entered the room, hobbling on his wife's arm. Anne Randolph's hand went to her face in astonishment, while her recovering husband nearly choked on his laughter at the sight of his eldest son's bruised and swollen face, his favored side.

"Looks to me like your brute elder brother 'fell' harder than you did, Ethan Blair!" his father proclaimed.

39

"She was sore peeved with Jordan Foster when he brought back that Scottish wife and lit out for Indian Territory, you know. Never in front of me, of course, but I heard her flinging glass and crockery over her room like the spoiled little girl I first married."

Ethan began to wonder if his father's head injury had affected his memory. "My mother, breaking crockery? Why?"

"Because of her plan for you, of course! To do what you've finally done on your own—study medicine under that Boston scholar. When her hope of it was finally dashed—when he went west to spoil all that expensive learning on heathen Indians—that was when I finally got you out from under her sphere, tried to make a trader of you."

Ethan remembered his mother taking to her rooms, the lifelessness of her eyes in the days before he went away to serve on board the *Ida Lee*. It was not his leaving Windover that caused his mother's distress, then? It couldn't have been, if she was going to apprentice him to the doctor in that time long ago.

"I almost succeeded, didn't I?" his father interrupted his confused thoughts.

"Succeeded?"

"Head out of your cloud, son. Succeeded in making a seafaring merchant of you, of course! Damned bad business, the British boarding of the *Ida Lee,* the wreck. But you survived it all and . . . whatever went on in Pennsylvania besides. You're home now."

"No. No, I'm not, Father. My home's upriver."

"Of course, of course. Commendable, you taking on a second profession, a healthy wife. Planting a family while you wait for your inheritance. I approve! Much better than wasting my fortune at the gaming tables and whorehouses. Just the profession, in fact, when you've got a father riddled with age and greedy brothers trying to hasten his end with bloodsucking surgeons. Ah, then, come in, Mrs. Randolph!"

Judith stood panting by the door, wondering if Ethan's mother were behind her, until she realized Winthrop Randolph was addressing her.

She stepped into the room, the threshold of which she couldn't cross in her fear the night before.

"I beg your pardon, sir. Learning Ethan was hurt, I ran—"

"Now, that you should not do, *madame*! There's much underfoot. Your husband is well enough. Stand up, Ethan. Take my stick. Banish the concern remaining in your lady's eyes!"

When Ethan reached for the griffin-headed cane, Judith saw the chaffed bruise around his wrist. These people were savages, she decided. Bullying, insufferable, full of pride. She had had enough of them. She wanted to go home. The suffering look in her husband's eyes stopped her. Did he think she included him in her seething indignation? She turned her attention to his cut mouth.

"I have my medicinals."

"It requires nothing. I fell, Judith."

One of his artful truths. "I have my sewing kit as well. If you will allow me your coat?"

"Yes, sit with us—hands busy!" his father commanded. "Such a resourceful woman you are. You must be a great asset to my son in his practice. I have been most fortunate in your timely presence."

Judith had almost forgotten that the elder Winthrop Randolph could be gracious. And she hadn't even inquired about his health. She should apologize for not joining Ethan in attending him the night before. But the residue of anger, along with her recent propensity for bursting into tears, would not allow it. Or was it pride? How she missed her own father at times like this.

Judith busied herself at her needle and thread and torn sleeve as the two men talked of Windover's family, black and white, and harvest and politics and the merchant marine fleet out of Norfolk. It was as if her husband had no other life than this one he was born into. Ethan was not her confused, battered seaman here anymore, she had to remind herself. He had a place in this family. A history. Did he have a future with them?

"You wear a ring, *madame*," brought her to attention.

"To honor my husband."

"Still no vanity? Still a Quakeress, then?"

"No. No longer," she whispered.

"Speak up!"

Ethan covered her hand with his. She raised her head. "I am no longer considered a Friend, sir."

"Why not?"

"My marriage."

"Damned fools, to let go such as you! No matter. You're a Randolph now. Deserving of more rings, and some finery, I think. For a celebration."

"Father," Ethan interceded, "we have no desire for—"

"I haven't a care in the world for your desires, rascal! And it seems to me," he continued, scanning Judith's form, "you are already getting those fulfilled in ample measure!"

He pulled her harder up the hill. "Stop," she urged.

"Too fast for you, Judith?"

"For you. Your leg. Ethan, Jordan would be so angry—"

"Then we should give thanks he's not here to scold. It's just ahead, the place we can escape them."

The tiny brick structure in the woods was so overrun with greenery that Judith could not separate it from the landscape until her flushed young husband opened a vine-shrouded door.

Far from the ruin she expected inside, the plastered walls were whitewashed—simple, clean, maintained. "Sit, sit," he said grimacing, impatient, like his father. No. Pained politeness. Waiting for her to sit before he could rest his own overworked leg, that's all. He wasn't like his father, his brothers. She took her place on a chair with a tapestried cover. He collapsed in its twin.

"Here." She patted her lap. He slouched but allowed her to lift his muddied right boot to her knees.

"What is this place?" she asked, beginning her massage.

"The start of Windover. Built by the first Randolph to marry a Blair, in sixteen twenty-two. Would that my family had remained so simple in our needs."

Judith closed her eyes. At first she thought she was becoming ill. Then she nodded, giving the vision leave to come, and welcome. She saw the faces of women. Giving birth, nursing their sick, dying. They all resembled Ethan's mother, and so him. They all pointed westward, toward the setting sun. When Ethan's hand took hers, they faded. He remained respectfully silent, so she sought out more, there behind her eyelids. She saw a small boy, surrounded by black children. He wore a smock identical to theirs. His dark hair was tied back in a queue, so she could see his round, angelic face, his intense eyes. The children listened as he read from a book half his size, as he made letters in the dirt. An older boy seemed to see her. That boy raised his head from the circle, and nodded, smiling.

"Ethan?" Judith called. "Aubrey had eyes like Martha's."

"Yes."

"And a tiny scar," she touched her cheek, "here."

"From a fishhook."

"You taught him to read. And other slave children, when you were smaller than Betsy. You taught them here."

He shrugged. "All with an interest in it. I was just playing at being Sally. It helped me remember my own teaching."

"It was dangerous, you were breaking the law!"

He frowned like Fayette. "Since when have you been concerned about the laws men make, tree climber?"

"You knew? What we were doing, that night in Pennsylvania?"

"Eventually."

"Why didn't you ever—?"

"And lose my ability to surprise you? You'll throw me over when that day comes, Judith Mercer." His dark eyes sobered. "You must allow me to work on these matters my way, at Windover," he admonished. "Nothing would give my brothers more pleasure than to have my abolitionist wife tarred and feathered here in the Tidewater."

"I'm not going to—"

"No?" He fixed her with a pointed stare.

She looked away. "I follow my Light. I'm obliged to do that."

"Without a doubt."

"Are you laughing at me?"

"No, *madame,* I am trying to stay clear of you. Look. My hand is scorched from your communion with my ancestors."

She touched it. Warm. "Ethan," she said in wonder. "You saw the women?"

"Briefly. Your Light is blinding."

She sniffed her indignation. "And what of yours, causing you to swim the depths of the ocean with your dolphin kinsmen?"

"That was the Atlantic shelf—hardly the open sea. My ocean days are behind me, thanks to my ties to certain wicked women."

Judith laughed as she looked around the well-kept room. "I believe this place is still used for your purpose. Who teaches now?"

"I don't know. They didn't trust me with that information before I left for Pennsylvania. Phoebe, I expect. She is so quick-witted, and a wonder with—"

"You're a wonder, Ethan Blair. How can my heart expand further, to hold this new vision, this new depth of love for you?"

He kissed her behind her ear. "Oh, you're expanding, sweet wife," he teased slyly, "but not for me."

She brought his hand to her bodice. “For you,” she assured him, coloring at her own brazenness. Since that afternoon of his fall she knew that her breasts pleased him, and now he took delight in her pregnancy’s changes causing their enhancement.

“Why, Judith,” he proclaimed, even while he unlaced her, “this place is a hallowed hall of learning.”

“Let us teach each other, then.”

He kissed her bared shoulder. “Mrs. Blair,” he admonished, “without even a bed?”

“Since when have we required a bed?”

He laughed, taking her down on the cool dirt floor of his schoolroom.

That night Judith dreamed of sitting on the tapestry chair, prepared to thank Ethan’s ancestor women for their vision. They came, pointing again, west. A broad-banked, flowing body of water awaited.

She sat up. Ethan took hold at her disappearing waist.

“What do you need, love?” he asked, his voice still drenched in sleep.

“Water. Yes. The Ohio River,” she answered.

He rubbed his stubble beard. “Aw, Judith,” he sighed, “would a drink from the well suffice tonight?”

She laughed, burrowing down in the featherbed, resting his head beneath her still-racing heart. “We must leave, husband,” she announced. “West. Your mother’s people urge it.”

“The frontier? Are you mad?” his father bellowed.

“It is merely a borning contemplation. But consider: You have said yourself that my years abroad have made me unfit to be a Tidewater planter.”

“Twisted! You’ve twisted my words, you . . . Frenchman!”

“There! Exactly so. It was once French-held, this land along the Mississippi, the Ohio. My second language will aid us there, yes?”

“It is not your country.”

“Father, the Louisiana Purchase expanded the United States to number—”

“*Virginia* is your country!”

Ethan frowned, regretting he’d even introduced the subject. “In the years I had no memory, I dreamed of a flag. The American flag, Father. Its field had many stars.”

"Dreams fueled by that French revolutionary. Do you wish to end up like him? A man with no country, no family, no—"

"He had family. He had me."

"Little good you did him!"

Ethan saw his friend's broken body again, felt a twitch beside his eye. "Perhaps. But we had each other," he maintained quietly.

"As you have me, and your brothers, and— Oh, I see. It is they you would flee? Because you think you are powerless against them? Ethan, you are not powerless. You have my protection, son, so long as you—"

Ethan swallowed bitter retorts and willed his voice calm. He would make the old man understand. "Not flee. I do not wish to flee. Father, Judith and I, we move *toward.*"

Winthrop Randolph's eyebrow cocked. "Nonsense, utter nonsense! To anger and distract me from your real purpose. What is it you came here for? What do you want?"

" 'Want,' sir?"

"Yes, yes, I know a ploy when I hear one. Rather late this time, I'll admit, as your eyes are still a child's and it's difficult to decipher your cunning."

"Cunning?"

"You returned home at whose behest? Your mother's?"

"Yes," he admitted.

"To get into my good graces before I died. And now I have not died. Because of your skill. You stay, visit. Tantalize me with the new generation in your wife's belly. Then you talk about emigration, which will mean the end of our family. Cunning devil, you want it all, don't you? You want Windover."

"No, sir."

"Look at me, Ethan Blair. What is it you want?"

Locked in the old man's stare, Ethan resorted to the whole truth. "Aaron."

"Aaron?"

"Yes. And his family."

"Perhaps I should allow your brothers to lock you up in the attic. Do you understand what you're asking?"

"Yes, sir."

"And I put it to you that you do not! You have no sense of family!"

"I know that Aaron is our family! I know I do not want to see his family split, scattered asunder because of my brothers' greed!"

"Ethan, no one is going to—"

"Sell them off? Sell any off? What will you have to say about it when you are gone, and my mother powerless in this world you've made?"

"Your brothers will be honor-bound."

"My brothers breed people instead of crops. Do you think your servants will be any different than your sticks of furniture, your acres, to them?"

"That's your wife speaking! Come out from her skirts."

"My wife speaks more sense and has more courage than all the Randolph men who ever walked the earth, sir!"

"Damnation! You have no feelings, even for the women, who have mediated your every move since you turned up on our doorstep again, as unexpectedly as when first you arrived. I thought I had everything then, I thought you were your mother's middle years' indulgence. Now, you are all I have left. Insufferable boy, insufferable notions! Get out of my sight. I have had enough of you!"

Ethan did as he was bid, then leaned his back against the door. He wanted to go home to Richmond, to become the bastard son of Jordan Foster and a French whore, with a Quaker wife who gives away his shirts to the poor and can't cook. Because the truth was too painful. He was chained to this man, by iron as cold as that of his cell in Pennsylvania and on the deck of the *Standard*.

How could he keep his promise to Aaron while chained?

Ethan pulled the sturgeon from the river, gutted it quickly, and wrapped it in the broad wet leaf before stacking it on the rock with the others. No time to think, they were coming so fast. And he had come here to think, more than to fish. He dropped the line in the creek's flow, unbaited this time, and sat back against the willow's trunk. He heard Aaron's low chuckle behind him.

"Who you feeding? Jesus and all his Apostles besides?"

"I thought Martha might like them. For you and yours."

"Well, then. We can have us an outside feast, once she finished feeding you and your brothers up at the big house tonight."

Ethan groaned. "They're coming again?"

"Along with the elder Harrisons and Ruffins. Best get used to plenty company. I think your daddy's inviting most of the seaboard to the baptism, come summer!"

"Or maybe he'll disown me and I can go home."

"No hope of that. He laughing, conniving again. Just ordered me to seek you out. Seen him twice as peeved with your brothers, with much smaller cause. What you go talking about leaving again for?"

"I thought he'd be glad for my enterprise, my finding a place. I thought he might help us."

"Only place your daddy knows is Windover, Ethan. And he sees it going down without an heir. You and your lady, you be his hope."

"His hope will end yours."

"How is that, sir?"

"The manumission laws. Free, you'd be banished from Virginia within a year."

"The law say this?"

"Yes. So you see, while our father still lives, before my brothers tie up any inheritance in the courts for years, I need to get you all from him." It felt good, unburdening his predicament, one not even the mind of Thomas Jefferson could solve for him. Jefferson had proclaimed, "All men are created equal," but now the best advice he could offer was that it was up to Ethan's generation to find a way to make it so.

"You wants to buy us from your daddy, child?" Aaron asked.

"Yes, exactly. Then we've got to get you west, into a new free state."

"Ethan. We—Martha and me and ours—we be the reason you goin' west?"

"Yes. Judith's dreamed it, Aaron. Dreams are a gift of God, aren't they? It seems the only course open to us, if you're willing, if I can convince my father that he owes you something, after all the years you've been the best, most dutiful son of the sorry lot of us. Would you accept the hardships this law thrusts upon us, Aaron? Would you travel a thousand miles to be free?"

The big man knelt beside him on the rock. He stretched his muscled arm until Ethan felt the weight, the strength of him come to rest on his shoulder. "Brother," he whispered their connection for the first time, "I want you to listen to me now, with your whole learned being. Take anything. No matter how good you treat it, it wants to be free. You can feed it good, and give it every blessed thing it seems to want, but if'n you open the cage, it flies. It's happy."

Ethan grinned. "Well, then. Let's continue our joint pursuit of happiness, shall we?"

"This here's Aubrey's rock we talking these things on."

"I figured as much when the fish wouldn't stop sacrificing themselves, just as they used to under his spear."

"His grandmam taught him that, spearing the sturgeon."

Ethan saw Hagar again, with her proud eyes, her cardinal's feather. The hanging branches of the old willow wafted in the breeze, reminding Ethan of the tree he'd courted Judith under in Pennsylvania. Sacred places. He understood his father's draw to this beauty. He would be sad to leave. He would trace Windover in his imperfect memory. But he needed to fly, too.

"Got another tug on your line, young one."

They pulled out the largest of his catch together, laughing.

"Maybe we can even get Paris out from his duties tonight with this feast of fish!" Aaron declared. "Phoebe misses him sore when he gone."

Paris. Winthrop's coachman. Damnation. He should have bargained for the coachman before he'd done his brother harm. He'd need to buy Paris, too, or Phoebe's heart would break on their way west.

40

Judith watched for the schooner's billowed sails, hoping Captain Atwater would recognize her from Windover's old dock, now a deserted place of narrow inlet and a small, splintered, pontoon bridge. He'd described it to her on his last official stop, laden with Jordan's letters and medicinals. They'd planned to continue delivery of her sewing undertakings from there.

In this quiet, deserted place, and at the height of the day, Judith felt most invisible at Windover. She wondered where Ethan was. Not cooped inside with Windover's account books, she fervently hoped. On those days he visited her accompanied by the stale smell of old tobacco. On those nights his dreams were bedeviled with numbers and ruin. What would he think of her being here, waiting for Captain Atwater? Would he forgive her? Of course he would. Continuing this part of her life in Richmond was helping her chase her own blue devils of doubt and confusion.

And she was doing her part in their new life among his family, was she not? They dined with his parents and sister and visiting relatives at three each day. Together with Windover's mistress, they called on the sick and new children in Windover's slave community. Judith treasured seeing mother and son assist each other. The slaves even treated Mrs. Randolph a little less regally with Ethan beside her, teasing the children, and making the sick and their caregivers alike smile.

Deep night had become their time together again, as it had been on board the *Standard*. They refused to be separated then, and laughed about Winthrop Randolph's thundering admonitions to his son not to visit his wife's bed with such frequency. Mother Ballard had already rid them of any concerns about disturbing the health of their well-planted child with the joy they found in each other's arms. Afterward, they would curl up and talk of their time apart.

Judith was grateful that her husband's nocturnal visits gave her the excuse to retire from the family at the height of the day. Still, it had not been easy to carve time from this family's obligations in order for her to follow her Light. Pregnancy had its uses, and she thanked the growing child inside her for providing this claim to solitude.

She'd been careful to establish her resting time from noon until the family's three-o'clock dinner, so Judith felt safe as she worked. No one came near their room in the west wing of the Main House during those hours, not even Ethan. At first she'd longed for him to join her sewing the simple frocks, trousers, the capes, the warmer woolens—all to help the human cargo Captain Atwater brought deeper south before shipping up the coastal waterway to Philadelphia.

No one questioned her requests for Windover's woven-goods supply, assuming she was sewing for herself and the baby. She sighed. Her poor baby had not a thread yet. Even her sisters-in-law had contributed fine silks toward making herself and her child more their equal in finery, though their generosity was more to impress Winthrop Randolph than to honor her and the Randolph heir she bore. No matter. She now had a lady's traveling-clothes ensemble for Captain Atwater this time, a wonderful disguise for a brave soul, perhaps a mulatto woman light enough to pass for white on the journey north.

Her deception both from her husband and his family had been so easily accomplished that Judith felt twinges of guilt. She reasoned hers was but a small contribution after the thrilling night of the lanterns in the trees, of the rescue at Del and Ida's lighthouse.

She'd partnered with Ethan before in her efforts. But that was in their wild time, when he was courting, when they had no names. In Richmond, her activities would jeopardize his apprenticeship with Dr. Foster. And here such business would be even more dangerous for him, Winthrop Randolph's son.

He'd called her an abolitionist in the hidden house, without a hint of judgment in his voice. What would her doting husband think of her if he knew what she'd done in Jordan's house, and here, in his father's? Would he still be accepting? Would he be angry at her pursuit of her

Light's precepts? Her blue devils were back, she realized. Were they the price of her deception of her guileless husband? *Banish them, Judith. Follow thy Light.*

She saw the captain tuck his spyglass under his arm and wave. He'd seen her! God forgive her—Judith prayed, as the launch was lowered with its single occupant—for needing what this man gave her in an embarrassment of abundance, praise for even her small contribution to the *Opal* and its escape route north.

"Kindly stay where you are, Mrs. Blair," the captain reprimanded her gently as she reached for the bow of the launch. "She'll beach nicely, and I've boots to take the mud in stride." Judith stood on the higher ground, impatient, beached herself, until the captain took her outstretched hands.

"It is good to see you again, friend."

"I have yet more letters from Dr. Foster."

Judith tucked them into her deep side pocket. "He is well?"

"Well, but pining for his missing family."

"As we are for him in this time that cannot be helped. But tell me of your own needs now, Captain Atwater."

"I hope your brave stance onshore indicates goods. We are in sore need of your services, having added two to our cargo of tender years, and barely clothed."

"These might suffice," Judith said, presenting her wrapped bundle.

Captain Atwater's face dimpled in a grin as he hefted the package's weight. "More than suffice, I'll warrant. How I wish I could ship you to Philadelphia myself, to tell of your part in our work for one of our scribe's pens."

She smiled. "Your sometime cargo takes risks much greater than I, Captain."

"For a chance at a much greater reward. What is your reward, friend of the Friends?"

"It is in this moment, sir. I suspect you know that to a much greater degree."

"Do I?" he asked.

"Surely! At what other endeavor might we indulge a high moral purpose with the bedeviled high spirits of our vanished youths?"

He threw back his head of weather-bleached hair, reminding Judith suddenly of Fayette. "And you, Mrs. Blair, are forever young!" he proclaimed with a suitor's abandon.

Judith bowed her head, scanned her hands. She must not encourage this, she realized suddenly. She made her voice tranquil again. "Are the stories of the runaways really being written down in Philadelphia, Captain?" she asked.

"They are. And published. The pamphlets are dangerous to carry in Virginia, of course, but I will endeavor to bring you one next time. They're whacking good tales!"

"I hope they inspire others to end this blight in our country."

He frowned. "Sometimes I wonder. We all thought it ending of its own accord. But the peculiar institution thrives. What use even are heroic stories against the cotton gin, the growing, vast plantations of the Southern Frontier? The money to be made of the sweat of these people's backs?"

"You sound like my husband at table, Captain."

"And how does your husband's time here progress, Mrs. Blair? Surely with the master of Windover's health returned, you will be released from your duties soon? Dr. Foster complains that your garden likes him not at all and will not show a single shoot."

"I shall be home within a fortnight, I think. My husband has promised to leave once the cotillion planned for us is over."

"For you? But the word on the docks proclaims the cotillion is for the youngest son of Winthrop Randolph."

"That is true."

"Then you are—"

"Blair in Richmond. Randolph, here."

The captain blinked as the comprehension of her words began to take root. "Ethan Blair, the doctor's assistant, is Winthrop Randolph's son?"

"Yes."

"Natural or legal?"

"Legal."

"An heir, then? This man who visits the sick of all colors in Richmond? Who has you for his wife? How came this to be?"

"He is the same good man here, Captain."

A slight stiffness rode through his form. "Of this I could not testify. But you, ma'am, I find most courageous in both places."

"No. Captain Atwater, think on it. My way is clear. It is my husband who is torn between our shared beliefs and his loyalty to his family."

"What would he do if he discovered your part in our excursions?"

"I take great care that he does not. For the sake of harmony between us." She smiled. "Have no fear for me. It's you who have muddied your fine boots for a poor parcel of clothes."

"A parcel beyond price, Mrs. Blair," he corrected, squeezed her hand, and returned to his launch.

Judith stood in the shade of the scrub pine. She'd trusted the captain of the nimble schooner with the knowledge that the master of Windover's doctor was also his son. It should not have grieved him. Captain Atwater knew Ethan's reputation in Richmond. He knew her husband would become no lazy planter's son in their time here.

"Imagine, Judith," Hester declared between pursed lips less than a week later, "the very man who delivered your correspondences to and from Richmond—caught! It's a disgrace!"

"Caught? Captain Atwater, caught?"

"Exactly so."

"They've seized his ship," Clara chimed in. "He's ruined."

"They speak of imprisonment. And worse."

"Worse?" Judith whispered, her hand hovering over her expanding middle, feeling ill for the first time in weeks.

"They ought to treat him to the same punishments inflicted on the property he was stealing!" Hester declared watching Judith closely. "They ought to whip him to within an inch of his life!"

"He'll be lucky if he survives long enough to go to trial," Clara's handkerchief signaled back, "from what I hear about the mobs of Norfolk."

"Ladies . . ." Judith heard her mother-in-law's steely voice. "That is enough of this venomous conjecturing about a man who never did us any harm, and performed a valuable service for Ethan and Judith."

"Oh, yes. I suppose now you will have to wait for the post rider like the more humble of us who don't have schooner captains at our beck and call, Judith," Clara said in her sweet-sick voice.

Judith stood, speechless in her anger and misery. She wished Sally had not returned to Richmond with her little ones. She needed badly to cry into Ethan's sister's lap. Sally would be all comfort, no questions.

Anne Randolph answered the entreaty in her eyes. "Lie down a little while, Judith. I will finish entertaining our guests."

Judith left the room's confines—not for her own rooms, but for Martha's kitchen. The cook was leaning into her baking oven. She turned. "Why, Miss Judith, where's your hat, child?"

"I need my husband."

"But I don't rightly know where—"

"Who does, Martha? I need Ethan now."

"You well?"

She nodded fitfully, trying to keep back her tears.

"Up to setting yourself on a saddle, miss?" she asked, pulling a cloth bonnet from its peg on the wall.

"Yes."

"Well, then, come along. We find out where your man is. And we get you into his company right quick, don't fret no more. But put this on, it's cool yet."

It was easy to spot him among the black men mending the roof of one of the older slave cabins on Blackberry Lane. He lifted his head from his hammering when one of the men touched his shoulder, pointed toward her with his chin.

Ethan climbed down a ladder as Judith dismounted. He took her hand, leading her under a tulip poplar. Like his sister, no questions.

"I would go to Norfolk, Ethan. I would speak for Captain Atwater," she explained.

He listened in silence to the circumstances of the capture of the *Opal* and its runaways. Then she waited, startled by the change in his eyes. Eyes like his mother's, not in color, but in their evasive veils.

"By water would be fastest, I think. Would a sail at first light suit you, Judith?" he asked.

He joined her in bed that night with the scent of bourbon on his breath and his brothers still reveling below. He kissed her cheek, then circled her waist and nuzzled like a child beneath her heart. She waited for him to speak. He did not.

"Ethan?" she called softly.

"Hmm?"

"First light?"

He groaned. "Already?"

"No. A few hours yet. Are we still leaving then?"

"Aye, *madame*."

Her blue devils were back, wanting her to shake him, ask him why he drank bourbon and caroused with his father and brothers deep into the night before their mission to save a good man's life began. Or was it not his mission, but hers alone? She silenced her devils, and pulled her husband as close as their growing child would allow.

41

Ethan's hand felt clammy in hers. The smell of iron, the closeness of the keep. So familiar to him, over his long impressment, and his time held for her father's murder. Judith suddenly wanted to pull him away and beg his forgiveness for even asking him to bring her to this place. She saw bushy gray eyebrows, there beyond the unlatched square in the heavy door.

"Your name, again?"

"Randolph," he repeated.

The eyebrow cocked. "Which Randolph?"

"Ethan Blair. Son to Winthrop, of Windover."

"Aye. The Federalist merchant. You the young one, then? The mad one? Who was lost at sea, hauled off by the British to fight Napoleon, then went chasing a Quaker woman with your French manners, then—"

"Guilty on all counts," Ethan conceded quickly. "And you, sir?"

"Me?"

"As you have the advantage of me, I ask your name."

"Morgan Carr, who ain't been out pirating ships and Quaker women for amusement, but who keeps slave-stealing prisoners right secure."

"I'm sure you do, Mr. Carr. You have no cause for concern. My wife tells me that she would only sit with her kinsman Captain Atwater today."

"Kinsman? I didn't hear that part of the story. This captain's related to Randolphs?"

"It can start with you, then, that part. You look hungry, Mr. Carr. Does he not, Judith?"

Judith nodded. "You do, sir. I'm sure my . . . my unfortunate kinsman would share what we've brought for his refreshment in return for a short visit."

"What's brought, missus? Do I smell cinnamon?"

"Indeed. Baked into the lightest rolls your tongue ever met. And there's a sea pie, pickled sturgeon, onions and cucumber."

"Like to cause me gut rumbling, the cucumber."

"My husband could make up a powder for that ailment. He studies medicine in the most diligent manner. That way you might enjoy all, and the Shrewsbury cakes, spruce beer, and a peach cordial besides. All prepared by the best cook on either bank of the James."

Ethan smiled affably, as if this man were a patient, or a neighbor. "Open your door, Mr. Carr," he urged. "See our bounty for yourself."

But it was she herself Morgan Carr was interested in seeing, Judith decided as they entered the stone keep. She held her husband's hand tighter as the man peered under her wide hat. "She don't look like no terrible Quaker scold, sir, any more than you're my idea of a French-ified lunatic."

"We're sorry to disappoint you, Mr. Carr. Now"—Ethan thumped the basket on the oak table—"feast your eyes. And tell my distressed lady she might comfort her cousin a little while."

The man raised his head from Ethan's tantalizing glimpse of the contents of her basket. Judith saw a gap-toothed smile and gave thanks for Martha's skill. Morgan Carr rubbed his stubbly chin. "All right, then. I want full half, though I'll trade the cordial for the spruce beer. Your wife only, in there with her kin. I'll hold you, Dr. Randolph, to assure her good behavior, and for your powders and advice on joint-achings as well." He closed one eye. "After you surrender me your weapon."

Ethan took a light hold at Judith's shoulders. She nodded. He lifted his knife from his boot, placed it on the table, and held out his hand to Morgan Carr. "We're in agreement, sir."

Judith set her lightened basket down on the small table in Captain Atwater's cell. "You should not have come," he whispered.

"I have been in worse places than this, friend."

"Is your husband—?"

"Ethan entertains your guard. Are you well?"

"Better than my passengers. To be sold on the block this afternoon."

"Together? Will they sell the brothers together?"

"Yes, perhaps."

"Well, at least they have each other."

His eyes met hers. "Do you see good in everything, Judith Blair?"

"Yes. It's tiresome, is it not?"

He shook his head. "No, not in the least." Then his voice lost its brief flirtation with mirth. "The men who boarded the *Opal*, arrested us, they have your package with the lady's traveling clothes inside," he said. "I tried to send it overboard, but everything happened so quickly. Judith—"

"Do not concern yourself with that."

"But the silk. If any should trace it to your hands . . ."

"I am not known for my work with silks, Captain." Judith touched the bodice of her lavender lawn gown, ornamented only at the neckline and wrists with the Battenburg lace Anne Randolph had given her.

"True. That's how my mother knew to trust you, there in Richmond. Because you wore the dress and had the gentle, generous manner of a Quaker. Were you once a Quaker, Judith?"

She began to empty the contents of her basket. "Captain Atwater. Would you rid me of all my mystery?"

"No." He sat, stared at the floor. "I would rid you only of your handsome, philandering husband."

Judith felt her cold hands becoming colder. "You must not speak so," she whispered. "It slanders a good man, and does yourself no service."

"Forgive me. Mrs. Blair, please. I have had too much time to think. To dream." He bowed his head. Judith saw a dark form crawling near the crown of his sun-bleached hair.

"Stay still," she summoned.

"What?"

She knelt beside him on the corn-husk mattress. "Still, I said!" Judith locked his head between her hands. Her fingers sifted until she captured and cracked the vermin between her nails. She flung it aside and searched his scalp for companions. Two more met their deaths, while the captain of the ill-fated *Opal* sat in stunned silence.

"There," she said, satisfied. "You are fortunate I have been able to vent my anger on those vexing creatures."

"Where in heaven's name did you learn to do that?"

"A long way from Heaven. Dartmoor Prison, in England. I could destroy twenty-seven in a minute's time. We made a game of it, the prisoners and I. It passed the time."

"I'm damned."

"Not nearly, Captain. Come. Eat. Your mouth will be better served in giving yourself nourishment."

He took her hand. "You must not do anything that would put you in harm's way. I charge you—"

"You are not on your fine vessel now, Captain Atwater. I will take no orders from you."

"For the love of all that's holy, woman! This is not a game!"

"Oh, but it is. A dangerous game, I'll grant you. We both know that. Eat. I have brought worse than you up from the depths. And you do not know half of my Ethan's talents."

"Judith, listen to me. I have confessed all, in return for my crew's release, uncharged. I am sentenced tomorrow. I will lose my ship. I will leave my mother almost penniless."

" 'Leave'?"

"If I can escape the gathering mob's fury, I go to prison. You must not visit me there, no matter your skills finding head vermin, understand? If you will only look in on my mother from time to time . . . Judith, are you listening to me?"

She was not. She needed to speak to Ethan about the thought birthing itself in her heart.

At the close of the day they finally sat together in silence near the shoots of crocuses in the public gardens on Lancaster Street. Ethan's time with Morgan Carr had netted paper and a quill for a letter to Captain Atwater's mother and a raise in his drinking-water allowance. Both concessions were echoes of another captive's needs, Judith now realized. Silver had passed between the men's hands, because there were limits, even to Ethan's charm.

Then he had left her in these gardens while he secured their room, in the attic of an old Counting House friend of his father's. They were lucky to get that, in the crowded city, on the eve of Captain Atwater's sentencing. But Judith sensed the echo of another place in her young husband, one that reeked of tobacco and commodities and the salt of the sea. Where had he gone, leaving her to the public garden, unattended by any but his traveling book of an English playwright's poetry? As one hour turned to two, she'd grown so worried she'd actually opened the book. The words were beautiful, but she was distracted by the child's drawings of ships and sea serpents in the margins.

But the afternoon had taken its toll on the man that child had become, Judith thought as she stole a glance at her silent, troubled husband. He'd favored his right side, leaning heavily on his walking stick. She had asked so much of him. And she was about to ask more.

"Ethan. Tell me how you have devised Captain Atwater my cousin?"

A sly half-smile broke through the strain on his face. "Why, Judith, are we not all kin by way of our common forebears, Adam and Eve?" He sniffed. "I thought you knew the Bible better than I."

"Rogue," she whispered, feeling herself blush.

He turned, took her face in his hand. His smile was gone. "I love you, Judith. Remember. Always."

Now. It had to be now. "He must not go to prison."

"No," he agreed, releasing her, staring down at his hands.

"What can we do?"

"Watch. And wait," he advised, "for an opportunity."

When the judge held up the woman's suit of clothes, Judith felt her husband flinch there at her side in the courtroom, for her sisters-in-law had made a great demonstration of showing him their gifts. But he stared straight ahead, his expression unchanged. She should have told him. She should have risked his censure. Captain Atwater remained steadfast, refusing to divulge where the silk originated. The angry judge raised his sentence from seven to ten years, and ordered him branded on the hand.

Fear entered Captain Atwater's eyes, finally, giving the first measure of satisfaction to the courtroom's audience. Now. Dear God, they were going to do it now, Judith realized, before the man had a chance to compose himself toward his fate. He breathed hard in his effort to maintain his dignity. The overflowing crowd leaned closer. The red iron was brought from the outside forge by a man whose face ignited her very veins with fear.

"Who is he?" Judith whispered.

"Boswain's mate. Punisher," Ethan said. "Do you wish to leave?"

"No." She buried her hands in the crook of his arm.

Ethan faced full forward again, the twitch dancing madly beside his eye. Judith prayed to God to forgive her this new hell for him to witness, but she could not leave, not with Captain Atwater's eyes fixed on her as if she was the North Star in the sky of a storm-tossed Atlantic.

The *S.S.* brand's meaning was clear: slave stealer.

Steady. She must keep her gaze steady, focused on Captain Atwater's face only, even as it contorted in pain, even as the smoke rose and the stench of burned flesh filled her nostrils. When would it stop?

"You have made your mark, sir," the judge commanded. The burn continued. The judge leaned over. "Cease . . . " he began, but got no further. As Captain Atwater finally burst forth with an agonized wail, Ethan leaped to his feet, then flew over the railing. Was this her once-crippled husband, flying? He whacked back the wrist of the punisher, sending him sprawling, sending his instrument to the floorboards. Captain Atwater slumped in Morgan Carr's arms, his steaming hand buried in his coat.

"It appears Dr. Randolph got him ceased for you, Your Honor," Carr commented.

The judge left his bench as Judith fought her way through the crowd. He glanced down at an unconscious man. "Dr. Randolph, may I now call upon your healing skills?" he asked.

Judith watched Ethan blink, turning himself from avenging angel back to healer again. He yanked open Captain Atwater's cravat and neckerchief, lifted the man's eyelids. "If you'll mind the hand and bring him forward, Mr. Carr?" he instructed. Judith rummaged her wide pockets for a vial of clove oil that might help revive their patient. The clerks and bailiffs struggled to maintain order outside their haven.

She found the vial as the jailer sat Captain Atwater up. But Ethan stayed her hand, before beginning his calm assessment. "Nerve damage. In two places, burned to the bone. And, Judith, what's this?"

"What? Ethan, allow me to see—"

The vial was knocked from her hand as Ethan reached down, taking his knife from his boot. Why had he done that? A gasp. Ethan's grip tightened. A red stream spurted up his arm. Everything was happening so fast. He shook his head, blinking blood out of his eye as he pressed harder to staunch the flow. "Judith!" he shouted. "Ice! Get me ice!"

She turned and tore through the crowd to the doors.

When she returned, a bailiff took her straw-packed cake of ice and left her with orders from her husband to wait outside the judge's chamber.

Judith felt abandoned, alone, and achingly tired in the emptied courtroom. Why was Ethan leaving her out of Captain Atwater's care? She tucked her ruined slippers under her mud-splattered skirts and lay across the length of a spindle-backed bench. A strange serenity came, punctuated by the gentle, butterfly roaming of the child inside her, saying, *No, not alone.* She wanted to tell Ethan that here, among all this turmoil, their child was moving. She wanted to press his hand against her middle. She even dreamed she was about to do that, and he was not bloodied and shouting, but her gentle Ethan again, swaddling her in his coat, lifting her close against his heart.

Judith opened her eyes to a billowing sail in the starlit sky. Ethan, without coat or vest, was helping the sailors raise the sail. . . . They were the familiar, lively young crew of the *Opal,* though this fleet river vessel wasn't the *Opal.* Ethan fit splendidly into their company.

He approached, knelt, the smell of the salt wind vanquishing the courtroom's polished woods, the whiskey and tobacco of the judge's chambers. The scent of blood remained, as did the dark exhaustion circled under his eyes. When Judith tried to sit up, he placed his hand at her shoulder.

"Rest."

"Captain Atwater—"

"Below." He looked away.

"The judge changed his mind? Oh, Ethan, that's splendid, a release! I must—"

"Stay here. Sleep. Please, Judith."

"But I cannot. You look so tired, darling boy. Allow me to tend Captain Atwater's needs now."

"He has no needs."

"N-no needs?"

He looked over her shoulder, at the stars. "I did the best I could, Judith. I'm sorry."

"What are you saying? He is not dead."

"The veins, at the wrist—"

"What have you done to him?"

His face darkened. "Done, *madame*?"

The nervous twitching, again, beside his eye. Who was this man? Judith heard her own voice make a screeching, foreign sound. *"Look here,"* she charged, *"in my eyes, Ethan Randolph. You will not tell me he is dead!"*

Ethan took her arms, shook her. "Stop! This is unseemly, such grief for a man you barely know. Unseemly from my wife. Enough!"

She pulled back, breaking his hold, and slapped him hard across his face. "How dare you?" she charged.

Judith became aware of the silent stares of the seamen, black and white, surrounding them. She'd never lifted her hand to a living creature in her life. How had they come to this? Her cheeks burned with indignation. She was Judith Mercer. How dare this man she'd given up so much for treat her like an unchaste wife? How dare he shut her out of the judge's chambers? How dare he allow that good man to die?

His soft white shirt billowed up around his shoulders, transforming him, suddenly, into a misshapen monster.

He stepped back, returned to his sails. This was all he wanted, this spoiled, rich planter's son, her blue devils told her: to be captain of the mizzenmast.

42

"I would be in Richmond with Mrs. Atwater at this terrible time, husband," Judith said with quiet insistence.

"That will not be necessary." His gaze did not shift from their destination, Windover's great house. Nor did his step falter.

"We must not send him home to her alone, Ethan!"

"Ease your mind on that account."

"The ship waits," she said, confused.

"For me."

Judith stopped at the steps. She saw his brothers, their wives, standing at the opened windows. "I would be home in Richmond," she beseeched quietly.

"Climb with me, *madame.*"

She fisted his waistcoat, but could not lock his eyes to hers. "What are you doing? What are you doing without me?"

"Judith," he breathed.

"Don't leave me here, please."

"It cannot be helped."

Panic shook her frame. "I'm going back to the ship. I don't belong here." She turned to the glowing lantern path. "I need to see Captain—"

"Have you not humiliated me enough?" he shouted at her back.

The night air rang in silence. He caught her arm, turned her around. When she resisted, he clamped a hold on her wrist. His eyes dared her to test his strength. He lifted her high and carried her inside the house.

He ignored all of his family's entreaties until he reached his mother, standing on the stairs' first landing.

"Ethan, what are you doing?" Anne Randolph demanded.

"Placing my wife in your care until my return, *madame*. Somewhat against her will."

"And how are we to keep her?"

"In chains, if you must."

His mother stood aside. "Oh, very well," she said with a sigh.

He kicked open the door of the room before placing Judith on the bed. She looked down at her hand. Blood, where he'd held her wrist. But it didn't hurt, she told her racing heart. He'd held, not hurt her. He'd never hurt her. It was not her blood, but his.

"Ethan." She could almost feel him bristle before turning. How could those warm brown eyes she knew transform so completely? The veils, again. Almost transparent, seldom-used veils.

"How much more am I supposed to endure?" he demanded.

"More?"

"Of their laughter, their taunts, about you playing me for a fool in your pursuits? About them making a game out of guessing . . ." He faltered here, and Judith saw his bad leg betray him and threaten to take him down. Tears shone in his eyes, back behind the veils. "Guessing who has fathered the child you carry."

"Ethan," she said quietly, "thy mind is poisoned."

"Do not you turn high and mighty Quaker priestess on me now, Judith Mercer," he railed, "with your '*thys*,' your kind euphemisms! Poisoned? I am not poisoned, mad, an imbecile, an idiot, except perhaps in my pursuit of women, yes? Well, what's done can be undone! *Maintenant* . . ." He faltered, blinking. "What is it?" he stormed. "The English?"

"Now," she whispered.

"Now, yes, for now, the time being, madman or not, I am a Randolph and you are my wife. You will obey me. You will remain in this house until I decide what to do with you!"

Ethan leaned against the closed door between them. Judith was weeping. What had he done? Was it all unraveling, all turning to madness? He ran his hand through his hair, heard the whistle from the ship. Stand fast—finish. His mother approached. He felt her scent. Roses, wild roses from their dancing time. He rested his hand at her neck, dropped a kiss on her cheek.

"Were you attempting to inform only Windover of your displeasure with your wife, or three counties around?" she asked tartly.

"Windover will suffice."

"You've succeeded."

"Aye, *madame*. But will that keep her until I return?"

She lowered her voice. "And hold your brothers' mechanizations at bay?"

Ethan sighed. "I see I come by this loathsome ability honestly. Send for Sally, will you?"

She nodded. "If you will meet with Jordan, accept his help."

"Mother. I cannot ask—"

She touched his face. "You will not have to ask. Ethan, promise me you'll meet him."

"I suppose I can hardly avoid it," he grumbled. The whistle, again. "Mama? Take care of her."

"We will. Don't be long, darling."

Judith pleaded for the beautiful woman's understanding. "These things he claims . . . I have given him no cause. And, Mother, I have endured much more for his sake in Richmond."

"Oh?"

"Whispers, taunts. That I must be some eccentric adventuress to have captured such a young, handsome man as my husband. That his beautiful eyes seduce all the women he meets, that he charms them, treating all like treasures."

"But he does see most of us that way, poor boy. That was one reason I was glad he found you so soon in his manhood, Judith. Before his heart became as scarred as his back. You know his way with women is innocent. Well, innocent mostly. What man is innocent? His devotion to all manner of females is, I think, misconstrued by others, because he is . . . well, as you say, a striking man, and unaware of it. This way of his, it is his appreciation of us, that's all. I rather like it."

"I do too! But certain people always assumed—"

"That is their concern, is it not? Not yours."

"Yes. But should he not afford me the same grace now? Especially after I defended him against the very man—"

"Judith. Did Captain Atwater defame my son?"

"He . . . Oh, Mother, I didn't understand—"

"That he had feelings for you? While you were engaged in your exciting, beneficial undertaking together? Feelings fed by the Richmond rumors of Ethan's own unfaithfulnesses? I warned Sally that would come to no good! Don't look so astonished, Judith. I have been a participant in this play myself."

"When?"

"When I was almost exactly your age. Don't worry. I think my son is secure in your love. It stems more from his protection, this intemperate growling of his."

"Growling?" Judith almost laughed. "Granting me no measure of grief for my friend? Then doubting my child is his? Threatening to put me away? This is growling?"

"Were you listening carefully to his words?"

Judith stared at her mother-in-law, astonished.

Anne Randolph laughed. "I know, every member of this household could hardly avoid hearing your . . . altercation. But perhaps that was as purposeful as the words he chose."

"The words he chose! My only hope is that he barely chose them in the heat of the moment. He was so angry he lost command of his English!"

"Judith, Judith. He does not forget his first language when he's angry, but when he's afraid."

"You're right," Judith realized suddenly.

"Of course I'm right, I'm his mother."

"But, why?"

Anne Randolph held up a long, graceful finger. "His mother, not his God. Ethan's ways might even perplex the All-knowing. He always had peculiar notions, that child. And he's found a kindred spirit. He will not so easily put you away; he is not a stupid man, a fact he seems strongly adamant about himself, does he not? It must have been born at sea, this sensitivity about his intellect. He was always too clever by half for his brothers' liking here."

She shrugged her graceful shoulders in the same way Ethan did when something was beyond his understanding. "Well," she continued, "neither of us knows what my wayward son is out and about doing now. But when he comes home, all will be set to right.

"Now, don't let the rest of this family know that, Judith," she said in a low, conspiratorial tone. "They are so enjoying feeling superior in your downfall. And they are meant to believe they have succeeded in casting doubt in his heart, I think. They may even show signs they pity you, about to be cast aside. Let's enjoy that together, shall we?"

"Enjoy?"

The mistress of Windover giggled behind her hand. "Do you think me the source of my son's peculiar nature for harboring such a notion?"

Judith smiled at her mother-in-law.

"There. Much better!" Anne Randolph approved. "No more weeping, it's not good for the baby." She held out her hand. Judith took it. "I've determined this time we'll have together is my son's gift. You must warn me when I'm being insufferable. Come, let's invite Sally and the children to keep you company. Then let's wash out a few things I've saved of Ethan's. I have the most charming array of baby caps!"

Ethan soaked his hand in the basin of salt water the sailor had brought. Climbing the rigging must have reopened the wound. But it was not swollen or hot to the touch. He dressed it quickly. Then he turned to the man in the berth that barely held him, checked the eyes' dilation nervously. They blinked. He thought the combination of mandrake and henbane would keep him down for another hour at least. He was a big man, her captain, a good thirty pounds heavier than himself. Perhaps that's why the dose was off. He'd make a note of it. But for now, he must be a good doctor. He smiled, stroked his patient's cool forehead. "How do you feel?"

"Like I've slept the sleep of the dead."

"You have."

"We're on the water."

"Aye."

"Not my ship."

"No, but a worthy one. Hired out." Ethan stared wistfully through the porthole at the lights along the shore.

"But . . . Dr. Blair. I was sentenced."

"Yes, well. Corpses stink up prisons something dreadful."

"Is that what I am? A corpse?"

"Officially, yes."

He moved, winced. "In the courtroom. Your knife. You cut me!"

Ethan frowned. "I did not. 'Do no harm.' How far would I get in my training if I ignored my profession's basic precept so soon?"

"But—the blood?"

"Mine."

"You cut yourself?"

"I was improvising. Had I more time to plan, I would have avoided it, believe me."

"Judith?"

"Was determined you remain out of prison."

"Does she know?"

"Not yet. You will go home to your mother, submit yourself to a decent burial, then disappear, if you please. North. Where will your kind help you in this?"

"Philadelphia."

Ethan winced. "How did I know all you lawbreakers come south from Philadelphia? We will bring you there, then. But not before writing my wife a letter. To help me win back her affections."

"You care very little for your wife's affections, Doctor."

"Of that you know nothing, sir."

"I have eyes, Dr. Blair! I saw— Wait. Not Blair. You are a Randolph." He gave a sudden, short snort of laughter.

"This amuses you?"

"So is she!"

"Who?"

"The woman—the one you meet in the park, take by the hand. Mrs. Gibson, the surveyor's wife. She is a Randolph. She is your sister!"

"You should remain on the water, instead of spying on people in parks."

He laughed. "The children who call you 'Uncle.' You *are* their uncle!"

"You are too loud for a dead man. And I am out of henbane."

"I didn't pay heed to any of the whisperings until I saw you and Mrs. Gibson that day. How you made her laugh and kissed her hand and . . . I am overfond of your exceptional wife, I confess, and that might have tainted my judgment."

Ethan frowned. "Maine is a very fine state, I hear, Captain Atwater, with a good, long coastline. Perhaps your kindred slave stealers might resettle you there? You and your mother and her chickens might do very well for yourselves in Maine."

"And it is as far north as I can get from your beautiful Judith."

"Exactly."

"Bring on your ink, paper. Sharpen me a quill with that deadly weapon of yours, Dr. Blair. I'd best write a left-handed letter, before we are boarded and both hurled into prison."

Finally, with Jordan and Mrs. Atwater below to take over her son's care, Ethan sat in the ship's stern and let his head drop into his hands. He saw himself loving Judith, on the lightkeeper's beach. She was laughing, her whitened petticoats spread out like a lacy fan beneath them as he worked toward their mutual delight. He leaned over, kissed that sweet, salty spot below her ear. Was that all he had left of her? Memories? He felt a hand at his shoulder.

"What are you going to do now?" Jordan asked quietly.

He opened his eyes, lifted his head. "Travel overland, to Philadelphia. I know the way. Their people can figure what to do with my dead man then, yes?" Ethan waited for a host of objections. He felt only a healing massage of his shoulder.

"This has cost you a great deal."

Ethan turned his attention to a woodcock flying past.

"How much?" Jordan pressed.

" 'Much'?"

"How much money, Ethan?"

"Five thousand dollars."

"Five . . . ?"

"It is very expensive—bribing jailers, hiring this schooner and her crew, buying slaves."

"Buying—?"

"Then sending those slave brothers north, clothed by Judith, free papers signed by her husband, whom she would never tolerate if he owned slaves for more than an hour's turnaround."

"Good God, Ethan, do you have anything left?"

"Thirty-seven dollars, fifty-eight and one-half cents. Can I hire a funeral coach for that? And get us to Philadelphia?"

"Where in hell did you get the money?"

"I borrowed it from my brother."

"Winthrop?"

"Yes."

"Against?"

"All future claim to inheritance."

"Ethan, does your mother know of this?"

"Of course not."

"Terms?"

"Thirty days. At thirty-percent interest. He made it easy for me to remember."

"Nonsense." Jordan sneered. "Winthrop was a terrible student of arithmetic. He made it easy for himself to remember. Do you need a hearse driver? I charge a very reasonable rate."

Ethan raised his head. "Jordan—your patients."

"All farmed out to other physicians. Even Mrs. Willard found me so pitiful she said she only wished us to be together, even if we were no longer peering down her throat."

"Thank you. I did not expect . . . Jordan, I thought—"

"I'm glad I can still surprise you." He tousled Ethan's windswept hair like the sheet anchor men on the *Standard* used to. "Clever boy."

Ethan turned away. His mother had been right. He did not even have to ask for help. How did he deserve this man as his friend, agreeing to share yet another burden?

"Stop that!" his master exploded.

Ethan wiped his eyes with the backs of his hands. "Forgive me. I am taught better than this. So rude."

"Not rude," the doctor insisted. "You're just exhausted even beyond your celebrated endurance. Where are your handkerchiefs?"

Ethan shrugged.

"Good," Jordan decided, pulling one from his waistcoat. "I will have a subject to reprimand your peerless mother about upon our return. 'You sent your son into the wilds of the north country again, Annie Randolph, without handkerchiefs?' "

"It wasn't her fault." Ethan defended his mother stoutly. "I left so abruptly. No one calls her Annie but you. Jordan—"

"I'll keep the first watch. Rest now, son," the doctor urged.

"I wish I was your son."

"Ethan—"

"I'm sorry. I am as bad as my father, am I not, trying to arrange destinies? I have been at Windover too long, that's all. It is good to be in your company again, sir."

43

Ethan lifted Mrs. Atwater into the funeral coach. She turned, touched his face. He could not see her features distinctly beyond her heavy veils. Her silence astonished him, even more than the tender gesture from this woman so parsimonious with her eggs.

"All will be well, *madame,*" he whispered.

"I know, sweet boy."

"Sweet boy"? She was frightened, perhaps. Jordan, her remaining black-clad sentinel, now waited for him in the driver's seat of the coach. Ethan climbed up, joining him.

Rarely was a funeral procession disturbed, Ethan realized. It was a perfect place to hide stolen cargo, to travel without an excess of questioning. He must tell Judith. *Dieu*—his gentle wife's intrigues had him thinking like a criminal.

"Stop grinning. You're supposed to be in mourning."

Ethan snorted softly. "For that slave stealer?"

Jordan shook his head. "You can be quite convincingly Virginian," he admitted.

"I am Virginian."

"When shall we let him out of that hot box beneath the seat?"

"Another mile of bouncing might do it. Make him think twice about approaching my wife again."

"Ethan!"

"What is it?"

The physician grinned now. "This is spectacular, what we're doing."

Ethan shrugged. "An old sailor's trick."

"I wish Judith were here."

"I'm glad she's not. Jordan, once we secure Captain Atwater and his mother in Philadelphia, I need to . . . to finish business in Harmony Springs. I have to find that stake, the one Eli Mercer had in his hand as he died. Because my wife is not safe, now that our name is known. And . . . Jordan, I think she sometimes wonders if I killed her father." He stared forward. "It has grown, this small seed of suspicion. Now she thinks I allowed her captain to die, too."

"Atwater was never hers, Ethan. Judith is devoted to you."

"And to her Light."

"They are not incongruous devotions."

"No," he admitted.

"There. Do not nurture your own seeds."

"I have already done that."

"How?"

"In my time at Windover, my brothers have taunted me, in the same way they used to when I was a child. Small, dark, not a proper Randolph. Now about . . . about Judith not being faithful."

"Ethan, you never truly doubted Judith?"

"No. But I was afraid, and she had Captain Atwater and her secrets. I used my fears. I gave them free reign to keep her there with Mother, so I could do this part alone. I did not lie, I never lie. But I let her think Atwater was dead. That was so much more difficult than I thought it would be. You know those eyes, that voice raised in her indignation! Jordan, I said terrible things to keep those eyes from routing out what I was about to do."

"She will forgive you, when she understands."

"Or go back to her people, feeling betrayed, out of patience with me. She must be safe, even if she throws me over and chooses that way. I need to pick up the scent, track the one who killed Eli."

"Ethan, to most of Harmony Springs you are that murderer. Freed by way of your family's influence, then audacious thief of their traveling minister besides."

"Perhaps. But not all see me that way. Not the one who knows better."

"Do you think Eli's killer is among them?"

"Yes. Judith now suffers the company of my imperfect family until I can find him. My mother and Sally will keep her safe until my return." He laughed softly, without mirth. "I wonder if she will be able to bear the sight of me by then?"

"What if Eli's tree stake has been destroyed? What will you do?"

Ethan bowed his head. "I don't know."

"We should talk with all who will receive us at Harmony Springs. About that day. We should begin with the children, I think. You got on well with the children, didn't you?"

" 'We'?"

"Of course, *we!* You're my associate. We're partners now, Dr. Blair. I need you. And you'll need someone to watch your back. Now, Ethan, you have Captain Atwater's letter of explanation. And you have your wife's love. Please let the poor man out of his box and into his mother's arms."

Judith sat in the vine-shrouded, one-room house, praying for a vision. None came. She began to doubt the meaning of the first ones. Were they angry about her doubt, the Blair women? Or were they all along telling her to go west without Ethan? Were they trying to rid their family of this slave stealer who was now stealing the only Randolph son who could give Windover an heir? Did they ponder putting her away, the same way Ethan did?

Clicks. Reprimanding clicks sounded at her ears, even after she pressed the heels of her hands against them. Another visitation by the slaves in the hold of the *Standard*? Or the descent of madness?

Judith fled the house and stumbled toward the river. She sat on the gentle bluff above the old, ruined pier, weeping. A nudge. Judith smiled, weaving her hand through her deep pocket to get closer to the tumbler in the secret sea inside her body. This child was the keeper of her sense, she felt, over these strange days. Her hand touched Ethan's letter, folded and refolded, there, beside their child. She removed it, read again the bold, sweeping hand she knew so well:

Dearest Judith,

If it were within my power to undo the events of the past days, believe me, they would be undone. I regret any grief the course of my future may bring you as well. I am called upon a journey with Dr. Foster, one that does not allow for further missives. Kindly tender my regards to my family at Windover and my further regret in having to include them in this wilderness of correspondence. Will you strive to be content in the women's care, Judith, and not place any of my faults at their feet?

My return will carry with it hope for your forgiveness. I will not return otherwise.

—E. Blair

"Not return" shocked her less this time as the paper warmed between her hands. She ran her fingers over the ink. Dark, black, determined. But something else; tired, she realized now. Perhaps he did not mean to frighten or threaten her with that phrase. Perhaps it even pained him, too, this parting? *"Dearest Judith"* . . . Was it just his habit, from their previous letters, to address her so? And why had he signed it *"Blair,"* except that he wished to be returned into the grace of their lives together as the physician's assistant and botanist's daughter?

How Judith missed her father's good counsel, his gentle reprimands of her pride. She'd slapped her husband because he'd wounded that, her pride. His brothers were eaten with envy. Of course they taunted him about the parentage of the child she carried. Ethan had endured their company, for the sake of family harmony. It was she who needed forgiveness. What were his transgressions beside hers? What were her fears that she would peel aside his veiled eyes and find a murderer? Her own madness, surely.

"I hope thee is in good health at this place, Friend Judith."

She crushed Ethan's letter between her fingers and turned.

Prescott Lyman stared down at her from the bluff.

44

Judith felt as if she were underwater. And heavy, rooted with the burden of the child within her. Ethan's letter turned to pulp under her fingers.

"What are you doing here?" she whispered.

"Visiting. Upon the invitation of thy sister-in-law, Clara Randolph. Judith, did thee know nothing of it?"

"No. Nothing."

"Oh, my dear. Here. Take my arm."

She stumbled in the opposite direction, toward the river.

A lace-edged handkerchief appeared over the hill, attached to Hester's hand. "Judith, stop! Where are you going? Have we not made you a fine surprise?"

Hester was quickly joined by stern Clara. "Mind the marsh, dear, or you'll ruin yet another pair of slippers. Your husband will be circuit-doctoring for another month just to keep you shod! Now, I do hope you might be our guest long enough to see the prodigious changes in our brother Ethan, Mr. Lyman. He didn't leave your church's company on the best of terms, we understand."

Judith barely heard the women. She could not stop the riot of clicks going off in her head as she surrendered herself to their company.

"Here's our chance to make all right, were that wandering boy to return from his latest . . . adventure," Clara continued.

"We thought our poor new sister was looking frail in Ethan's absence. We sought to cheer her with an invitation to one of her own church."

"Meeting," Prescott Lyman corrected Hester softly.

"Yes, forgive us, Mr. Lyman, Meeting," Clara said. "Oh, Hester, for shame. And you, a churchman's wife?"

Hester pouted. "Judith used to be very good at correcting all of us about titles and lifted hats and such," she insisted. "But that's before Ethan . . . That is to say . . . when she was still a Quaker."

Clara took Prescott Lyman's arm as they walked up from the river. "Well, little did we know that our open invitation to Harmony Springs Meeting would bring the very man to whom we are indebted for taking on our little brother in his courting pursuits last year. This is God's Providence, is it not, Hester?"

"Providential indeed," Clayton's wife agreed, absently sniffing the air. "Ah. I believe Martha is baking almond puddings."

Clara smiled again, showing teeth so even, they looked filed. "Almond puddings? You are an honored dinner guest of our dear father-in-law, Mr. Lyman."

Judith looked past the live oaks and tulip poplars to see Anne and Winthrop Randolph sitting in the spring afternoon's sun, like the king and queen of the fairy tales their Scots-Irish neighbors in Pennsylvania used to tell when she and her mother would make sick-visits. Judith had tried not to listen, for they were frivolous. But the stories had healing properties, she remembered thinking even then, to the sick children. The sight of Ethan's parents, waiting for her, concern on their faces, had the same effect on her now. She must learn those stories. To tell to her own child.

As they approached, Judith saw the elder Winthrop Randolph's habitual scowl deepen. Though her father-in-law remained a duty-bound host in returning the hospitality Prescott Lyman had shown his son, Judith felt again that she had an ally in the master of Windover.

Her mind scrambled in confusion when the old man asked for her company in his accounts room. He'd never done that before. Judith glanced up at Anne, who interrupted her own instructions to her servants to nod, smiling. Judith took her father-in-law's arm.

"Sit," he commanded, closing the door on Ethan's memory chamber.

She did.

He began, as always, without preamble. "Did this man court you, there in Pennsylvania?"

"Yes."

"What is he doing here?"

"Clara invited—"

"I know who invited him! And what those two insufferable women are after. I want to know what *he's* after!"

Judith shook her head.

"Damnation! First the slave-stealing sea captain, now this mealy-mouthed Quaker! Have you been playing my son for a fool, woman?"

"I have not, sir."

"That child you carry, who is the father?"

"My husband is."

He paced to the window, looked out at Martha's cookhouse, and farther, at the stables. She stared at the knot of hands behind his back. "Good, then. Established." He turned. "God's blood, Judith, I am too old to be put in charge of these affairs. Your husband should be dealing with you and these leftover suitors of yours! How long does it take to bury a man? Where is he?"

"I don't know!" Judith stifled her sob with the back of her hand.

"There, there, don't cry now. I promised her I would not make you cry." The master of Windover rifled through his waistcoat pockets until he found a handkerchief, then pitched it into her lap. He approached, retrieved it, then fanned it out beneath her nose. "A good blow now, there's the girl," he urged quietly.

She obliged.

"Good, good. I am not such a beast anymore, am I?"

"You have never been. Not to me."

"But you don't discount the stories?"

"No," she admitted.

"It's well you should not. I have regrets I will carry to my grave, if that husband of yours will allow me to take my overdue leave of this world. But as for this present predicament—you have no love for this man, do you?"

"No, sir."

"That is apparent, even to me. Well, don't fret yourself, brave little Quakeress. You're among your family, in my house. My capricious son left you in the right place, if he had to leave you anywhere. We'll look after you here. Do you understand?"

She nodded, blowing her nose again.

"Good girl. Now, let us figure our strategy, shall we? Clara has filled this Quaker with stories of Ethan throwing you over, no doubt. But you're growing with my son's child. You've made your choice. Why does he still want you, this cold-fish farmer?"

"I didn't know he wanted me the first time!"

"When?"

"In Pennsylvania . . . when my father was ill. At first I thought he was being kind, you see."

"Good God, woman, did you know my son was courting you?"

"Oh, yes, once he . . . Ethan was much more direct."

The old man's grin turned mischievous. "That's good. Learned something from that Frenchman, did he?"

Judith bowed her her head, feeling her cheeks flush at the thought of the willow's trunk at her back, supporting Ethan's deep kisses.

"Well, I don't like something about the look this farmer has for you. And if a woman of your sense has never recognized it as ardor, perhaps it is not. Perhaps it is something else. To hell with my Virginian's reputation for hospitality. Let's feed him one dinner, then get him out. Let's make him those damned interfering women's problem, shall we?"

Judith smiled. "Yes."

"Good, then. He'll not be welcome here. He can pitch his tent between Winthrop and Clara and Clayton and Hester. You may refuse all their invitations to visit, too. I hope he stays the season and eats them out of both their houses!"

A bubble of laughter came up her throat. Startled, Judith reached up to suppress it.

Her father-in-law took her hand. "Laughter's allowed here," he told her, "encouraged, even. By my taskmaster, your husband." He squeezed her hand gently. "The look about you now. It puts me in mind of his mother's when she was carrying him. She was very dear to me then."

"So I understand, sir."

"She was so frightened when first I looked in the cradle. Why? Because he came early and was small, not as robust as the others? 'Do not fret yourself. I am well pleased,' I told her. The look she bestowed on me then. . . . Judith, I almost believed she was forgiving me for never loving her. Even for taking her too soon, when she was still a child. For all my transgressions. He accomplished that somehow, her dark, tiny, kicking boy, in that moment. Imagine. I envy the love between yourself and my son, Judith."

She pressed their clasped hands to her cheek.

"Stop that. I have no more handkerchiefs. Women get so sentimental when in breeding. My wife was worst of all with him. I hope this means you are carrying a boy? Your Quaker visions have not foretold—?"

"No."

"Ah, then. It doesn't matter, this time, what you've planted together. Women are lovely adornments. And you are both young. Almost younger than I can remember being." He walked back to his window, frowned at the dark-clad figure walking beside Hester. "That man is pure purpose. He won't leave until he's sure you're lost to your husband. Your increasing middle would deter most. It seems to fire him somehow. Damnation. I don't like him," he muttered.

Judith was glad when the one dinner she was required to attend with Prescott Lyman was over. She was glad to be out of the stifling dining room, with too much color and talk. But Prescott Lyman had rid himself of her sisters-in-law, and followed her.

"Judith, please wait! Allow me to walk with thee."

She turned. Aaron was at his shop, quietly making boot adjustments Winthrop had demanded. Micah was close, too, at his wheel. Their vigilant eyes tracked her movements. And she could hear Martha's song rising from the kitchen. They were all watching out for her. She'd be safe, if she stayed in the yard. And perhaps she needed to purge herself, finally, of this man and his cold, angry eyes. She slowed, but did not look at him.

"It was kind of thee to sit with me at dinner," he began.

"I was honoring my family."

"Are they thy family now, Judith?"

"Yes."

"The food was pleasing. I wish I could have eaten without discomfort."

"Discomfort?"

"At being served by . . . them."

"Them?"

"It doesn't bother thee? Even at table, indeed everywhere we might go on Windover land, to be surrounded by all this blackness."

"They are not black. Coal is black, jet is black. These are people. Fine people, of many shades of color."

"That is because—"

"I know the reason. It does not make them lesser children of God. It does not make them less beautiful to me. They are my friends. And they are my husband's family."

"His family? Thee sounds like the other frivolous Randolph women. The drops of whiteness in their blood have been swallowed by the black! They are thy husband's property."

"He was born into this world. He does not choose it now. Go home, Prescott. See how many you can send to Africa so their presence does not disturb you so."

He was silent for a long time. Judith walked, taking her refuge in the children's laughter that flowed out of Martha's kitchen, the soft chinks from Micah's forge. She thought he would leave her side, when Prescott

Lyman spoke again. Softly. Contritely. "I understand thy dismay with me, Judith. I was severely reprimanded by our Meeting for my words at parting. But none has castigated me more for my behavior than I have myself. I have tried to find thee—"

"You have tracked us like runaways, Prescott Lyman," she challenged him.

"Yes. For that I was sat upon at Meeting. Judith. I begged the Elders to allow me to accept thy sister-in-law's invitation, now that thy presence here has been revealed to us. By one of your husband's own family, seeking help for thee."

"Help?"

"Clara Randolph says thee has suffered a great deal in thy marriage. She suspected his punishments. And she says there are great burdens on thy heart since thy husband abandoned thee."

"My sister-in-law is mistaken. I have been neither abandoned nor punished. My husband is good and true and riding circuit with the physician who teaches him. He will come home soon."

"I see. Windover is thy home?"

"No. We live upriver."

"At thine own plantation? Surrounded by black slaves?"

"No! We live modestly." No more, no more. What was the use? Clara or Hester would tell him everything they knew, and he would find them. She thought of the days of running, of relentless trackers who'd driven them to the shores of the Atlantic. She would never feel safe in their Richmond rooms again. Another home, lost.

"I see there is no mission here, except perhaps one that humbles me further." He finally ceased his silent walk in her footsteps.

She stopped, felt the evening breeze in her skirts. "Prescott?" she called quietly.

He turned. "Yes?"

"How fare the children?"

Silence. Then, "Still suffering from the events of last spring, there at the farm."

"That grieves me."

"I have considered moving Ruth and Hugh away. Or even joining a migration west."

"West?"

"Yes, there are several begun. Quaker settlements in the new state of Indiana, along the banks of the Ohio River."

Judith saw the women from her dream and vision again, pointing. Her hands shook. "Ohio?"

"Yes. But I am determined not to leave without resolution of our invaded, disrupted time together, Judith. Of thy father's murder."

Judith fought the remembrance of the blood, all the blood. Eviscerated. Like what Ethan had done to the rat. "Perhaps there can be no resolution."

"Why not?" He stepped closer. "Does it not haunt thee?"

"It does," she admitted. "As did the slaughter of my mother, and her babies. But I went on, after that."

"Yes. Touched by God. Who touches you now, Judith Mercer?"

45

Ethan paced the small, chestnut-paneled room.

"Sit," Jordan commanded.

He slammed himself into the chair, rocked back on his heels.

"Still!"

"I don't like it here, Jordan. It's so dark. Why is the window so high? How will I get out?"

"The door is customary."

"I will not be put on trial again."

"That was a hearing. You're not on trial now. I'm telling you, Ethan, Seymour Hess sounded . . . remorseful."

"Remorseful? Why? He and the other two magistrates did not hang me. They only took my brothers' bribe and depended on Winthrop and Clayton's promise to keep me locked away at Windover."

"That is speculation. Don't mention bribery. Damnation, Ethan, I don't know why he wanted this meeting! That's for us to discover. So behave yourself. Stifle that caged-convict head of yours. And keep that Randolph arrogance in check, too."

Ethan smiled. "What will be left of me?"

"Be Judith's devoted husband and protector," his friend suggested. "My dedicated assistant."

"Assistant? I thought I was your associate!"

"What did I say about arrogance?"

Ethan sighed. "I should have seen that one's approach."

"Yes. Your mind would be quicker if you weren't so worried about being locked up."

"It has foundation. I have not been the most fortunate of men here in Pennsylvania."

His friend smiled sadly. "Perhaps you're due for some more favorable winds."

After a soft knock, a tall, steel-eyed man entered the room. Ethan recognized him immediately as the middle magistrate he'd had listening at the hearing, then had lost. Seymour Hess was followed by Elder Oakes, whom Ethan remembered from Harmony Springs. An old man, but strong, one of the hard-shod farmers who'd kicked him into blackness the day of Eli's death. Could he and Jordan get past these two and out that small door, if they needed to? Were there any on the other side, waiting to take him captive again?

"Friends," Elder Oakes said quietly and stepped back, becoming a silent mass in the room's shadows.

Then Seymour Hess offered his hand. He even smiled. "Ethan Randolph. Judith Mercer's sailor home from the sea has returned."

"Her husband now. Devoted," Ethan blurted, making Jordan cringe.

The towering man laughed softly. "It's been brought to my attention that your name is on the papers of a pair of brothers who were destined for hard labor in the iron mines as branded runaways."

"I did not steal them," Ethan protested. "I bought them free and clear and legal!"

The magistrate crossed his arms before his chest. "Then sent them north with your wife's stitches to keep out the cold. You are a most peculiar slave trader, Mr. Randolph."

Ethan realized that this man was not meaning to lock him up again. His mouth twitched. "I couldn't have my wife's fine sewing buried in a mine, sir."

"Nor have our Captain Atwater buried on land or at sea just yet."

Ethan frowned. "He's buried, Mr. Hess. As sure as I was thrown to the sharks a dozen years ago."

"Fellow Lazaruses, you and the finest captain in our little fleet."

"Our fleet?" He was not the only lawbreaker in this room, Ethan realized, glancing at Jordan as Seymour Hess continued.

"The network now thrives, in part, because a child—a third son of a Tidewater planter—secretly taught slaves to read many years ago."

"Aaron and Martha helped you?" Ethan whispered.

"Along with many others they and theirs have taught, now spread up and down the River James. There, then. Enough information to send us both to prison for the remaining years of our lives. If it's earned your trust, tell us how we can help you, friends of Friends."

Jordan Foster nodded his full assent, so Ethan began. "Judith and I, we left Harmony Springs in haste."

"So I understand."

"Eli's death remains unresolved."

"That is true."

The Quaker in the shadows finally spoke. "Have you returned, then, bent on finding the killer and vengeance, Ethan Randolph?" he demanded.

"No. . . . I mean, yes, I have a powerful need to find Eli's murderer. Judith and I have been in hiding under another name, aided by Dr. Foster. But our circumstances have changed. Our name is Randolph once more, and so my wife is vulnerable to her enemies again."

"Again?" Elder Oakes prompted.

"Yes. I believe Eli's murderer has attacked her family before. Judith remains, the last of the Mercers. I would have my wife safe," he told both men. "I am determined to find him."

"You know of the Loyalist raid," the magistrate said.

"I do, sir."

"Who told you the story?"

"Eli Mercer."

"Perhaps he is directing you now."

"I am not good at directions. Not on land, Mr. Hess." Ethan turned to the Quaker elder, and appealed to both men. "Please help us. Help Judith, who has served her people and Pennsylvania so well. She follows her Light, still. I have not prevented it. We are innocents in this. As is the child growing within her body."

"Child? A child?" the Quaker demanded now. "Announced? Apparent?"

"Both."

"Where is your wife now, Mr. Randolph?"

Ethan's eyes narrowed. "Safe," is all he would allow.

He wanted to shake the men. But he sat quietly, though on the edge of his chair.

"That Loyalist took a stand after the raid on the Mercer farm," Seymour Hess said, finally. "He was killed."

"But one of the party was never found."

"His brother. Younger brother."

Ethan bolted upright. "How do you know this?"

"Recent, very recent communications, I assure you."

"You have picked up the trail again, yourself, Mr. Hess. Why?"

"Because of a little boy disturbed by everyone calling his friend, a friend who taught him how to catch minnows with a handkerchief, a liar. Once the frozen ground thawed, this boy dug up a small stake buried next to a dead rat and brought it to me. Here in my chambers."

"Hugh. Did the stake bear a message?"

"Only bloodstains. Indiscernible scratches. But it planted a seed," the magistrate admitted. "And I had never gotten over the . . . the ring of truth to your testimony, sir. I began inquiries. To Canada. I knew the Mercers, watched Judith's flowering. We all took a great pride in her, Mr. Randolph. I could not believe she had left her work for her father's murderer. Then when I heard from Captain Atwater, of this herbalist seamstress and her work for our slavepath north, I knew she had not." He glanced beyond Ethan. "Is it not time, Elder Oakes?"

The Elder hesitated. "This is happening so quickly, and is a matter I should consult others on."

Ethan turned, ignited with suspicion. "What have you done?"

The Elder finally came fully out of the shadows. "But, the woman who wrote to Harmony Springs Meeting—she said he'd beaten, then abandoned Judith. That she was sick of heart, and sought to return to us. She asked for our help."

"Good God. Who?" Ethan breathed. "What woman wrote this?"

"Thy brother's wife, Clara Randolph."

Ethan nailed the man still with his gaze. "You know that other brother, don't you? The brother of the Loyalist, who came down from Canada on the raid twenty years ago. He returned. He became one of you. He's been waiting, watching, for years. Still bound by a promise. One that allowed him peace, while Eli Mercer remained a widow, while his daughter lived her celibate life. But Elder Oakes, the Mercer line is growing again."

"Judith. She is on your father's plantation now, is she not?" Seymour Hess prodded gently.

"Yes," Ethan said, from a mouth dry and tinged with the metallic taste of his own fear.

"You must go, Ethan Randolph, and you, Dr. Foster," the elder said in a ragged remnant of his powerful voice. "The Meeting, we will help you get home the fastest way possible. I fear we have delivered Eli Mercer's murderer to your doorstep."

46

The three men were still dressed in mourning there on the dock. Ethan didn't like the feel of black on his shoulders, directing the sun's heat to his skin. Grieving black, biding its time, waiting to have its purpose. His Quaker wife's aversion to the color had seeped into his being. Captain Atwater offered his good hand. Ethan took it.

"My mother and I sail on the next tide. Maine, I think you stipulated."

"Requested. Captain. You'll be welcome at our home."

"Mother, too?"

Ethan managed a smile. "Even her chickens."

"Spoken like a courteous Virginian."

"Don't tell Dr. Foster. He believes he's turned me into a coldhearted New Englander."

"I will repay you, for your purchase of my cargo."

"The cost was in something I have no use for."

Ethan released the hand of this man who loved Judith. He did not wonder at it, only at how there were not legions more.

Ethan hesitated only once, on the ship's gangplank. In heading out on the open sea, he was breaking his promise to his mother to remain landed.

Jordan shoved him gently. "I will defend you for taking this fastest route home," he said. "She will understand, and forgive."

"Thank you, sir."

They walked to the port side of the schooner, where none of the other passengers seemed willing to brave the salt spray. Ethan tapped the ship's rail nervously.

"I wish I was as clever as Daedalus and could make us both wings," Jordan offered.

"No need. Prescott Lyman will wait."

"When he's got Judith defenseless? Why?"

"She is never defenseless. He will make one more try for her. He was her suitor in Harmony Springs. He would have been her celibate husband, were it not for me. It was I spoiled his last chance to fulfill his promise to his brother without blood."

"You and Eli."

"Prescott Lyman must have been listening that day, when Eli gave me his permission to court. A madness came over him then, I think."

"A calculated madness. To use your knife, to desecrate Eli's body so even Judith was paralyzed by the sight . . ."

Ethan turned into the breeze. Revulsion soured his stomach, sending bile up his throat. When would they set the sails? He would feel better once at sea, he was sure.

"Ethan?"

Get it out. Get the rest out, before it poisons. "I left Judith full of doubt about me. He will prey upon that. Jordan, where was my sense? I should have trusted her with the knowledge that Captain Atwater lived, should have listened to her pleas not to be separated. Just as I should have known from the hatred in Prescott Lyman's eyes when I came for her, there in Harmony Springs. I should have known that he was the one."

"You had other objectives then."

"I am now the father of her line, and so, even more, the spoiler of his plans. *J'ai espérance . . ." What is the English, Fayette?* his mind asked through its fear.

—Hope.

"Hope. I hope he waits for me."

Jordan Foster smiled. "That thought sustains us both."

Ethan's eyes traced a gull's flight. "Jordan. You must have a care, stay safe. My mother loves you."

"And I love her. I have all my life."

Ethan turned to his friend. "All your life? Is that why you couldn't love the dulcimer woman, the way she loved you?"

"Yes."

"Your Maggie, she knew this?"

"Yes."

"She had a great heart, I think, to have taken you to husband just the same."

"Ethan, there is so much I have yet to tell you."

"I know. I'm slow, a poor student."

"That's not what I mean! Listen. What you said to Captain Atwater . . . it was about your brother's loan, the one you made against your inheritance, wasn't it? Does that inheritance truly mean nothing to you?"

"The Randolph one?" Ethan snorted softly. "Jordan, this avarice of my father and brothers, the conniving of their wives and this wealth that slips so easily through my fingers—it is based on the sweat of bondsmen and -women. Now a small portion of it has gone to free others, black and white. Perhaps these three, the brothers I bought back and Judith's captain, they will go on to free more. That from my small investment—that has value, yes? The money was not nearly enough, after generations of Randolph slavery, but it is all I am likely to lay my hands on.

"I have no further interest in that legacy, believe me. My true inheritance is of my second life—Fayette and Judith and you. I treasure your gifts beyond measure. And I cannot lose you or Judith, or the child she carries. I am still a selfish boy, a brat. I am so unfinished."

His friend looked at him long and hard, searching. For what? He was so hopelessly transparent, was he not? "I cannot—" Jordan Foster finally whispered. "I cannot do this without her."

"Without who? Do what?"

"Your mother, damnation!"

"You will not blaspheme that lady's name, sir!"

Jordan merely sighed in response to the hot flash of anger. "Oh, keep your dueling pistols in their box, Virginian," he said. "I've done worse to that woman."

"Not while sober."

"What in hell do you mean?"

Ethan laughed. "Has your memory tripped again? How else could I have tolerated you making her a whore?"

What was the source of the rage filling Jordan Foster's face? Ethan wondered. Did he not remember his insult to his Annie when drunk? But Ethan had barely time to open his mouth to ask before he felt the hard slam of the doctor's fist at his jaw. That and a launching sea swell unbalanced him, sending him sprawling to the deck, dazed. And Jordan Foster was still coming at him.

"You know nothing about it!" the doctor shouted.

"Know nothing? I was there when you called my mother a French whore! I did not challenge you then, I carried you home!"

Suddenly, Jordan's face filled with discovery. "My God," he whispered. Ethan crawled backward until his head hit the railing. Jordan's voice was a whisper. "You meant what I said in the tavern."

"Of course. Why did you hit me?"

Jordan crouched on the deck beside him. "Ethan, forgive me."

"Bloody hell! Not this time! Why did you hit me?"

"I misunderstood."

"What?"

"Your words."

"What words? *Dîtes-moi!*"

" 'Dîtes'?"

"Tell me! Damnation! I am not stupid, addle-brained, empty-headed! I am not an imbecile!"

"No," Jordan soothed. "You are Annie Blair's clever boy. And mine. Ethan, you are my son."

"What?"

"I loved your mother, and she returned that love. I am your father."

47

Suddenly the bright clouds, the waves, the calling gulls, were too much to bear. Ethan closed his eyes, shutting them all out. But pictures started there, behind his eyelids. "Oh God. You did not flee the Tidewater, like the dancing masters, and craftsmen, and tradesmen. When my—when her husband was away in Europe. At the time of the epidemic."

"Yes."

"And I was not born early."

"No. Only obligingly small."

Ethan opened his eyes. Jordan Foster was holding his arm in that curious warm grasp from their first meeting. "You abandoned us, then?" he whispered.

"No. Your mother sent me away."

"To Scotland. Your studies. To Maggie. Another family. Children. West. Indians."

"Yes. Let me help you—"

Ethan pushed the hand away. "Why hasn't my mother ever told me?"

"She was protecting you, in the only way she knew. It was hard for me, young, as you are now, to accept her choice. But it was made for you. So you would not grow up wanting, and in the shadow of her disgrace. When she lost you to the sea, there was no consoling her. Now that she has you back, after all these years, I think she fears losing you all over again."

"Losing me?"

"Yes. Your love, your forgiveness."

"Forgiveness?"

"I—I need it, too."

Ethan grabbed the iron railing, letting his eyes warn Jordan Foster back as he rose to his feet on his own power. When the healing hand approached his face, he turned away, clenching the rail. "It requires nothing." Ethan watched the swells. "Why did you not tell me, before this?"

"I promised her."

A promise. To his fragile, steel-eyed mother. This he understood. His voice turned quiet. "So. We both broke promises to her today."

"Yes." The doctor waited until he turned away from the sea, a long time. "Well?"

" 'Well?' " Ethan echoed with a perverse satisfaction.

"Well . . . say something!"

A gull swooped down to the water's ripple, caught his prize. "If you wished to distract me from our encounter with Prescott Lyman, you have accomplished your goal."

The schooner's sails moved them away from sight of land, and out onto the open sea. That was all Ethan needed to bury the remaining shock, to banish the childish anger over what-might-have-been from his heart. The time of Jordan Foster's punishment was over. He felt the physician's hand on his arm. Warm, familiar. "Please. Let me check your jaw."

Ethan locked his eyes on this man, his father. "I have dreamed of snow. Sleighs, bells, Jordan."

"Have you?"

He must stop. It was very rude, this mental tracing of hairline, eye color, height, shoulders. But he was a new man. Again. Not an improper Randolph. A Foster. Mrs. Willard had surmised long before he had that he was not a proper one of those, either, of course, but a Foster. Hands. Hadn't Eli said his hands were like Jordan's? Did Eli know? Did Judith? Would Sally love him less when she discovers herself half a sister?

He looked out over the Atlantic, as wide and deep as his women's love. It would not change, no matter who he was. Of that he was certain, as certain as the realization that this was his last time riding these waves. His beautiful, determined wife would draw him into the western wilderness, where the Ohio's waters would have to content him. "Good God," he whispered suddenly, "my ancestors hanged Quakers? For that alone Judith will go back to Philadelphia."

"I don't believe any of our people did," Jordan said earnestly. "Some of them founded the town of Providence with Roger Williams, based on religious freedom for all. And, Ethan, our coloring . . . There are persistent rumors that the source was a marriage into the native population."

Ethan grinned. "Indians? We are Indians? What kind?"

"Wannopeg. One of our grandmothers married a survivor of King Philip's War, I believe." He frowned suddenly. "Now, how did I know that my family's best-guarded secret scandal would not be a source of dismay?"

Ethan laughed. "Walk the length of this fine ship with me, Jordan. Let's see if Fayette or your dulcimer woman has sent us some dolphins, for Godspeed."

"There, Judith. It's so fortunate the styles of the day are such to keep your interesting condition an enhancement! And there's still room for you to remain lithe in dancing with your husband upon his return."

Judith stared down at the sea green silk that flowed from her high waistband. She could dance now. Anne Randolph had brought in the fiddler every day and kept her busy learning quadrilles, line dances, and even the scandalous waltz, Ethan's favorite.

Judith had suffered his women's attempts to give her grace, glad for their company, their lively, open hearts. And she loved his cantankerous father's courtly efforts to please her with French delicacies from Martha's kitchen. Their daily talks in the scrolled bench he had installed in the corner of Sally's flower garden were now treasures of her heart. He'd been a man of his word. Prescott Lyman had been banished from Windover since that first night.

But he remained the guest of Winthrop and Clara, a mere three miles away. It kept Judith close to the big house, and in the company of family. Still, the feeling that Prescott Lyman was watching her came at odd moments. It came now. She was afraid of those eyes, always intense, now burning. They said her eyes had been like that once, fired with purpose, when pursuing her missions. Would there be no more missions, if she submitted to her husband? If she still had a husband.

Where was Ethan? Would he return? Would they remain here at

Windover? Would he become an indolent planter's son? Worse? Was he already worse? No. That was poison, Prescott Lyman's poison. She knew Ethan Randolph as she knew her own soul. She had chosen him—a difficult choice, but wasn't she the same for him? He was a healer, not a killer. A devoted, loving husband, whose touch she missed beyond reason. *Am I beyond reason, Papa?* Her mind pleaded with her father's spirit. *Am I beyond God, and—what Prescott Lyman believes—blinded by my desire for this man?*

"Why, Judith, the color has quite left your face," Anne said. "Are you tired, sweetling?"

"A little."

"In need of your solitude, perhaps? Away from our chatter?"

"I love your company," she admitted to women and children who would have never been in her sphere of influence had she remained a dutiful Quaker.

"Still, what if Ethan should come home today, and you were the least bit wan?" her mother-in-law asked now.

Sally rolled her eyes. "We would be subjected to that imperious French tone of chastisement. Mama's right, Judith."

"Let's get these dreadful pins out of you."

Judith laughed. "They're not sticking me anywhere, Mother. Please finish the hem first."

"You're sure?"

"Yes."

The women continued their work in a happy, full silence. Even Sally's daughters played more quietly, there by the big casement windows—open, so tall, like Randolphs and Blairs, like these Virginians' hospitality. The sheer lace blew in a salty breeze, reminding her of her sea-loving husband. Where was Ethan? she wondered again. Would any of their efforts lure him home?

Betsy called from where she held a spyglass to her eye. "A new ship, Mama! It's docking!"

Anne Randolph raised her head. "From upriver?"

"No, Grandmama—from the great Atlantic!"

"Pirates?" her younger sister asked.

"I spy two, the first two disembarking. Yes, all handsome and dressed in black—pirates! Dr. Foster and Uncle Ethan!

"Give me that glass, you silly creatures!" their mother demanded, then held the instrument. "Mama, Judith . . . it is they!"

"From the open sea?" Anne demanded. "Those two have some explaining to do!"

"They will, Mama, they will. But they must be hungry. And no wonder Martha and Phoebe have been boiling plum duff all morning! They must have known! Let's tell them to bring it over. Come, girls. Close all the shutters but the one on that window, yes, that one casts such a lovely light on Judith. Hurry now, that recalcitrant brother of mine is not minding his leg at all. He's quite ahead of our Jordan. Judith! Stand here, so he will look up and not regret his return from the sea."

Slowly, in the ringing silence of the women's wake, Judith raised the glass to her eye. There, below, so close now. Her young husband, handsome even in black, was being ambushed by his nieces. He swung them high in the air. Then he embraced his mother and sister, whose words, as Sally directed his gaze to the window, transformed his tight-with-worry face into one beaming its relieved joy. Joy. At the sight of her. She must get out of this gown, Judith realized, feeling her blood race. She must not stab her fine-formed man with a hundred dressmaker pins.

Footsteps. And the fear, searing her being.

"You allowed that man your body, Judith?"

Prescott Lyman. In her room. *Impossible,* she thought. "You"? Where was his Quaker "thee"? *Talk.* Her only hope. *Through your fear, Judith. Find your voice. Talk.* "He is my husband," she whispered. "A good man. One my father loved as his own—"

"Murderer!"

"Stop it!"

He shook his head. "Stop. Of course. There is no going on, for either of us, is there, Judith?"

"You must leave. I do not want you here."

"Are you afraid of me? Or the truth I bring?"

"Perhaps only God will know the truth of that day."

"I think you know."

" 'Know'?"

"I am sent here to lift the veils."

"What veils?"

"The ones within which you have shrouded this man, your husband. These slaveholders, they have enslaved you in that whore's satin, in their sensual world. You are victim of them, of your murdering husband's carnality. When the veils are lifted, when you are cleansed of his seed, your powerful Light might shine again. I am the instrument. God has sent me to do these things, Judith."

48

"Now. Come away from the window," Prescott Lyman com-manded. "Unless you wish to have an unfortunate fall."

Judith's eyes judged how far away Anne Randolph's sewing basket was, its scissors within.

"My new daughter has the grace of a deer. She will not fall, sir." The master of Windover stood in the doorway, displaying a shining saber. "This weapon has been in my family for seven generations, Mr. Lyman, no Quaker stranger to killing."

"Neither am I," Prescott Lyman proclaimed, pulling a pistol from his coat and pointing it at the man's head. "Stand aside."

Judith rushed forward. Prescott Lyman backhanded her hard, knocking her off her feet.

The elder Randolph raised the sword in both hands, whacked her attacker soundly, then turned the blade, slicing his side. Prescott Lyman stared at the gleaming blood, then fired his weapon. Judith watched the old man stagger back. The close-range burn mark at his abdomen turned red. His eyes held their determination, but his powerful body had no function.

Prescott Lyman threw down the pistol in disgust. "Damned old man!" he muttered, kicking Winthrop aside as he pulled Judith through the doorway.

Ethan lifted Winthrop Randolph into his arms. He packed his handkerchief against the wound. "Didn't like that man," Winthrop muttered, "from the first. Now. Hurting her, your good choice, Ethan. Not in my house! Stop fussing, child. Go—give chase. West. The river. The falls, where we lost Aubrey. Go."

Ethan rose. Jordan grabbed his arm.

"Look after my father. Please."

The physician released him, nodding.

Ethan rushed past his advancing sister, slowed by her clinging little girls. He grabbed the children, one under each arm without breaking his stride.

"Charlotte?" He asked after his youngest niece.

"In Martha's kitchen," Sally said.

"Mama!" Alice screamed.

"Go with your uncle, girls," she commanded, rolling back her sleeves. "Take care of the babies."

When Ethan burst through the doorway, Martha and Phoebe turned from their baking-day fire in astonishment.

"Keep mine with yours, yes, Martha?" he asked, breathless.

"Always welcome, but—"

"All children inside. Bolt the door."

Her eyes widened. "Yes, sir." He felt her long, strong fingers grab his head in a curious, familiar hold. She'd done that on the dock, the day he went to sea. And before, long before, after she'd broken the bag of waters, and eased his way out of his mother's body. How was he remembering that? All of her strength seemed to flow into him as she planted a hard kiss on his forehead. "Godspeed," she said, and released him.

Her unfinished gown was leaving a bright trail to her, as parts of it unpinned, taking root in brush and branches, Judith realized. Prescott Lyman didn't seem to comprehend this, or anything, except pulling them higher, and toward the rushing spring waters.

"An innocent is within me, Prescott," she warned quietly. "You must not hurt us."

"I have done so already, don't you understand yet? That first time. I only held the horses then. The children, like lambs to their slaughter. The woman, her screams echoing in my head ever after. My brother charged me to finish with his dying breath. It would not have been so painful for your father if he hadn't turned that damned Virginian toward you. I would have spared you both. I had found a bloodless path!"

"What are you saying?"

"You had to find him like that, Judith. So that it could be planted in your mind that your sailor could dispatch a disapproving father like a rat."

"Dear God."

"But his carnal hold on you was too strong—rutting you against a tree's trunk like an animal! Or perhaps my laudanum made you without resistance to his abduction that day at Meeting? I'm sorry if that was so."

"It was not the laudanum. And it was no abduction."

"You married him freely?"

"Yes."

"Not my fault, your choice. A comfort to me, then. You still seek to comfort. Extraordinary. Extraordinary woman. And so difficult to kill."

"Come back to the house with me, Prescott," she urged.

"No." He yanked her wrist. "Higher. His leg is bad. I need him weakened, after what his meddlesome hulk of a father did to me. I took his spoiled, lovesick son into my household. I offered that worthless brat a life with my Ruth. Look on this!" He offered her his bloodied hand. "That was not very hospitable of him! I do not trust fathers. Yours caused all this, with his terrible choices, in army, in land, in husband for you."

"You slander a good man."

"I keep my promise to a better one."

"Promise, or curse? You can stop it here, Prescott. You have that power."

"Do I, wise Judith, my counselor in ragged finery?" He swung her in an arc until she fell on the flat rock, scraping her palms on the blue stone as she protected her middle. His look hardened further as he finally took in her ballroom silk, turned to rags. "Do you remove your gown to entice me?" he demanded. "You, whom I once thought dwelled only in the realm of the Spirit? How far you've come to earth, Mrs. Randolph. Shall I cut out your eloquent tongue, so it will not entice me? Shall I let your husband discover you then? Perhaps that will send him into one of his mad fits. Will that finally finish him?"

The image of Ethan thrashing about the library's bed suddenly blinded Judith with tears.

"For him! Still you weep only for him!"

She struggled to rein in her grief, her shame for ever doubting Ethan.

—*Calm. Calm, Judith.* Whose thought was that winging its way into her being? "Let it be clean," she whispered. "With dispatch. I would not cause my husband any more pain."

He pulled a vial from his vest pocket and crouched beside her. Blood from his side stained the rockface. Was he weakening? "Drink this," he said with an icy coldness.

"No."

"Judith," he reprimanded. "Find your courage."

She raised her head. "Swear it. Swear on your brother's memory that you will not cause my Ethan any harm, after."

He raised an eyebrow. "A Quaker demanding I swear?"

"I am no Quaker. Neither are you. Swear."

"You think me heartless, don't you? I am not a heartless man. What you ask for him is not a mercy. I would I had died with my brother. Once your husband has been punished with the sight of you, I would not leave him to become the shell the years have made me."

"That will not happen. He is not you. He has endured worse trials than you have. And he answers with goodness, always."

He laughed. "That's what she used to tell me, that woman, my Quaker wife, who led me back to you. 'Answer it with goodness,' when my brother's death grip was on me, when his voice would rise up in the night and charge me again."

"Hear her. Hear us both now."

"Too late. It grows within you, Judith. A future. That cannot be allowed. This man who made me kill, he will see you cleansed before I kill him."

"Cleansed?" Judith asked softly.

"Of the child. Lay back."

Judith's fingers found Anne Randolph's sharp-bladed scissors, slid them soundlessly open. He would not hurt her child while she had breath.

"Stay away from us," she warned.

"It can be so much easier, dear Judith. Drink first. Let the contents take you beyond the pain, to that place of visions you're always seeking. There." He came closer. But there, in the tree above them, a flash of silver. The buttons of Ethan's vest? Closer. "That's my love," her tormentor soothed. "I will leave you to God, I promise. If you survive the cleansing, I will take you back. With him gone, we will form our chaste union."

Now, before he laid a hand on her. She thrust where she thought his heart was. Wrong. The scissors pieced his skin, but hit bone. She tried again. He laughed, grabbed her wrist, pinning it to the rock. She screamed the scream she'd been holding, waiting to release since she found her mother and siblings dead by the hearth, her father dangling in the chimney. Its sound drove the birds skyward and Ethan from the tree.

49

Ethan came down squarely on both feet, bootless, after climbing the notches he and Aubrey had carved in the rockface when children. The right leg buckled. Prescott Lyman circled the air with bloodied scissors as he spoke.

"This Mercer and I had an appointment which far preceded yours."

"Ours was from Time's beginning."

"You can barely stand, Virginian. And I have nothing left to lose." Prescott Lyman thrust his weapon, the scissors.

Fayette had taught Ethan how to dodge. He did. Again. And again. It felt strange, doing it standing up. The scissors only sliced the space between his coat and waistcoat. Startled, his attacker retreated, smiling that eerie, unnatural smile Ethan remembered.

"So, there are some things your black slaves don't do for you."

He threatened again, forcing Ethan backward, toward the ledge, trying his weak leg. He pulled his knife from his waistcoat. Where was his pursuer's weakness? If only there was more room. Prescott Lyman's heel caught under Ethan's bad knee, sending him down, driving the knife from his hand and over the ledge. Judith screamed. Lyman's boot landed squarely in his side. Ethan grabbed it and twisted until the bigger man came down with him.

Prescott Lyman's fingers crushed around Judith's hem, dragging her closer. She pulled some pins from her high waistband and he suddenly possessed nothing but a handful of silk. Wondrous woman, his wife, Ethan thought, barreling into her attacker. The big-boned farmer howled, then finally fell still.

Ethan rose, yanked Prescott Lyman's head back, then let it fall. He felt Judith wedge herself under his right arm. Her palm was sliced open, bleeding. It was raining. He must finish this, he thought, and get Judith away. He removed his coat, placed it around her shoulders. She smiled in response, before her eyes widened in horror. Her silk became a noose, suddenly, around his neck. Prescott Lyman leapt over the sheer-drop side, dragging Ethan after him.

Ethan's back slammed against the rockface. He saw a patch of dismal sky, the rushing water. Above, Judith's bloodied hands holding his foot. Below, Prescott Lyman's weight tightened the silk noose. He was upside down, he finally realized. Like the holy fool in Fayette's deck of fortune-telling cards. No wondrous flight, no landing, this. Suspension, anchored only by Judith's sobbing, fervent pleas. Captain Willis, laughing—finally getting his wish to hang Henry Washington as a spy? Purple spots before his eyes began to blot out the gray sky.

—*Arms,* petit général, *use your arms to relieve this torment,* Fayette advised.

Ethan reached out over his floating hair, found the silk line. Both hands closed around it. He pulled. A semblance of his breathing returned. Along with Prescott Lyman's voice.

"You're as tenacious as her father in the chimney, little husband," he said, annoyed. Securing himself in the rock's footholds, he reeled his tether around his broad hand, then held the scissors over Ethan's heart. "Watch, Judith," he called, "watch it done properly."

Judith screamed, her powerful voice splintering, causing an avalanche. No—a pistol's shot, Ethan realized. He endured her cry of despair as he kicked out of her grip, holding fast to the line of silk that attached him to her father's murderer. Together they fell into the rushing water below.

Clayton smelled of gunpowder.

Large Randolph men, Judith thought vaguely, as Winthrop lifted her from the ledge without effort, even in her state. Sally rushed up behind them.

"I let go?" Judith whispered.

"No. Ethan broke your hold."

Clayton touched her brow. "I don't know how you held on as long as you did. He wouldn't allow you to fall with him. Do you understand?"

She was in two worlds. One clear, too clear, despite the rain. The other world was blurred, rushing. Ethan's world. Judith clutched his coat around her as the man who held her came into view again.

"You tried to help us—"

"Too late."

"We're sorry." They sounded like brothers, at last, to her.

"The water won't take him," Sally argued, wrapping Judith's hand in a remnant of her petticoat. "Not Ethan. He was born in the sack."

* * *

Ethan felt Prescott Lyman's desperate strength even as the spring flow pulled them toward the James. *Hold. Hold on, until this man is dead.* But his fingers grew numb.

—Let go.

"No. He's so strong."

—You got healing hands. Not made for killing, the voice coaxed gently. *—I got him now. Don't you be worrying 'bout him no more.*

He did as Aubrey asked. His burden lightened, then disappeared. Aubrey wore a wide straw hat. He was taller than when Ethan left on the *Ida Lee.* The grin—warm and welcoming—was the same.

"You weren't finished growing, then?" Ethan asked his friend.

—No. I be a big man, like my daddy. You needs to keep your promise to him, to my folk. You gots to go back.

"Back?" Ethan asked, confused.

Aubrey directed his long arm below them, where Ethan saw Aaron leaning on his spear, like a mighty sentry. Weeping, as the others gathered around a fish he'd plucked with that spear and landed on the creek bank. A still, coatless, bootless fish. Himself.

"Am I dead?" Ethan whispered.

—You? Who I teached to swim? You gonna spoil the women's birthin' stories?

"Born in the sack?"

—There now, your memory ain't so bad!

"Judith's coming. With Sally—"

Aubrey touched his back. *—And my mama's been cookin' up your plum duff all morning'. Find your way home now.*

Ethan nodded, then called out to the people below. No one heard, except the tiny, bruised child inside Judith, who leaped, startling her. There. That got her attention. "Help me, Judith," he whispered, through the rain, wafting the curling wisp of hair beside her ear. "You know what to do."

She knelt, fisted her bleeding fingers. Struck his back.

Aubrey laughed. *—You got yourself one mighty lady!* he proclaimed. *—I'd stay on her good side.*

With Judith's second clout, Ethan leaned over, coughed up brown sludge from the creekbottom. He was breathing, though every breath pained his throat, and he had no voice. Away. Why were they pulling Judith away? He looked at his hands. Empty.

"River's done got him, sir," Aaron soothed.

No. Aubrey. Aubrey's got him, Ethan wanted to tell Aubrey's father. Aaron smiled, as if he had. Ethan took an unsteady grip of the bondsman's massive shoulders. He only managed to pull himself into a sitting position. Aaron laughed. "Easy, now, brother. You ain't long back 'mongst us. Let's get this wicked noose from your neck, make you more presentable to your ladies, shall we?"

Ethan made a guttural sound.

"You don't needs to talk, young one. I hear you," Aaron reprimanded.

Other hands pulled at his neckerchiefs. Jordan, chest heaving from his run. Not looking into his eyes. Smelling of death. Winthrop Randolph was dead, then. Ethan had broken his promise to see the old man out of his life. But he'd sent one father to look after the other.

He began shaking. From the cold, only the cold. Mouth, trying. No sound to answer Judith's calls. Battling the hands, all pulling at him. *Leave me alone.*

Jordan yanked open his eyelids, issued curt commands—Look up, down, right, left, at my shoulder, toward the sun—when all Ethan wanted to do was comfort his powerful, weeping wife.

Aaron began to interpret between them—with his new father, just as he used to with the old one. "Excepting that mean neck-burn, the boy seems sound to me, sir. And he has a mighty need for Miss Judith just now, Dr. Jordan."

Jordan shook his head. "Blood. From his mouth. May signal internal injuries."

Ethan growled.

"His lip, sir," Aaron interpreted. "Chomped down on it in the waters, is all. That right, young Ethan?"

Ethan nodded vigorously, though it started his teeth chattering.

Jordan's eyes finally locked on to his own. Ethan saw fear there, which gave him a touch more patience.

"You bit your lip?" Jordan whispered.

He nodded, more slowly.

"And, aside from your throat, you feel no serious injury?"

Ethan shook his head.

"Didn't I tell you?" Sally's voice demanded. Ethan saw her over the doctor's shoulder. His sister, another go-between, the full measure of her love shining from her swollen eyes. "Now, Doctor, kindly give Judith leave to her husband, before she breaks poor Clayton's arm!"

Ethan stood, then staggered on legs that felt as weak as a new fawn's. He blinked, trying to clear his vision of beaming faces, black and white.

"Landsickness," Jordan Foster diagnosed. "He's better on water."

"Or flying, sir," Aaron agreed. "He soars like a hawk."

The doctor snorted. "One direction. Down."

"Stop teasing my brother," Sally defended him stoutly.

Ethan didn't care. He was holding Judith, and she was warming away all fear of fits. She led his hand to her middle. Larger then when he'd left her. Round. Perfect. And, what was this, alive? Of course alive. Leaping. This new go-between. Judith pressed his hand to the undulation, laughing. "Your child welcomes you home," she proclaimed.

When he opened his eyes, he was in his bed at Windover, his beautiful wife curled against his side. She stretched as drowsily as a cat. "You are a wondrous good patient, husband," she whispered at his ear, "in need of barely anything but sleep and my warmth." Ethan felt his face flush with shame at his intense physical reaction to her, but she only smiled wider. "Well, perhaps something more? To help us both fall into a deeper sleep?"

He glanced at the room's doors. She'd latched them all securely.

He woke again to fingers parting and reparting his hair. His mother's, his wife's, his sister's tender, nervous habit had given his mane its wildness, not his years below the decks of the *Standard*, he realized, looking up at Anne Randolph.

Her long, rose-scented fingers beat gently against his mouth. "No talking, Jordan says, or I must leave. Judith will return directly. Jordan's rebandaging her hands. Oh my darling, don't look so worried—they will heal in time for her to hold the baby."

He curled his hand around his mother's fingers, set them on his chest.

"Good, then," she approved. "Now. Shall I tell you a story, Mr. Washington? One those beautiful eyes have been asking for all your life?"

He nodded slowly.

"Very well, then. It is about a woman of three-and-thirty years, who should have known better than to fall in love with the young man who taught her growing children, who would not leave her side when a terrible sickness came. But he was so brave and handsome, and possessed such a lively, all-encompassing intelligence, that she came alive again, after so many years of duty and care of others and neglect of herself. She had never been allowed to be a girl, can you understand this?

A girl giddy in her ripe body's power, giddy in her love of this man.

"But the sickness left, and her husband returned and she was bearing the young man's child. She was seldom more than a breeding mare to her husband, but she had seen the power of his anger when any was caught stealing from his estate. She feared her lover and child would not survive that anger, so she chose deception and, she thought, safety for them both. She had not seen the wide world as you have, my darling, she did not yet know there is no place, no decision safe.

"She learned. When her child's father accepted her gift of a profession, but did not patiently wait for her to give their beautiful boy up to his care. When he chose a wife, a family, a wilderness, a war. When her son turned toward the sea. There he was lost to all of us, while yet a child, writing beautiful, oil-packeted letters to a mother who had never deserved them or him."

"Mmmm—" Ethan tried, as tears threatened his already swollen throat, but her fingers against his mouth pressed him silent again.

"Then, one day," she continued, "another woman, one who had never been allowed to be a girl, either, she found the boy, a young man now, and brought him home. And this wondrous woman and my son's father, who'd never stopped loving a child he'd never seen, they joined forces and gave him back to us all, and . . . Well, you know the rest, don't you?"

He nodded.

"Do you still love me? Do you forgive us, Ethan Blair?"

He frowned, shaking his head at her need to ask this question. "Mama," he whispered, sounding like a hoarse, disapproving ram.

She laughed. A girl's high, musical laughter, through the shining tears. He grinned. If Jordan Foster ever so much as attempted to extinguish that girl, he'd best be standing by, Ethan decided.

50

Ethan stood beside the door of the cookhouse at the appointed time. Aaron stepped out in his best clothes, and shook his hand. "Thank you for coming, young master."

"I'm not your master, Aaron."

The big man looked contrite. "Have patience with us, sir." He shifted his mighty, tree-trunk legs. "I asked you to come so's we could talk 'bout that time, back. To release you, before you listen to the will-readin'. You ain't got to keep that promise made to me and mine."

"Why?"

"You done made it to a brother, sir. Swore it out real fine on our common blood, remember?"

"I remember."

"And now we come to find out there's no blood between us. We ain't related at all."

Ethan smiled. "Aaron, that is the only thing I regret about the circumstances of my birth. I should have liked very much to call you brother."

"Truly, sir? Friends do."

"Might we continue, then?"

"You asking my permission, young Ethan?"

"Of course."

"Them's fine French manners you got, my Martha says."

"Martha doesn't think less of my mother, does she, Aaron?"

"I think my Martha, she always knew, down in the heart of her. Think most of us did, child. You was just too different. A Blair, for sure of course, as kindhearted, as good with your healing hands as your mama and Miss Sally. So we never minded you much around, even when you almost tripped us up in our . . . well, less-than-strictly-legal pursuits."

Ethan grinned. "Is that as close as I'm going to get to finding out how many of the Tidewater runaways found passage through Windover?"

"I expect, sir, yes. Now, old master, he took such little notice of you we all thought we could see you safe, keep you tucked away, too. Until no babies come from your brothers' marriages. Until you got sent off to sea till you could have your own try at the babies. You and your lady and the one that's to come, you made old master die happy, and feeling himself brave, Ethan. You needs to think on that, when you feel lonesome for him."

Ethan pondered his friend's words. Was it possible he would ever feel lonesome for the man he'd been ashamed to have for a father? Who would have most likely put him out on the road, along with his unfaithful wife, had he known who his youngest son really was? Of course it was. The would-haves had not happened, and this intemperate, arrogant man had done the best he could with Windover, with him. And in the end Winthrop Randolph had sought to protect Judith as fiercely as he had.

"I'll bring you the news after the will is read," Ethan said. "And your family will not be separated or sold off while I have breath, brother."

The oldest son of Winthrop Randolph again shook the hand of the youngest son of Anne Blair, and each returned to his life's separate station.

Ethan had none of his Quaker-like stillness today, Judith thought, as she took her place beside him in the accounts room. He was as uncomfortable around his family as when she'd first brought him to Windover without memory. He'd told her then that these were not his people. He knew it instinctively, this man who told the most artfully concocted truths, but never lied. She only wished Jordan had told him the revelation in her presence, so she could have delighted in the moment Ethan found out that this man he loved so dearly was his own father.

He shifted again. "I don't belong here. Couldn't we take a walk outside until it's over?" he asked, tugging at her sleeve.

"Unhand your lady and sit still, pest," Jordan commanded.

Ethan's brow furrowed. "You of all people should know I have no business here. I gave up all claim I had, remember? For Winthrop's loan."

"My memory is perfectly sound. Yours is deficient. You repaid your brother in full, with the usurious interest agreed upon."

"I did?"

"By way of a small portion of our dulcimer woman's estate, which she foolishly left to her miserable husband. Now sit still."

"That's why Winthrop and Clayton look so worried?"

The doctor smiled. "Exactly."

Judith stifled a giggle behind her hand.

"Jordan, I cannot take anything from this man's estate," her husband insisted. "I still have my honor."

"Honor! I'd like to see Fayette just long enough to knock him into the middle of next week, do you know that? What about your promise to Aaron and his family? Has that promise got about it no honor?"

Ethan grinned. "You sounded exactly like Fayette just then, Jordan."

"That comes from listening too long to you mangling English. Hush now, you great magpie. I think I liked you better without a voice. Honor your mother's choice, the old man's delight in you, and your promise to his eldest son. Ponder them all and keep still."

"Damned Boston preacher," Ethan muttered.

"Enough," Judith whispered, finally quieting them both.

After a prelude of what seemed like a thousand admonitions about his youngest son's past sins and neglectful behavior, and explanations that his brothers had been given their own lands and plantations while he was alive, his mother's guardianship and Windover was left to Ethan Blair Randolph.

Jordan abandoned him without a word or a look. Ethan sat, stunned, his left hand warmed between Judith's arm and her side as his right was pumped with congratulations by the solicitors. His mother finally drew them away with an offer of rum punch. Ethan released Judith onto Sally's arm. His brothers approached.

"Give it to him," Winthrop demanded of Clayton.

Clayton laid an oversized ledger across Ethan's knees.

"The actual, undoctored books of the estate since the sinking of the *Ida Lee,* little brother. We kept them from our poor aging father's knowledge while you plowed the salt seas and had your landed adventures."

Ethan stared at his brothers. "You are both wealthy men. You could have prevented this. You could have spared our mother her worry, her selling off her dowry to keep the servants clothed and well."

"Yes," Winthrop agreed. "But that course of action would have given us no leverage if ever you returned, if ever our foolish father did what he has done. As it is now, the debts you so cleverly suspected, the ones that Clayton tried to warn your ambitious Quakeress about? You have just inherited them, too. By the time you sell off goods, your people, and half the acres, if you are very lucky, you will be left with this grand house and no one to run it, no one to till the lime-enriched soil of your magnificent new corn- and wheat-fields."

They hovered above him as Ethan's hands turned the pages on years of red ink, unpaid expenses. This was so familiar, being bested by his brothers, of them being one step ahead of him no matter how diligently his parents tried to look out for his interests. It would go on forever, if he stayed here. He raised his head.

"Let's trade," he said quietly.

"What?" They quickly called servants to bring forth chairs. Ethan didn't like his brothers so close. He wanted Jordan to advise him, he wanted his gentle wife's approval. Nonsense. He wanted the courage to withstand the lightning bolt the old man was sure to hurl at him now.

"Now," Clayton asked. "Trade what, Ethan?"

Ethan willed his rough, still-healing voice calm, respectful. "Windover. What you've wanted so much that you've hidden these debts. And thereby made your father's last years free of that complication. It was good of you to do this, in the years I was away, and I thank you. Well, now, I will trade the entire estate, with its debts."

Both brothers leaned forward. "For—?" Clayton asked.

"Its people."

"Its people?"

"And Paris."

"Paris?"

"Yes. Phoebe needs Paris. He's her husband."

"What in hell good is Paris?" Winthrop stormed. "You've got the breeder, you damned idiot!"

The name stung. It shouldn't have, but it did. *Use it. Use their low opinion of him, for what really matters,* he told his bruised heart.

Clayton hushed his brother with a fan of his fingers. "Ethan, our father hasn't sold a slave of Windover in years."

"I know that."

"Is that your intention? To drive them to Natchez, to New Orleans, to market? To acquire cash for your start in life?"

"In a different state? A territory? The Southern Frontier?" Winthrop continued, obviously liking his brother's conjectures more by the moment.

His eyes were telling them too much, Ethan decided. He had so little experience at working his mother's veils. He closed them. "That is not your concern."

"Mother will not stand for it."

"Leave our mother to me," Ethan informed them coolly. "This is your only opportunity. Before I consult with wiser minds than mine, what is your answer?"

"If . . . if you give us your word that Mother will be provided for, that her needs—"

"Our mother's needs will be met," he ground out between his teeth. "Your answer?"

Winthrop held out his hand. "Done."

Ethan shook it.

Clayton lifted the account book from his knees, and called the solicitors from their punch.

When all the signatures were supplied, Ethan sprang from the room that had haunted him enough to re-create it in miniature without memory. Judith was waiting in the great hall. He pulled her under the curving staircase. "You should be outside now, in the cool of the day," he said.

Her brow furrowed. "So should you, you're as pale as—"

"Judith, can you travel before the month is out? Can you climb over mountains, west? To your Ohio River Valley?"

"Yes."

He kissed her soundly. She gasped, then returned it, carefully shifting her expansion between them. The child inside her kicked against his hand.

"Was that a yes too, do you think?" he asked.

She nodded, tears tracking her cheeks. He flung a handkerchief at her. "Stop that! Where's Jordan?"

"In the garden with your mother. But, Ethan," she resisted the pull of his hand, "I don't think we should . . ."

He released her. "I will, then."

"Will what? Ethan Blair, come back here!" she yelled, as he flung the tearoom's doors wide and stepped out into the garden.

He found them under a leafy pear tree, in each other's arms. He flung back the doctor with a twist at his shoulder. His mother's lips were swollen with kisses.

"Propose," he demanded.

"Ethan, I—"

"Now!"

"At least allow me to take her hand, son."

"No hand. Propose!"

"Mrs. Randolph, would you do me the honor of becoming my wife?"

"Within a fortnight," his apprentice stipulated further.

"Ethan! This lady's mourning—"

"My mother has spent too much of her life in mourning. And my wife must travel with us while it is still safe for her."

"Travel?" his mother whispered.

"Yes. I have traded Windover and its mountain of debt for the slaves, Mother."

"You have?"

"Yes. And I will be writing the papers to free them once we reach the Virginia border."

"I see."

Her veils. Closing her down, one after the other. No, not veils, this time. Tears. She was crying. Damnation, Ethan thought, was she so attached to Windover?

"No more debt?" she whispered.

He took her hand. "No, Mother."

"No more selling off my dowry?"

He winced, shook his head, wondering for how long she had been doing that. She smiled, touched his cheek. "I so wanted just a few things. To pass on to Sally's children. And yours, beautiful boy."

"You'll have them, *madame*," he promised.

"Oh, Ethan," she said. "What about Phoebe's Paris?"

"She's got him as sure as you've got Jordan and me, homeless as we are at present. You may stay here with Winthrop or Clayton if you choose, but you must give up Windover if you marry this man. We're going west."

Her eyes widened. "We are?"

"Yes."

She smiled. "How splendid."

He grinned. "You'll do it, then? Make me legitimate before my own child is born?"

Jordan stiffened. "I don't wish her to marry me to make *you—*"

"Hush, Jordan," Anne Randolph reprimanded. She smiled sweetly at her son. "I think it's the least we can do, Ethan. You've been very patient with us." She kissed his cheek. "Now, run along, dear—there's poor Judith, out of breath from chasing you. Kindly enlighten her further, as Jordan will enlighten me."

She took her lover's hand and pressed it to her lips as if she'd been doing it for a lifetime. Ethan stepped back, suddenly startled and bereft. "I—I'll never be far from her again, Jordan Foster. You'll treasure my mother always or you'll reckon with me!"

His young father cocked a brow. "Now who's the Boston preacher?" he accused.

Epilogue

Ethan raised the spyglass to his eye, here, on the edge of Virginia. The red sun was hanging low in the west. Astonishing! The Allegheny Mountains looked like the rolling waves of the Atlantic. He thought suddenly of Fayette's vision of long ago, just before he fell from the mizzenmast. He smiled. "Lafayette, I am here," he whispered.

—Not yet, precious bane. Find her.

Ethan closed down the glass, turned toward the camp, where the women were starting the fires for their evening meal, swaying in the late-summer breeze. He was still amazed by the numbers of their traveling companions. Though a few of the former Windover slaves had chosen other states or territory to settle, most were on their way, via Barton Gibson's accurate maps, to the rich bottomland Jordan Foster had cleared for his first family.

He must write to his sister tonight, Ethan reminded himself. Description of thesc hills. He'd leave the urges to join them to her already westward-drawn husband and the tiny revolutionaries he'd planted in her midst.

The scent of Martha's open-fire hearth mixed with the rich pine of the mountains around. He tried to steal a slice of corn pone, but got burned and slapped at the same time for his effort.

"Ethan Blair, don't you know nothin' about protecting them healing hands of yours?" Martha scolded.

He grinned. "I'll bring some food to Judith. Where is she?"

"Off to higher ground, when your mama say lay herself down. Wouldn't listen to that good sense. She lit off over the trail instead is what." She indicated the place with her chin. "Go on. Fetch her back, child. Got water?"

"Yes."

"Good." She offered two of the corn cakes wrapped in the linen towel she'd grabbed off her shoulder. "I am sore uneasy about all Miss Judith's restlessness this day."

"She's been restless?"

Martha eyed him suspiciously. "And you have a care with her in your spooning. Please her all gentle, if'n it's the same kind of restlessness got you sparked now. And don't you be gone long without a lantern. Don't fancy hauling you's both out of a tree prowled by wildcats!"

"Anything further, *madame*?"

"No need to Frenchify me, young one—you just get her to eat all her share of them cakes—her appetite been poorly today."

"She says she can't find her stomach."

"Well, you the doctor! Find it for her, and make her give it a little nourishments."

Ethan began climbing the small, winding trail. It had been a fine day's travel. Nearly twenty miles, a good distance at this altitude. Why were the women so testy that not even his French could win a smile from one? All seemed restless, worried.

—*Hurry,* Fayette said at his ear.

He turned. His friend formed out of the evening midst. He was not the ghost from other visits—joking, confident, knowing everything. This was Fayette falling, suspended between Heaven and Earth. Confused. Terrified.

His Washington went cold with fear at the sight. Judith. He must find Judith. She would know what to do.

He stumbled, climbing higher. There, ahead, her beautiful hair shining through the loose weave of her sea green shawl, almost blending in with the pine trees. From behind, she was the Judith of the night they met, without the enormous burden the child inside her had become. She stumbled, fell to her knees.

He ran to her side, helping her support her pregnancy as if it were a bundle of wheat from the fields of Windover. She leaned back in his arms. She looked at the sky, drawing in a long breath. A cry burst forth from her then, a wild, ecstatic sound, that ended in laughter. "You see, Fayette? He's come," she called out. "Go on to your reward, and bother us not about the aspects of Heaven that do not suit your taste!"

Ethan raised his head. She saw him too, then. The falling Fayette turned into the confident, all-knowing one. He held up his hand to them before disappearing into the mist.

"He's well now?" Ethan asked his powerful wife.

"Yes, love. I think our Fayette is going on at last."

"And you?"

"I?" She erupted in girlish laughter. "I am far too grounded to fly away with him. My husband has seen to that."

He bowed his head, kissed their clasped hands. "You have all the women worried by—"

She squeezed his hand until the pressure made him gasp.

"Judith, have your pains begun?"

"No. Not pains. Only . . . Ethan, I can hardly bear to keep my eyes open, the world is so beautiful to me."

"The world?"

"Yes. At first I thought it was the sky's hues, the hills about, rolling like the ocean. So I tried to concentrate on smaller things—my ring, the wildflowers, the pine needles at my feet. Then the gold, purples, the softness became richer, deeper than I can bear. Then Fayette going on at last, and now . . . now, you!"

"Me?"

"Ethan, look at you!"

"Mais, ma chère femme, je ne connais pas—"

She rose to her knees and pulled him close, laughing. "No, no, speak English, sweet boy!"

He blinked. She laughed harder. He didn't care that she was laughing at him, just so she laughed. She was well if she laughed, wasn't she? She pressed his shoulders. Hard. Harder.

"Those eyelashes your mother and sister envy, will our child have them, you think?"

"*Comment?* . . . Pardon?" he amended quickly.

More laughter. "Oh, Ethan, if you kiss me as the first stars come out, I think I will die with the joy of it!"

"Non," he breathed. "Don't die, Judith."

She took his face between her hands. "Your kisses bring life. Don't be afraid for me."

He touched his lips to hers, remembering Martha's injunction. But their chaste kiss turned into waves of tasting each other's mouths, of breathing each other's breaths. They kissed long and deep and closer than he'd thought possible. Then profoundly sensuous trills. Which one of them was causing that? A wave bursting from Judith's secret sea suddenly soaked the ground beneath them.

She smiled, looking thoroughly wanton, besotted. "Ah. That's better. Thank you."

"Better? Judith, if your time has come, we need to get you down to—"

"The ground."

"Ground, love?"

"Yes, down, on the ground."

"Is the baby coming? Now?"

"Yes."

He yanked off his coat, spread it out beneath her. "It doesn't happen like this, Judith. You must have pains first, coming, going, for hours, to drive me to distraction!"

She smiled. "Perhaps I've driven you enough?" She took his sleeve. "So soft," she mused, rocking back slightly on her heels. "And how I love the scent of you, husband, even in your fear."

She grabbed his shoulders again, squeezed hard. "Oh, Ethan," she breathed. "Help me."

"I will, Judith," he said, kissing her temple, whispering at her ear. "This is a good place to be born—soft ground, gentle breeze, a perfect place." He eased her out of one petticoat, stuffing it with the forest floor's abundant pine needles, placed her back against it and the trunk of the sheltering tree.

"Good?" he asked shyly.

"Yes."

"Thirsty?"

She nodded and he offered her the spring water from his bag, then poured a stream of it over his hands.

"Judith, may I—?"

"Of course."

He folded her skirts back over her knees, then pulled his shirt's cuffs to his elbows. She closed her eyes, but still did not appear to be in pain, even as he eased her legs farther apart.

"Close?" she asked.

"Feel," he whispered, leading her fingers to the slippery mat of dark hair.

"Oh!" she marveled. "Girl or boy?"

"I can't tell from the head, love."

She laughed. "No? What kind of a doctor are—" But her *r*'s continued, grinding into his soul, becoming long, deep grunts of effort. The baby's head eased out into Ethan's hands. Steady hands. They didn't seem to belong to him, these patient hands, stroking tiny cheeks that turned from blue to pink as the mouth opened, gasping, caught between water and land worlds. One shoulder, the other, then all the rest. Small, perfect. Child. More water, splashing out, soaking his shirt. A child, their child, Judith's and his. Moving, breathing, reaching for his face, then turning to a mother's beautiful voice, calling.

After he'd cut the cord and examined the afterbirth, Judith helped her resourceful husband remove three more petticoats, swaddling the baby in one and herself in the other two. He attended them as he had the birth, quietly, moving around their pine-needle carpet like a crab in the hold of the *Standard*.

The swaddling, the hand-fed feast of spring water and the most delicious corn pone Judith had ever tasted had combined to finally defeat her efforts to stay awake, to not miss a moment of this vibrant new life she'd sung and suckled to contentment. So it was through half-closed lids she saw Jordan and the lanterns, the women.

"Lord, Miss Judith, that be you?"

"Yes. Ethan said you'd find us soon. It's wonderful up here, isn't it?"

Martha came closer. "Wonderful foolish of that man of yours!" she complained.

"Foolish?"

"I done warned him about having his way with you in the cool of the evening, on the top of a mountain, with you so close to term! You look worn-out."

"But Martha—"

"Where is that scoundrel?"

She smiled, watching Jordan's eyes change, grow as wide those of his new wife's. "He's close," Judith assured them all. "He's brought the baby to see the constellations," she told them all.

"He didn't take him no children when—"

Martha stopped suddenly as she saw the bloodstains. Jordan knelt beside the earthen bowl Ethan had dug for the gleaming afterbirth. Anne Randolph rushed forward.

Judith gasped against the feel of the women's hands kneading at her abdomen.

"Good," Anne whispered.

"And hard," Martha pronounced.

They were like sisters, these women, Judith realized, in the way Ethan and Aaron were still brothers, even without a kinship link. Jordan Foster grasped her wrist, feeling for a pulse.

"Good Lord, Judith."

"Steady, yes?"

"Yes, but it hasn't been an hour since Ethan left us. How could you have—?"

"It didn't have a great deal to do with me. There was no time to come down, even to call," she explained. "So fast. Almost no pain at all. In moments the three of us were very busy."

"Three. Do you hear that, Annie?"

Tears. There in Ethan's young father's eyes as he grasped for his wife's hand.

"There now, love," she whispered.

Oh, Ethan must not miss this, Judith thought, just as he stepped into the small fire's light. He looked different, this man who had shed his skin yet again. This man with too many names was now a father, by the grace of God and the love they shared, her heart whispered to her own sweet father. And to the other, the gruff one, who'd praised her hips and called her Ethan's good choice.

Ethan raised his eyes to the steady, silent stream of fellow homesteaders. Judith found his scent mingling sweetly with the night air, the lifeblood, the downy newness of his burden. He responded to the children's tugs at his waistcoat and knelt.

Judith took a measureless pride in her husband as she watched him open the layers to their child's first circle of hushed company.

"Her name is Memory," he announced.